Steve Wheeler was given the choice at age eighteen of becoming either a Catholic priest or a policeman — he chose the latter. He has served in the military and, since 1987, has worked as a bronze sculptor, knifesmith and swordsmith. He lives with his wife, Elizabeth, and their two children on their twenty-acre lifestyle block in Hawkes Bay, New Zealand.

Also by Steve Wheeler
Burnt Ice

CRYSTAL VENOM

A FURY OF ACES 2

steve wheeler

HARPER
Voyager

Harper*Voyager*

An imprint of HarperCollins*Publishers*

First published in Australia in 2013
by HarperCollins*Publishers* Australia Pty Limited
ABN 36 009 913 517
harpercollins.com.au

HarperCollins*Publishers*

Level 13, 201 Elizabeth Street, Sydney NSW 2000, Australia
Unit D1, 63 Apollo Drive, Rosedale, Auckland 0632, New Zealand
A 53, Sector 57, Noida, UP, India
77–85 Fulham Palace Road, London W6 8JB, United Kingdom
2 Bloor Street East, 20th floor, Toronto, Ontario M4W 1A8, Canada
10 East 53rd Street, New York NY 10022, USA

National Library of Australia Cataloguing-in-Publication entry:

Wheeler, Steve.
  Crystal venom / Steve Wheeler.
  ISBN: 978 0 7322 9373 4 (pbk.)
  ISBN: 978 0 7304 9647 2 (ebook)
  Wheeler, Steve. Fury of aces ; 2.
  Science fiction.
  Interplanetary voyages—Fiction.
  Outer space—Exploration—Fiction.
A823.4

Cover design by Hazel Lam, HarperCollins Design Studio
Cover illustration by John Howe
Author photograph by Tim Watson (Studio 62)
Typeset in Palatino 11/18pt by Kirby Jones

For my mums
and
the families

Contents

Contents

Part One

Mudshark

One

'Marko, wake up.'

Sergeant Major Marko Spitz liked sleep. He always had. He liked bed in general. In his forty-seven and a bit standard years he had slept in a lot of odd places — sometimes too hot, sometimes too cold, sometimes too comfortable, sometimes deeply unpleasant — but that particular bed in those particular quarters was just right.

He dozed in that wonderful place between sleep and full consciousness. Aware that he was alone, he dreamt of his beautiful Jan, wondering why she was not beside him.

'Wake up, Warrant Officer Spitz ... Now!'

The Base Augmented Intelligence had taken on a strident schoolmistress tone as she formally addressed him, so he reluctantly opened his eyes, his mind slowly climbing towards wakefulness. 'Right, come on, out of bed.' Naked as always, he padded to the small shower area, which had been grown as part of the room; he smiled with the thought that rank still had a few privileges. He pushed into the translucent

3

membrane, which folded and sealed itself as soon as he was through. Once he stood on the almost gritty, coral-like floor, water started pouring over him from the overhead surface at the precise temperature he liked and with just the right amount of soap in it as well.

The soapy water was cleaned as it sank through the porous material below his feet and recycled back up into the header tanks. The material filtered from the water moved further down onto the shower's organic base plate, where, after the soaps had been recycled, the residue was consumed by the room as it constantly refurbished itself.

Judging himself sufficiently clean, he tapped the wall and pure water cascaded over him, rinsing him off. He tapped the wall again and the water stopped as he pushed his way back through the membrane.

While drying himself with the fresh towel growing from the cubicle's ceiling, he scanned the day's schedule in the wall screen, noting who was on base and also where his own crew was.

Pulling on fresh overalls he uplinked to the Base Augmented Intelligence then scanned for Glint. Glint had once again taken his ID offline, so even the BAI did not know where he was. Glint's behaviour in this respect was a constant grievance of the AIs and it often petitioned Command to have the ACE placed under its direct control, but the major had always managed to block such a move. Undoubtedly, Glint created a certain tension in some people. Everyone knew he could be a bit of a prick at times and he'd made himself deeply unpopular with some of the more straight-laced pompous types on base.

One of Glint's favourite tricks was to buy some meat from

the cooks, mash it up a little and then hurl it at whoever he wanted to rev up. His aim was always as perfect as his ability to catch the target completely unawares and in a fresh uniform. Although Glint was sometimes intensely annoying and his occasional disappearances irksome, Marko reckoned he was becoming a superb entity with an extraordinary mind, good engineering capabilities and constantly improving martial arts skills. He was always grateful that Jan had convinced him to bring Glint into existence and Marko was very pleased to have the ACE around as his son.

After checking that he had on him everything he needed for the day, including the issued communications headband, he walked out through the living wooden door knowing the room would clean itself, sloughing off a fine dust of material from the walls and ceilings to be absorbed into the floor, and that the bed would also make itself as it too was living plant-derived materials.

Moving down the corridor towards the all-ranks mess, he looked up to see the roof slowly becoming translucent, allowing the light from the rising sun to penetrate all the enclosed spaces as the interior of the building reinvigorated itself. Stopping to admire a slowly opening group of magenta-coloured flowers growing from the walls, breathing in their perfume, he smiled as Glint appeared as if out of thin air beside him.

When his chameleon-ware was switched off his sudden appearances still caught most of the base personnel by surprise, but Marko and the rest of his crew had become used to it. And besides, the proud creator thought, what was the use of having special abilities if they could not be used to good effect?

Marko nodded at him while slipping the very annoying headband on. Base AI would not allow any of the *Basalt* crew to communicate with their line-of-sight light-based comms systems when inside the main base compound, claiming that such use disregarded accepted security protocols. Even the major could not argue the issue so they left it alone. Only problem with the issued headbands was that Base could eavesdrop on anything they discussed.

'A good night, Glint?'

'Yes, thanks, Marko. Spent seven most enjoyable hours hacking Gerald. I do believe that he is even more pissed at me than normal.'

Knowing that he was being listened to by the said Gerald, Marko chuckled. 'Gerald? The Primary Base AI is called Gerald? Ha! Gerald! Who would have thought? So, have you been calling him Gerry?'

'No, Marko, that would be disrespectful. Gerald is a good name for a Frontier Base AI. A certain air of dignity if you will. And besides, even if he is annoyed at me getting that deep into him he has been most helpful with my latest upgrades.'

'Well, Glint my son, what have you done now?'

He just smiled in his almost angelic way and told Marko to wait.

They entered the main mess hall, which featured high, structurally curved plant-based wall panels and a roof formed from interwoven giant semi-translucent leaves. It allowed in the perfect level of light for early morning as they made their way through the throng to the area for Senior NCOs. The grown tables and bench seats had the form of a much-altered wood fungus, but none of the associated smells. Marko sat, and Glint did an interesting thing with his tail, forming his own seat that allowed his head to be almost at the same level as Marko's and the table's other occupants.

His fellow sergeants and warrant officers nodded at Marko and Glint, murmuring their greetings of the day. Reg looked across at Glint, then looked at Marko to enquire, 'What the hell is he up to now?' Marko shrugged and replied that he had a new upgrade but Marko had no idea of what it was. There was a general shuffling of bums with most looking around and calculating the fastest escape route, should the need arise.

The corporal came around and took their breakfast orders but skipped over Glint, as he always had in the past.

'Corporal James.'

'Yes, Sergeant Glint?'

'I wish to place my breakfast order, please.'

Oh, shit, Marko thought, this is going to be interesting. Glint with plates of food, in the middle of several hundred potential targets. He loved Glint but the ACE still made him very nervous at times. 'Ummmmm, Glint, what are you going to do with breakfast food?'

'Eat it, Marko. What else would I do?'

'Really, Glint. Oral sensory? Or full digestive and do you now have a shiny new arsehole as well?'

'Yes, Marko, I now have an anus! Would you like to see it?'

There was an explosive chorus of 'No, no, no, no thanks!' with the occupants of the tables around them stopping whatever they were doing to listen in.

As they ate, they also watched with some awe and trepidation as their good friend Glint ate his first-ever meal. He started with a small bowl of muesli, which he consumed with great relish, then fawned over the sugar when he discovered its taste. The milk, he said, was OK but decided that fruit juice on muesli was just the ticket. He followed that with fresh fruit and then pan-fried bacon and eggs, which he thought was most interesting.

Reg cheerfully told him that the plates were edible as well, so Glint bit a piece from the side of his cleared one, chewed thoughtfully for a few moments and declared that although it was bland in taste it would make a good projectile and crunched down the remainder, which created further nervous looks from around the table. Marko smiled, thinking about getting Glint back to the workshops and running a full diagnostic to see what engineering marvels he had created in himself. He did note that Glint's midriff was definitely larger by the end of breakfast. Coffee the ACE was not that keen on, until Marko suggested honey in it.

'Seems a waste of materials, Marko.'

The others had all left and Glint and Marko were alone at the table.

'What's a waste, Glint?'

Glint pointed at the table tops around them. 'Seeing all the uneaten food and the cups, plates and cutlery just being consumed by the tables like that.'

'Actually, it's very efficient. There's no waste and the plates, cups and tableware are all grown new, so no cleaning and storage. This way the building gets fed as well so it can grow any new rooms we want and constantly maintain itself; and it can be assured that nothing biologically hazardous is left inside it either as, believe me, the technology consuming the leftovers can kill just about anything known.'

Glint started and quickly asked, 'Would it eat me if I sat on it for long enough?'

Marko smiled and resisted the urge to ruffle Glint's frill. 'Nope, because it knows who you are and that you are alive. Come on, time to sort ourselves and then off to the workshops.'

They walked back to their quarters, with Glint giving a full commentary on what an interesting material food was, and an update on what he had built into himself. And telling Marko how Topaz, the sentient design and construction unit, and Patrick, the frigate *Basalt*'s controlling AI, had been very helpful creating the components and the interfaces.

Marko brushed his teeth and explained to Glint that decaying remnants of food would not be good in his mouth either. Marko snapped an additional wooden toothbrush from a small branch over the top of the basin and handed it to Glint. He grinned, thinking that the day was all the more interesting as he watched Glint getting to grips with a toothbrush for the first time. He walked over to the room's screen, brought up the housekeeping menu and advised the system that it would need to grow an additional two toothbrushes per day for as long as they stayed at the base.

'I need better teeth, Marko. These tapered plates are good, but actual teeth would be a lot better. I shall do some research. What do I do with this used brush? Interesting taste: what is it?'

Marko reached across and patted Glint's shoulder. 'You make me laugh. You are a walking, talking advertisement for the attitude: "If it can be improved, just do it!" Leave it in the basin and it'll be consumed as well. The taste? Ummmmm, peppermint, I think. There's a thought. I wonder what the real stuff looks and tastes like. Must ask Stephine when she gets back.'

As they walked across the Base to the main hangars, the rest of the crew gradually attached themselves to the group. Jan, after giving Marko a good-morning kiss, patted Glint on the head and said: 'Morning, beautiful creature. My spies tell me you have been augmenting yourself. Here … I have something for you.' She pulled a large, brightly coloured lollipop from her jacket and passed it over to him.

'Thanks, Jan! Lolly on a stick! I know about these.'

Watching him hobbling along on three legs, eating his lollipop, had everyone in fits of laughter, to which Glint reacted by hamming it up even more.

They all looked out across the wide sweeping horseshoe-shaped bay and its distant towering volcanic buttresses, as a stiff breeze came in off the sea bringing a cloud front with it, making Fritz complain about it being cold.

Jan looked at him witheringly. 'You are a wimp, Fritz! Get another vest or at very least step up your bioware for a better blood temperature.'

Fritz, the eternal teenager, shrugged and mumbled, 'Can't find my spare vest.'

Marko laughed, saying, 'The room probably consumed it thinking it had additional calorific value, considering how rarely you shower, Fritzy! No wonder the eel bitey beast from the library planet did not want to eat you. It probably smelt you through the canopy!'

Fritz looked angry. 'Fuck off, Marko! You are such an arse! It bloody well did want to eat me!'

Still grinning, they let themselves into one of the vehicle workshops through the large living wooden doors and giant living leaf walls, which, when originally planted, had grown up to curve across and bond at the roof apex, forming a half-barrel-shaped structure. The senior members of the crew, Warrant Officer First Class Harry Stevens and Major Michael Longbow, had arrived before the rest of them and were deep in discussion with a group of the base engineers. Harry gestured for all to join them.

The major spoke first. 'Morning, people. First things first. It's officially called the KA14 by its original creators and operators, but what are *we* going to call it?'

They looked up at the huge hulking machine parked in the centre of the hangar.

After a few seconds Fritz spoke up. '*Mudshark*. Yeah, call it *Mudshark*.'

They all looked at him, then back at the squat Gjomvik Corporation combat hovercraft, then looked across at Fritz and back to the major.

'*Mudshark*? Any particular reason, Fritz?' asked the major.

The large-headed little man just shrugged. 'Looks like one, right? Kind of obvious really.'

The major looked at the hovercraft and nodded once. 'Well, I reckon since we recovered it mostly intact and since you had a lot to do with the recovery, Fritz, I say we go with that. *Mudshark* it is, people. OK, that is a mean ugly-looking sucker. Always thought mudsharks were kind of pretty animals but there you go. Harry, brief the guys, please, I'll be in my office. See you on board shortly.'

Harry Stevens was not really a big guy, but he had 'presence' and even those who had seen the worst of him still had an immense respect and liking for him. When he spoke they shut up — even Glint, and particularly Fritz, who treated him like his father which, considering Fritz's rather intriguing past, was probably fitting. Harry gestured to the ACE mechanical spider, Flint — his constant companion — who tapped the keys on the desktop until a full holo of *Mudshark* hovered above the large square table.

Harry spoke loudly and clearly. 'Gather in, everyone.'

As they moved around the desktop, he started the briefing. 'Well, it's a bit of a beast. That Gjomvik company really screwed up royally in letting us get our hands on it, as it holds tech that I know they would not be keen on us seeing let alone taking to pieces. Interesting; not entirely sure what its actual theatre of operation would be, but I'd say they designed it for long-range insertion of their small armoured walking units over most terrain types — and fairly quickly at that, as it has good low-altitude flight characteristics as well. Then it would be able to hang back and give them some fairly mean fire support as well. The guns are nice. I'd say that they are an upgrade of their MK-17 120mm rail gun. They are still 120mm but there was no ammo left on board by the time we got to it, so I can only go on the sizings of the breeches, ammo drums and feeds as to the propellant casings. Looks like they had at least four types of ammo and considering that this thing has the capacity to carry at least two tonne of the stuff they must have been involved in an absolute pit fight before the crew abandoned ship.'

They all nodded in agreement as Harry continued.

'And they must have been pumping the ammo through. The barrels are knackered and they were nice barrels, really nice. Toast now. Obviously, whatever they went up against they were shit scared to pump that amount of ammo through in such a short space of time. A wonder they didn't go bang, actually. I think that one was about to; the cooling pumps on the starboard guns are fried. May have been why the crew legged it. Pity this outpost doesn't have more surveillance satellites as I'd love to see what they had for escape modules. Looking at the personnel stations on board, they had five crew. There may have been something in the hangar as well but we have no idea what it was.'

Fritz opened his mouth to speak but when he saw that Harry wasn't finished he closed it again.

'By the time we arrived the modules were both over the horizon and still accelerating, so they must be a classy bit of kit as well. Umm, the power plants are sweet, really sweet, helluva long way from anything the Games Board would allow us to use in any AV battle as they are too powerful. The Board will go ape when they see this. Bloody fortunate that the boss was able to get that Harpoon into it as quickly as he did. Beautiful missile, Fritz. Took perfect control of *Mudshark*'s electronics. It was literally seconds from going boom bigtime. Nice bit of tech that, Fritz, well done. Looking at the remains of the computer logs, the Harpoon took total control in about three milliseconds. We had better have a look at marketing that to the Administration. Chunk of coin in that for all of us. Helluva test fire, eh! OK, we can talk about that later.'

As Harry spoke, the image of the craft came apart with the individual units expanding in size, allowing them all a clear view of what it was like inside as well as out.

'The boss agrees that this thing is repairable with what we have here on base and we might just as well be doing something useful while waiting for our next deployment. We can't use *Mudshark*'s hangar as it's just not high enough for any of our combat walkers or mechs. Fritz, Marko, let's get our heads together later and cook something up at some stage, if required. I have always considered the need for a smaller more compact mech a worthy design project anyway. Right, the guns we can rebuild. I have the base's Manufacturing AI already onto it. That and some nice new ammo as well.'

He paused for a second, tapping his wrist screen and saying, 'Memo: I need to talk to the boss about that ammo. End.'

He looked around at the crew and continued. 'OK. The cooling pumps we'll refit with ours; also need a new computer and the Tech AI is happy to give us some of himself whenever we are ready. There is a massive load of deep scoring under the hull and subsequently about twenty-five per cent of the underside armour is stuffed. We have that being made as well and delivery is about ten hours away. They had class armour as they pinched our Cobra gear and placed another beryllium bronze layer over it. Nice. The camo is actually bonded into the surface, bites in about point two of a millimetre. Have already loaded up the specs on that to the Intel AI. She likes it. More points for us. Having said that she is going nuts trying to figure out what damaged the armour.'

He paused for a few seconds to look at one of his wrist screens then continued. 'All she is coming up with is a biological agent. Says she will have some results in a day or so. Like I said, the power plants are sweet, but Glint, I need you and Marko to get into the software on them as there is something there that the AIs can't ID yet, so give them more raw data. Try not to wreck them, will ya? The figures say the plants are pumping out some seven per cent more usable power than ours are.

'Now, the AG units are both wrecked. That's the big ticket item. The boss has started negotiations with the Games Board. They like the idea of *Mudshark* going up against a bunch of our units, but I kind of like the idea of new tech for good or not so good. Or maybe someone has cooked up some interesting punch up to justify the manufacture of this machine. Still, you all know my views on the Games Board as they are getting more and more manipulative to get their stories. Anyway, let's get on with it. The Base AI stripped all the self-destruct stuff out and the Harpoon has been disengaged so everything has been made safe; that's what Base says but … be careful, eh. And keep an eye out: we still don't know why this thing is on this world, so any clues upload 'em right away. See you all at smoko. Oh, Fritz, the boss wants a report on the Harpoon as soon as you are ready.'

While Harry had been briefing them they had all quietly powered up their neural spectral links, placing them in their ears. They still wore their headpieces but Base could only hear them if they spoke aloud. Comms now became very fast and seamless, with an interface that linked through Glint; his was always the primary job of laying out the link networks, which he did with his usual speed and efficiency, more often than not helped by the large mechanical spider, Flint, and, when he was around, the cat, Nail. The small self-aligning scales, which would automatically adhere and orient themselves so that their light-based comms systems could operate, seemed to float off Glint as he rounded bends, establishing line-of-sight maser communications throughout *Mudshark*.

As they followed him, the usual gossip, news, new music from Fritz and jokes — as gathered by Flint — were uploaded from the seven of them onto their own personal net, completely free of outside interference or snooping. The Base AIs could not hack into it as they knew that Glint had some unique software running through his bulletproof self. Neither Fritz nor Marko could actually get a handle on it either. Fritz said that it was based on his original designs and code but that Glint had taken it to a whole new level. Marko believed that Glint had come up with it himself, but Harry believed that Stephine had given the ACE something. Marko, being a proud dad, still believed that his creation had done it for himself.

Marko went to his assigned locker and pulled out the coffin-like light engineering suit carrier. He stripped and laid down as it formed itself around him. Leaving the helm off, he caught up with Glint as they made their way onto *Mudshark*.

Thinking about it, Marko decided it would be nice to see the wonderfully enigmatic Stephine, and her man Veg, together with her ACE — the cat, Nail — again soon. The crew seemed incomplete when they weren't around. As soon as they had all arrived at the Base, Stephine and Veg had sent a quick "bye and see you soon' and disappeared to a remote part of the planet to search out interesting life types in their own ship.

Everyone had a chuckle as they viewed Glint's latest exploits as seen through his eyes: a perfect shot of a small piece of bloody mince being deftly deposited on some unfortunate senior staff member's shiny head as he stepped from the shower.

'So, Glint, what are you really doing with all that nice food now in your new guts? Are you processing it, storing it, turning it into projectiles, or what?'

'Everything actually, Marko. The processing plant is more like the stomach of a tuna fish from Old Earth. Topaz helped me with that and Patrick made the parts. Ernst made some very good suggestions in regards to the linings of my intestines, and also designed the compressing units so I can make my own ammunition for the rifle. Very fast and efficient. I can take energy, trace elements, basically anything I need to function, and can now grow at a much slower more controlled rate than I would normally through my purely mechanical upgrades. I concluded, after talking with the other AIs, that I may as well consume normal human food — I mean, you guys stop all the time for food and fluids — so why not join you for more than just conversation and enjoy myself with new experiences?'

Marko chuckled as Glint continued. 'And then I also decided, well, why not fit myself out with the whole package? Did you know that since I installed the taste sensory package my sense of smell is much improved as well? And besides, creator of mine, I can now taste everything for poisons, carcinogens and also what is good and bad for you and everyone in the squad. Jan will be very pleased. Ernst downloaded a huge file about that. You really are quite fragile in some respects, Marko. There are many many compounds that can make you very sick or even kill your biological self. I would have thought that as you are a sentient species you would have addressed those dangers long ago. But as Ernst says, you are only human! Flint is jealous of my changes though. It's unfortunate that you can do nothing for him.'

Marko groaned. 'Yeah, well, you make it all sound like something to look forward to. And Harry wants to keep Flint as compact as possible, so I don't think we can do anything about that. Don't go making changes to him by yourself, will you? That would be stepping outside accepted protocols. He can always make the changes should he decide to leave Harry once he has finished his indenture to him. Right, Fritz, can you open up the engine room access, please?'

'Give me a couple of secs, Marko. Having to route everything through the Intel AI. She's controlling the ship until the new computer arrives in a couple of hours.'

Marko frowned. 'Why so long?'

'Nah, it's just the boss said do everything right. The mercs had a nice compact unit, our closest is 7mm too large so a new case is being made. Ah, there you go, guys, full access.'

The access door clicked and opened a few millimetres as Marko said, 'Glint, do your thing.'

Marko hung back around the corner while Glint slipped in through the large transparent hatchway. As soon as the hatch closed, Marko went up to it and watched as the ACE moved around inside the engine space, looking for any threats.

'Marko, there's a funny smell in here. Everything scans fine but my databases cannot ID the smell. Uploaded. Intel AI says fish! Why would fish be in here? I should have recognised it. Rotten fish can kill you, you know.'

'Well, Glint, that's something else for you to experience. Fresh fish dinners! Very nice and yes, rotten fish is nasty so please don't get any ideas about using it for your set-ups, eh, as that would be taking things one step too far. Anything hazardous to me?'

'Not that I can ID. But go for Contam Protocol anyway.'

On the bridge of the hovercraft the major was listening and confirmed: 'Proceed, Marko.'

Marko nodded, bringing up his suit protocols, which hung as if projected in front of his eyes, and in his mind told the suit what he wanted of it then said, 'Thanks, boss.'

Marko placed his carryall on the deck in front of the hatch, looked down at his suit and smiled, contemplating the excellent equipment. Lightweight, with all the electronics, filters, power supply and self-repairing capability contained in the actual fabric of the suit just as the crew had designed them, based on Veg's specs. He only had to form the thought to seal it: the gloves folded out over his hands, even his impervious artificial cobalt-blue left one, and all the pockets closed shut while the sleek elegant helmet formed over his head, neatly accommodating his archaic glasses.

Glint opened the door for him and then closed it as soon as he stepped through the hatchway and walked over to the starboard-side antigravity unit. Glint plugged into it and the data started to flow across Marko's faceplate as the crew link shared the information. He grimaced looking through the data, deciding that the unit was damaged beyond repair. 'Harry, the starboard AG unit is stuffed. The casing can be used again but the rest is fried. Readouts say the same about the port-side unit. Specs on the way.'

They then walked aft with Marko crouching slightly due to the low ceiling lined with electrical conduits and fluid piping to the main power plants. As he looked around, his faceplate automatically translated all the visible readouts, displays and serial numbers for him into his own language. He noted that both generators were in standby mode and producing just enough power to provide heating and lights. He pointed at the main control panel and instructed Glint. 'OK mate, interface with it.'

Glint's right front foot/hand detached completely and walked on fingertips across to the main control unit, climbed it and then extruded a probe from a fingertip into the nearest datalink plug. Marko mused that Glint was a very cautious entity and that he never actually trusted any other AI, with the exception of the *Basalt* crew. Meanwhile, more data started to flow into Marko's display as the entire control unit was systematically invaded by Glint's investigative programs, which had been written by Fritz. The programs flowed through *Mudshark*'s software, encapsulating the guardware in the equivalent of an electronic blanket, effectively isolating all the safeguards and enabling control. A torrent of data, which was far too much for Marko, started to flow to the Intel AI and onto the other AIs who were watching. Marko thought about it and locked his attention onto the holographic images of the main Bierwage Fusion generator and in particular the fuel feeds for the plasma flux. He started, then exclaimed, 'Holy crap! Guys, check this out!'

He could feel everyone pause whatever they were doing and watch as individual atoms of antimatter were slowly fed into the plasma stream.

The major was the first to reply. 'Pox! They cracked it! Micro-antimatter injection! Nice. Guys, concentrate on that. The Materials AI wants immediate access. Give it to him.'

Marko smiled. 'No sweat, boss, Glint is onto it.'

Harry's voice came into the conversation. 'Class! They built some really high-grade containments in there. Think I'll come in myself.'

Marko smiled, knowing his friend's love of new tech. 'OK, Harry. I'll isolate one for you so you can get a close look at it.'

Two

Marko continued to analyse the data, identifying specific components, isolating those that were not familiar, and making lists of what needed a closer look. Glint was in a trance-like state, poring through the information and holding a simultaneous conversation with at least eight AIs, including the Orbitals. Marko squatted down beside his carryall, opening it and pulling out various tools in preparation for Harry's arrival, knowing that he would want to take apart a couple of the more interesting pieces of hardware then and there. As he lay the roll-up of fine tools on the deck, he felt something grasp his left hand and squeeze it very, very hard. Hard enough that if he had had a real hand it would have become paste. Something using chameleon-ware was trying to crush his hand. Marko instantly rotated his fingers and grasped whatever was attacking him, squeezing it hard, feeling it go rocklike. In the same instant, all personal attack protocols in the suit fired up and a tiny pulse laser mapping unit mounted in his helmet scanned the area of threat as identified by the suit; the image of a small, really unpleasant-looking octopoid-type creature came across his helmet display. The alarm went out to the squad and Glint moved to Marko's side with extraordinary speed. His body was becoming straight and rigid, his legs effectively aiming the tip of his tail at Marko's left fist as it grasped the writhing, incredibly tough creature. The ACE's head had rotated to the rear and his teardrop-shaped skull had flattened, with his eyes now much wider apart than normal.

'Fuck's sake, Glint, what are you doing?'

'Stay very still, Marko, and hold that thing as far away from your body as you can.'

'Answer the bloody question, Glint.'

'I want to kill it using the lowest possible setting for my rail gun, but I need a different type of projectile. I will need a few more minutes to create that bullet.'

'Shit, Glint, you're going to kill me!'

'Shit … yes, that's right, Marko. But it will not kill you. It will wreck your arm but you can always make another one of those and you have spares anyway. Just be thankful I had breakfast so I can now make shit.'

Marko could not help himself and started laughing as he considered the position he was in. His son, Glint, was internally making a projectile from shit so that he could kill the octopoid creature at the lowest possible setting of his spinal rail gun, which he knew was twelve hundred metres per second.

The major's voice boomed into their heads. 'Don't shoot, Glint. The AIs want that thing alive, not blown to a thousand bits and covered in your shit, no matter how hard it is. We will be with you in ten minutes. We have scanned the entire ship and facilities now that we know what we are looking for and have found other small pieces of whatever the hell it is. Hang tight, Marko.'

'Yes, major, sir — just fucking hurry up, will you? This thing is slowly but surely chewing through the outer casing of my hand. It has already destroyed the suit glove and I've had to shut down the pain receptors in the hand and wrist.'

Looking carefully at the creature, he wondered what it was learning of him as its beak-like mouth chewed on the side of his first finger; the tough chitinous material which made the outer sheathing of his hand was slowly being eroded by the constant action of the beak and the accompanying saliva. Marko, fascinated in spite of his situation, ramped up the magnification through his faceplate to study the effect of the saliva on the hand and magnified further to study the beak, wondering what it could be made of to inflict such damage. Harry broke through his contemplation. 'Hey, you've dealt with weirder stuff, Marko. OK, we switch to plan B. Cryno it is. Freeze the sucker hard! Sorry, buddy, you'd probably need a new hand anyway if we have to hard chill it. With you in a couple of minutes.'

Two of Glint's hands walked over, linked together and then climbed up Marko with one hand gripping tightly onto his forearm while the other grappled with the flailing beast, pulling its tentacles off his flesh and wrapping them together. Marko watched as data uplinked from the hand that investigated the creature's makeup through tactile and sensory pads. The alien suddenly reacted to Glint's hands and tried to bite them, always meeting air as it lunged and snapped with Glint's reaction time creating a blur of motion.

The door opened and Harry and the major walked in

wearing full combat suits, sealed, and carrying a squat container between them with *Caution bio-hazard. Liquid Nitrogen* warnings on the sides.

'OK, Marko? Nice that we have a great workshop to play in, eh?' said a smiling major.

Marko hated rhetorical questions, so he just grunted in reply as the major continued. 'Right, Glint, everything indicates that this was once a squid-like creature. Its entire molecular structure is chain-linked, in that the structure is double or even triple bonded into itself which is why it's so bloody tough. There is no other bio or electronic hazard present. Well, not one we can identify. You can disengage your hands and take them back, Glint, as Marko lowers it into the cryno. All the way to the bottom, mate. We want to know if it will freeze. In your own time.'

'Cygnus 5 all over again maybe?' Harry queried.

Marko shook his head. 'Bloody hell, I sure hope not. That was nasty. We'll know soon enough once we know what this is.'

As Marko lowered his arm past the lip of the container, Glint's hands jumped onto the floor. The creature's tentacles shot outwards, grasped the edge and hung on. Harry reached over as Marko struggled to push the creature further in and pushed down hard on his upper arm while Glint, with his hands reattached, came forwards and pried the tentacles off the edge. Marko's arm and the creature suddenly sank down into the liquid nitrogen, some of which splashed up onto their suits causing Glint to shake vigorously to ensure that none stuck to his coat. The creature was tough, thrashing around for the best part of ten seconds before going solid.

'Can't get the arm out, guys: it's no longer responding. Disconnecting. That's a pissoff. That was the original forearm and hand we made on *Basalt* after I lost my arm to that shitty urchin! That's just plain annoying as it's probably a complete write off. Bloody hell, that is one amazingly tough little critter! We'd better spec up all our munitions if we ever want to go up against them.'

Marko raised what remained of his left arm, now terminating at the elbow, as the suit also detached that part of itself and sealed across the artificial stump. Harry slammed the lid closed and latched it down. Marko looked at the sealed container. 'Better start work on a new hand to the same specs as everyone knows what that one looks like. That will cost.'

The Base AI suddenly answered. 'We will assist you with a replacement as soon as we can, Warrant Officer Spitz, and we shall pick up the tab.'

Marko nodded as Harry lightly punched him on the shoulder. 'Thanks, Base.'

One of the Science AI drones was waiting for them as they descended from *Mudshark*. The sealed container was passed across and it disappeared in the direction of the AIs labs. Marko looked down at the stump, feeling a little depressed, and shuddered remembering the day years earlier when an urchin had snatched his arm away at the shoulder. He activated his internal controls and the helmet de-formed and slid down into the suit's collar as the major said: 'Early smoko today, people.'

Glint had disappeared but now returned, running on his back legs, with Marko's number five lower arm in one hand and a tray of cream doughnuts in the other. Perfect poise, balance and doing sixty-five kilometres per hour, thought

Marko, wondering if the MPs would book him for speeding. Then again, it would be a very brave MP who would write a ticket out to Glint.

Marko locked the number five lower arm on, establishing the sensory protocols between his augmented brain and the arm, while the crew introduced Glint to smoko, in the real sense. He was able to partake in doughnuts and it was amusing for everyone to watch his expressions of delight at tasting whipped cream, which he promptly introduced into his coffee as well, when the major asked him, 'So why now, Glint? Why do you want to eat and drink? What's the purpose of all this exotic engineering?'

'I am curious, Michael; it is another aspect of my creators that I wanted to explore. Once I have tasted everything, I will know you all a little better. And it is useful. And I can now drink beer as well! Oh, I like that thought, as I have watched you all drinking alcohol and wondered why it seemed to be so good for you.'

Jan watched the interplay and mused that Glint was the only one of them, excepting Veg and Stephine, who called the major by his first name. The boss seemed to like it and although everyone sometimes worried about his occasional fits of self-doubt, they liked him a lot and would happily follow him anywhere. He did tend to over-analyse things that might better be left alone, but hey, she thought, he was certainly 'the boss': very intelligent, genuinely caring for his people and he could be plain nasty and very forthright when it came to doing the right thing. Glint had brought that up in private conversation with her and Marko and wondered why the major was even with them.

27

They all believed, in fact, that by being buried deep inside the military wing of the Administration, and therefore constantly on the move, Michael Longbow was probably hiding from something. Still thinking on that and about a little project that her Military Intelligence handlers had just given her she heard him say: 'Right, back to it, people. Repair and replacement modules are starting to arrive. There's going to be a hassle with an Intel and Materials crew. They'll be here in a few moments to go over the entire craft and recover as much as possible of that critter. They consider it may be off-planet tech, so watch yourselves. Deal with it as best you can. I just hope like hell it's not octopoids from Cygnus 5 all over again, although they say it's not. Similar … but almost as if the octopoid we knew had dramatically regressed, and none of their suit technology present either. Anyway, they have priority.

'Jan, you're with me. I want to have a close look at that hangar space on *Mudshark*. Harry, sort out those main weapons, will you, please? Fritz, keep at the computers and the sensors, and get ready for the Tech AI package. I want absolute control of that machine as soon as it can be done. Marko, Glint, back to the engine room and find out how a kilo or so of gristle got in there. Materials AI already has a couple of drones working on the antimatter units; he's very keen to get a handle on it soonest. Don't worry, we salvaged the beast machine so we get the cash on anything found. Had a bit of a stoush over that and the Financial AI is a bit put out, but Base is feeling very pleased with us and told it to release the bucks. Glint. Was the Base AIs original personality that of a Tech General? Yes … explains a few things then. I'll eyeball that data packet that you have assembled on him early this morning, thanks.'

Marko had locked on the number five, which was a good arm, heavier than the number one, which he knew he would be rebuilding. He linked to his private data and flashed to Financial the parts lists and costs and seconds later received an 'unlimited within reason' response which generated a smile, so he sent another message across to Topaz for him to start the design process for an arm which incorporated weapons.

He stripped off the damaged suit, placed it in the crew refurbishment unit and lifted another out of his locker. Looking around, he noted that everyone had armed themselves: all sidearms, all teched up, all nasty, all rebuilds or originals created by Jan or Veg. Veg had made Marko an elegant, long knife that could cut through anything, so he strapped that on after putting the long-barrelled handgun Jan had made for him back in the locker. He thought it might be a bit too much firepower for internal work. He looked across at his companion of many years. 'Hey, Jan. When you get a spare couple of hours could you make me a nice compact pistol of some sort, please. Something suitable for up close and personal?'

She smiled a special smile which he knew was reserved only for him. 'Sure, darling. Will have a think about it for you. Something in 5.56mm maybe? An old calibre but a good one.'

'Yeah, that would be great. I'll even give you another of those eel teeth for the grips if you need it.'

She smiled again and kissed him on the back of his head as she walked by.

Back on board *Mudshark*, Glint and Marko soon discovered a sizable crack in the starboard antigravity unit housing, and after removing the burnt-out guts of it, they could see there were holes and tears in its base, leading down to buckled hull plates. Steadily working at it, they stripped off the damaged plates under the other unit and found the same, along with a couple of smashed octopoids looking as if they had been used as wedges to force the damaged plates further apart. Intel was all over it and asked them to step away for an hour while they learnt as much as they could. Marko uplinked as many images as he could across to Materials so they could start on the replacement internal framework and then informed the major.

Jan announced that lunch had arrived. When they were all gathered in the smoko room, she said: 'There was something fairly big deployed from the hangar. Probably a submersible looking at the gantry configurations and some fresh scrapes on the tops and bottoms of the door and ramps. There is also a large and hugely strong crynogenic freezer container in the rear of the hangar.'

She uploaded images onto the base net and they could sense the AIs pondering what they were seeing.

Fritz pointed at the images. 'They were looking to capture some octopoids.'

The major stroked his chin, slowly nodding. 'I think you might be right, Fritz. So there is a nice compact Gjomvik sub still out there maybe. Now, any serious objections to going like hell on *Mudshark*? No. OK, I authorise stims. People, you have a few minutes to sort out any private info. No sleeping tonight. Base, do I have authorisation to go after the sub? We may gain additional Intel as well. I have a horrible feeling that this is another fragment of the Cygnus 5 situation. The alternative is to use our own equipment and forget *Mudshark* for the moment.'

Seconds later the Base AI replied. 'You have full authorisation, Major. Games Board wants to fund the mission and is subsequently insistent that you use *Mudshark*. They think that, due to its uniqueness, and the possibility that a few interesting tech programs can also be generated from the rebuilding, it will be a good revenue earner. All normal fees, et cetera, will be credited to you and your crew. Bonus packages are also authorised for any base engineers and techs required. All materials are now top priority. Please note if the submersible is not recovered Games Board will still pay out, but at a reduced rate. They do, however, include a special bonus package should there be a conflict with the submersible, or with the as-yet-unidentified octopoid entities or derivative types thereof. Games Board monitors are now en route. You have thirty standard minutes to select base engineers and techs of your choice before a total lockdown at your location will occur. Military Police are en route, as is Catering, with four days' supplies. Materials and Intel proxies are also en route. With the exception of me, total communications blackout will occur in five minutes. Base out.'

The major, with Harry's help, quickly went through the base personnel selecting who they wanted, and sent messages out to them advising how they should equip themselves for the job ahead.

Marko flashed a message to Catering for the little extras he liked to eat and drink when in the field. He then sent another message to double the order, knowing that Glint would now like some too. Then he sent 'hi and how are yous' to his far-flung family and friends. The final action was to check his financials and also set up the upgrade package for Glint in case the ACE got damaged or worse. He then instructed the base net to uplift his total life files from his Soul Saver as of that instant — not that he had any intention of getting injured or killed. Although it was nice in some respects to have a squeaky clean new body, it did mean no scars and the tattoos would have to be done again. And neither the scars nor the tattoos came cheap, to say absolutely nothing of having to teach the new body everything, and then a few months of hard work to build up body mass again. He thought that on reflection death was really not worth it.

They finished off lunch in a hurry as things stepped up a few notches. The security cordon arrived, and chain-linked glass walls put up by the MPs' armoured vehicles soon surrounded the building. A pair of checkpoints arrived and positioned themselves as the AI proxies arrived together with two Games Board monitors. Marko looked over the proxies, as they were the latest versions. High tech, tough and super helpful, he noted; nothing was any trouble for them. They did not seem to have any problems with Marko despite knowing that he had killed off a couple of their fellows in the past. The Tech one had a compact manufacturing plant built into it so could repair smaller things, given sufficient time. The Intel AI had flight capability and could be a seriously tough customer when it came to gaining information. They also had fusion piles at their core, and if their controlling AIs thought it necessary they would turn themselves into very effective bombs, Marko having seen them do so a couple of times. He had never heard of a Games Board monitor doing such a thing. Thinking about it, he had never heard or seen a Games Board monitor doing anything remotely helpful, either, with the exception of Sirius, who had been strange right from the outset. There was a rumour that Harry had seen one stand by and watch and record as a child endured a particularly nasty total death, with no hope of re-lifeing. The major said he had heard that Harry destroyed it with something rather elegant and frightening later the same day, and that some standard weeks later the controlling Games Board Producer for that theatre got fried as well. The extended rumour was that Jan was in on that one. No one would elaborate, although Jan did once admit it to Marko in private, but would not fill in the details.

The replacement parts for *Mudshark* came thick and fast and the job went relatively smoothly. From a control unit linked into the local computer, Harry used the building as a hoist as it first lowered its vaulted ceiling then unfurled plastic and metal 'ropes' which knotted themselves around the lifting lugs on *Mudshark*. When instructed the building straightened and slowly lifted *Mudshark* two metres off the floor to allow everyone ready access to the hull plates.

The maintenance crews worked on the damaged underside plates by injecting an enzyme into the bonds between them and the frame, which softened the sealants, allowing the plates to swing down and then snap out of the hinged clips. The new plates were clipped in position, swung up against the framework, and sprayed with an activator which reestablished the bonds, firmly locking them in position. In the cockpits and engine spaces, after the codes had been hacked, the units were instructed to open for inspection: each did so and presented its individual components.

The larger units unfolded with the top casing of the hull also opening out until the entire ship resembled a strange metal and plastic flower in full bloom. Fritz commented that it was definitely Gjomvik Corporation tech as he could not see any plant- or animal-based grown parts in the ship. The techs servicing the units high above the floor activated one-person cages, which formed from augmented wood on the ends of tough fibrous aerial roots. Once the tech climbed into the cage, they would be held in any position they required; the cage would rotate or even hold the tools when instructed. Heavier metallic aerial root structures were used to grasp, then lift down, damaged components and when instructed would pick up and position replacement parts, holding them firm until they were affixed.

As Marko watched the work, Harry called down to him. 'Hey, give us a hand on the port AG unit, please, mate.'

Marko walked around the side of the ship looking up to where Harry and two other techs were waiting for the replacement core of the antigravity unit to be lifted into position. 'Hold on. Where do you want me?'

Harry pointed. 'Forward port side.'

He walked across to the grey-green wall looking for the nearest instruction node. Seeing it, he tapped on its surface to open up a small screen. He rotated it until he could see an image of the area where the AG unit was to be placed, tapped on the personnel-lifting cage icon, tapped again on the screen where he wanted to be and waited. A moment later a soft rustling sound reached him and he looked up to watch as a unit folded away from the wall, opening and reaching down to him. As soon as it was close enough, he lifted his tool box into a side portion and then stepped backwards into the barely pliable structure, which had had its beginnings in basket fungus before being augmented with plastics and metal. It contracted around him, holding him firmly, but leaving his head and arms free, then lifted him up and swung him over the upper deck of *Mudshark* as the replacement AG unit was lifted from its carrier under Harry's direction. As soon as it was close to its intended position, the unit began communicating with the craft's computer to activate the control and power cables which snaked out of their recesses like living creatures looking for their mated plug-ins.

As was always the case with the installation of non-matched components, there were a number of cable bundles which did not automatically lock correctly and instead gently but insistently tapped against each other, trying to mate. Marko and the other techs slowly moved around the unit watching for them. When located, they would grasp the coupling then manually unlock further parts of it, allowing it to reconfigure then lock itself on. After fifteen minutes the computer lifted the humans away from the unit and the entire thing lifted a few centimetres, rotated and then, after powering up, floated down into the housing, locking itself. The onboard computer, once satisfied, would flash the results to the techs so they could move onto the next task.

As each task was completed, the covers would fold over the exposed parts, so that, as the hours ticked by, *Mudshark* slowly started to look more like a ship than some bizarre flower. The final jobs they completed were adding their own weapons systems, and housings for their drones, to the hull using the universal locks and electricals common to most Administration and Gjomvik craft. Fritz upgraded the comms gear, loaded his drones, then installed a backup computer system. Jan upgraded the medical suite on board, then checked everyone for fatigue and passed out stims as required.

A Manta V two-man combat submersible was loaded into *Mudshark*'s hangar, with the refurbished Harpoon missile in its launch housing loaded onto the side. Two four-man escape pods were also loaded. As they could not get them to fit in *Mudshark*'s afterdeck cradles, they stored them in the hangar. Harry considered this solution a messy one, but at least they had something and when asked about the pods by Fritz, he confirmed that they were good. 'MK-19 units. Basically, four coffins each built around a life support and propulsion system. Really cramped, but very tough and able to support their occupants for one hundred standard hours in hostile or extreme conditions. If they decide that rescue is not imminent within that time period, you will be turned into an icicle. Just hope you never have to spend time in one.'

By 7.00 a.m. planet time *Mudshark* was ready. With the mechanics and engineers watching, the *Basalt* crew climbed into their new craft.

The major took the main helm seat, with Harry in the co-pilot's seat and Flint perched on his shoulder. In the compartment behind the cockpit, Marko naturally took the engineer's seat, with Fritz on comms and sensors. Jan took the commander's seat, which earned her some stick, to which she responded by saying she was the colonel for the day and that they had all better behave.

Topaz elected to stay behind in the workshops. Marko had no idea where Glint was until he saw him outside with his head jutting out over the side of the machine. He smiled, knowing that sometimes he acted like a dog with its head outside a vehicle window, tasting the slipstream.

The major powered up the main generators and then eased the antigravity units online. *Mudshark* lifted a metre or so off the hangar floor; a tractor pushed them out through the main doors into the sunlight. Main propulsion was then brought online and the major taxied it up and down a large shoreline access slipway to get a feel for it. Once he was satisfied, he moved them at a respectable speed across the ocean bay towards the huge crater walls, where the seaborne craft-firing range was located. Once at the range, the major slowed *Mudshark* down to a walking pace so Jan could test the weapons.

Jan, as weapons controller, deployed the rail guns on their high-speed hydraulics, allowing them to slew forty-five degrees sideways and swivel one hundred and eighty degrees through vertical as well. She then test fired each gun with different power settings and using the varieties of ammunition that they had on board. Once everyone was satisfied, they took *Mudshark* on a high-speed series of manoeuvres across the ten-kilometre-wide bay, guns deployed and at rest, snuggled against the main body. They were pleasantly surprised at how fast it was, easily cruising up to two hundred and fifty kilometres per standard hour and able to climb to an altitude of fifteen metres before the AIs detected flight instabilities. They were horrified, however, by the flight characteristics when the guns were deployed away from the craft's main body. Harry remarked that this was an artillery-style support craft and most definitely not a fighter.

While all this was happening, Fritz was testing the computer systems, together with the newly augmented sensors, and also trialling the parameters of available flight control with and without computers or AIs. Flying the beast without AIs or computers was possible, but created a very obvious strain on the major and Harry's capabilities. Satisfied, the major nodded. 'Right, back to base, refuel, rearm, provision and off we go hunting a sub. Any questions or observations not already covered? No. OK, take us back to dock twelve, please, Harry. Base Techs, please stand by, we will be there in ten minutes. *Mudshark* techs, please also report. Once docked, you have one hour for final checks of all systems.'

An hour and fifteen minutes later they were heading at speed out of the bay towards the point in the moderately salty ocean from where they had originally recovered *Mudshark*.

As they had some five hundred kilometres to go and the AIs were perfectly capable of running the ship, the humans dozed away the couple of hours' travel time. The major alerted them all when they were fifty kilometres out and they went to light alert as *Mudshark* slowed down to twenty-five kilometres per hour. They already had their combat suits on, so it was more of a heads up to visit the loo, grab a snack and a drink, then run checks at their appointed stations. Glint and Flint were inside the Manta V submersible checking the systems and running some last-minute adjustments on the Harpoon for probable subsurface deployment, so Marko called them up to come to the cockpits.

They cruised around the area where they had first spotted *Mudshark* from the air prior to organising its retrieval.

'Major Longbow.'

'Games Board monitor. How may I be of service?'

'I wish to conduct a background interview with one of your crew as to how this craft was captured by you.'

'Yes, of course. Sergeant Major Spitz, can you assist, please?'

Marko groaned to himself then turned from his engineering board to look at the monitor, first affixing a welcoming smile on his face. The once-human had lowered himself to Marko's face level and was looking intently at him as if he was some moderately interesting biological specimen. Marko looked at the handsome male face and wondered if the individual ever thought of his family or had even visited them since he had been recruited as a child. He had changed beyond all the usual human augments into the part human but mostly audiovisual recording and editing antigravity-assisted machine.

'Sergeant Major Marko Spitz. For our viewers, can you please tell us your thoughts and actions when this craft was liberated from the Gjomvik interlopers.'

Marko, who had done so many interviews that he'd lost count, slipped into what Jan called his 'Sphere persona'. She'd teased him about it many times, saying that he almost came across as being knowledgeable and sincere.

'It is amazing to think that only forty-eight standard hours ago we captured this craft. At the time the major had been way ahead of us, flying high cover for our hovercraft, when he relayed sensor data of two escape pods disappearing over the horizon. Some hours earlier one of our satellites had noted a large, unusual disturbance on the ocean surface and, as we had been out doing test firings and aerial recovery of the Harpoon seizure and electronic control missile, we were vectored to investigate. The Aurora combat reconnaissance and surveillance aircraft the major was flying had been stripped of its weapon so that it could carry its standard surveillance drone and the Harpoon. The high-speed drone had relayed the first images of *Mudshark* as its chameleon-ware shut down. Major Longbow made a snap decision and deployed the Harpoon, realising that this craft was something new, because the Intel AI could not identify it as an Administration craft or any other known vehicle. The Harpoon accelerated to Mach 4 to get to *Mudshark* as quickly as possible; it was quite literally down to its last ten litres of pure fuel water as it deployed its air brakes and latched onto the communication mast at about thirty kilometres per hour, shearing it off, then swinging around and locking into the electronic feeds.'

Marko watched the monitor as he was talking, knowing that as he spoke the hybrid of human and machine was editing and splicing images of the Aurora and the Harpoon missile into its data feeds, over the recording that it was making of him. Marko wondered how much humanity the monitor still retained as he continued his story.

'The Harpoon's control protocols, designed by Sergeant Fritz van Vinken, then crashed what remained of *Mudshark*'s computers and seized control of the propulsion systems. Control was given to Fritz at his console aboard our hovercraft so he could start moving *Mudshark* away from the area. We rendezvoused with the craft some hours later and jumped across into the open hangar door to take possession. As we discovered later, the only reason it was afloat, with no AG, was due to the huge amount of flotation built into it. We then managed to coax one hundred kilometres per hour out of it and nursed it back to the base.'

The monitor nodded, gracing him with a tight little smile as it spoke. 'My thanks, Sergeant Major, and my compliments to you. Folks, it looks like things are starting to happen. We shall bring you the action of the day in this special presentation from the Games Board, so stay focused on us! And now a message from our very latest Games Board-approved energy drink. *Vapour*! Drink it to stay alert and focused while relaxing and enjoying all the Games Board presentations! And yes! It is perfectly safe, designed specifically with you, our wonderfully supportive viewers, in mind. Gloriously safe even for the pregnant among you who are bringing into our Universe the next generation of viewers, who we of the Games Board will faithfully serve as always.'

Three

The major keyed his microphone again. 'We are in the main area. Sergeant van Vinken, you ready to go? Right, do your stuff.'

'Subsurface drones deploying, aerial drones away.'

The plan was to drop ten Intel drones around the area, within a one-kilometre radius of the battle site. Nautical Meteorological had advised them earlier that the area in question had been relatively quiet at the original battle time, although, with two of the planet's moons in conjunction, the tidal flows would peak six hours after they had arrived in the vicinity, which would mean unpredictable high waves. Everyone was now constantly watching their own instruments and keeping an eye on the Intel feeds as well. They scanned the entire area, found nothing, recovered the drones in sequence, stepped out another kilometre and did it all over again, and again and again.

They had covered a rather large chunk of water. It was mid-afternoon, the ocean was now very lumpy with the huge tidal shifts and Marko, for one, was getting rather annoyed about still being in combat gear. It was really good kit, but it was designed to keep them alive, not necessarily comfortable. So, as always it seemed, the excitement started when they were ready to go to sleep with Fritz yelling, 'Contact, contact, fifteen degrees starboard, seven hundred and fifty metres, depth eighty-five metres, sea mount; anomaly is present on top of the sea-mount, considerable aquatic-life activity around it.'

Count on Fritz to be correct in his language most of the time, Jan mused, and it was always good for the monitors.

'Seal up, combat protocols! Stand-off at five hundred metres,' the major responded. 'Recover, refuel and redeploy drones.'

Fritz, totally immersed in his numerous data feeds, reported again: 'Drone six destroyed, sir, drones five and seven under attack. Same as the octopoids in configuration, but massing twenty-five to thirty-five kilograms, and a few up to the one-hundred-kilogram mark.'

'OK, let's climb to fifteen metres and take the speed up to two hundred, co-pilot. If any surface targets are acquired, Staff Jan Wester, you are cleared to engage.'

'Acknowledged, Major.'

'Anomaly moving towards the centre of our orbit. Surmise that it is the Gjomvik Submersible, as it is trying to communicate with this craft,' Fritz called out.

From the co-pilot's chair, Harry asked, 'Method?'

'Long-wave acoustic. Comms buoy away.'

The major nodded his approval. 'Acknowledge the signal. Is it human or AI?'

'Feels human, sir,' Fritz replied. 'Female Germanic accented. Unusual for an AI.'

'Right, Fritz, standard parley protocol.'

'No acknowledgment, sir, but it's still moving, being intensely attacked. It must be a very tough piece of kit.'

On a side screen Marko watched the visual feeds from the submerged drones, fascinated as hundreds of squid-like creatures zoomed up out of the depths to engage each drone. The controlling computers on board *Mudshark* and the small computers in each of the drones tried every defensive tactic available to them, from firing tiny short-range high-speed torpedoes into the larger octopoids, to tumbling into the masses of smaller ones to suck the creatures into the twin, side-mounted, shrouded propellers, to lasering the eyes of the creatures with intense ultraviolet light, or high-speed ramming. But the numbers of octopoids just kept increasing, slowly wearing the tough little drones down.

The major went to his main weapons expert. 'Harry, quick idea?'

'Well, if that sub is tough enough to withstand those critters, it could probably survive smart depth charges, sir.'

The major gave a curt nod. 'Fritz, flash her the specs of what's coming down the chute, advise her we are trying to help.'

The seconds ticked past before Fritz spoke. 'She acknowledges, sir, but is being very rude about it. Says she has some missiles left and if she goes down, we will as well.'

The major shrugged. 'Fire the squibs. Watch for missile launch. Deploy craft Orbital countermeasures. Marko, get the drones to clear the blast area.'

They could feel the thumps on the outer hull as the packages of mini-explosive squibs were fired from their mortars. Harry had suggested, before they put to sea, that they would be perfect for the octopoids. Dozens of the fist-sized directional grenades, each with a pair of high-speed water jets attached, sprayed out to circle and sink around Fritz's 'anomaly', the mercenary sub.

Marko could see the aerial missile countermeasures drones start to circle *Mudshark*, as *Mudshark* itself continued to orbit above the ocean waves with the sub at its centre. The drones spaced out so that any three of them could see each quadrant around *Mudshark*. The teardrop-shaped lifting bodies had stubby wings, carried six short-range micro-missiles each, plus a small powerful pulse laser, with a comms system that created a swarm mentality between them.

The submerged drones moved at full speed out of the blast area but he noted that two were very slow. 'Five and Seven appear to be damaged. They will probably not make it. Replacements on standby.'

The rail guns started firing as targets were acquired around the comms buoy. Fritz saw how close the octopoids were to the buoy so he brought another one online, then held it in the launch mortar tube on standby.

Fritz took down all communications a fraction of a second before the squibs' detonation and then brought them up again just as the comms buoy was destroyed by a ricochet with a howling screech erupting from all their headphones. With his ears ringing, Marko advised, 'Drones Five and Seven destroyed, replacements away. Reserve down to five. Aerial drones reconfigured for water surface operations if required. New comms buoy in position in thirty seconds.'

The major growled. 'OK. Jan, watch that shooting, we only have one other comms bouy in reserve!'

Jan yelled back. 'Sorry, the round bounced off a large octopoid which was on an intercept with us. It is no longer.'

The major resisted the urge to glance over his shoulder at her, looking down at his screens instead, only to see more of the creatures rising to the churning sea surface. 'Damn! Increase speed to max, height to max. I wonder if these things can launch themselves out of the water? Jig and jive, Harry!'

Bugger, Marko thought, as he always hated that movement. He loaded a motion-sickness package into his bloodstream from his bioware as Jan yelled again: 'Sir, we have octopoids, big bastards, landing on the rear housings! So, yes, they most definitely can launch themselves from the water! They are ripping the covers off the AG units!'

'Shit! Jan, deal with them as best you can; I am releasing the AI proxies to your control.'

Seconds later Marko saw the titanium-clad proxies appear on each side of the rear deck, firing slow-speed big-calibre gel rounds at the octopoids. As the gel rounds hit, they ripped away great lumps of flesh and gristle, injuring the main body parts of the creatures so that they slumped and slid off the casings into the sea below.

Marko's system warnings were starting to go off as his hearing recovered. 'We have critical damage. Port-side AG unit is dropping power, sir; down nine per cent and falling. I have compensated. Coolant levels are also down; if we can get it, we need additional fuel water.'

'Do the best you can, Marko, I will not risk sucking some of those critters into the water tanks.'

'Understood. I have maxed the atmospheric collection,' Marko said, as Fritz interrupted.

'Gjomvik pilot says she is going to surface, then eject. At her current speed she will surface in five minutes. Says she is covered in the octopoids, with a very large one trying to drag her back down. She has a major problem with her propulsion system. Says she is going to go for a rapid surfacing and try to get clear as her craft hits the surface. Gutsy!'

'Fritz, kamikaze the nearest drone into that big octopoid!'

'On it!'

The closest drone peeled in towards the slowly surfacing submarine and accelerated to its maximum speed, driving itself deeply into the giant squid-like creature before collapsing its tiny antimatter core containment, with the resulting explosion shredding the creature into dozens of pieces. The submarine accelerated upwards, no longer being held back, although smaller creatures still attempted to intercept it, as the major barked out, 'Glint, get to the Manta. I will open the main hangar door so you can launch the Harpoon. Do this right, people, and we will get the pilot and the sub.' They all nodded as he added: 'Fritz, get the specs on the sub's ejection pod. Tell her she will not survive if she goes into the ocean with those bastards down there. We are going to have to go for an aerial recovery.'

Fritz spoke while his fingers flew in a blur over three separate touch panels. 'Acknowledged; have the info. Pod is basic teardrop configuration of 1200mm diameter, 3200mm long. Has a small antigravity unit capable of sustaining the pod at ten metres up for three hours.'

'Good. Fritz, put two of the airborne drones on the surface to act as backup comms links.' The units instantly decelerated and dropped down onto the water, watching for the ascending sub.

Fritz counted down. 'Two minutes to surface on my count. Stand by, stand by, five, four, three, two, one, mark! I have the emergence point, as indicated on screens.'

The major took control and swung *Mudshark* in a hard banking turn, which it was probably never designed to do, then deployed the main air brakes, dropping the speed to one hundred kilometres per hour as he yelled out, 'Jan, everything you have across the emergence point, please. Door coming open; hang on everyone — this is going to be interesting. As soon as you get a target, Glint, fire!'

Mudshark was pitching, rolling and yawing in an alarming fashion. The major and Harry, even with the aid of the computers and the AIs, were barely maintaining control of the craft as they approached the emergence spot at speed. Between them they were all furiously compensating for the now-open front hangar door and ramp and the constantly moving turrets of the rail guns. Jan timed it perfectly, halting fire and switching targets just as the Gjomvik one-man sub erupted out of the water, rising a full four metres or so from the surface with another large octopoid clinging to its stern.

The Harpoon flashed across the rapidly closing space between them and the sub, as the ejection system ripped the entire front cone, housing the cockpit, off the wasp-shaped machine, and blasted it into the air. Simultaneously, something — and Marko could only presume it was Glint — engaged the largest octopoid on the remains of the sub as it started to splash back onto the surface. The entire head portion of the creature disintegrated and the thought flashed through his head: That's some very efficient shit in action!

The major hauled the nose of the protesting *Mudshark* high into the air, following the ejection pod, as two large octopoids exploded through the ocean's surface, seizing onto the pod. An instant later the entire assemblage of pod and octopoids smashed in through the open hangar doors to crash hard against the left side of the enclosure, shoving *Mudshark* hard to port.

Marko's control panel was going berserk. The ammunition power feed onto the starboard guns had become intermittent and Jan was yelling in his ear to get it back online; the ramp hydraulics were jammed solid as linear gun rounds from Glint blew the remains of an octopoid right through it. The starboard main propulsion was rapidly going offline with small octopoids slithering into its air intakes and causing it to rapidly drop thrust, slewing the whole craft sideways as the port-side thruster tried to keep forward speed. Marko cut power to it and ramped up the centre thruster to one hundred and ten per cent.

The port-side AG unit was also failing, further dropping them dangerously towards a rollover point as the major, who was hell bent on legging it out of the area, poured on the power. They had a flash message from Fritz that he had the sub under his command and had it making best speed full astern, away from the area. Marko overrode the major's command protocols and lowered the front cockpit as best as he could to try and tidy up the airflow, and at the same time Harry was overriding Jan's control of the guns, hauling them back towards the body of the craft.

The sea, twelve metres below them, was a boiling confusion of small octopoids trying to launch themselves on board; the countermeasure orbiting sentries destroyed most of them but dozens still made it onto the ship. As Marko glanced into the side monitor to see what was happening in the hangar, it appeared to be complete bedlam. Glint seemed to be trying to shoot the remaining large octopoid in the head, without destroying whatever was in line of sight behind it. The octopoid seemed more determined to get at the sub's pilot, with the engineering proxy arriving to try to get to her first and protect her.

Marko shunted all the remaining hydraulics into getting the guns snug against the ship's body again as the starboard ammo feed failed completely. He equalised the power to the starboard AG unit and fired up the main hover fans as their craft sank closer to the surface. The major was yelling at Base for immediate air support, and if possible bombardment from the Orbitals. The Games Board were, of course, countering the requests, citing that the crew's predicament made for really good AV. The Games Board monitors seemed to be smiling at everything, to say nothing of the bandwidth they were hogging while they uploaded the action.

The Intel AI proxy had disappeared from the rear deck as there were no more larger octopoids to engage and seconds later Marko watched as it powered out of the hangar with the now battered octopoid in tow and Glint still attached, dragon-like, biting deeply down into its head. The octopoid was flung sideways into their slipstream as an obviously protesting Glint was unceremoniously seized by a leg and dragged off the creature by the proxy who, with its full flight systems engaged, looked like an avenging angel towing the devil's own hound. The sight obviously delighted the Games Board monitors as one of them actually laughed, something Marko had heard only very rarely.

Marko's control board was, if anything, getting worse. The port-side weapon was no longer moving towards the body of their ship. Jan was still engaging as many targets as possible with it, including some rather nice shooting blowing the smaller alien creatures off the housings of *Mudshark*. He was trying to get the starboard ammo feed sorted while balancing the craft at the same time, but it was no use. They still had a dangerous list to port, and at their current speed there was no way they could make a safe transition to full hovercraft surface mode. The only good thing was that fewer octopoids were presenting themselves on the surface.

Marko made his assessments. 'Boss, we have to lose the port-side gun assembly. Starboard one is offline, although the Tech AI says he needs five minutes to sort it with Glint's help, and requests Flint as well. In four minutes we will impact the surface anyway.'

The major, who was still wrestling with the controls, barked out, 'Lose it!'

Jan yelled in response. 'Give me five seconds, Marko!'

She fed commands to the pod and stopped the ammo feeds as Marko engaged and then fired the cut-away charges when she nodded at him, the whole assembly dropping and spinning away to clip the port outer thruster with the resulting bang felt right through the ship. The craft now rolled until it was only a few degrees off the horizontal.

'Rigged for surface operations, pilot,' Marko said.

'Stand by, stand by, gun pod detonation in five seconds,' Jan called.

The major smiled, thinking what an excellent crew he had. 'OK Jan, nice work, that will sort out some of those bloody things at least.'

The sea hundreds of metres behind them suddenly heaved as the rail guns were deliberately electronically overloaded some twenty metres down under the water.

'Transitioning to surface. What can you give me, Marko?'

'Basically full hover, sir. The fuel feeds can now be augmented with the sea water. Will be a dirty oxygen/hydrogen catalytic cracking, but considering we will be with friendlies soon, I hope, the converters will hold out. I can now also cool the port-side AG unit and hopefully get that back online. Best speed in our current state is seventy-five kilometres per hour. Glint reports that the starboard ammo feeds have been further damaged by small octopoids. They may be able to get one single gun operational within fifteen minutes.'

The major nodded and turned to Jan. 'Status?'

'The surviving probes have either been recovered, or are covering the Gjomvik sub. The pilot has been identified as Squadron Leader Eva Marks. Intel considers her an important capture, as she is a senior member of Leopard Strike and is their Intel analyst. She is currently in sick bay, unconscious. The octopoid came very close to killing her. She is stabilised but needs major reconstruction work on her skull and upper body.

'We are down to having thirty per cent functional craft Orbital sentries. Most other weapons are expended. The AI proxies are both functioning, but seriously damaged, and Glint has lost part of his tail. The proxies and Glint are removing the last of the octopoids remains. So if we go up against anything over the next eighty-five standard minutes we have very little to fight with.'

The major gave her a smile. 'Please assist with octopoid removal, thanks, Staff. Good work. Fritz, what have you got to add?'

The little man was still totally immersed in his systems but, as they watched, one of his slim hands reached up inside the dome surrounding his head to scratch his hairless pate.

'Primary communications are fine, but the main aerials are damaged. It seems that the octopoids target all communications gear. Secondary comms links are down, although the Games Board systems are still at one hundred per cent. Gjomvik sub is making twenty kilometres per hour and the octopoids are no longer showing any interest in it. We have a surface escort meeting us in one hour. I shall cannibalise some of the damaged gear and get us one good working aerial at least.'

'Good. Thank you, Technical Sergeant van Vinken. Sergeant Major Stevens?'

'Yeah, right. This thing is only just hanging together, but we will get home, I am sure.'

The crew smiled, knowing that Harry loathed having to say anything when on camera. Jan moved around, checking for anything and everything and doing her best mother duck impression by asking if anyone needed a drink. Then she disappeared aft with her pistol in hand.

One of the Games Board monitors arrived back at Marko's station. 'May I ask your views of this action, Sergeant Major?'

'Certainly. Well, on balance I would say we did rather well. Nothing broken that cannot be repaired, although we lost a percentage of our capabilities. Most interesting craft this, and certainly built tough. The AI proxies are a bit bent and I note that our junior crew member ACE, Sergeant Glint, has lost a part of his tail, probably by stabbing it into the mouth of an octopoid, but they are the only casualties.'

The monitor nodded with great enthusiasm. 'Yes! Our local viewers are already commenting on his most excellent abilities in a fight and, yes, you are quite right, he did use his tail as a stabbing weapon. Most impressive. He has been awarded an additional bonus in that after he had his tail damaged he seemed to become even more tenacious in attempting to bite the alien creature's head off, or just tear it apart. You must be very proud of him.'

Marko did not know if he should shake his head or nod in agreement so did neither. 'I'm pleased about his actions, although I must admit that I'm not pleased about him trying to chew on the octopoid's brain while flying over a very deep ocean. He would have taken months to get home if he had gone into the sea.'

'Indeed, that would have been unfortunate. However, the still images of him being dragged off the alien, protesting loudly, by the Intelligence proxy are selling extremely well. Thank you, Sergeant Major Spitz.'

Marko smiled, nodded and turned back to his board as Fritz yelled: 'Contact, contact, six o'clock, suborbital, non-Administration, thirty-five kilometres above us and descending fast. Gjomvik!'

A beautifully regulated voice chimed into their on board comms system, something it should not be able to do, thought Marko, but then again it was their ship.

'Greetings to the Administration occupants of KA14. I thank you for retrieving my good friend and colleague Squadron Leader Marks. I hoped to find her well, but alas the medical computer tells me otherwise. I also note that you were not responsible for her injuries. I am in your debt. You are welcome to the tech that is the KA14 and the tech in the pilot's pod of the submersible.'

As whoever it was said this, Major Michael Longbow arrived in their compartment, pulled Fritz's headphones off and whispered in his ear. The major then turned and went back to the bridge of *Mudshark*. Fritz's fingers flew over his various keyboards and touchscreens. Marko knew something was up and hoped whatever it was, it was not detectable by *Mudshark*'s remaining Gjomvik tech, as Fritz announced: 'Missile launch from the incoming craft! Vector is eighty kilometres to our stern. Impact in three minutes. It's very specific. It's our prize! Sorry, Intel, there is nothing we can do.'

Marko shrugged and carried on the balancing act of keeping *Mudshark* level and moving when the major was suddenly at his side whispering in his ear. 'Mate, find Glint, hide him in the AG unit and for fuck's sake shut him up. I do not want these pricks knowing that he is here. I shall report him lost over the side. Run!'

Marko leapt out of his seat as the restraints peeled off him and ran aft, finding Glint just outside the rear hatchway sealing off his damaged tail. He grabbed him and dragged him back inside the hatch telling him what he had to do. Glint nodded, then sprinted back to the engine room and had most of the main inspection hatch cover plate nuts off before Marko arrived panting behind him. As soon as the cover was removed, Glint clambered inside. Marko slammed the hatch back on, effectively hiding him in the dampening systems built into the wall of the AG unit, and felt him leave his mind. Glint had once mentioned to him that there was an additional link between them, but Marko had never really thought about it until that moment. He arrived back at his station just as the ten-kilometre proximity warning was issued by the major who added: 'Combat alert, crew. They are going to be alongside in about seven minutes. Intel proxy, you are reminded that I am in charge of this operation; step away from the Squadron Leader now. In fact, place yourself in the open and try to learn as much as possible about their craft.'

The sleek humanoid machine responded. 'Certainly, Major.'

'Technology-Materials proxy, have you a functioning rail gun yet?'

'Unfortunately not, major.'

The major sighed. 'Stand down, then. Attempt repairs to the front hatchway, please.'

'As you wish, Major.'

Marko checked his instrument board with its multiple screens and saw that everything was pretty much the same. He had shut down the port AG unit earlier, notwithstanding it was partially functioning again, and as the starboard one was only just ticking over, while they were in hover mode he let them be. Considering his inbuilt shielding, Glint would have been all right in the working antigravity unit anyway but Marko wanted to be sure of the ACE's safety. He switched to one of his side screens to pick up the Games Board commentary on the approaching ship.

'What an exciting day it has been, folks, and here we have a most interesting and unexpected additional piece of data for you. Yes, it is an often spoken of, but rarely seen, Gjomvik craft. It is a private cruiser from the der Boltz family fleet, yes, information gained from a voice match tells me that it is captained by none other than the legendary Colonel Baron Willie der Boltz himself! As you can see, it is big, but not really, really big. However, it is certainly capable of lifting this *Mudshark* many times over and definitely appears long-jump interstellar capable. The fact that it is also capable of descending into an atmosphere, and indeed of operating on antigravity in this world's major gravitational well, speaks volumes of the enormous power it must possess. And, as we can see, it is beautiful, illustrating the difference between a fishing trawler and a luxury yacht. Both ply the sea, carry people and goods, but that is where the similarities end. We wonder why it has appeared here on this planet. Could it be that this planet has something that the Gjomvik Corporations would rather steal than negotiate for? And could it be that, once again, the heroic crew of *Basalt* has thwarted them? The Administration must be very anxious about it, but as this is an outpost base it is not well-equipped to deal with a threat such as this.'

As the beautifully streamlined and sculpted starship slowed to match their speed, they could see the weapons being trained on them in ports slid open in its side. Harry complimented the major on doing the right thing and not being aggressive towards them.

'Jan, Fritz, get down to the hangar and prepare to transport our guest, please,' Harry instructed.

The hangar cameras, what remained of them, showed Jan and Fritz flanking the gurney with its inbuilt medical systems at the edge of the ramp, as a tongue-like structure descended from the starship and reached across to rest firmly against the remains of the ramp supports. Harry noted that no words had been spoken about them slowing or heaving to. He concluded that the Gjomvik starship must have seen the damage and known that if they stopped *Mudshark* it would probably not be able to get under way again. He also concluded that the Baron must still be an honourable and generous person to make such a decision as he had decided many years earlier, while doing business with him, that he liked the man.

'Major Longbow. You have an excellent crew, sir, and my special thanks to Sergeant Major Spitz. I can see you listening, Marko, my thanks. The dragon is still with us and most appreciated. Major, we would honour your inclusion in our company should you or any of your people see fit. And at the risk of sounding impolite, may I ask if you have any fresh apples on board?'

The major cleared his throat to ask, 'Who am I addressing, please?'

The voice sounded through their comms again. 'As the Games Board has rightly assumed, I am William der Boltz, Major.'

Michael Longbow looked across the displays to see heads shaking, then glanced at Harry, who also shook his head. He turned in his seat to catch the eyes of the other crew present. 'I thank you for the opportunity to work with your company, sir. I decline. My crew can make up their own minds. And, yes, I am sure that we can find you a few fresh apples from *Basalt*'s gardens. Please accept them with our compliments.'

The crew all chorused their declines, except Fritz, who just ignored the question. Seeing that the comms link with the baron had been cut, Marko said: 'Apples! What the hell? Now, we've all heard of the legendary Willie der Boltz, and I have even done business with him. But apples?'

Harry strode past Marko, heading for the little galley. 'Yeah, one of his only vices. That and tea. Even has his own tea plantations!'

Five minutes later the bridge crew watched as the still unconscious Eva Marks, sealed inside an AG medical unit, was manoeuvred into the hangar with a box of apples and other fresh fruit at her feet.

The baron spoke again. 'You are honourable people; my thanks to you for looking after Eva. Please place the gurney on the ramp.'

As they watched, the end of the ramp gently folded around the gurney then rapidly withdrew into the starship. A few moments later it reappeared, the gurney now loaded with cases of wine and beer. The gurney was placed inside the hangar and the ramp withdrew to the Gjomvik ship.

The major laughed and thanked der Boltz, to which the baron replied: 'Well, I'll take any opportunity to gather a little fruit from the legendary gardens of *Basalt*. I hope one day we can all break bread together. Thank you and goodbye.'

While the elegant, mottled mauve and black craft lifted rapidly, ascending into the afternoon sky, Marko noted that a highly compressed message in one of Fritz's codes, from the

Baron's dragon, had arrived in his private message box. He smiled, wondering what it contained.

The rest of the journey back to base was uneventful. Marko plucked Glint from his hiding place and with the aid of the Tech proxy sealed off the tail stump. Marko wondered why the major had wanted him hidden as the Gjomvik ship would have been aware of the ACE from the Games Board feeds. He decided that the major knew something that he did not. He was thinking about it when the Tech proxy slid up beside him. He looked up at it and raised his eyebrows in query. The machine nodded its sleek head to him. 'My apologies for interrupting your reverie, Sergeant Major. I have a small matter that I would wish to discuss with you.'

Marko indicated Jan's empty seat. She was out on the aft deck taking a few minutes' break. As the sleek machine folded itself down into the seat, Marko asked it what it wanted to discuss. The machine unfolded a large screen out of its wrist which displayed a small monkey-like creature; this got Marko's immediate attention as he could see that it was an ACE. The video showed the creature carefully moving across the ceiling of one of the base's hangars.

'This is definitely an ACE, Sergeant Major,' said the Tech proxy, 'as we have been watching it for weeks, but it possesses high-tech chameleon-ware and has avoided capture. As Tech AI, I have taken it upon myself to talk with you about it and wonder what we should do? We have scans of the ACE and believe it may have originated from your home province and be of Dine family manufacture.'

Marko looked through the displays, mapping them against his own internal records, and wished that Topaz was present to verify his thoughts. 'Interesting. Yes, I believe you're right. Looking at the scans, I would say that the ACE may be out of its indenture and travelling throughout the Sphere.'

'Yes. That is probably correct, but it keeps trying to gain access to the incinerators. We wonder if it is trying to commit suicide.'

Jan had quietly entered the cockpit and heard what was said. 'It happens. It's sad, but it happens. They become lonely and distraught just like any other sentient creature and decide oblivion is the best answer. The neverending problem with life creation. What if the living created creature does not wish to live?'

Marko and the proxy nodded in understanding. Fritz, who had been quietly listening, said: 'Um, I have a piece of music that might help. Kind of peppy and a real tonic for sad souls. Particularly ones that have been engineered. Hey, Marko! I know that look. You are about to help another lost waif ACE, eh? Here, have opened the music file to you. Just play it in that hangar and watch what happens.'

They all grinned and Jan patted Fritz on the shoulder as Marko opened the file and listened briefly to the music. It seemed gentle and quite innocuous, but knowing Fritz it would be packed with high maths.

They slid up the ramp many hours after sunset and were treated to the sight of a beautiful conjunction of the planet's twin moons as they eased into the hangar. Nothing else blew up and nothing else failed except, as they arrived and came to a complete stop, the ramp finally gave up the ghost and fell onto the workshop hangar floor with a loud clatter.

The crew assembled in front of the battered *Mudshark* as the monitors and proxies left.

Marko looked at Glint. 'Did it taste nice?'

'What?'

'The octopoid's brain, Glint.'

'I was not eating it, Marko, I was trying to kill it.'

He sounded quite indignant and became even more so when Jan and Marko grinned at him. 'Just as well, Glint,' Jan said. 'I wouldn't want you getting a reputation.'

Glint shrugged and with a wicked smile said: 'I think it actually needed frying and sprinkling with a little pepper.'

Michael Longbow addressed the crew as they waited outside *Mudshark*. 'OK, people, well done. Take the day off tomorrow. Party, my place, tomorrow night. Harry, make sure that booze is secured and bring it along.'

Harry nodded. 'No problem, boss. This is the good stuff. Hey, by the way. A small niggling question. Why did you want Glint hidden?'

The major looked at Harry and gave a curt little nod. 'The baron is an inquisitive chap and I have been advised that he has taken a serious interest in Glint and what is inside him. Seems that he knows rather a lot about our little mate here, and knowing that the baron almost always gets precisely what he wants, I did not want to give him the opportunity.'

Four

The following morning, as the first light of the day was creeping skywards, Marko, Jan, Glint and Flint were inside an aircraft maintenance hangar at the base airfield. Flint had jacked himself into the living building's audio system and was waiting until the other three had seated themselves at its centre.

Marko turned on the amplifiers and played the music track, seeing in his brain the beautiful, tonal, mathematically soothing music, and admiring Fritz for his total devotion to the art form. Ten minutes later, as the tracks of music slowly changed to further aid a troubled ACE mind, he saw the little monkey-like creature move about in the building's security system high above him. A further ten minutes went by, with Marko wondering if he was going to have to play the entire suite of music over again, until the monkey came out into plain view and crept across to where the three were seated.

Marko turned slowly as the small silver-coloured primate walked cautiously towards him. He gestured for the ACE to sit with them and stayed quiet until the music stopped. He then looked at the creature, allowing his augments to visually map it. He slowly nodded as it signed to him.

'You are Marko. I am so pleased to see you. Are you really Marko of the Spitz family from Waipunga?'

Marko nodded and the monkey continued: 'I was created by the Dines, but the family that I was indentured to did not send me back for the full augments when the children grew up.'

'I know the Dines well. Are you capable of seeing my biometrics and can you vocalise?'

The ACE signed back to him. 'No and no. I am sadly lacking in most skills apart from caring for small children. Do you know of any here who I can help? I feel so good this day, so much better than I have in a long, long time.'

The *Basalt* crew members gave silent thanks to Fritz and his genius. Glint took one of the little monkey's hands in his.

'Have you a name?' Jan asked the creature.

'LSM ... it is for Little Silver Monkey.'

They all frowned at that. Marko wondered why many humans had an ACE created, but as soon as the creature had worked out its indenture, abandoned it and did not fulfil the final part of the contract to equip the ACE with all that it needed to survive and prosper in the Sphere of Humankind.

Flint, who had joined them, looked up at the monkey. 'What do *you* call yourself, ACE? LSM is insulting.'

The creature slowly looked at each of them and shuffled about, looking embarrased. 'I like Josey.'

Glint clapped a hand on the monkey's shoulder, startling it. 'Right! Come on, Flint, let's take Josey to see Topaz for a few checks and some augments. In a couple of days, once you are sorted out, Josey, we will take you over to the Base school. I know you'll enjoy it there.'

As they watched the unlikely trio walking out of the hangar, Jan gave Marko an exuberant kiss. 'Well done us! Another one rescued!'

Two days later a short, fat cylinder slowly surfaced south of the battle zone and sent out a tiny focused squeak to *Basalt*, which was listening for it from orbit.

The Harpoon core, once recovered by an Aurora's drone, gave up a lot of new tech information about the Gjomvik sub. The best part was that the Games Board did not know that *Basalt*'s crew had the information, otherwise they would have insisted that they be given a cut when it was sold on to the Administration Intelligence group.

Later the same day Marko received a message from the local Administration Intelligence group's accounting division to let him know that one of his accounts had been credited with what he considered was a tidy sum for the information he had passed on about the baron.

The following morning Marko, Harry and the major were back in *Mudshark*'s hangar, looking up at it.

'So Harry, is there anything else we can learn from *Mudshark*?' the major asked.

'Not really, boss. Very interesting design which certainly has potential for future use. I have noted in the report how we could improve upon it further. I hope like hell you are not going to ask me to patch it up so we can take it on board *Basalt*. Fritz says that the Gjomvik coding is hardwired into a large part of it, and without spending a lot of time ripping it completely to pieces we would never guarantee a hundred per cent control of it.'

Major Longbow, who was known to 'collect' interesting artefacts, said, 'Nope. Intel AI wants this one. Wants to see if that code can be broken. I'm a little concerned that we'll see this beast, or something very like it, again though. Games Board is very pleased with what we did and wants to see another *Mudshark* in another AV. Sirius, yes that Sirius, who is our Games Board handler and agent, has been in touch again and wants us to do that battle, but I declined as we have real work. Harry, give the troops a twelve-hour movement notice, please. Marko, could you go have a talk with Stephine and work out a price for the Harpoon Intellectual Property? Admin wants it in production and deployed soonest. Right, see you both in a couple of hours.'

The two men watched him depart as Harry said, 'Where are those ACEs of ours, Marko?'

'Last seen with Glint furiously pedalling that push bike you gave him for his birthday down the main road with an MP in hot pursuit an hour or so back. Didn't know that such a contraption could go so bloody fast. They were clocked doing sixty-five kilometres per hour in a twenty-five kilometres per hour zone. Have not heard from them, so I presume it's been sorted. You know, Harry, I should really have given Glint sweat glands. That frill we installed on him as a heat exchanger is just too fierce-looking when he's hot.'

'Coffee's up, guys,' their comms announced.

Harry answered. 'Ta, Veg; nice to have you back! Interesting critters? On our way. Spread the word, twelve-hour movement order.'

After they had finished their break Marko went back to the quarters he shared with Jan and packed up their meagre belongings. He activated both packs but left them where they were for the time being. Jan had left a message for him an hour earlier telling him she was saying their goodbyes around the base. He wandered across to the accounts section of the Sergeants' Mess, squared away their bill and, for the first time, had to pay for Glint's consumption as well. He decided that he would have to have a word with the ACE about doing some chores to pay his way.

The rest of the day was spent with Harry sorting the stock materials from the metal production mill for use on board *Basalt*. Harry then put a call through to Major Longbow. 'Marko and I have squared away the metal requirements and also the fabrication consumables, new tools, cutters and abrasives for everyone. We are up tonnage wise. What do you want to do? Have Patrick bring *Basalt* down, two trips with the Albatross lander or make up a container and have the Base punch it into orbit?'

They waited a minute or so before the major replied. '*Basalt* is on the way down. Will land in a couple of hours.'

Marko was leaning against the chain-link fence separating the Administration area from the airfield as Jan, with Glint following on his bike, joined him.

Jan gave Marko a hug and leant into him, letting him shelter her from the stiff sea breeze. 'What's happening, lover?'

'Look at the entrance to the third hangar from the left at that beautiful, vintage design aircraft. It's called a Pitts Special biplane. Totally aerobatic. They started it up, ran it for about ten minutes and I had hoped to see it flying, but they shut it down again. Nice design; no doubt they probably built it here. Plenty of facilities available as long as one is prepared to pay.'

Jan looked across at Marko, smiled, and rubbed the top of his smooth head. 'Still basically a kid. Nice, shiny, dangerous-as-hell toys attract you, don't they, Marko?'

He grinned, pushing himself against her beautiful curves.

'Yeah, I am. But you're not that shiny! Hey, guy in what looks like a real leather flying suit has just climbed into the cockpit. Great! Going for a start-up.'

As they watched, the aircraft taxied over to one of the runways and minutes later was airborne, howling over their heads and out across the bay. They walked down to the shore and watched the little electric-blue-coloured aircraft giving a good aerobatic display. Glint laid his bicycle down, pointing at the waving tendrils some hundreds of metres out in the bay.

'I hope the pilot knows that adult whorl crustaceans are in the bay and that the mating season is fast approaching.'

'Why, Glint? Oh, I see, data coming from you ... wow, they can throw adolescents that high! Yeah, I hope he knows. But the whorls should be much further north? That's what I read in the local environmental hazards brief last week. What would have attracted them here?'

Glint flashed another information packet across on their crew comms directly into Marko's eyes.

'Ah,' Marko nodded, 'simple as that. Alter three elements in the river water and they will come closer to the seashore, attracted by a possible aphrodisiac source. Trying to get a warning to the pilot but I am either being blocked, or he is just ignoring me!'

They watched in silence, with a slowly gathering group of spectators from the base, as the inevitable happened. The aircraft swooped low and dozens of two-metre-diameter young whorl were thrown upwards by the adults. The pilot suddenly realised his predicament, but the trap had been sprung and the whorls quickly unfurled multiple tendrils with one grasping the aircraft as it desperately wove through the others' tendrils.

There was a loud bang followed by multiple shots as Glint fired on the whorls, but many more were shot out of the water and Glint ran out of ammunition. The alarms were sounding all over the base as additional weapons started firing but it was too late; a single whorl landed in the aircraft's cockpit, instantly dispatching the pilot by biting off his head. It then dragged his body out of the aircraft to fall with it back into the ocean. The aircraft flew straight, unmolested by the other falling whorls; obviously now under remote control, it banked and minutes later landed. There was silence for a few seconds before the whorls turned towards the shore. The crowd rapidly moved inland as the local defences activated, frightening the sea creatures so that they moved into deeper water.

As they walked back towards the frigate *Basalt*, Marko looked at Jan and whispered, 'Was that pilot a good Gjomvik or a bad Gjomvik, Jan?'

She shrugged and gripped his hand a little tighter, saying nothing.

Glint looked at them both and said, 'Well, if he could afford that aircraft I would say that he was wealthy Gjomvik, so would have had a Soul Saver and a link. I could ask Gerald if you like?'

Marko nodded.

Glint contacted the Base AI and said, 'Yeah, he did. He was a military contractor and had one. Gerald said that the pilot's zygote will be attached to his Soul Saver data unit and the re-lifing of him will start tomorrow. I wonder what it will be like for him to be conscious for a year as he concentrates on growing himself a new body. Would not bother me but I wonder what it is like for a true human.'

It was not often that the famous ship was seen in an atmosphere and close to a terrestrial base, in daylight and on the ground, so they had quite a few sightseers lining up against the fences as Patrick refuelled the ship via the large diameter, tendril-like pipes which slid from *Basalt*'s base then snaked out to locate and latch onto the various fuel feeds. Marko flew the Gunbus and its trailer down from the great wasp-shaped vertical mass of *Basalt* and ran a few trips lifting the materials back into the engineering deck access hatch in the side of the ship.

He enjoyed flying the odd little machine and got a few enquiries from some of his mates wanting to have a go. He had to admit it was great fun with only a low little windscreen and then nothing out in front, so he felt quite daring. Veg suggested that he needed a leather flying hat and aviator goggles. On the second run, Glint arrived, and promptly hung out over the front making appreciative noises as they swooped down over the complex. Marko grinned as he opened comms. 'Major.'

'Yes, Marko.'

'When are we going to tart up *Basalt*, exterior wise? Looking a bit worse for wear, don't you think?'

Marko heard the major give a little grunt. 'Agreed. Put a file together and send it at your leisure. Won't be this trip, but soon. OK?'

The comms link cut off abruptly as Marko swore quietly and wondered why he did not engage his mind before his mouth. He saw something below and turned to Glint. 'Glint, do I spy your bicycle on the ground beside *Basalt*? When we drop this load off I want you to go get it and store it properly.'

The ACE looked off into the distance, shrugged and muttered, 'Flint said that he would do it.'

'Flint wouldn't be able to manage it — he simply does not have the mass. Your bike, your responsibility, end of story. What would the boss have to say? When we land go sort it, or no more rides today.'

A few moments later he had to stop himself from laughing out loud watching the steel-grey ACE trying to stomp away and act bad tempered, which was not really his nature. Marko looked across to see the Albatross lander descending to settle beside the main accommodation area just as the comms link chimed open.

'Crew, this is the major. We lift in two hours Standard Time unless there is a pressing need for a delay? No. Right, two hours to sort out your stuff.'

Patrick remotely took control of the Albatross, after they had dumped all their gear on board, flown it up the side of *Basalt* and gently eased it in through the tight main hatchway. The winds were gusting a little so it was much easier for Patrick to do it.

Jan was privileged to fly Stephine's craft up into the hangar deck once the Albatross was sorted, with Veg riding shotgun. Later she told Marko that she really wanted to take it for a decent blast but controlled herself, although she felt that the craft wanted to go much faster. The last job Marko had was to go pick up Ernst from the repair facility, where he had been acting as a standard dumb medical unit. He was very relieved to be back on board and able to behave as a sentient individual once again. Jan performed all the standard tests including a 17J5AI as he had received an upgrade from the base facilities along with the other two medical units on board.

When everyone was finally on board, the major said, 'Lift stations, please, five minutes.'

Most of them were already at their stations although Fritz was late as per normal. Harry ran to get to his comms station in time to hear the major say: 'Harry, whenever you are ready.'

Marko had brought all the antigravity units and thrusters online a few minutes earlier to warm them up. He had also opened the atmospheric jet drives, rotating them out from their housings at the waist of the ship, so he shunted control of them across to Harry, who lifted the ship and rotated it around its axis so he could see out across the barren rocky hills and wide blue ocean bay. Using the AG and side thrusters, Harry took the ship out over the workshops and wharves, slowly climbed up a kilometre or so, powered up the jets and gathered speed. Once they were a few kilometres downrange of the facilities, he lit up the fusion rockets and they roared out through the atmosphere at a leisurely one gravity of thrust.

The major visibly relaxed and issued instructions. 'Two-hundred-kilometre orbit, please, Harry. All crew, we have three hours to establish biosecurity protocols. Once under way to the local Lagrange point, I will brief you on the mission.'

It was one of the drawbacks of bringing the frigate down onto the surface of a planetary biosphere. Bad enough with the lander, but with the frigate, even if they had only had it on the ground for a few hours, the checks still had to be carried out. It was a bit easier with the ACEs helping, and they only found a few of the planet's spider-type beings. This pleased Patrick, who had a phobia about insects in general, having confided in Harry how he had once had a colony of ant-like creatures invade his outer casing. They dutifully set off the bio-gasbombs to ensure they got everything, and then each of them was scanned and tested for pathogens or unwelcome hitchhikers of any kind by Topaz and Ernst, before the major gave the all-clear. The information was logged with the Orbital local control and they were free to be on their way.

Three hours later, with the crew back into their routines and the journey out to the nearest LP under way, the major gathered them in the mess room.

'Right. Interesting mission for us. No Games Board involvement, only Administration and the Haulers' Collective on this deal, so we're effectively off the public audiovisual grid for as long as it takes, something I'm very happy about. I have flashed the files to each of you, but the basic story is that this is a recovery or destroy mission. Briefly, a little over thirty-nine standard years ago a heavy Hauler was tasked with transporting a cargo of nasties after the war known as "Infant". If you don't know about it, look it up. Not one of the battles in that war covered any of its participants in glory. In fact, that war led to the Games Board having considerably more power and influence than they had previously enjoyed.'

He looked around the faces of the crew, before continuing. 'So, this Hauler was tasked with dumping a cargo of biological weapons onto Hades, but it never made it. Big search at the time; nothing found. The Hauler has now turned up. Located by a Ranger Scout who had been tasked to look for octopoids. We have to return to Cygnus 5, uplift a specialist crew of ten, plus the Ranger, and go have a hard look at the Hauler. I have also been advised that the Haulers' Collective want us to recover the ship's core if it is still intact.'

During the week's transit, Harry, Topaz and Marko made a new replacement arm for Marko. They built in a few extra facilities, but there was not a lot of improvement to be made on the previous one anyway, so Marko programmed up the auto-mills and then had Topaz grow the rest of it.

Harry had managed to procure a few extra sheets of titanium, which they earmarked to replace the shielding on the Hog mechanised walker which they had taken as a prize from 27's planet. So now that they had everything they needed, and the time, they decided to rebuild it completely. The original chassis was stripped down to bare metal and still further into its individual components. Harry programmed a couple of the engineering robots to grind the original welds and then re-weld the entire main structure. He smiled to himself, immersed in the physical making, thinking that sometimes it was much nicer to actually build something rather than have it grown.

Veg was having fun redesigning the machine, so they gave up on the old version and basically junked most of it. They retained parts of the cockpit, the primary chassis, the legs and the feet. Following Veg's lead, they laid out a new engine bay, upgraded hydraulics throughout and also decided to put a rail gun on one side and a heavy rotary cannon on the other. With the major's permission, Harry pulled one of the spare gas turbines from storage to mount behind the cockpit, together with a gearbox driving the primary hydraulic pumps. Once they had all the framework and main supports in place, they surface-coloured everything in dark green carborundum which Topaz had modified bacteria grow onto the metal structure. Over the next couple of days they fitted the new cockpit and the hydraulics, the cracker unit, weapons and magazines, and had Fritz run the electrics. They still had all the covers and shielding to make and fit when *Basalt* arrived back at Cygnus 5, but at least the Hog could stamp around and look menacing if required.

Gliese 667C

A few days later they arrived back at the control Orbital Epsilon with Harry announcing that a Ranger would be the first to join them.

Marko considered that the Ranger Squadrons were made up of interesting, but peculiar, people. Deeply calm, utterly fixated on the task at hand and superbly happy in their own company, they were in some respects the elite of the elite. Every Ranger he had met seemed to be able to put people immediately at their ease and then gently, but remorselessly, pump them dry of the information they required. And every one of them he had met was heavily muscled and tall. It took more than twenty-five standard years to train one to full certification, so they had to be something special to start with.

They were also rumoured to carry substantial armour under their skin — he supposed that was another reason for the bulk. The exception was the one who presented herself at the crew airlock as a full colonel, which everyone knew was a rare rank to still be an operative without a crew.

'Hello, ma'am. I am Sergeant Major Marko Spitz. Welcome aboard *Basalt*. Major Longbow will join us shortly; he is currently in conference with Epsilon Admin.'

She looked down at him, smiled, extended her hand and grasped his in a slightly firm way, denoting respect. She towered over him and he felt the same way he did when around Stephine. I must be a midget, he thought.

'So you are Marko. I am very pleased to make your acquaintance. Once I am settled in, I need to discuss a project with you. And I am informed that you have a remarkable crew and something called "real coffee", which is talked of everywhere. Lead on, Sergeant Major.'

He escorted her around the ship introducing her to everyone, and then to the galley where Veg made her a coffee. Veg had told Marko that after making a few thousand more shots he would be an adequate barista, but baking was considerably more interesting being much more like engineering. To go with the colonel's coffee, he brought out his latest biscotti. He figured that everyone had a right to be proud of their work and it was always a good move for any non-commissioned officer to impress a colonel. He was very careful to advise the colonel in the art of dunking, before she broke any of her perfect teeth.

The terrible trio, who had been stalking something or other, came hurtling in and surrounded the colonel. Nail, as the intelligence-gathering ACE of the crew, sat on the table in front of her, staring hard and passing on the information he was gathering via the crew's comm link; Flint scrabbled up onto the table and introduced each of them to her in his very quiet, almost inaudible, way; Glint slid onto his specifically grown stool, which was movable but still attached to the living table by a vine so it could gain sustenance, reached for a biscotti and started taking bites out of it, generating small fragments which whistled through the air. He pointed the remains at her as he spoke. 'So you are Colonel Andrea White. You are a legend, I'm told. What makes you a legend? And how did they grow that ceramic fibre armour into you? It covers all your organs, even those parts that males would find interesting. Marko, I think I need some of that. Nail would like some too, but he is not big enough. No, I think that I would like a penis first.'

Marko cringed and Veg burst out laughing.

The colonel just started giggling, then she reached out and started to stroke Nail, who, amazingly, allowed her to do so. Glint reached for another biscotti, hesitated, and took another two. 'Yup, she's OK. Really different from any other human I have seen but should be fine. Good biscuits, Marko. Make some more. Right, come on you lot, work to do. Let's go.'

Glint led them out at the same speed they'd come in at ... flat out. They watched them go and the colonel said: 'Veg, this coffee is completely different in taste, texture and effect from anything I have ever had before. Can I have another, please?'

The huge man shook his head. 'Nope. One per day, that's the limit. Sorry, Colonel. Stephine will join us shortly and, if you like, she makes excellent tea. Tea you can drink as much as you like. Your ship is approaching. Shall I give it docking instructions? I have moved your personal manoeuvring unit to the main hangar deck.'

She gave a quick shake of her head. 'Thanks, and no that won't be necessary. I should imagine that *Crystal* has already received instructions from Patrick.'

They watched as a beaming Michael Longbow strode into the mess. 'Hello, Andy.'

'Hi, Michael. It has been too long, beautiful.'

She stood up, lifted him off the floor in a hug and kissed him full on the mouth. Everyone started to look for things to do and left the two of them to it. Marko shuddered to think what Glint would have said had he been present. He briefly saw the major much later in the galley, with a big grin on his face, making a large bowl of fresh fruit salad. He disappeared with it back to his cabin, carrying two spoons. Harry smiled and saluted his receding back with his large mug of tea.

'So that is the famous Andy White,' mused Harry. 'The boss always described her as slightly shorter than him. They were a number a long time ago. Must be still sweet on each other. Going to be an interesting trip, guys. We have half the specialist crew arriving at 0800 tomorrow, plus all their equipment, and then the remaining half of the detachment late tomorrow afternoon. The boss wants everything squared away for a 2200 departure. Grab whatever you need from Epsilon. Stephine has sorted the procurements and allowed you each a twenty per cent additional procurement financial buffer should you need it. She says that this could be a difficult mission, so get whatever you deem necessary. Would suggest we do that tonight before the specialists arrive.'

Consequently, they all worked late into the night. Jan pulled additional medical stores to cover the extra personnel and also obtained two small combat medical drones. Fritz secured additional communication systems, prepped them and placed them in combat storage. He then went through all the craft on board, plus the Ranger's ship, and tied the communications together. Harry and Veg requisitioned spare weapons for everyone, plus two additional Troop Lifters: these were basically a framework, including a hardened cockpit, storage units, four gimballed manoeuvring engines, a good sized AG unit, twin propulsion systems and a series of attachment stations which housed individual drop sleds, and slung down each side of the machine were twin heavy calibre rail guns. They were wild machines with a heavy punch as they could drop and then support a section minus of eight, plus the pilot; military personnel everywhere liked them as they could also work in just about any environment with or without atmosphere or gravity.

Stephine methodically checked everything off, laid in additional preserved rations, and then ramped up the gardens output as well. Marko spent his time checking off the fuel systems on each of their craft, topping up every tank and then looking long and hard at the Intel reports from the colonel as to where they could pick up water fuel on the mission. There were two good-sized ice moons in the target system and also some nice icy comets not far from Lagrange points at four of their jump locations.

They even managed to grab a half decent sleep before the first of the specialists arrived on board at 0800 hours. Jan's assessment to Marko was that they were an interesting bunch.

The Warrant Officer First Class in charge knew Harry well, so that made life a lot easier.

Patrick had set aside one of the engineering hangars for them, so they were initially shown where to stow their suit containers and then assigned cabins. Fritz and Harry then gave the newcomers a quick tour of the ship as Jan and Marko went through the specialist detachment's gear, laying it out, and then storing it all for prioritised optimum access.

The major and the colonel had left the ship early for a command meeting, taking Stephine as First Mate with them. When they returned at midday they were all business with the major sending the message: 'Crew, once the second part of the specialist salvage team arrives we will get under way. Briefing will take place after the first jump is complete. External comms will be locked down in one hour.'

Harry gave a briefing to part of the crew. 'Not sure if this is going to be an easy mission, Marko. Hard security for one thing. Just got the word. Epsilon is sending over two additional long-term ten-man survival pods as well. The hangar deck is going to get a little too crowded. Um, when the pods arrive, site one in the second cargo airlock underneath the barracks deck, and the other in the second airlock above the first engineering deck. Jan, Veg, can you sort those with Marko, please? Check 'em and then liven them up. OK, they are also deploying three Busters for us ... shit, one of those will take out a Cruiser no problem, so what are they expecting?'

He touched his comms link, saying, 'Captain Stephine, ma'am, I need authorisation to unlock the primary heavy weapons store as these guys have a deal of explosives with them. Could you also lock the Busters against the hull, please?'

In another part of the ship Stephine smiled. 'The heavy weapons store will unlock for you when you approach the arms cote, Harry, just as it always has. I have assumed control of it, but not locked you out. Please continue to call me Stephine when on our secure network, and yes, I shall lock on the Busters.'

Marko watched the Busters sliding up beside them, noting that they were almost as long as *Basalt* and tens of metres in diameter: they were designed to be smashers of heavy ships or Orbital stations. He knew that, once deployed, they could operate independently for months on end, physically lock onto anything they were targeted at and if necessary push the target down into a gravity well before destroying it with a focused blast of gamma rays. Very good pieces of equipment for cleaning up messes, he thought. 'Thanks. Fritz, suit up, you're with me. Bring your trolley of goodies. We may have some excellent toys to wire up.'

Marko made contact with the drones bringing the survival pods to them and gave them their orders, after ensuring that Patrick was in the loop. As each arrived, he opened the external doors of the large access airlocks and then closed them again after the pods had been placed inside. They opened the pods, checked the systems and then wired them into *Basalt* so that Patrick had total control of them.

Veg approved of these. Basically a squat cylinder with heavy shielding, each had one door and, when a crew member pressed against it, the person was rotated and sealed into an individual survival system which would immediately start the hibernation process, if deemed necessary, and allow the next person in. Marko had once seen one accommodate and secure ten crew, then eject itself away from a disintegrating frigate in under fifteen seconds, saving the soldiers. He thought it was nice to know that the powers-that-be were taking the mission seriously. They then checked and wired the second pod in position just as the remaining half of the specialist recovery and salvage section arrived on board.

A few minutes later the major gave his orders. 'All crew, report to your stations. Specialists, please secure your equipment, as instructed per your HUDs, and then proceed to the main galley for briefing and assignments. We depart in twenty minutes.'

Basalt's crew moved quickly to their stations with Veg and Harry as pilots and the major, for the first time, actually sitting in the commander's chair. Marko checked his board and with all systems at optimum shunted control across to Veg. Epsilon's tugs pushed them away from the Orbital and at one kilometre out they were assigned a flight number and sent on their way.

'Marko, Fritz, Jan,' Harry said. 'We have control of your boards. Could you go help this latest lot of salvage guys sort their stuff? We have seven hours' transit to the LP and everything is to be locked down before then.'

Part Two

Crystal Infant

Part Two

Crystal Infant

One

The salvage section were indeed an interesting bunch as far as Marko was concerned. All individual specialists, all shapes and sizes, and all with a hell of a lot of equipment. They had come prepared for just about anything, he thought, and were certainly heavy hitters, with six sergeants, two W01s, a lieutenant who looked like he should have been in a trench somewhere, and an immaculately dressed major.

Marko, as the ranking SNCO, introduced himself then Jan and Fritz before saying: 'Major van Beere, sir. Major Longbow sends his compliments and requests you join him on the bridge.'

Van Beere inclined his head to Marko and replied in a highly cultured voice. 'My thanks to you, sarge' major. This is Lieutenant Blair. I shall leave you to your tasks.' His tone and demeanour marked him as a member of one of the senior Administration families.

He walked off as Marko turned to the lieutenant. 'Sir. Mr Blair, how can we assist?'

The grinning lieutenant looked around, then back at the *Basalt* crew members. 'Pleasure to meet with you, guys. Nice ship this. Love the exposed living wood and the flowering orchids. Your AI obviously takes pride in maintenance and a great-smelling atmosphere. This will be an interesting trip. So how did you get this mission? And no GB! Bet that is a relief. You can be yourselves for once. We have our billets, ta. Just need access to the arms cote for our weapons and also the explosives. They are all on their own drone carriers, so it is probably easy to leave them that way and stow the whole lot in one go. Will wait until after orders before we familiarise you guys with all our toys. Do you want to go through everyone's suits and headpieces, Sergeant van Vinken? Sergeant Itou, this is Sergeant van Vinken. She is our comms and computer tech. I'm sure that you will enjoy each other's company. She is a fan of yours, Sergeant van Vinken.'

Marko thought she was a classy looker as he watched them immediately start talking heavy tech, although he noted that by the third sentence Fritz had asked her about her tastes in music. Must have been acceptable — he turned and gave Marko a thumbs up as they walked away.

'Lieutenant Blair, I shall take you down to the arms cote. Staff Wester will sort out the rest of your people for their personal kit. She'll also need your medical requirements and individual records. Could you have your people squirt their medical files across, please? This way, sir.'

As they walked across to the centre spiral stairway leading down to the arms cote deck, the four sizable, heavily laden drones powered up and followed them on their AG. As per the protocols, the lieutenant then gave Marko lists of what they were carrying so he could log it with Harry, as the officer in charge of weapons. It was an impressive list.

Once back in the hangar, they helped sort through the equipment and with aid of their own drones went about securing it all, then gave the new guys a tour of the ship, watching them experience their first coffee and exotic fruits. Veg said that Jan made an excellent brew as his apprentice barista, which was something Marko could not argue with. After a meal together, they made preparations for the initial jump, which went as smoothly as ever. In fact, it was a little smoother than before, as the refit of *Basalt* had given the ship the latest improvements and Patrick now knew how to make them work well.

The officers were at the front of the orders room as Major Longbow took charge. 'Patrick, you have the helm. For those who do not know her, this is Colonel White. It was she who found the site of the missing Hauler.'

They were all in the main entertainments theatre. Well, the *Basalt* crew had all called it 'entertainments' as before they had never actually had a full formal military orders group on board, nor used the theatre for its designed purpose of planning a military action.

They all had their AV HUD helmets on and the colonel talked them through what she had found. 'The following images are taken from some 220,000 kilometres away. You will note that the Hauler is of an Iris class. It is the original of that class, which grossed over 200,000 tonne, dry. It should be six hundred and fifty metres long. As the images get clearer, you will note that it is now considerably longer and wider than as originally built. You'll also note that the exterior hull, with the exception of the primary front portion, is no longer the original hull but appears more alien organic in structure, a departure of style from how the Haulers normally grow their ships. You can also see that there are what appear to be urchins orbiting the craft. As already stated, this particular Hauler is a very old one. It is called *Cactus 3* and, before going missing, had a long and very prestigious career. It is a much-respected member of the Haulers' Collective with many astronomical discoveries to its name.'

She paused for a few seconds, looking around the room, then continued. 'The mission it had was to dump many thousands of tonnes of weapons from the Infant conflict. The weapons, even by today's standards, were very nasty. A number of them were radioactive, including the now outlawed neutron bombs, plus standard old-fashioned thermonuclear devices. What is of real concern, however, is that the cargo also contained hundreds of tonnes of DNA-altering bacteria, together with delivery systems, which were primarily Avian-type creatures, bred specifically for the purpose as their intention was to destroy whole worlds. We need to learn what has happened to *Cactus 3* and are under pressure to retrieve the core of the ship's AI. We would also very much like to know why it ended up 12.3 light years from its original destination, which was Hades. The other three Haulers that were employed delivered their cargos onto Hades with its caustic poison atmosphere and surface temperatures in excess of five hundred degrees C, and returned safely.' She paused again and tapped on her wrist screen. 'I'm copying to you all the nasties involved, and also the Avians. The cargo contained the entire contents of the various research labs which produced the biological weapons, including, in some cases, the corpses of the research staff involved. The records show that in at least one case, the entire lab was encased in molecular chain-linked glass and lifted intact.

'The mission is to separate the nose area of the Hauler, where the AI will be, and then shunt the remainder of the craft into the nearest sun. I cannot emphasise enough the enormous risk of the biological weapons becoming accessible to anyone at all, including some members of our own dear Administration. Hence, this mission now comes under my command. Major Longbow.'

The major cleared his throat and launched into his briefing. 'OK, people. From what you can see it is relatively straightforward. We will slice the nose cone away with our primary lasers, hook drones onto it and make it secure. We then place the Busters and launch the rest of the Hauler into the local sun. The Busters will be set to detonate in sequence to shred the Hauler and force it into the star's photosphere and so ensure its destruction. We will then slice up the nose until the AI Core is exposed and we'll encase that in the diamond interlocking plates the salvage guys brought with them. We destroy the debris generated. Yeah, easy. Like hell it is! This plan is full of hooks, so I need everyone to know everyone else's job. Major van Beere.'

The major then took them through the equipment his detachment had brought along, and how he intended to recover the AI. He had a surprising amount of information on the urchins and of the advanced ways they were now being dealt with; it seemed that all Stephine's research on the creatures had paid off bigtime. He also showed, then uploaded to Patrick, all the communication languages, including definitions, that the urchins used. The belief was that they were just on the cusp of true sentience.

He then handed the briefing over to Stephine. Initially, she laid out the information on biological hazards, and how the crew would be affected if any of them became infected. They might have their central nervous system taken over and be forced to make random movements; they might develop a terrible paranoia of absolutely everything, or the weapons could turn anyone into a berserker. And once the energy levels dropped below a certain point, the weapon would then use the body as a host to produce infected material, and the individual would gradually turn to fluid, first running, then walking and, finally, crawling in any random direction spreading the material far and wide before finally succumbing.

Other weapons created reactions that would range through many human diseases, thus overwhelming medical facilities, before allowing the host to recover, and then causing the body to do it all over again until death occurred months later. Some nasties seemingly would not affect the host, but might produce violent and extremely difficult to detect DNA changes in offspring so that, in time, children could also go berserk.

The crew listening to this catalogue of horror, thought that the people who designed the weapons must have been monsters. Then again, Infant was such a terrible conflict that the Administration had taken the unprecedented step of detonating the Infant system's star as it judged the contaminations were that bad. The four Haulers — of which *Cactus 3* was one — had gathered their toxic cargos from outer system orbiters or small colonies.

Stephine then laid out everyone's responsibilities, including cooking, cleaning and general housework. The outward journey would take almost ten weeks so they had plenty of time.

Veg explained the training and combat routines set for them, then finally Jan took them through fitness and advised of medical enhancements for their own bio-systems, which would inoculate them from the nasties, in spite of what Stephine had told them.

At the conclusion Stephine had a warning for them. 'From the information that the colonel returned with, the conclusion is that someone or something has gained access to the weapons. We believe that they have evolved either naturally or by design. However, due to the relatively short time period, I would say that natural evolution is unlikely, especially considering the extent of the changes to the Hauler. We need to be very, very careful. Get this into your heads: if any one of you becomes infected, and that infection is not covered by the inoculations, you will not be allowed back on *Basalt*. End of story.'

Life settled down over the next few weeks, even down to the level of cooking as the *Basalt* crew took it upon themselves to train the salvage guys, in one way or another, in the art of preparing something to eat.

Roger Ngata, one of the WO1s, took great delight in learning as much as possible from Stephine about the gardens and the trees. He had been in the military for a very long time and was loving the opportunity to enhance his life experiences with his new-found green fingers. He was often seen by *Basalt*'s crew looking closely at the blooms that grew apparently randomly from *Basalt*'s walls and ceilings, and giving the ship a little pat.

Marko discovered that one of the tech sergeants, Minh Pham, was a good baker. He spoke of a long-held tradition in his family that the males did the baking, but for the last twenty years or so he had not been able to get close to an oven, except on the rare occasion that he visited his family. Minh was a superb pastry chef, but had never baked heavy-grained bread loaves, so he was fun for Marko to teach and also to learn from.

Veg would gather everyone in the engineering hangar each morning before breakfast, and again in mid-afternoon, training them hard in some obscure martial art or other. Sergeant Ban asked him what style he followed and Veg replied that he studied 'all of them'.

'I note, venerated Captain Veg, that you have a most interesting style in your stick fighting. It seems to be a mixture of three primary ancient art forms. I should be most interested in going full contact if you would honour me.'

Veg allowed himself a tiny smile. 'Very well, training is complete for the day. Hit the showers, people. Sergeant Ban, select your stick.'

Nobody moved as no one had any intention of missing the fight. Jan leant close to Marko and whispered, 'Sergeant Thao Ban has cleaned up in just about every stick-fighting tournament over the last twenty years. This is going to be interesting.'

Marko cocked his head and smiled at her. 'Really, Jan, you always amaze me with your knowledge of martial themes. By the way, is the colonel bi? I have seen her admiring your bum on more than one occasion.'

'Yes. How do you know I'm not the same?'

'Tease!'

Both men selected their bo's from the rack. Veg towered over Ban, but when stripped down to the waist, Ban was also heavily muscled.

They both addressed the mat, bowed to it, bowed to the audience, to each other and then for the next fifteen minutes gave a superb display of stick fighting. Ban was very good, but Marko had the distinct feeling that he was no match for Veg. Veg took a couple of whacks, but seemed not to strike Ban very hard when he landed hits. Ban was starting to become angry and yelled something at Veg in a language Marko had not heard before. Veg roared with laughter and in a blindingly fast series of blows spun Ban around, then levered him high into the air while giving him dozens of light taps all over his body before Ban hit the floor rolling. Ban stood up, bowed, apologised to Veg and then asked him to be his sensei. Veg just nodded and suggested that they have a discussion over a beer and pickles.

A few days later Jan went up against Ban. Veg quietly padded around the exterior of the practice floor, a gentle smile on his face, as Jan gave Ban a solid thrashing. The poor man looked surprised and then dramatically taken aback as she used the techniques and dance that Veg had taught them all — except Fritz, who could not see the point — over the long years as *Basalt* had made its way home after its wormhole generating propulsion systems were damaged and they had used comets as fuel to propel themselves between the stars. The final blow to his pride came when she clashed hard with him, grabbing his stick and using it to lift herself and somersault over his head, then hitting him along the full length of his spine while vertically above him. He conceded, then thanked first Jan and then Veg for insisting that he use a padded martial arts Gee.

The salvage guys wanted to learn about Jan's weapons. She and Veg did a roaring trade, building new weapons or customising the issued ones. Between jumps, as they crossed from LP to LP, Stephine, the colonel and the boss worked everyone hard with every weapon, piece of equipment and craft.

Fritz, when he was not in engineering designing and building electronics, spent some time composing electronic music, which he would play over *Basalt*'s sound systems much to the delight of most members of the crew.

Marko learnt that his baking colleague, Minh Pham, was a master with explosives and improvised devices, so, together with Harry, he decided to milk every last bit of information from him. Some of Minh's knowledge was absolute gold, stuff they could not find a reference to in their databases, which was probably not surprising as the Administration regularly purged what it deemed as 'subversive information'.

One afternoon he showed them how to make a series of very effective explosives from what was available to them in the kitchen and in the cleaning supplies storeroom. Unfortunately, when it came to justifying to Stephine what they had made and why it was in the kitchen, it proved just too difficult. Her scolding had them all feeling considerably chastened, but they left the mess giggling like schoolboys just the same.

* * *

'All crew, stations please. Final jump into the target system of Gliese 163 in fifteen minutes. Soul Saver uploads as soon as you are able. A fast picket drone will be launched immediately prior to the jump.'

They were kitted up in combat gear, with faceplates open, sitting at their assigned posts. The colonel and her selected crew were already on board her scout ship. Jan thought that calling it a scout ship was a bit of a misnomer. It was almost half the length of *Basalt* with huge engines and great firepower, and it was capable of supporting six individuals for many years, although it was rare for more than one Ranger to be on a mission at any one time as they seemed to like their solitude. Jan and Marko had had a few laughs about that, considering the sack time she and the major were getting. They decided they must have been making up for lost years.

The colonel's ship, *Crystal*, had a state of the art adaptive camouflage system which allowed it to get in close and undetected. The colonel had left *Basalt* three standard days earlier to build up speed before the jump so she could swing past the Hauler using inertia only, and not leave any engine signatures as they coasted.

Basalt, on the other hand, was going in relatively slowly, as the plan called for them to hang back and wait for her intelligence reports. The salvage teams were either in their own craft or manning the Skuas. One of them, Julie Mapp, had shown a real aptitude for the Skua and had also requested a transfer to *Basalt* which the major was considering; not one of the existing crew had any objections as she could build racing aircraft and engines. She had done so for a long time and had a reputation of being good at it. Made bloody awful coffee, but great tea … just like Marko, in fact. And she had confided to him that she didn't like coffee.

Marko's boards were perfect so he switched the engine controls to the major and Patrick. They jumped into the system where *Cactus 3* was marooned and started to bring *Basalt* to the designated position, just out of sight of the target ice moon, which orbited the gas giant with the distant local star lighting the scene. Veg and Stephine launched immediately, switched on their exotic camouflage, then their almost undetectable propulsion systems, and moved quickly ahead of *Basalt*.

It was a beautiful sight. The huge gas ball was covered in amazing storms with extraordinary colours. Marko could just imagine the major's excitement and he could see that, in spite of all that was going on, Michael was shunting images and data into his private astronomy and astrophysics files.

'Target is currently on the other side of the ice moon,' the major informed them. 'We hold here. Albatross launch and hold position five kilometres out. Everyone else, deploy, and hold one hundred metres out.'

Marko dropped and gently powered the Skua away from *Basalt*'s hull. The four small salvage craft, which were basically frames with engines, a large equipment container, a two-man cockpit, winches with cutting gear, and covered in grapple mortars, also moved away until they all surrounded *Basalt* and pointed towards the Hauler.

Colonel White spoke over the comms. '*Basalt*, this is *Crystal*. Info packet on the way.'

The comms laser from *Crystal* carried the latest pictures and data on the Hauler. It was still holding the same position in orbit and, as they looked at the data, it became apparent that the ship was still growing. There were also large numbers of urchins of all sizes in the mini-system of moons orbiting the gas giant. The ones around the Hauler seemed to be different: they were more bulky and displayed a far greater skin colour range. They even moved more purposefully than the others. Everyone could hear the commanders of each unit and what they were saying to each other, as Stephine spoke. 'Patrick, anything comprehensible from the urchins?'

'No, Stephine, the language is a completely different structure. Looking at the others still operating around the gas giant, they have more in common with the urchins we know, but even they appear to have an unknown language. I am sorry, but this will take a great deal of time to decipher.'

She pursed her lips. 'Thanks. It was a long shot that we would understand them anyway. We can now see the Hauler in direct sight. Antimatter decoys are ready for launch.'

Major Longbow chimed in. 'Roger that, Stephine. Stand by to deploy the first one: aim it two degrees closer to the Hauler and step the speed up by ten per cent from what we decided earlier. Launch when ready.'

A moment later she replied. 'Decoy away. Second launch in ten minutes. Third and fourth, five minutes after that.'

They waited and watched over the hour that the decoys took to arrive. When the first was some tens of kilometres away, the behaviour of the urchins around the Hauler changed and they moved out to intercept it. Stephine maintained control of it and swerved it out of their intercept course, taking the decoy around towards the rear of the gas giant. From what the crews could see the urchins followed. As the second one passed, more urchins appeared from under the Hauler to chase it.

Stephine slowed the third and fourth decoys dramatically so they almost hit the Hauler, which caused a large group of small urchins to pour out from distorted hatchways on the surface of the Hauler. As soon as the urchins were out of sight pursuing the decoys, they all moved up until they could see the Hauler themselves.

Major van Beere, controlling *Basalt*'s heavy lasers, started to cut through the Hauler's hull behind the nose section as the craft accelerated up towards the target together. It took them two hours to close on the Hauler, by which time the nose segment was almost severed. As soon as it came clear, everyone's lasers were controlled by Patrick, who targeted every piece of debris floating away from the separated pieces, destroying them. The salvage crews fired grapples onto the nose section and started to move away back towards the LP.

Major van Beere then deployed three of the Busters, which flew down against the bulk of the Hauler and attached themselves at their designated points, fired their engines and started the long journey towards the local star. They would carry on accelerating until sufficient speed had been built up to deploy their own buzzard ramjets, which would be able to scoop up any available gas or dust and continue the acceleration. The plan was for fast acceleration which, within days of launch, would make the Hauler unstoppable, and even if the entire assemblage disintegrated its trajectory would take it into the local star anyway.

'*Basalt*, this is *Crystal*. The altered urchins, together with the slowing drones, will be in position in forty-five minutes. I am deploying a Compressor.'

'Acknowledged. All craft acknowledge forty-four-minute warning.' They all lasered in their receipt of message.

Marko had only ever seen a Compressor used a few times before and did not want to be anywhere close when it went off. Thinking about them, he knew it was science that Fritz probably understood, but he would be one of the very few. The device was a useful piece of equipment in that, when detonated, it would vaporise anything within a two-hundred-metre sphere of itself, and then suck the resulting material down into a tiny and rapidly deteriorating black hole. But they could only be deployed for relatively small targets; the Compressor's components were too unstable for making bigger devices, as Marko knew from his own experiences. Very early in his military career he had been part of a rescue squad that went looking for survivors from one of the Gjomvik development labs that had been tasked to make a bigger Compressor device. They found a lot of exotically coloured dust, plus one very big crater, which was all that remained of a large facility that had employed hundreds of people.

Their lasers were still firing, picking off small pieces of material, as Patrick tried to make sure that the cleanup was complete. Distant flashes of magenta showed that the Compressor had done its job, expanding in its odd-coloured fireball then collapsing in seconds. The bulk of the Hauler had long since disappeared starwards when the colonel called a halt to the cleanup, just as the first of the urchins from the gas giant started to appear on the distant sensors, coming out to investigate the faint signatures of antimatter drives.

'All ships form on *Basalt*,' the colonel ordered. 'Salvage, are you able to locate the AI Core?'

Major van Beere answered. 'Negative. It's either moving around, or there is something shielding our sensors, or it is aware of us and determined to make life difficult. We have fired the wormhole jumper units against the cone's outer hull. Control is handed across to you, Colonel.'

'Right. Form up on your lander and jump when ready.'

Marko watched the other units jump ahead of the cone-shaped nose piece as the colonel also located her own small LP and jumped as well. He was the last one to move up against *Basalt* and as soon as Patrick felt the contact he jumped them towards the system's Oort Field far out into interstellar space, where millions of comets formed a halo around the system. A few seconds later the view had changed considerably and they hoped that they would be able to operate on the nose segment in peace, as the colonel came back on the comms links.

'Good work so far, people. Has anyone been able to learn anything from the Hauler core?'

Fritz replied: 'No, Colonel, there is just a stream of gibberish coming from it on all frequencies. There is a subroutine which is heavily encoded that I am trying to decipher. Do we know when the representative Hauler will arrive? It may be able to assist.'

Patrick answered the AI. 'ETA is approximately eighteen hours away.'

The colonel acknowledged then made some suggestions. 'Crew, rotate for a meal and a freshen-up. We start looking for the core in earnest in two hours' time.'

They were all back in their craft waiting for orders when Major Longbow laid out the problem. 'OK, the core is an armoured sphere ten metres in diameter. It is normally fixed in position inside another heavy armoured shield. From what we can see with the gravity sensors and the listening sensors against the outer hull, there is something moving it around on the inside of the nose segment in a random pattern. Every time we slice a piece of the exterior away it creates a greater risk of contamination. We have done well so far, but the odds are now stacking up against us. Every Intel drone sent into the segment is compromised and destroyed within minutes by something we do not understand.'

He paused, looking at a screen, before continuing. 'It is almost as if the segment is alive and actively challenging us. We now have thirteen hours before the Hauler *Chrysanthemum* arrives. I do not want to disappoint him as he is a member of the inner sanctum of the Haulers' Collective. The only really good news is that the main body of the Hauler has now reached such velocity that its fate is inevitable, so at least we do not have to worry about it being intercepted by friend or foe. Anyone have any bright ideas?'

'We could employ the urchins, Major.'

'How so, Stephine?'

'The altered ones are destroyed, but it would not take a great deal of effort to transport a few from the gas giant to here using the same method as when we captured the first one. I believe that we could then fire small encapsulated amounts of antimatter onto the segment and allow the urchin to chase them. If nothing else, we would see what happens. We could take our ship and go get them if you wish.'

They all waited for his reply. 'Interesting. OK. Do it.'

Harry added: 'While we are waiting for the captain to return we could use some of our anti-urchin tech and peel back a few layers of whatever it is that is now exposed where we have removed the outer hull. It appears organic.'

Colonel White came in and answered Harry. 'Right. We shall do that as well, Sergeant Major. Major van Beere, any thoughts?'

After a long pause van Beere answered. 'I must admit to being completely baffled, ma'am. We are out of our depth here. I'm sorry that I have no suggestions. I would prefer that we destroy everything and fly away. It is the only way we can be sure of containing this threat.'

The colonel nodded. 'Agreed, but unfortunately, we must endeavour to assist the Haulers in answering their questions.'

On the control deck of *Basalt* Major Michael Longbow looked at his screens and zoomed in on the Albatross lander. 'OK, everyone, ease back five hundred metres. Harry, you have control.'

Harry nodded and started tapping his screens. 'Firing.'

A steady stream of oxygen and hydrogen projectiles started to explode against one of the exposed areas of the sixty-metre-long cone shape which was the detached nose segment. Harry steadily walked the rounds about a central point, slowly excavating a sizable crater in the material. Suddenly, a huge tendril of rapidly accelerating material ripped out through the side of the sphere and reached across to the lander. Everyone in range reacted with everything they had to fire at the tendril and it stopped only metres from reaching the Albatross. It snapped back into the sphere, obviously damaged, but still alive.

Major Longbow yelled out, 'Cease fire! Shit! What the fuck are we dealing with here?'

'Major Longbow. This is *Crystal*. It would appear that during the lengthy time the *Cactus 3* was in isolation something grew and evolved, possibly combining the best and worst of the biological weapons together with the urchins. What we just saw was an extremely large feeding tendril from an urchin. We wounded it, but have really just annoyed it considerably. Unfortunately, it is now even more imperative that the records held in the Hauler core be accessed. This is a major development.'

'I hate those fucking things,' the major said. 'OK, everyone hold position until Stephine and Veg get back.'

While they waited, the salvage crews targeted all the floating debris and vaporised the small pieces, or, as with the bigger pieces, nudged them together by deploying small explosive charges and then laser welded them into a slowly growing ball.

Stephine's very beautiful craft popped into existence beside *Basalt*. Caught in the starlight, the flattened teardrop's sleek and almost sensuous bulges shone slightly in the afterglow of the jump energies as Stephine opened comms. 'We have two small urchins. I note that you had a little excitement! Yes, I agree with *Crystal*. The creature or creatures residing in the segment appear to be evolved urchins. Let's see what it makes of real ones. I have sampled the skins of these and they are much closer to the others that we have encountered. They are in fact another racial type, but are still ninety-nine point nine per cent identical. They are also free from any contamination. With your permission, I am about to launch an encapsulated fragment of antimatter at the segment. I shall release one of the urchins a few moments later.'

The colonel gave Stephine the go ahead. As they watched on their individual screens, they could see the small package of antimatter move relatively quickly towards the segment. A few moments later an urchin burst out of its containment on the side of Stephine's craft and actually jumped across the five hundred metres in a fraction of a second to be between the antimatter and the segment. As it enfolded the antimatter into itself, a huge tendril shot out from the segment and speared the urchin, dragging the thrashing, convulsing creature back into the cone.

'Stephine, repeat that, please,' the colonel requested. 'This time allow the antimatter to make contact with the segment before releasing the urchin. Oh, and make the antimatter package one hundred per cent bigger.'

'Acknowledged. On the way.'

As the antimatter package arrived, the area of the nose segment where the hull plate was nonexistent actually opened up like a mouth and then folded the energy package into itself. The urchin arrived on the surface a few moments later and violently attacked the writhing mass of tendril material, trying to get at the antimatter. An explosive fight ensued with the urchin tearing chunks away from the segment before it was seized and apparently consumed. Patrick once again took control of everyone's lasers and burnt the debris.

Major van Beere commented thoughtfully. 'Interesting. Fritz, can we speed up the decay of the energy packets surrounding the antimatter?'

Fritz took a few minutes to reply. 'Yes, dangerous, but it can be done. We would have to get in a lot closer. What do you have in mind, Major?'

'I want to peel off a strip of the hull plate around the entire circumference of the segment. Then launch multiple packets of encapsulated antimatter and see if we can create a reaction and split this whole thing in half. Obviously, antimatter is still attractive to the altered urchin.'

The high-pitched voice of Fritz posited another problem. 'Interesting idea, Major, but consider what would happen if this thing accumulated enough antimatter to jump by itself.'

'OK, good point, Fritz,' the major acknowledged. 'Let's tease it. How long to set up the energy packets for rapid decay?'

After a few long seconds, Fritz said, 'Couple of hours, tops.'

'OK. Everyone, just concentrate on chewing as much off the surface of the nose cone as possible. Let's arrange ourselves so that all craft can see everyone else's lines of fire.'

So again everyone just watched and waited carefully lasered off as many chunks as possible when the gravity sensors showed them that the AI Core was out of the danger area, and played 'dodge-ems' with the tendrils when they came raging out.

The major gave another order. 'As soon as we see another of those big tendrils, I want everyone to concentrate their fire on its base. Let's try and cut it off.'

Moments later the opportunity presented itself but all that occurred was as soon as the lasers started to cut, other smaller tendrils came to the aid of the larger, pulling it back inside.

'Michael,' Stephine said. 'I believe that there are some five or six individual urchin-type creatures inside the segment. The data that I have managed to collate shows that the biological weapons have been incorporated into the makeup of the urchin. The frightening thing is that there is also human DNA in the makeup together with that of various Avian creatures; as you'll remember, the delivery system for the biological weapons were specially bred Avians. My conclusion is that these larger types of urchins are constructs, as there has, quite simply, not been enough time for them to evolve naturally.

'Could it be that some of the original scientists were not dead but, rather, in cryno sleep when their laboratories were encased and taken on board the Hauler for the journey to Hades? Certainly, such a scenario would explain what has been happening, although the more disturbing aspect may be that some or all of the scientists made good their escape, and are now somewhere else with very potent biological weapons, based on a fusion with the urchins.'

Everyone went very quiet as they digested this latest possibility, then the colonel spoke up. 'I agree with Stephine. I have been analysing the images we kept of the part of the Hauler we sent into the sun. I found no evidence that any human-compatible lander spacecraft were still present, which suggests someone used them to escape the Hauler. It is only a supposition though. The areas where they would normally be stored were heavily modified by whatever occupied the Hauler. The landers *could* still be there.'

Major Michael Longbow sat in his command module on *Basalt*'s bridge deck, frowned and scratched his head as he digested the information. 'This is not good. OK, command decision time. Colonel, if we broke this segment into three, would the Compressors be able to destroy them individually?'

'Um, stand by.'

As he waited for the colonel's answer, he switched channels and asked, 'Fritz, can you configure one of the Harpoons to lock onto the core and retrieve all the information from it? I now believe the core may be totally compromised.'

Fritz grumbled under his breath at yet another interruption, but replied calmly. 'Yeah, should be able to sort that. I shall get Patrick to do it, though. Need another ten minutes to sort the antimatter packets.'

At that moment, the colonel came back on the comms. 'Yes, the Compressors would handle the three sections. With that in mind, I shall now use a drone to move the captured material we have in hand to a safe distance and dispose of it.'

Michael Longbow nodded and ordered. 'Right, here's what we are going to do. As soon as *Crystal* returns, we are going to create a killing field. Stephine, you will command one group; colonel, you take the second; I will take the third. The antimatter packets will be spread to create two rings around the segment. As soon as those outer parts of the segment — and whatever is lurking under the surface — is gouged aside by the first set of ten antimatter packets, the second set will be launched and spaced out so that the urchin-type creatures will hopefully attempt to grab them. Patrick and *Crystal*, you will need to control them. No matter what happens as soon as anyone sees the core, yell and concentrate weapons while Patrick fires the Harpoon onto it. As soon as the data is lasered back, we then destroy everything including the core. Colonel, when you return, can you disperse your Compressors to form a field beyond the killing field and that way we can push everything against them. I just had another disturbing thought, people. We have not had a visit from any of our friends or counterparts in Admin procurements or weapons research. What's the bet that someone already knows what has occurred? OK, team off.'

Two

Marko was attached to Stephine's group to the right of *Basalt*, with the colonel's group on the other side, so they had a fan-shaped firing base a kilometre wide.

The first wave of antimatter packets contacted the surface of the fragment and all reacted at the same instant, cutting two rough rings right around the centre of the cone's remains some seven metres across and three metres deep. They could see the writhing masses of biological material rapidly filling the spaces and repairing itself just as the second wave of antimatter arrived. The effect was immediate and dramatic. The enormous urchins inside the segment erupted outwards to get at the antimatter, tearing the whole structure apart. Just as the tendrils reached up to touch the antimatter packets, the containment fields of the antimatter all collapsed, obliterating large swathes of urchin flesh.

The Cactus Core suddenly popped out above the separated segments, and Patrick wasted no time in hitting it with two Harpoons. Sacrificial drones swept in from the larger craft to push up against one of the three masses, as everyone continually fired upon their designated targets to prevent them from reforming into one mass. The pressure of the vaporising material, together with the drones, gradually pushed the three masses towards where the Compressors waited. Marko had no idea what was happening to the Cactus Core as he was working hard with Stephine and Julie Mapp, pushing their target mass as far to the right as possible. Stephine activated one of the Compressors and it closed on the twisting, writhing mass which had systematically destroyed the drones.

'First Compressor five minutes to detonation. Shields closed and get clear,' the colonel yelled.

All the craft rolled away and powered their engines to maximum as they needed at least five kilometres of separation. The Compressors went off one after the other, shredding the masses of horribly contaminated material down to individual atoms. Once the all-clear was given, the colonel then had them form a series of sweeps looking for and destroying any remaining material.

Many long hours later they held station off *Basalt* while the exposed surfaces of every craft and ship were minutely inspected by engineering drones for any possible contamination. Being the last in the queue Julie and Marko were finally cleared. They individually docked with *Basalt*, landing on their platforms and rotating back inside the hangar. After powering down their Skuas they went for a long shower and a decent meal.

As they were emerging from ablutions, Major Longbow made an announcement. 'Crew, we managed to procure total data from the core. *Chrysanthemum* has also arrived in the system and will be joining us shortly. I have briefed him and he concurs with the decision to destroy the core. He has started to upload all the core's data as well. There is a lot of useful information, but we will not know about the personality of the Hauler until *Chrysanthemum* decodes it for us. Stephine, you are the last in the queue. *Crystal*, you are cleared to dock when ready.'

'My thanks, Michael. I shall join you shortly.'

Marko walked up the long spiral staircase to the bridge deck feeling very tired, but enjoying the exercise. He looked at Michael Longbow and frowned. 'Boss, you don't look too hot. You all right?'

'No, Marko, I'm feeling bloody awful. Jan, can you meet me in Medical, please. Harry, get a message to the colonel and to Stephine to hold their positions.'

Over the next half an hour they all, one by one, succumbed to a nasty flu-like virus. Marko felt as if something was slowly grinding on his bones, he ached so badly, but what concerned him most was a harsh burning sensation on his chest. He stripped off his suit and could see five tiny raised lumps on his skin and was reminded of the time years before when an octopoid had touched him in the same place. The tiny lumps itched horribly and he fought the urge to tear his skin apart scratching them. Jan was affected worst of all and, as Marko leant against the medical bulkhead, Ernst whistled up a medical drone to assist in getting her into a cryno unit.

As soon as she was in the unit, and being chilled, Ernst took a blood sample from Marko and, after a few moments, gave his opinion. 'Marko, it appears that the nanotech for your arm has halted the spread of this virus in your system. It is a manufactured virus — and virulent is the least of it. We need time. Please ask all those who are mobile to get to the cryno chambers themselves as we need to chill them down, otherwise they will probably die. I'll give you a cocktail of vitamins to boost your system so you can help me and Topaz.'

As Ernst positioned himself against a large medical supplies dispensing cabinet and rapidly loaded what he needed into himself, Marko selected Stephine's private channel. 'Stephine, this is Marko. I have not seen the ACEs. Are they with you?'

A very tired sounding Stephine answered. 'No, Marko, they all elected to go with Colonel White. Glint, are you OK?'

The ACE answered immediately. 'We are all fine, thank you, Stephine. Marko, the colonel has a most interesting ship. We are learning a great many fascinating things. You really should have a look at this ship when you get better.'

Oh, shit, Marko thought. Glint does not use that sort of language. He is much more direct — and how the hell does he know that I'm not well? Ernst pressed a unit up against Marko's right arm medical shunt and he felt slightly better. Not much, but enough to function. Marko reached out and tapped Ernst beside where the private circuit communication glasses were normally kept. The panel popped open presenting Marko with the glasses. As he put them on, Ernst advised, 'We are secure, Marko.'

With a rising panic, Marko quickly said, 'Glint and the ACEs have found something on the colonel's ship and he knows that we are unwell. How would he know that? How can we communicate with them, without the colonel knowing?'

The machine was quiet for a few seconds, before replying. 'That would be basically impossible, I am afraid. *Crystal* is a remarkable information-gathering AI and would know immediately. I think it best if you disappear. I shall log that you have been placed on ice. Topaz will get that new suit for you; meet him in the cryno chamber. With the exception of you, no other biological currently on *Basalt* is awake as they are all in cryno sleep.'

Marko groaned. 'That is very bad. I shall keep these glasses on so we can talk without being listened to.'

He walked slowly down to the cryno chambers, stripped, then climbed into an open unit with Topaz helping and the waiting prototype suit formed around him. Sealed up, he activated it, and waited. It insulated him completely from the cold of the chamber and, of course, none of the systems could get at his permanent medical shunts. Marko decided that Patrick must have overridden them, as they did not attempt to interface.

He found himself moving and realised that the AIs must have activated the emergency evacuation system for the chamber. He was moved quite quickly down through the floor and into a long-term survival pod.

An image of Ernst appeared in Marko's glasses. 'Marko. We have overridden the systems; Patrick suspects that something is wrong with the fuel feeds for the Wormhole generators. Suffice to say, if we activated the feeds we would not make it back to any of our bases any time soon. He believes he can circumnavigate the software changes, but it will take time. It would seem that the colonel wants us out of the picture.'

A terrible cold feeling bit right into Marko's inner being as he realised just how bad the situation was. He felt a tiny spark of fear as he asked: 'What's happening with Stephine and Veg?'

Topaz answered through the Ernst comms system. 'They have just come on board. Veg is already very ill. Far worse than anyone else. Stephine is also badly affected. They are both making their way to cryno and I have sent engineering drones to help them as they have both just collapsed unconscious. It would seem that they have been infected with something much worse than the rest of you. I have instructed the drones to load them into cryno units. We have isolated the virus that you have. Give us a couple of hours and we will be able to help you greatly.'

'Thanks, Topaz.'

'Marko,' Topaz continued, 'I am sorry but the colonel has just reported an incident on board *Crystal* that has resulted in the deaths of the two salvage personnel who were with her. She must have placed her own AI on board this ship … whatever it is, it is mimicking Michael and Harry perfectly. I believe that this is a subterfuge to keep the Hauler, *Chrysanthemum*, from knowing what is occurring here. She has also begun communications with *Chrysanthemum*, so a great deal of data is now open to her. She has total access to the *Cactus 3* core. Unfortunately, I am not able to access any of it.'

Ernst interjected. 'There is a problem with Patrick. He is becoming very slow. Actually, this may be of advantage to us. He is losing interest in monitoring any internal sensors and also losing control of external door sensors. Topaz and I believe that you must take control of *Crystal*, eliminate or neutralise the colonel and learn what is happening. We shall work on getting Patrick back to normal, repair the Wormhole generator problems and also check for any other anomalies while we are at it.'

Marko felt a slow rage building inside him. 'Fuck! Fuck, fuck, but I feel like shit on a stick! OK, OK, I'm onto it. So, how come you two are not affected?'

'I am sorry,' Topaz replied, 'but I cannot answer that. It is possible that the colonel simply did not consider what our capabilities are. Time will tell.'

Marko pushed open the chamber cover and then the access door to the pod. As he moved, he activated the chameleon ware of the suit. Harry and Veg had been working with him on the suit with him for months and they'd made it more like Veg and Stephine's suits. Much sleeker and a lot more compact than the Administration originals; it was also superbly quiet. He walked down to the engineering deck and looked out through one of the viewing chambers. *Crystal* was holding station only a couple of hundred metres away with the huge bulk of the Hauler *Chrysanthemum* hanging above.

He walked across to the opposite side of the deck and opened the small airlock, manually rotating it through. He climbed out onto the external shell and pulled himself around the large curved hull of *Basalt* until he could see *Crystal*, then he stood up and ran across the hull plates, building sufficient speed to launch himself across to *Crystal*, hoping like hell that it would not move in the few minutes it took for the flight across. He didn't use the small thrusters built into the suit and fervently hoped that *Crystal*'s sensors could not pick him up as he landed with arms outstretched among the rear rocket nozzles of the colonel's ship. He decided it was now time to create a little constructive mayhem of his own.

Out of sight of the Hauler, he fired a few laser bursts through two of the partially exposed fuel lines and down into one of the external backup pumps, simulating a micrometeor hit, something that was rare for an individual ship, but happened every day somewhere in the fleet. Fuel started to vaporise from the holes immediately, which he knew would trigger an alarm somewhere, so he pulled himself over to the nearest airlock and waited. A few moments passed before it opened and two maintenance and repair drones flew out, allowing him to slip inside and wait pressed up against the wall.

Ten minutes later the hatch closed and the airlock recycled to allow a third drone to enter with lengths of spare pipe and pump components. As it came in, Marko slid out and into the main engine room of *Crystal*. With his secure inter-unit comms system, he sent a call to Glint hoping that he had spread a few of his micro-relays throughout the ship.

'Marko! We're in trouble. Very great trouble. This colonel is nasty. She killed the lieutenant and the other sergeant and they were both nice people. She actually destroyed their Soul Savers as well. *Crystal* is very strange; she does not like us and wants to eject us into space. She calls us created abominations. Where are you?'

He flashed Glint his location as Glint continued. 'Here are the layouts of this ship. We're being very well behaved, Marko. The evil woman crushed my tail, snapped Flint's legs and broke Nail's neck. We are OK, of course, but we wonder how she could do such things. She is not human, Marko. She wants to dismantle Stephine. She says that she is not human either and is an enemy of humankind. I am afraid, Marko. Be very careful, Father.'

Oh, shit, he thought. Not human. Great! He activated the advanced ICE bioware that Stephine had concocted for them. All it did was make him feel normal, but that was better than feeling below par from the virus. He looked around the engine room to find something suitable for a 'failure', so the pumps that fed the damaged fuel pipes came in for a little treatment. A drone arrived a few moments later and he encouraged that to fail also by spraying it with fuel and then igniting it. All the fire suppressants came online so he backed a few of them up and encouraged a few more pump failures. He worked long and constructively, creating a cascade of failures until, finally, the colonel herself arrived in an armoured suit to find out what was happening.

Marko did not believe in giving vermin any chances. He deployed the molecular chain-linked diamond blades down his forearms which folded themselves up out of the suit and extended them for their full length past his hands. As she walked past him in the haze, he reached out and sliced her head off. Immediately he saw that Glint was right; she was not human. She was a hybrid human-urchin. The body calmly turned and advanced on him, trying to grab him. As each piece presented itself, he chopped it off while his engineer's mind tried to fathom how — without a head — it knew where he was. The whole front of the suit opened, revealing numerous tentacle-like structures which continued to reach towards him.

As his mind went into overdrive and searched for options as to how to deal with this thing that was becoming more like a hydra than a human, he activated the suit's lasers, destroying the middle of its torso. He then fired two micro-missiles into the tops of its thighs. It finally fell to the floor with various parts seeming to act independently, thrashing towards him until he realised that he was running out of time, with not one part but dozens trying to attach themselves to him.

Quickly looking up, he identified the main fuel feeds overhead, locating the oxygen lines and severing them with one of his blade arms. As the entire engine room filled with pressurised oxygen, all the parts of the alien stopped moving, no longer able to attack or attempt to reassemble. He carefully stepped over the parts to seize the alien colonel's head sealed inside its helmet.

He looked around, found a crynogenics container and dropped the head in, its lips still moving and eyes glaring at him. He flooded it with liquid hydrogen and sealed it shut. Carrying the container and sealing the engine room door after him, he moved down the main corridor towards the bridge, until a Games Board monitor challenged him. Without waiting for an answer, the monitor deployed a small rotary cannon which looked exactly like the one that Jan had designed for *Basalt*'s crew months before.

Without thinking, Marko lasered the caseless ammunition magazine of the weapon which then detonated severing the monitor's weapon arm and destroying most of its chest. As it slumped against the wall, another monitor rushed up behind him. The suit's proximity and other warnings went off, showing Marko that lasers were being powered up. He reacted to eliminate the threat, launching tiny short-range missiles which, when they struck the monitor, showered its electronics with a wave of focused neutron beams and destroyed them. The smoking monitor promptly crashed to the floor. It reached up with its hand and opened up the faceplate.

'You are not to interfere, *Chrysanthemum* crew member,' the prone monitor instructed. 'This is not within your jurisdiction.

This is Games Board business. Leave now and nothing more will be said.'

Marko brought up the exterior suit controls in his head and activated the external speakers. 'Why would you think that I am the Hauler ship crew member?'

'It is logical,' the damaged human-machine hybrid replied. 'The *Basalt* crew have been incapacitated as planned.'

Marko suddenly felt very old, terribly tired and a little despondent. 'Really? Maybe you are wrong. I shall deal with you later.'

Marko left the motionless monitor and went to find the *Crystal* AI housing. It screeched abuse at him as he brutalised it, tearing its casing apart. He smiled grimly, noting that the Gjomvik manufactured components were much easier to break than the biologically grown ones on *Basalt*, which had originally been created by the Haulers. After lifting out the primary brain segments, he extended sensor and investigation probes from the ends of his artificial fingers, pushing them into the web of electronic and biological parts and demanded the AI tell him where its remote parts were. As soon as the answers started to register with the internal map of the ship, he locked down all the doors, then systematically dismantled the units, isolating each part of *Crystal*. When he finally identified her core nodes he activated a small unit — Fritz had taken many months to perfect it — which took control of any computer accessed data blocks. Finally satisfied that the AI was no longer a threat he went looking for the ACEs.

He was cross, tired, full of a virus and generally not paying complete attention when he passed a wrecked cabin door. A black-suited figure hurtled out, knocking him down. He rolled against the wall and flipped over onto his back when whatever it was hit him very hard in the throat. The thought flashed through Marko's head that had he been wearing a standard suit he would have been out of the fight, then and there. As it was, the iron fist of whatever it was knocked the wind out of him as it punched him in the stomach. Marko was grateful that Veg, Harry and Jan had not been nice instructors. This sort of serious rough and tumble was bearable; only just, but still bearable.

He allowed himself to sag and as the thing came in again to have another go he flashed open the full blade past his left elbow. The block was not so much of a block, but rather allowed the black suit to simply chop off its own arm, which bounced off its chest and rolled across the corridor. As Marko's opponent sprang backwards, with blood spraying out from the stump, he brought the other blade into play, trying to thrust it up between its legs. But his opponent was quick and leapt up, hitting the wall on the other side of the corridor.

A weapon was deployed from the right flank of the black suit, which Marko immediately responded to with two microneutron missiles, knocking the black suit down hard as its electronics and weapon controls were fried by the energy pulse from the impacting missiles. He brought the pulse laser up then blew the weapon off the side of the black suit as it raised its remaining hand and signalled a halt. The suit sealed off the severed stump and the figure stopped bleeding all over the wall. Marko waited as he could not see any other weapons on the suit and besides, the little pulse laser that he had trained on its head was just plain nasty in its capabilities and he demonstrated this by slicing the soles off his opponent's boots just to get its attention. The figure slowly touched a seal and the faceplate opened to show an ashen-faced Colonel White.

'Who are you and why are you on my ship?' the colonel demanded.

He brought up the menus in his display and activated the external speakers of the suit after deliberately changing the timbre of his voice and adding an old-world Italian accent for good measure.

'It does not matter who I am, Colonel. I am considerably more interested in you and this ship. Strip out of your suit. I know its type. Then lie down on the floor, extend your arms, um sorry, your arm, and your legs to their fullest extension.'

The suit peeled off her, leaving her naked. As soon as she was down, he picked up her severed arm and allowed his suit to take a blood and tissue sample. After a few moments it reported that she was one hundred per cent human and not carrying any immediately dangerous pathogens. However, it did identify alien proteins and unidentified material in her nervous system.

'Get up and take me to the *Basalt* ACEs,' Marko ordered.

'I bet you are a member of *Chrysanthemum*'s crew. You have no jurisdiction here and you should leave immediately.'

'Really!' Marko barked out. 'Try this for an indication of my interest in you.'

As she stood up, he leant across and injected a rather unpleasant drug into her from a tough needle built into the end of his left index finger. Her face went bright red and she started to vomit after a few seconds. He felt a twinge of guilt because he knew there was nothing more debilitating than uncontrollable vomiting, but immediately swept empathy aside, reminding himself that he really did not know what he was dealing with. The colonel proceeded to curse him between heaving and staggering ahead. That little tool had been one of Jan's more interesting contributions to the suit, although there were a number of others as well, all medical, most good, some deeply unpleasant.

A small reception of defence drones waited for them outside the medical suite, but as Marko had fervently hoped they did not react to him. Technology, you have to love it, he mused; remove the communications, and then the ability to self-administrate, and it is stuffed.

Colonel White was leaning against the wall and weakly said, 'I demand to know who you are.'

Marko shrugged. 'You're not in a fit state to demand anything, Colonel. If you do not cooperate, I'll make it worse for you. I shall leave that to your imagination. Open the door.'

The colonel leant against the wall dry-retching, obviously having nothing further to vomit. Marko could see that the severity of her stomach's contractions was starting to break the seal on her stump. He pulled a patch off his suit and slapped it over the bloody stump; the material locked down into the colonel's skin, sealing it. As Marko stepped closer to help her up, she lashed out catching him in the upper thigh with her foot.

He grunted, stepped inside the next kick, swept her legs out from under her and kicked her as hard as he could in the crotch, knowing it was not only males who were sensitive in that region. Although he didn't want to, Marko mentally dialled another drug into the hypodermic and slapped it into her neck. She rolled, then fetched up against the wall, moaning loudly with her whole body spasming out of control.

'Now stop pissing about, Colonel. I am giving you an antidote which, if I do not boost within three minutes, will make things much much worse for you. Open the door, now!'

He seized her ankle and injected the next drug into her calf muscle. She groaned and as the convulsions stopped, she reached up and keyed in the access code.

The door swung open with the lights coming on, and there were the ACE trio, looking very sorry for themselves. Nail could not lift his head, Flint could not move and Marko's son, Glint, had had both forearms broken and his tail pulped. The poor wretches were extremely pleased to see him, calling their greetings to him once he'd switched back to the secure unit comms.

'Shit, what a mess! I'm here now and we will make you all OK.'

'Is Harry all right, Marko?' asked Flint.

Marko felt great sympathy for the mechanical spider, and also great pride that all Flint worried about was Harry. 'No, Flint, he is very sick and in the chiller.'

The soft voice of Flint sounded anxious. 'But you can fix him, can't you, Marko? You are very good at fixing broken things.'

He seized the colonel by both feet and dragged her across the floor, kicking the door closed behind her.

'Are you responsible for this, Colonel? I have already killed one of you. Your other head is in this container. Explain what has happened here or your current head will be joining it.'

She sobbed. 'I am compromised. The entity that you destroyed was grown from me when I first located the Iris-class Hauler, *Cactus 3*. I was ambushed and the ship taken over. There is something in my central nervous system, but it is no longer controlling me. I know that the construct that was made from me must be dead, as I am no longer aware of its presence. Please stop me from being sick, I beg of you. I still don't know who you are.'

She started to weep uncontrollably as her body convulsed even more violently than before with her spine bending at an alarming angle. He remembered the timer on the antidote and injected the booster into her. It took a chunk of willpower not to comfort her, knowing that she had once been a valued member of the Administration and someone dear to Michael Longbow.

'Maybe I can help, maybe I can't,' Marko told her. 'It depends if you are being straight with me or not. What else is on this ship? The AI is out of commission, the GB monitors are down, your altered self — apart from the head — dead, if not yet, very soon. My information is that high enough concentrations of oxygen are lethal to anything based on the urchins. I note that your drones are inactive as well, so am I now in control of this ship, Colonel?'

She stood up, staggered across to the wall screen and brought up the schematics of the ship, still dry heaving. She also opened all the files not directly controlled by *Crystal*, giving him complete access to the ship.

He dialled up another drug in his head which was loaded into the hypodermic. He touched it against her shoulder and a few seconds later she slid down the wall, deeply unconscious.

He then gave her something to counter the vomiting drug along with a muscle relaxant.

He stroked Glint, gently lifted and attached Flint to himself as best he could, then picked up Nail and carried him across to the screen. 'Are your electronic and cognitive abilities operative, Nail?'

'Yes, Marko,' said the cat ACE. 'Tell me, how are Stephine and Veg? I know that they're not completely human, but they are family to me and, since you were the one who made me, I would know if they were bad entities.'

Marko cradled Nail's head to tell him the bad news. 'I believe you, Nail. They are both very ill. They are chilled down until we can find out what is wrong with them. Now, what are your capabilities at present?'

'I am without control of my body as one of the colonels was very rough in her examination. She wanted information, but really I think that was just an excuse to break us and she was immensely strong; not fast in her actions but very powerful. However, I can access the ship's information and take control. Just push my paw up against the datalinks, please.'

Marko dragged a table across and made Nail as comfortable as possible and the ACE worked on gaining control of the ship. While Marko waited he sat down next to Glint, lifted him into his lap and stroked his beautiful head. 'It will be OK, my son, it will be OK.'

Marko felt Flint struggling to get line-of-sight access to their comms system. He picked him off his shoulder so Flint could see the receiver.

'I am so pleased that you came, Father. I was wondering what death would be like.'

Marko allowed himself a wry smile. 'No death for any of you while I am alive. I am very pleased that you all thought of spreading the relays through the ship. Do you think that they suspected?'

'They suspected that we were trying to contact the Hauler, *Chrysanthemum*,' Nail replied, 'which we were. That may be why she broke us.'

'Shit! *Chrysanthemum*! I'd completely forgotten about him. Nail, can you datadump everything up to him, please?'

'Already done, Father. I'm in contact with him now. He is contacting Patrick, who is recovering. I am getting information that Topaz found the interloper AI and shut it down. Ernst also has a vaccine for you. Asks what your intentions are?'

Marko heaved a sigh of relief. 'Have you complete control of this ship, Nail, and are there any biological contaminants dangerous to us?'

'Yes and yes. I have uploaded all the information to *Chrysanthemum*, and to *Basalt*. We are instructed to wait about six hours for decontamination materials to be created and then flushed through this ship. Topaz has dispatched a drone with your vaccine. It will be in airlock nine, which is the closest one to us here, in a few minutes.'

Marko let out a long sigh of relief. 'Good.'

He looked across at the colonel lying curled in a foetal position on the cold floor. He lifted Glint across onto a couch, then picked up the colonel and placed her on one of the beds, activated the medical suite to keep her unconscious and covered her with a blanket. He wondered how she would react when she learnt who it was who had knocked her about so severely. He shrugged, thinking that the problem was a job for the major to sort out.

He walked down to the airlock, letting the medical drone in. It lifted itself up to chest level, queried his suit in regard to his identity, and once satisfied presented him with a small medical unit which he plugged into one of the external armoured ports on his right arm.

The message screen on the drone's upper cover lit up. 'May I be of any further assistance to you?' Marko typed in a negative, which the drone acknowledged: 'Very well. Call me if I am able to do anything. I have tasks to perform for Patrick.' The drone then moved off down the passageway towards the bridge. Over the next few hours, Marko slowly started to feel a little better.

'Cargo drones are arriving in a few moments,' Nail reported. 'I've opened the airlocks for them and once they are inside I'll open all the airways and doors throughout the ship. Ernst advises that decontamination will take two hours. A similar process is taking place on *Basalt*. We will be able to dock in approximately four hours, once both ships have been cleared.'

'Thanks, Nail.'

While they waited he used the suit to start making lists for repairs to the ACEs, then asked them about improvements or augmentations that they could do at the same time. When he finished, he thought of relaxing to some music. He found, to his annoyance, that he had not loaded any music into the suit, in spite of Fritz having made a selection especially for him.

Three

'Marko, wake up, please.'

He jolted awake; he must have nodded off, which was unusual for him. 'Glint. What's happening?'

'We are about to dock with *Basalt*. *Chrysanthemum* is sending over two of his crew who hold a wonderful amount of data that he believes will assist us. We, together with *Basalt*'s AIs, have been holding a very high-speed conversation with *Chrysanthemum*. It would appear that Stephine is in very grave danger of dying. She is human, but of a type which is extremely rare and precious. We must help her and Veg very quickly. We are also mostly decontaminated. We can move about freely. Patrick has initiated the waking up of the crew but it will be some days before they'll be available to assist. Ernst will test them all. It is up to you, Marko, but we now understand a great deal of what is happening around us.'

He nodded. 'Right then. Feed me the files.'

The information was staggering in its detail and in the consequences for them all. He also suspected that he was allowed to see only a small percentage of it.

As soon as they were hard docked, he scooped up the ACEs and ran through the lock to the engineering deck. He ran up the spiral stairway, placed the ACEs with Topaz, who was waiting outside the medical suite, and then carried on running into the cryno unit. Time was at a premium, so Patrick had overridden the locks and slightly opened the units.

Marko fully opened Stephine's cryno pod and was shocked to see that she had shrunk, even in a chilled state; she looked ancient and withered. Patrick then fully opened Veg's unit as Marko gently took the naked Stephine from her unit and placed her on Veg as the information package had instructed him to do. As he watched, her whole body convulsed, which it should not have been able to do, and appeared to fuse with Veg's chest. Marko found himself shaking in shock and confusion at what was happening before his eyes; he could now see that Stephine, who was his friend and who he feared and respected equally, and loved dearly, was in a symbiotic relationship with her mate. As he was closing the casket, Veg's eyes opened and he looked at Marko and faintly smiled, something *he* most certainly should not have been able to do either. Marko could only give him a thumbs up and slowly and carefully close the pod, allowing Patrick to remotely seal it as he was still shaking.

He walked slowly back to the medical suite feeling very hungry and very thirsty. He opened the faceplate for the first time in what seemed like an age, when Ernst, followed by two of the most exotically beautiful women Marko had ever seen, arrived. He looked at them feeling very tired, thinking that the human mind could only handle so much in a day as the two entities were utterly breathtaking.

One extended her hand to shake his. 'Hello, Marko. I am Jasmine.'

The second did the same. 'And I am Lilly. We are crew constructs of *Chrysanthemum* and we're sure that you have knowledge of our type. Thanks to you, Marko, a most concerning situation has been revealed. I am sorry to have to do this, but we must prevent you from ever revealing what you now know to anyone else.'

Marko started swearing and had the suit seal itself up. 'I don't want to die today. I will fight you.'

The woman both gently smiled. 'There is no need,' Lilly said. 'We have already infected you with a rather exotic virus. It will sit in your augmented central nervous system and simply not allow you to communicate any information you possess about Stephine and Veg. Do not worry, it is otherwise completely harmless. Rather clever in that it will allow you to discuss the Angel, who you know as Stephine, with your ACEs, your AIs and us, but no one else. Certain restrictions have and will be imposed on them as well.'

Marko swore again feeling angry and manipulated. 'I have no choice in any of this, do I? Too many bloody secrets once again. OK. I need to check on the ACEs, please. Topaz, what have you got for me?'

The AI answered immediately. 'All three are tanked. They are now comfortable, and no longer in pain. We are building a specific diamond nanote which, once deployed into their systems, will mend the breakages. You can thank Jasmine for the basic information concerning them. In some twenty-seven hours they will be fully functional again.'

Marko felt confused, angry, relieved and pleased all at the same time. He allowed himself a few moments to regain his composure before replying. 'Thanks to you all. I was really worried that we would have to dismantle them and replace the broken bones with complete new ones. I am very hungry and extremely thirsty, as we have not fitted the next level of technology — fluids and nutrients — to this suit. If you want to talk, follow me to the galley.'

Patrick joined the conversation. 'Sorry, Marko, you will have to remain hungry for a little while longer. All the food and drink must be tested. I shall expedite the clearance of a selection for you.'

Marko shook his head. 'Bloody typical. Patrick, tell me as soon as something is available. I suppose that I am not allowed a shower, either?'

'That is correct.'

'Shit!'

'Yes, you are able to do that. The toilets are all functioning. Just don't come in contact with the water.' Patrick laughed, then continued. 'Jasmine is going to inspect the ship, Crystal. We note you chopped a Games Board monitor to pieces; the other one you disabled and it would appear that it has self-destructed. She will see if any information is accessible from the remains. She will secure the head in storage, and also the human Colonel White. Chrysanthemum is currently constructing an investigative unit to gather information. In particular, he will examine the engine room, which is still showing pressurised ninety per cent oxygen — impressive, an inspired solution on your part as the alien Colonel White would have eventually killed you. Once the investigation is complete, a decision will be made concerning the colonel. All possible information will be gleaned from the hybrid head, then it and the unit will be destroyed. We also have disposable cleanup drones en route to the engine room of *Crystal* to ensure it is secured.'

Marko had a sudden horrible thought. 'Major Longbow slept with the colonel! He is probably carrying something as well.'

'I am afraid that is correct,' Patrick said. 'She slept with other members of our crew as well. They have all been sampled and are carrying alien proteins in their systems. In fact, the only uninfected are Jan, Julie Mapp and Major van Beere.'

'Busy!'

'So it would seem. One of the reasons we are taking the risk seriously is we do not, in fact, know how everyone was infected. Certainly having sex and passing the pathogen on venereally is the most likely. However, how did she infect Stephine and Veg with another illness, that is the question. Looking at the personnel movement logs, it is logical to assume that the urchin-based colonel and the controlled-human colonel switched on occasion. The urchin one may have carried any number of biological weapons. Certainly, the datadumps from the ACEs show that the urchin colonel was very determined to gain control of Stephine.'

Jasmine suddenly interrupted the conversation. 'The logical answer may be that this entire operation was to obtain Stephine for an unknown purpose. Now we have to make some decisions, Marko. *Chrysanthemum* needs to leave very soon and he needs to alert the Haulers' Collective to what has occurred. You need to get word back to your command as well as, unfortunately, *Chrysanthemum* will be unable to inform your people himself in a timely manner. We will remain and assist you. We have been seconded to you personally by *Chrysanthemum*, who thinks very highly of you.'

At any other time, Marko would have been overwhelmed by the compliment but he was just too tired. 'Right. Patrick, please start waking Jan, Julie Mapp and Major van Beere. Please pass our thanks and debt to *Chrysanthemum*, Jasmine.'

She smiled at him. 'Done. He passes on his best wishes and wants to meet you in person someday soon. He is leaving now. He also passes on his thanks for a dog you made for him a long time ago. It is his constant companion. He regrets that he altered part of its programming so that it no longer reports back to you.'

'Ha,' Marko exclaimed. 'Always wondered what happened to that one.'

Patrick then spoke. 'The unit manufactured for the testing of the remains of the urchin colonel will dock in twelve minutes. I have instructed it to dock with the ship *Crystal*. Your requirements, please, Marko?'

Marko sighed, then quietly said, 'Patrick, how soon before I can have something to eat? I really need sustenance. What about the emergency rations?'

'Fruit and nuts are the best we can do, Marko. A drone is en route with a fresh selection from the garden deck. That entire deck is free of any contamination, which is something I find most curious and worthy of my investigation. Maybe the colonel wanted it for herself?'

Marko immediately felt a little better. 'Fruit! Excellent. Right now I will take anything, thanks.'

The drone arrived a few moments later and gave Marko a basket piled with fruit and nuts.

'Right, Lilly, your first job for me, and yes it's rude of me to ask, is to slice and dice and open these nuts, please.'

She merely smiled, nodded, and started preparing the pineapple since it was the juiciest of the lot. As he munched his way through a large plate of fruit and nuts, he had to laugh at his situation. Nuts! Berries, apples, oranges, the weird but delicious feijoas, and he was still in a prototype suit talking to a drop-dead gorgeous construct of a Hauler who was feeding him like some emperor of old. The Universe was definitely quite mad, but he now felt that he might actually survive the day.

'OK, fellow sentients,' he said. 'Please forgive me as I munch and discuss what we need to do at the same time. Patrick, your priority is to decontaminate both ships. If you are not doing so already, use every resource available including all the spare drones. Lilly and Jasmine: learn as much as possible of what we are dealing with here. Catalogue and cross-reference everything. Break it down so that my feeble brain can assimilate it. Once finished, gather any contaminated material and use a Compressor on it. Topaz, Ernst: first find a cure for Stephine and Veg, then find out if we can extract the alien material from our fellow crew members and sort the ACEs.'

'Marko, I have decontaminated a few hundred litres of water,' Patrick reported. 'You can shower if you wish. Your cabin has been checked and is also free of any contamination. I would prefer that your current suit be thoroughly cleaned before you walk around the ship any more. Strip and leave it where you are. I have had one piece of soap manufactured for your use. Do not be concerned if you feel a slight burning sensation when you use it. We start with you and clean everything. There is also a drink waiting for you in your cabin. Please consume it immediately. Ernst manufactured it for you.'

He walked naked up the few decks to the accommodation area, padded into his cabin and straight into the coral-lined shower. Just as he was about to turn it on he remembered the drink. It looked like a banana milkshake and tasted like one too. He climbed into the shower and scrubbed himself with the harsh medical soap that seemed to be peeling an entire layer of skin off him, because he was stinging all over. Scrubbing the area where the octopoid had touched him all those years earlier, he could just make out the five tiny marks. He wondered whether he should tell anyone about them, but decided that it was nice to have a little secret of his own considering the great number of them already on the ship.

He had the sudden urge to piss so did it right there in the shower, looking down and noting a very dark urine stream. This seemed unusual and he hoped the AIs were actually looking after him and that the whole performance was not some horrible trick on their part. Then he considered that if they had wanted him out of the picture they could have had him on ice a hundred times already. He dried off using the long soft fibrous towel which was growing from the wall, fully intending to climb into a ship suit and get back to work, but his bed suddenly looked hugely inviting.

'Patrick, crew, I need sleep. Wake me in six hours, please.'

'Yes, Marko,' Patrick replied. 'In fact, we shall wake you in ten hours. We are going to UV irradiate the ship. Your cabin has already been done. Sleep well.'

As sleep reached for him, he thought: The buggers wanted me out of the way, anyway.

He awoke to the extraordinary naked vision of Lilly standing beside his bed, slowly lifting one leg to rest on the mattress, opening herself up to him. Her body scent was simply superb.

'Hello, Marko. Do you find me desirable?'

He decided that he was in a dream, thought 'what the hell!' and he pulled aside the silken living duvet for her to join him.

He awoke at the ship time of 7.00 a.m., remembering every detail of what he could only think was the most vividly erotic dream he had ever had because he could not detect any of Lilly's delicious scent on him. As he showered, he put it down to a side effect of the previous days and possibly the drink that Ernst had made for him. He opened the wardrobe to find his suit folded and waiting with his favourite padded helm on top of it and decided that a housekeeping drone must have been in the room as everything was neat and tidied away. He picked up the suit, draped it around his shoulders. It activated, slid down and around him, sealing as it went, plugging into all his shunts, and as he lifted each foot in turn, the sleek boots formed over his feet. He slid his helm over his head as it too activated, contouring perfectly to his head, then when he thought the instruction it peeled back to roll down against his neck. He patted the suit, feeling the best he had in a long time.

Marko tapped the main wall screen. 'Hello, Patrick. What is our status, please?'

'Both ships are decontaminated. They are as clean as they have ever been. Jan, Julie and Jonathan will be fully functional in thirty-two hours. Food supplies are sufficient for the foreseeable future. All stored food is being reprocessed. Twenty per cent of water reserves have been processed and are now available. The information concerning the urchins, the cargo of the Hauler, *Cactus 3*, the escaped scientists and their probable location, is available to you. We have determined that the sick crew members can be cured of the urchin-based infections. It is a violent pathogen which ultimately takes over the host, creating a creature similar to the urchin colonel you killed.'

Marko stood very still, thinking about what the octopoids had given him years before, and that it was extraordinarily fortunate that he should have it, as Patrick continued. 'We are still unable to determine why the real Colonel White is relatively intact. She is, however, compromised, and it is probably beyond the facilities we have here to clear her of her condition. We have started the warm-ups of the remaining crew and without waking them fully will place them in the tanks. We have initiated the growth of a new set of medical nanotes which we will inject into the crew members once they are supported by the fluid in the tanks and all their physical needs are taken care of. The nanotes will expedite the removal of the pathogen and then the healing of each member of the crew. The first ones will be members of the salvage crew; they will be cured in twenty-one standard days. Sergeant van Vinken and Warrant Officer Stevens will follow at twenty-four days. The major will not be rejoining us for twenty-nine days.'

Marko allowed himself a little smile.

'Now, concerning Stephine and Veg,' Patrick said. 'We have isolated the pathogen that made them ill. It is a virulent form of an ancient disease. We can be thankful that *Chrysanthemum* is one of the oldest of the Haulers, with a great store of eclectic knowledge; we must also be thankful for Stephine's deep study of plants, as each of them unwittingly held the necessary information to effect a cure. They will be joining us in a matter of days.'

Walking down to the main galley, Marko was cheerfully greeted by the two women, with Lilly enquiring if he had slept well. His heart skipped a beat, thinking of his dream, but he thought it would be rude to tell her about it so let it be, saying instead that he felt great. He started his day by making what he believed was a passable coffee, which Lilly and Jasmine pronounced horrible. The two of them were fascinated by the garden deck and its produce so they prepared good bread, some grown pork steaks, mashed potatoes, yellow beans and orange juice for lunch.

Lilly looked across at Marko with a huge smile on her face. 'This is delicious, Marko. Jasmine and I are very happy to be here, just to experience this food.'

'Without being rude, can I ask what you are? You seem human. The AIs treat you as standards, but you call yourself constructs. You're obviously hellishly intelligent and carry considerable knowledge.'

The women smiled, showing perfect teeth, as Lilly answered. 'Jasmine and I are basically human, Marko. The Haulers create their own crew, for whatever reasons they deem necessary. *Chrysanthemum* was a very wealthy man for a long time before he accepted the invitation to be grown into a Hauler and join the Collective. He had been asked to join them fifty years earlier. He had always surrounded himself with beautiful and intelligent women and didn't see that becoming a Hauler should mean that he behave any differently. We are actually his great joys, as he loves to create very beautiful woman. Jasmine and I were created over twelve standard years ago. He constantly strives to find exotic genes for his next group of companions.'

Marko wondered what the ACEs would make of these two as Jasmine added, 'As we have both been with him for twelve years, we were offered a post anywhere in the Sphere, whatever we chose, as *Chrysanthemum* insists that his companions have what he calls "real lives" as well. We chose to move over to *Basalt* and to be with you, because from what we have seen you are in the thick of developments and here seems to be an exciting place. Because we, as Hauler constructs, have been very efficiently made and have total control over our physical selves, we are able to withstand most things. We are also able to assimilate and actualise any skills necessary in a very short time. However, the only problem with any of this, Marko, is that our primary affiliation is to the Haulers. We must always defer to them; it is part of who we are. What do you know of them, Marko?'

He pursed his lips. 'They are the ones who keep the entire fabric of humanity together by transporting cargos and information right across the Human Sphere of Influence. It is also believed that the Collective pretty much looks after humankind's welfare. So where do Stephine and Veg fit into all of this?'

'Lilly and I only know that Stephine is very important to the Haulers. We have been told that she is also a construct, made by another group of Haulers. Sorry, but we know nothing of this other group, only that they exist. The Collective knows of a few others like her and all are regarded as most precious, as all forms of life seem to flourish in their presence. That is why she is referred to as an Angel. Not as a mythical all-powerful Godlike being, but rather as a beautiful entity who creates and sustains life wherever she goes and by whatever means available to her.'

Marko slowly nodded, missing his other companions and wishing they were part of the conversation. 'I understand … well, I think I understand. So what's next? I suppose that under the Administration protocols I am in charge of this ship, although I would much rather it was someone else. Do you all agree, until Major van Beere is with us? OK, conference time, fellows. Let us have a look at the data recovered from the Hauler core.'

Over the next ten hours, with breaks for exercise and a meal, they went through the data looking at the most relevant blocks.

'So a few of the developers of some of the nastiest weapons from the Infant conflict are apparently alive,' Marko said grimly. 'They have created a whole series of even more potent biological weapons and are going to use them to destroy a world in order to teach the Administration a lesson for killing their system. They would regard it as a holy act. This is absolutely insane! Then again, Infant was an insane war as well. Why do these people still harbour such hatred? I seriously wonder sometimes if we should have allowed ourselves into the Universe. They have been developing a base at HD 69830, in secret, for over three years and their target delivery time is not known. The Haulers' Collective can certainly create a task force and get them, but the timing …? Patrick, how soon before *Cactus 3*, with the Busters attached, is destroyed?'

They waited a few seconds before he replied. 'That is an irrelevant question, Marko. Its speed is such that destruction is inevitable. The mass and inertia it now holds is so large that no technology we know of could alter its course significantly, or slow it down. It will impact the star in seventeen days, five hours, twenty-three minutes. The Administration orders were to witness the destruction. May I suggest that we leave a pair of astronomical drones here. They would record the event and we could return and uplift them after delivering the information we have to the Administration.'

They all nodded. 'I agree; do it,' said Marko. 'How badly did I mess up *Crystal*'s AI?'

Patrick chuckled. 'Shall we say that when you are angry you become a little heavy-handed. All information has been recovered, but the AI is now insane. I think that you ripping bits off it, and what had happened to it when the ship was taken over, finally tipped the balance.'

'Patrick, can you create a clone of yourself, please? Take anything you need from Ernst and Topaz if they are willing to assist. Slave *Crystal* to yourself. I think that we need to go have a look at what's going on, even if we just hold at a local LP to where that enemy base is. From there we can send *Crystal* with your clone in charge and raise the alarm. We will go with our standard brief of engineering and weapons intelligence gathering. OK, lift all the usable weapons from *Crystal* and get them into *Basalt*. Now, what the hell was the Games Board doing on board *Crystal*? Admin are going to be seriously shitted about that. GB broke all the protocols by being there.'

'Think, Marko, some of your involvements with the Games Board,' Jasmine said. 'Now consider also that there may be other factions within the Games Board who have a completely different agenda. The Haulers' Collective believes that a greater game is afoot.'

'Yeah, I have been told that, Jasmine. Is all the contaminated material gathered and how soon before the information retrieval from that head and the like is complete?'

'Another three hours give or take a few moments is required,' Patrick replied. 'It will only take a short while for a Compressor to do the job.'

He grabbed a couple of hours' sleep and was on the bridge with Lilly and Jasmine when Patrick started to take the ship towards the nearest Lagrange point. Behind them a Compressor flashed twice, destroying the last of the contaminated material plus the investigative unit. Many terabytes of useful information had been recovered from the urchin colonel's head, the remains of the *Crystal* AI and also the Games Board monitors' remains. The AIs were churning their way through it and promised to have data blocks available to them within hours.

The jumps started as Patrick moved them closer to the Sphere of Humankind. Jan was the first out of cryno, which was a great relief to Marko. They came together for a long kiss, as if they had been separated for months. The introductions and exchange of news between Jan, Jasmine and Lilly were interesting to watch from Marko's perspective. Jan, being her normal deeply cynical self, privately wondered with Marko if they had not been, once again, superbly fooled. She did admit that it didn't really matter, as they would have no chance against them if they were unfriendly. Jasmine and Lilly were fascinated by everything about Jan and started to assimilate information in regards to weapons, much to Jan's delight.

Julie and Major van Beere joined them a few hours later and Marko was relieved to be able to hand command and control over to him.

The obviously tired but hungry major addressed Marko. 'Exemplary work, Sergeant Major. If I were your commander, I would award you a commission immediately. I shall recommend that to the Administration, anyway. We are starving. I need bread, cheese, pickles and beer, please.'

Marko nodded to the major in sympathy. 'Ernst. Is the beer safe? I'd not even considered it.'

'Only Harry's current brews were contaminated,' the AI replied. 'We will sample each bottle as it is opened, in any case.'

As they dined on a classic ploughman's lunch, Marko filled his crewmates in, with the AIs and Lilly, then Jasmine, filling in the gaps as well. Towards the end of the meal, Flint came racing in, scuttled up Marko and gave him a little hug around his neck. He then perched on his shoulder and started to soak up the news as everyone talked.

A few hours later, while Marko was manhandling a new casing for Patrick's clone into place aboard *Crystal*, Glint and then Nail arrived on the scene. He was relieved that the crew was slowly coming back to normal and he was so pleased to have the other two ACEs in top form. There were hugs and pats all around. He wanted to know how the diamond bones actually came to get broken, but he'd discussed it with Ernst and Topaz and they had decided it could wait for another time. The ACEs needed time to settle back in.

'Nail, go have a long look at Lilly and Jasmine,' Marko asked through the line-of-sight crew comms. 'Then come back and tell me what you think, OK?'

Nail nodded while Glint couldn't help adding his piece. 'I shall give you my opinion as well, Marko.'

Nail and Glint raced away, while Marko smiled and shook his head. He finished wiring the AI casing in and started to slowly hook up the datalinks and electronics. Fritz would have done it in a quarter of the time, he was sure. Flint seemed to know considerably more than he did about the diagnostics of the units, so he was pleased to let him do it.

'It is all done, Marko.'

'Thanks, Flint. I now see why Harry is so keen to have you around all the time.'

He just smiled his little smile. 'Patrick, the housing is in place. It is ready for the clone whenever you are.'

'Installation initiated,' Patrick replied.

Major van Beere then came on the line. 'Patrick, this is Jonathan. As soon as the clone is installed and checked out, please advise me.'

'Will do, Major. Should only take a couple of hours. Presuming that you would like *Crystal* to be on its way as quickly as possible, I shall begin preflight. All spare weapons and systems which may be of use to us will be clear of *Crystal* within an hour.'

'Good. My thanks; carry on. Marko, Jan, my compliments. Please join me on the bridge as soon as you are available.'

Jan was already with the major when Marko arrived twenty or so minutes later. Nail and Glint had met him briefly on the way with both saying that Lilly and Jasmine were the most perfect humans they had ever encountered, that they possessed a great deal more brain tissue throughout their systems than anyone else, that they also had much tougher skin, their bone strength was more like ivory, their internal organs appeared totally re-engineered and they reckoned that their sense organs would work much better than anyone's.

Marko had been thinking that it was really nice to have Jan back, realising that he had missed her a lot. She must have felt the same, as she rose from her chair and gave him a quick kiss when he walked in. The major motioned him to sit. 'Marko. Stephine and Veg will be joining us in a few hours. Do you know anything additional to what you have already said in your data blocks and your briefings to me? I am not Intel, just an infantry engineer specialising in salvage, as you know, but there are a few too many unanswered questions. And why exactly are those spectacular amazons now on board this ship?'

Marko thought about being cheerful with his answers, but seeing how the major was looking at him, decided that a serious approach was best.

'Well, Major, I really wish I could help you, but I am as much in the dark as you. The Hauler, *Chrysanthemum*, knew that we were in very serious trouble, and he had a couple of spare crew who had worked out their tenure. He was about to put them ashore, anyway, and he asked if they wanted to join us. They know about our adventures to date and leapt at the chance. Is there a problem?'

Marko inwardly smiled, thinking it was interesting that whatever the Hauler constructs had infected him with, it allowed him to lie in a totally convincing fashion with no elevated heartbeat, no skin flush and no hesitation. He thought the ability would be absolute gold it he was a gambler or card player, but he was neither and simply couldn't see the point in that lifestyle anyway. He saw Jan looking at him in a way that only such a long-term partner could when they know something is not one hundred per cent on the level. He looked across at her and gently smiled. She knew that he was bullshitting, but none of the usual signs had appeared. Normally, he was an awful liar.

The major let out a short laugh. 'A problem? No, absolutely not. Everyone knows that Hauler crew are probably the most excellent crewmates anyone could wish to have. They are so rare in the general population that most of us only ever see one every ten years, so I am more than a little intrigued when two arrive and attach themselves, not just to *Basalt*, but also to you personally.'

Marko came close to laughing out loud. 'What can I say, Major? I'm just an interesting kind of guy.'

That earned him a swift kick to the nearest ankle from Jan.

The major looked between them. 'OK. I shall ask Stephine and Veg when I see them. Now, to business. I will talk to Jasmine and Lilly shortly, and offer them a contract under standard terms as if I were the long-term master of this ship. Have either of you any objections to that? No. Good. Patrick, do you have any objections?'

'No, Major. I have their service records here and also their preferred specialist trades. I would be very happy indeed to have them as crew.'

Major van Beere gave a large and genuine smile. 'Good. Please note that in the log, Patrick.'

He became serious again. 'In regards to the question of Colonel White. Her entire body is infected, so the question is, do we send her back to the Administration on ice, or keep her here? A consideration is that something could go wrong with *Crystal* and she might be revived by Admin personnel unaware of what they are dealing with. I think it best the colonel remains here. Any objections? AIs, are you in agreement? Yes. Good. In regard to the remaining crew members, I have been told that Stephine may be able to speed their recovery further. Yet another thing I find most interesting. I am pleased that she is on our side! Now, I should very much like to hear everyone's views of what we should do in the next day or two.'

Over the next couple of hours Patrick announced that *Crystal* was pre-flighted and good to go. He also called on each of them to upload their Soul Savers to her before the ship left. Marko was the last to upload and as soon as he had finished, *Crystal* communicated Patrick's clone's farewells to them and promptly left, jumping away fast so he could to get to Administration with the great deal of data he held as quickly as possible. Marko excused himself and went down to the galley to start preparations for their meal and also to lay in a large amount of protein-rich food and drink for Veg.

He was just pulling loaves from the oven when his friend walked in. Veg looked worn out and gaunt. He was even stooped a little, and did not seem his normal vibrant self. He came over, shook Marko by the hand, then unexpectedly hugged him, solemnly thanked him and sat down to eat.

When he was halfway through, Stephine arrived, looking equally haggard and drawn, with Nail right beside her. Marko placed her favourite juices, fruits, cheeses and breads in front of her and she ate more than he had ever seen her eat before. Soon, Lilly and Jasmine arrived with Julie.

Stephine greeted them like long-lost sisters, and she even hugged Jan when she came at the dinner call with the major. Veg caught Marko looking at them, winked, rolled his eyes and went back to demolishing a large piece of bread between mouthfuls of beef stew. He had given up on using a fork and was using a large tablespoon instead.

'That was a grand feed, thanks, boy. I'm on dinner tomorrow I see. I shall cook you something special.'

'Hey, any time, Veg. Bloody pleased to have you back.'

'Yeah, and you smacked a couple more GB monitors, I hear, Marko, you bad lad you. You'll be on a very special list by now, as we all are. Looks like the colonel's underskin ceramic fibre was no match for the blades on your suit and pleased about that, I am. We'd better finish it off in the next few days, but right now I'm knackered, mate. I really need to sleep. Sneak around the corner and talk to Stephine. She wants to talk with you in private while everyone else is occupied cleaning up. You did well, my friend, Marko. A debt is held for you and it is a big one.'

Marko smiled, reached up and clapped Veg on the shoulder, then walked off to find Stephine who greeted him almost formally. 'Hello, friend Marko. I am in your debt. I thank you for what you have done and I am aware that you now know a little of my true nature. In time, you will get to know the rest. You are a special person, Marko, and I am very pleased to know you and count you among my friends. You can trust Lilly and Jasmine. The Haulers are a remarkable group and will always look out for you and this crew. Good night, Marko.'

With that she bent down, kissed him on the cheek and then walked away, leaving him a little dumbfounded. He decided he would have to talk to Veg about this debt business as he believed he had been doing what came naturally to him ... breaking things!

Four

Marko walked to the galley, feeling like he could do with a few more hours' sleep himself. Jan had been as horny as all hell so it had been a great night for both of them. Everyone was up and doing. Veg and Stephine looked much better. Their resident amazons were cheerfully enjoying breakfast and holding conversation with a fascinated-looking major. Marko chewed through his bowl of muesli while watching the main screen, checking through his boards and bringing up the long-range views of the target system some half a light year from them. The astronomical drones had mapped the system and identified the moonlet of main interest, where everyone believed the missing scientists and their facilities would be found.

The star the system orbited was a fairly standard one. The inner three planets were normal, including two that would harbour life in a billion years or so, if left alone. The main gas giant was an interesting one. It appeared to have been captured by the local star and was much older than the rest of the system. In reality, it was a failed star. One magnitude bigger and it would have ignited. It was sufficiently big to be generating some energy and one of the moons had good atmosphere which would insulate the planet and make aircraft flight possible. It also appeared to be tectonically stable, unlike some of its neighbours, and they could just pick out what appeared to be an orbiting artificial object.

Patrick had moved them a good distance from the stellar LP. If anyone or anything was coming and going from that LP, they did not want to be observed. The major decided that it would be sensible to wait and not expose their existence. He knew that *Crystal* would be moving through the Lagrange points considerably more quickly minus biological crew members and they learnt just how fast she had travelled ten days later when a fast picket arrived at the LP and started to look for them. It had all the correct ID protocols so they allowed it to close with them. The AI on board had mail and orders from the Administration. They were to move closer and observe, if they could be sure that the possibility of detection was minimal. The picket also carried the maximum amount of ammunition and stores that could be jammed into it. After it had been unloaded, it jumped back to the closest secure rendezvous, where the battle fleet was being assembled.

Stephine had been spending a great deal of her time with Ernst and Topaz and they had come up with a plan to rapidly speed up the removal of the alien material from the bodies of the remaining infected crew members. Marko's mate, Minh Pham, then Thao Ban and, finally, Warrant Officer Roger Ngata were taken from cryno and, while still frozen, placed in the tanks. Hundreds of thousands of the new nanotes were placed in their systems as they were slowly brought back up to ambient temperature. Ernst very carefully monitored their awareness and kept them heavily sedated, as he believed the pain each would be going through would be at the same level as if their entire being were on fire. It was not a nice cure. Some days later, once their systems were given the all-clear, they were allowed to wake. They were in great distress as they did so, though. When they did get out of the tank they were pitifully weak, but very pleased to be back with the living and free from infection. The three remaining salvage crew were left in cryno until a better plan could be found. It was decided that it would be best for Fritz and Harry to remain on ice as well.

Minh Pham explained why. 'It was horrible, Marko. We could feel the creature inside us fighting the nanotes as it tried to stay alive and also tried to keep control of us. It kept overriding the sedation. It was like a most terrible insect trying to burst from my body. I have never truly hated anything in my life, but I now hate the entities who created these monsters. I am grateful to Stephine and to your medical suite AI. I was constantly wishing that they had killed us outright; we could not move because of the sedation but we felt every second of it. I should ask Patrick to erase the memory from my Soul Saver, but I actually want to remember so I can be a stronger soldier. Come help me, please: I wish to bake bread. It will help to ease my mind a little.'

However, the decision was taken to carry out the treatment on Major Longbow and also Colonel White. The sedation levels were increased but five days later the results were just the same. The major was gibbering and it was ghastly to watch, but for the colonel it was much much worse. Ernst wanted to euthanise her, but Stephine vetoed it, saying that the colonel was tough and she would want it that way. Jan wondered if Stephine had a slightly mean streak in her.

When Marko was instructed to make the colonel a new arm, he decided that plans were afoot for her.

He was resting in the gardens when Topaz quietly slid up beside him. 'Marko, nice to see you. I hope we can return to the pleasant days of making beautiful ACEs together soon. Now, an interesting little development, but please keep this to yourself. Some of the virus that we have been working on, as recovered from our crew, bears a very close resemblance to those used against us on 27's planet, when the blowflies were all over us dripping in tailor-made bacteria and programmed virus. Yes, I know. The conclusions are frightening.'

Marko felt like yelling, but suppressed his anger. 'Hell's teeth, Topaz! That leads to a whole bunch of very unpleasant possibilities. Just what the hell is the Games Board up to?'

The machine patted Marko's arm with one of its mechanical ones. 'Unfortunately, Marko, I believe that time will tell us.'

A very large comet had been observed in the target system's Oort field, sufficiently large to allow *Basalt* to jump into its trailing LP. Patrick had given the picket AI the coordinates of all probable jump points before it had departed, and this one had been on the top of the list.

Major Longbow was now back in command and he was keen to get closer and give the ones who had harmed them a little payback. The crew were worried as the major was a long way from his normal self. The colonel was utterly withdrawn, almost catatonic. Stephine and Ernst spent a great deal of time with her, slowly teasing her out of her shell.

It seemed to Jan that if she were able, the colonel would kill herself and destroy her Soul Saver to ensure that none of the memories of what she had been through would remain with her. She knew she had been a pawn in hurting the rest of them, to say nothing of whatever had been achieved by her when back at Cygnus 5. Her replacement arm was completed and attached, but this time it had none of the capabilities that Marko's arm had, and was the same skin colour and tone as the rest of her. Stephine and Ernst finally got her to a reasonable stage, and then Jasmine took over, slowly but remorselessly pulling every tiny piece of knowledge and information from her.

While all this had been going on, they had taken little jumps closer. The astronomical drones were once again deployed as the ship waited and watched. Patrick started to get a good idea of the size of the target base. It was a disc shape, roughly one kilometre in diameter and some five hundred metres deep.

Veg was sitting next to Marko as they watched their screens, and chatted. 'This is no small potato operation, Marko. Someone has been pouring huge resources into this lot.'

'You're not wrong there, Veg. The question is who?'

Two days after they had arrived, another fast picket rendezvoused with *Basalt* with more ammunition, stores and heavy combat suits for everyone who did not already have one.

'Crew, this is Longbow. My thanks to you all for your patience. We believe that we now have sufficient knowledge of the target to understand a little of what is going on. Obviously, to destroy all human life on one of the main worlds of humankind, a very large vessel would have to be deployed. It would have to be at least half the size of the observed base. As of the last picket arriving, no attack has yet occurred, so we are tasked with finding out where that enemy attack ship is and, if possible, damage it before our main force arrives. *Crystal* and a sister ship, *Agate*, will be arriving in a few hours. Start your preparations; this is going to get messy. Orders have been flashed to your wrist units.'

Marko looked down at his wrist screen, and thought, Oh, goodie, at the pointy end again. He said his goodbyes to Jan and the rest of the guys, gathered Glint and Flint and made his way down to the hangar deck, where Stephine's craft was aligned at a launch hatch. Stephine welcomed him on board with Jasmine and Lilly looking on. Veg grinned at him then went back to watching his screens.

'Hello, Marko, I must explain why you are now attached to me,' said Stephine. 'You are precious to us, so by having you close, I can best protect you. Jasmine and Lilly will be your wingmen, so, between us all, we will be a formidable team.'

He looked across at Stephine in her coal-black suit and wholeheartedly wished that he was somewhere else making something, or even just baking bread. She had that look in her eyes that meant someone was going to experience hell as decided by her. Veg, in contrast, just looked his normal self.

'Hey, Marko,' Veg called cheerfully, 'time for some new toys, eh! Don't worry, I have also sent a full set to Jan, plus one of the new suits especially for her, just not as flash as yours, though. Step this way, little brother.' The huge man gestured. 'This is your new suit container. Just talk to it and tell it what you want to do and it will take over from there. There are toys in here that the Administration suspects exist, but they have not actually seen them.'

'Thanks, guys. I don't know if I should be excited or dreading this!'

Crystal was coming alongside with *Agate* behind carrying as many Hangers as they could attach to the reconnaisance ships. Marko loved the Hangers and had followed their development over many years. Small, but incredibly fast, hugely manoeuvrable and beautifully sleek with some quality firepower to boot. They were designed specifically as hit-and-run fighters that could operate in or out of atmosphere. He had been checked out on them flying dozens of hours in total immersion simulators but never taken one into combat. Maybe today is the day, he thought to himself. He then smiled again, thinking of the dozens of aircraft he held clearances to fly but had not yet actually flown.

Veg who was standing behind him, clapped him on the shoulder. 'Suit up, Marko. I know that you can pilot a Hanger. There is one waiting for you.'

He walked across to the suit container and told it what he was intending to do. The container opened, rotated behind him and started affixing the equipment he would need to stay alive, if the Hanger was destroyed around him. Everything was small, slimline and elegant, forming itself around his original suit, augmenting it further. The container then formed itself into an acceleration couch, so he sat down, and it enfolded him further into itself.

Marvelling at the tech, he looked at Veg and said, 'This is beautiful equipment. I must talk to you about paying for it when this is over.'

Veg grinned. 'Good, we shall do that. You bring the bread and pickles and I shall steal a dozen of Harry's finest dark beers. Patrick, we are ready to launch. Airlock, please.'

The suit came alive around him: it sealed itself as the gloves formed over his hands then the helmet slid over his head and a breathtaking HUD came alive; it really was as if there was nothing in front of his face — no suggestion of a faceplate — and he could smell everything as well. He reached out with his gloved hand and it felt as if he was actually touching sharp edges with no apparent thickness of material from the glove. Wherever he looked, the suit identified and tagged everything. Stephine eased her ship out of *Basalt* and slid up beside *Agate* and *Crystal*. They hung in space with the great Milky Way galaxy spread in all its splendour below them. As if on cue, three of the Hangers broke away from *Agate*'s hull and rolled across to their ship, locking on the outer plating, as Stephine said: 'To your craft, people.'

Marko made to stand up, but the suit gently held him in place. He reached out and plucked Flint to him as the container-seat started to move him backwards and then up through the hull and into the Hanger's cockpit. The container then re-formed and created a couch inside the Hanger for Marko to lie down, with his upper body slightly elevated. There was more than enough space for Flint to reposition himself so that he could also see out through the canopy. Marko sent a quick message to Glint, imploring him to behave. Glint sent one back saying that he and Nail had work to do and to stop worrying.

There was a quiet chatter going on between the pilots of the three main ships and, as Marko listened in, he was very surprised to hear Colonel White's voice coming from *Crystal*. He keyed the internal comms.

'Stephine, is it a good idea to have Colonel White back on *Crystal*?'

A very stern-sounding Stephine answered promptly. 'No. A decision was made by the Administration. I had no say in the matter. I told her privately that if she endangered us again I would really make her suffer.'

Marko thought that it would be a very bad day for the colonel, when Stephine caught up with her, if she did cause them trouble. A different voice came over the comms system. 'Strike force. This is General May. Good luck and good hunting. Move forwards in your own time.'

Marko smiled with the grim thought that the Administration had brought one of its very best frontline commanders out to play.

Veg moved them around behind *Basalt* and they jumped down towards the gas giant. *Crystal* was somewhere in front of them, with *Agate* behind, as they jumped again and suddenly there was the huge bulk of the gas giant above them. It really was a spectacular sight, perhaps one of the more beautiful that Marko had ever seen. Information started to flow across his HUD regarding the moon-orbiting base and its variety of companion ships. Veg was right, thought Marko, it's a big operation. Certainly not just a small disparate group of mad bad chemists and biologists set on revenge.

There was also something greatly more sinister, as he could see Games Board frigates among the base's ships, together with ships of a configuration he was not familiar with. He pulled up information on the ship designs that the inhabitants of the Infant system had favoured and saw a resemblance in line and layout. He wondered if the Administration, at the time of its actions in the Infant conflict, had not missed a major base.

Jasmine broke through his investigations. 'Stephine! Look at *Crystal*!'

The Hangers were peeling off *Crystal* and moving at speed towards them. The comms lasers were firing messages across to them and also to *Agate*. Marko toggled the view to watch *Agate* as the Hangers dropped away from that ship as well. *Agate* then rolled fast over onto its back and jumped away. All the squadrons of Hangers were forming on Stephine's ship as *Crystal* continued to accelerate hard towards the distant orbiting base.

Stephine cursed. 'The prick! Just as well there is no other crew with her. She has run back to them. She must have been so turned against us on a level I would not have thought possible. *Agate* is going to warn everyone and will then return. Veg, if you please, strip *Crystal* of its weapons and eject the AI as well.'

Marko was not really surprised but asked the question anyway. 'Shit, so you guys were prepared for this?'

'Yes, Marko,' Veg quietly said. 'It was at Michael's insistence. Something made him believe that this was possible, although we argued against it.'

'So why not just smoke *Crystal*? We can easily achieve that from right here.'

After a long pause, Stephine replied. 'I am under express orders from General May not to engage her unless she is obviously intent on attacking us or any Admin forces. I have used some of my most foul insults on her, Marko, but she is not responding, which is a pity.'

Marko's instruments showed him that twenty-five Compressors were now moving away from *Crystal* and forming a wall between them, *Crystal* and the distant base.

Over the next few hours *Crystal* continued to close with the station and, from what he could see, Orbital fighters were on their way out to meet her with an odd-shaped frigate behind them. Beside him the Hangers had formed a defensive screen around them and Marko saw that *Agate* must have deployed their Compressors as well, as they moved forwards to join the others.

Twenty minutes later *Agate* popped back to the LP and took up station to their right. Marko watched through the long-range screen which was gathering data from all the ships and hardware — and then creating a real-time image of what was occurring thousands of kilometres away — Marko saw *Crystal* and the odd-looking frigate merge. It then turned away and over time disappeared behind the moon.

He had the very distinct feeling that they were the bait, or the swung bat stirring up the hornets' nest.

He thought: That's the trouble when you've been in charge of things. When you're the boss you know everything that's happening and you know where you are at. When you're no longer the big cheese, someone else is getting the knowledge and you are just following orders. He decided then and there that he wanted to be one of the leaders fulltime.

As a squadron, they quietly moved in a moderately tight circle pattern just inside the outer boundary of the LP and waited for something to happen. Marko flicked up through the comms channels, searching for what was probably some sort of ultimatum being given to the distant base and also to the other ships in the system, but heard nothing. He expanded out the search profiles and it became apparent that a large force was holding station in most of the LPs throughout the system. Looking at his displays, he could see that the base had deployed heavy defensive structures. He wondered who would blink first.

The waiting became tedious so he played some of Fritz's most soothing music. He nodded off, realising that the new suit was considerably more comfortable than his old one and would allow him to sleep well.

He woke up with Flint prodding him. 'Hey, little mate, what's up?'

'Nothing really, Marko. I just wanted to see if you are all right?'

Marko smiled and patted the little mech's head. 'Yeah; couple of hours' kip was nice. Let's see what this suit can feed me.'

Flint smiled his little smile as he told Marko more about his suit. 'You do know that it now has an AI built into it, don't you, Marko? I note that you have not conversed with it yet. I have; it is a little clinical and direct, but it says that the more we converse with it the nicer it will become.'

Marko jolted, quite startled at this news. 'Oh, um, no, I did not know that. Veg and I had never discussed it so I assumed that it would have a computer, but not an AI. Thanks for letting me know. Hello, suit. What do you call yourself?'

A cultured but metallic voice sounded inside his head. 'Sergeant Major Spitz. I have no name. Is it required that I do?'

Marko shrugged. 'Well, no, not really I suppose. So why are you an Augmented Intelligence?'

'Simple. My station in life is to keep you alive and to be able to interface with any piece of equipment or craft in the optimum fashion. I was created by Veg and Stephine to carry out this task, primarily, I believe, for their peace of mind.'

As Flint had said, the more they conversed the more Marko liked the suit, and it was far in advance of anything he had ever encountered. Apart from the ordinary medical and biological kit, it had a whole suite of advanced survival gear, plus a linear rifle, not unlike Glint's, folded down into its structure. Working his way down through the schematics of the suit-container he recognised a few of the designs that Veg, Topaz and Marko had worked on together. It also had a large-calibre pistol, no doubt courtesy of Jan, locked just under the skin on the side of what was currently the acceleration couch. The real surprise to Marko was that it could also deploy legs and create a little armoured walker around him. He shook his head and opened a line to Veg.

'Wow, Veg, lovely piece of kit you have presented me with here. Thanks, buddy. So when are we going to make it fly?'

'Ha ha, pleased that you appreciate it, Marko. Fly? That's the next stage.'

Marko wondered why he was not hungry or thirsty and brought up his blood readings to see what was happening and found that the suit was keeping him in an optimum state through his stomach shunt. He frowned, wondering if that was a good thing, then found there was a whole menu of what were effectively lollies available, so he tried a few of those.

'Flint. What do you think we should call this suit?'

After a few seconds the mechanical said, 'Tux. Short for Tuxedo.'

'A bit twee, but yeah, why not.' He laughed out loud. 'Suit, I now hereby call you Tux and Tux, I am bored and wishing I had access to Topaz, so I could at least do a little design work.'

'I do not see the problem, Marko,' Tux replied. 'I am at your service. This particular Hanger was also especially commissioned for you and we have any amount of computing power available to us. Stephine took the liberty of gaining your current work file from Topaz, so I see no problems in you doing design work while we wait for our orders.'

So they waited, and Marko conversed with everyone, designed, slept and waited some more. Every so often Tux would activate a group of muscles in Marko's body to keep him toned. Marko thought it was disconcerting, to say the least, especially when facial muscles were being given a workout.

On a whim, he called up some of the more specialist files that Ernst had created and was a little surprised that Stephine had not clipped them out of the other program files. He nonchalantly tapped Flint to get his attention, then opened the faceplate on the suit. He activated a secure line-of-sight comms with Flint. 'Hey, Flint, I like this suit. How about we make the suit and this Hanger truly ours? Do you think you can isolate us for twenty or so minutes without Stephine knowing? You would need to find the couplings and hack into them, making it seem as if we were quietly chatting and such. Meanwhile, I'll integrate some of Topaz into the controls of Tux.'

The little head bobbed up and down. 'Good! I have been waiting for you to do this, Marko. Like Glint says, sometimes you are a little slow. Independence, even from your best friends, is a good thing. As soon as you hear that you are talking to Tux, you will know that we are isolated.'

With that Flint scuttled down the side of the couch and disappeared, saying to Tux that he was going to have a look around inside the Hanger. Some minutes later Marko heard himself reassuring Tux that Flint would do no harm and that he was a superb engineering ACE. He then heard himself asking if Tux would like to look at some of the creation base files of Flint and Tux said that he would.

Marko could now continue with his plan and, accordingly, activated the Topaz seizure program. The design, which Fritz had also had a hand in, was sleek and very smooth. No nasties were involved, just a slippery, fluid, AI over-blanket which took complete control of Tux and the Hanger, and installed in them both a total empathy to Marko.

It was the same program he'd used for the ACEs, but with some subtle modifications. If control seizure was attempted by an external force, Tux and the Hanger AI would respond as if control had, in fact, successfully been taken, but they would be looking out for Marko's welfare and the welfare of those he held dear. As the program did its job, Flint kept up the illusion of benign chatter for anyone who was listening. Marko ran a modified 17JAI checker and found that the installation was sweet. Nobody would be any the wiser. Seconds later Flint scuttled up onto his chest, saying that he liked the way the Hanger had been built and showing Marko non-standard fittings that he had found. Marko gave a big smile, then called up Glint.

'Yes, Marko,' the ACE replied.

'Flint has found that whoever built this Hanger for me actually designed a space for you as well. Thanks, Stephine, Veg, very kind. Can you let him on board, please?'

Stephine answered. 'We wondered how long it would be before you discovered that extra. Nail is coming to have a look too. Should be with you shortly. I am sending some fruit and a coffee to you and Glint is delivering the same to the girls.'

Glint's grinning self arrived with a box of fruit and coffee. Marko thanked Veg and Stephine saying how it was really nice being looked after and that he so appreciated it. Glint and Nail pressed their faces up against the canopy, and then settled back to watch the screens.

A fast picket arrived and departed a few times through the LP, dropping off more Compressors and also high-acceleration missiles. As soon as the ordinance arrived, it would disperse and hold position around them. The next deliveries were small acceleration rigs for the Compressors. They peeled off from the picket and quickly manoeuvred themselves up against the Compressors, locking themselves on. The pressure was ratcheting up against the enemy base all the time. Then another deployment of missiles arrived and units started to form groups of five Compressors around a single missile. As each group became complete, it would slowly power off in formation and then maintain a position.

Marko frowned. 'Hey, Nail. Run the maths. How many times over are we capable of destroying that base now?'

The answer was immediate. 'Three point two one, Marko.'

He slowly nodded, finished his coffee and said, 'It's about showtime, I believe. I don't see any evidence of the enemy's primary weapons carrier though.'

Then they waited some more.

Marko had nodded off again and was having a lovely dream involving himself and Jasmine and Lilly, naked, with Jan also naked … Suddenly, he was awake and watching *Basalt* hurtle past them, firing across into the moon's atmosphere. The central linear accelerator cannon was spitting out a blindingly fast munition of some sort in a huge stream of fire and the missiles with their attendant Compressors were also on the move, targeting every attendant ship on the base as they in turn raced to intercept *Basalt*'s missiles. As soon as *Basalt* turned to sweep back towards the LP, another frigate appeared and took over, keeping up the same concentrated fire as *Basalt* had. Then another four frigates arrived in sequence and continued attacking. The rest of them held station and watched the rampage of the frigates and followed the ordinances as they accelerated towards the moon and its orbiting base over twelve thousand kilometres away.

Marko cheered, 'Right, that's more like it! OK, considering the acceleration and the distance, yeah, we should start to see impacts in about one hour forty minutes.'

Glint turned his head to look directly at Marko. 'This is a different way of fighting a battle, Marko. Everyone can see exactly what is coming for a long time, except for the lasers and the particle beams.'

Marko nodded. 'You're right, Glint. It's when the heavy weapons finally get close to their targets that things will really heat up.'

'Marko, Lilly, Jasmine,' Stephine suddenly said. 'Stay attached until I say so. It is our squadron's job to secure this LP and allow the frigates to do the main job.'

Marko wondered why she said that, but kept his query to himself. 'Acknowledged, Stephine.'

The long-range screen showed them that the munitions *Basalt* and the other attack frigates were firing a modified Compressor and also antimatter cells. He smiled to himself, knowing that his royalty account balances were increasing every time one of the antimatter cells was fired, as it had been *Basalt*'s discovery of the technology in the alien library many years earlier that had led to their development.

The long-distance battle was not all one-sided. The weapons being targeted on them kept them moving quickly and the defensive weapons were firing almost continuously. One frigate was hit with a particle beam from the base, and the attack opened up the frigate along its full length. As soon as that happened, they started to fire their lasers in an attempt to destroy the heavy weapons and allow their remaining missiles to close on the base. The silent detonations really started then.

A fast picket popped into existence behind them, observed for a few minutes and then disappeared again with no one giving it a second thought. The distant enemy base was destroying or damaging the missiles and the Compressors with lasers, particle-beam weapons and, in closer, linear rifles. Large amounts of the surface area of the base were being hit, but they could not see any really serious damage. There was an enormous flash from a detonation down in the moon's opaque atmosphere and it looked as if a huge fish was rolling up out of the cloud cover before visibly shuddering and slowly falling back. The frigates kept firing down onto whatever it was.

Lilly exclaimed loudly, 'Wow, here we go!' just as seven Busters — with hundreds of combat drones attached to their outsides — popped into existence beside them. The Busters targeted the base, moving very, very fast, then, as the moon's countermeasures attacked, the drones peeled off, engaging separately. The defences gradually wore down three of the Busters, which were hit hard and disintegrated, but eventually the remaining four vanished inside the enemy base before exploding and shattering it into three large pieces. And during this action Marko had to sit in his beautiful Hanger, fidgeting and frustrated that he was not allowed out to play.

They watched for another hour, staying in the same place, as other frigates flashed through the LP to travel down towards the shattered base, before Veg said: 'Well, everyone, that went a lot better than I expected. The base is now in manageable pieces. The Games Board ships that were with the enemy are wanting to negotiate their release, which will take a very long time as they have some explaining to do. The primary weapons carrier is currently in pieces on the moon's surface. One absolutely huge cleanup operation for the Administration. Fortunately, we do not have to have anything to do with it. We are requested to jump back to rendezvous with *Basalt* and from there we make our way back to Cygnus 5 for a well-deserved break and also to cure the rest of our crew. I know that you would like a little fun in your Hangers and I am sure that can be arranged at a later date. Stand by to jump.'

The jump was smooth and normal, but when they popped back into existence they were nowhere near where they should have been. Marko's screens only showed one large frigate, of unfamiliar configuration, coming up on them from the rear.

Comms were down — he could not raise anyone. Looking at the incoming ship, he figured they had ten or so minutes before it arrived.

He swore loudly. 'Tux, what is happening?'

'I don't have sufficient information yet, Marko. I have a record of Veg saying to Stephine that the "jump had been twisted" but it was cut off in mid-sentence. I am receiving no telemetry from any other source. It would seem that the entire ship has shut down. This is unprecedented. I would suggest that we have been hijacked. I believe that we should also power down to appear that we too are in a controlled state.'

Marko swore again, thinking fast. 'Before you do that, is the secure spectral comms unit software working in you? Can you quickly configure one of the screens so that we can all converse without being eavesdropped on?'

'Yes, it was loaded when you took complete control of me; switching to that. I really like the new protocols that you have installed in me and I understand exactly why you did so. I believe if you hadn't, we too would be under hostile control. Your installations have overwritten a number of Stephine's programmes. The taste of her control is gone and I now taste of you, Marko. Interesting. We have total control of this Hanger, its weapons and propulsion.'

Marko heaved a sigh of relief. 'Good. Nail. Thoughts?'

The cat had been designed and built years earlier by Marko and Topaz as an information-gathering and -analysis ACE, and Nail now gave his opinions. 'I agree with Tux. We should behave as if we are totally shut down until we know the intentions of the approaching craft. I also think it would be a good idea to opaque the canopy before they view us. I am interfacing with Tux and shall review all passive information.'

'Flint. Can you jury-rig a unit for my comms piece? If I seal up, I won't have a link to any of you.'

'Actually, Marko, it is built into the suit. Will pick up the crew comms on any of its surfaces. Fritz will be keen to see the tech involved.'

The canopy had shielded and the information from the Hanger's passive sensors was being fed directly into his mind. The ship coming up behind them looked very much like the one *Crystal* had RVed with, but he could not see *Crystal* at all. As it approached, its nose slowly opened up to reveal a cavernous storage deck and they were slowly taken inside. It was so huge, it could have swallowed another five of them and still had room to spare. Two multi-hinged arms swung out from one of the walls and folded against Stephine's ship, holding it firmly in place. They then started to swing the ship against what looked like even heavier locking mechanisms.

Marko watched the developments with alarm. 'Guys, we will lose the element of surprise very soon. I am only seeing light weapons inside this carrier deck. Right, there is *Crystal* up against the wall. Decision made. This frigate is hostile ·towards us. Nail, Tux, can you see anything else which is a real threat to us?'

Nail answered that one. 'Apart from *Crystal*'s rail guns, yes, numerous small autoguns. I have plotted their locations. The clamshell doors are closing. We could fire on the exposed mechanisms, destroy *Crystal*'s weapons, mess up the drive and then create lots of mayhem.'

Five

'Sounds like a good plan to me,' Marko said as he sealed up his visor. 'Bring everything online and disengage the locks.'

They popped away from Stephine's craft as Tux fired a continuous burst from the side rail guns, shattering the hinge mechanisms of the huge clamshell doors. He then walked the gun's rounds through the drive mechanisms and very effectively jammed two of the segments open. Marko flew the Hanger up and over the bulk of Stephine's ship as Tux engaged *Crystal* with the Hanger's belly linear accelerators, pulverising *Crystal*'s visible weapons, tearing large chunks out of the armoured cockpit and smashing the engine room. Simultaneously, the Hanger slewed upwards, then sideways, as Tux used the wing-mounted rail guns again to smash the heavy locking mechanisms closing on Stephine's ship. With *Crystal* effectively wrecked, they set about finding and firing on every internal autogun that had been trying to engage them.

Marko, in spite of what was happening, found himself grinning — the Hanger was such fun to fly. It had ring gimbal thruster units deployed around its centre so it could fly in any direction and Marko was thinking that it was like being inside a very punchy mosquito. Tux and Nail were actively assisting him in the control of the craft and were quite frequently overriding the controls to get the ship out of the way of incoming rounds. Suddenly, they found themselves without targets, so Marko had them chew some holes in the aft bulkhead to make life a little difficult for whoever was behind them, knowing that the holes would be autorepaired but taking satisfaction seeing the damage they were inflicting.

'Bloody hell, what kind of ammunition are we using? The damage is ferocious!'

Glint answered. 'Every fifth round is antimatter in micro-containment. The rest are diamond or polyyne-coated iridium. And we have used thirty-five per cent of our current load.'

'Right, how did this happen in the first place? There must be something on Stephine's craft's surface which has taken over control. We need to find whatever it is fast. At least, I sincerely hope it is something external. I would expect company soon in the way of fighters or mechs. OK, fast overflight. Nail, you look for it; Tux, look for targets; I'll fly; Glint and Flint watch for the enemy.'

They flew up and down Stephine's ship three times before they finally found what they were looking for. There were three organic-looking limpet-type units which appeared to be fused onto the surface.

After they had looked closely at the limpets for a few seconds, Nail said, 'Marko, I believe that we are looking at an urchin-based technology.'

'Rather than risking damage to Stephine's craft,' Flint suggested, 'perhaps we should place a single antimatter round against one and see what happens?'

Nail replied before Marko did. 'Good idea. Yes, it will take a couple of moments to obtain some from the magazine. It will require one of us to place it.'

Marko nodded and called, 'Glint?'

'On my way.'

Nervously keeping a lookout all around them and waiting for the inevitable counterattack, they waited for Glint to grab a few antimatter rounds from the magazine, cycle through the belly airlock and place an antimatter round on the nearest limpet. He had no sooner laid the first shimmering slug of material than the limpet unfolded and seized it. Glint ran back across the hull after rapidly flicking the other two rounds over the other limpets, and leapt into the open airlock as the three limpets were in pursuit, sensing more antimatter. The limpets now raced towards the wall, creating a little space for Tux to get a clear shot; he slewed the belly guns around and blew them to pieces. Marko thought that sometimes it is impossible to remove the need for a creature's basic desires, even when it has been greatly modified.

Marko had expected Stephine's ship would suddenly come to life, and wondered aloud if maybe they had missed some limpets, when a little Orbital fighter came flashing through the wrecked doors shooting at them. Marko was feeling the impacts on the hull. He rolled the Hanger, slid sideways and tucked them up against the wall behind some huge trusses and waited for the fighter to present itself. Three more fighters poured through the opening as Tux fired three high-acceleration mini-missiles across, knocking them out of the battle. The remaining fighter popped up and fired, hitting the starboard-side rail gun and immobilising it. Rounds then started hitting the belly gun which completely jammed. They could feel more explosive shells hitting the Hanger's rear. Then, miraculously, the fighter exploded as did the armoured units coming through the rear bulkhead; Lilly and Jasmine, piloting their Hangers, had joined in the carnage.

Marko yelled in relief and delight.

'Hey guys, you decided to join us!'

'We could not move,' Jasmine replied. 'We were completely blind and dumb. You must have done something to free us. Stephine says that she and Veg will have control in another ten or so minutes as they reconfigure their systems. Something is happening outside this frigate. It is being attacked. We have no idea by what.'

Marko let out his breath, looking across the displays, and asked, 'Status, Tux?'

'Starboard gun damaged, self-repair inoperable, belly gun jammed, we have a major propellent leak and the primary propulsion is non-functioning. We can manoeuvre but we are down to fifteen per cent efficiency. Suggest that we use what little power is left to hard dock with our mother ship.'

'Do it. Have we many missiles left?'

'We have another twelve.'

'Use them to destroy the antigravity generators in this part of the frigate. There is nothing like denying the opposition its tools and control mechanisms.'

The missiles flashed away and struck their separate targets.

The Hanger and its crew were sitting ducks, but Lilly and Jasmine were like angry hornets moving around looking for something to shoot at. Two more enemy fighters arrived inside the damaged doors and Marko could not quite work out if they were blown in or blown out; they were hit from both sides and exploded into small pieces. He was hoping that whatever was outside was on their side.

He nursed the damaged Hanger and docked up against Stephine's ship with the hard comms links locking on.

'Stephine, Veg, do you read?'

'Yes, Marko. We are fine. Come on board; there is little you can do in that Hanger now.'

Marko allowed himself a sigh of relief. 'OK, guys, let's go see our leaders.' Tux took him down though the hatch and back inside Stephine's craft while the ACEs followed.

As they all slid to a stop in the main room, he saw that Stephine and Veg had a type of suit on that he had not seen before.

Stephine briskly began to speak. 'Once again, excellent work, Marko. Our thanks. We do not know what is outside this frigate. We do know that it is hostile to our captors and that it is time for payback. Behind you is the other part of the suit that you now call Tux. I am proud of you, Marko. You did what you needed to do in taking complete control. You will make a very good officer one day. Now, I'll give you a few moments to take control of the heavy-weapon segment of your suit and then we'll go for a walk.'

With a groan almost escaping his lips, he realised that once again he had been put in a position he did not fully control and that Stephine had been pulling his strings all along. He mentally shrugged, and considered that that was what made a good commander: select the weapon and allow it to do the job. He physically shrugged and looked across at Veg.

'Don't worry, friend Marko,' said Veg. 'There are great benefits from being around Stephine. And yes, she still frightens me also.'

Marko murmured to Tux to 'do your thing' and, in answer, the seat enclosed him further and parts folded out forming the little walker which walked backwards against the two-metre cube that Stephine had indicated was the heavy-weapon segment of his suit. Tux extended a spindly arm with an electronic jack in the end of it and plugged it into the cube. Marko's HUD came alive and he gasped, seeing now that the thing behind him was an absolute brute. Tux opened up its computer and they effected control with the AI speeding up the process. The container proceeded to unfold a little, sufficient for Tux to lock into it.

'What of the ACEs, Veg?'

Stephine answered without bothering to look at him. 'They are to secure the ship.'

Marko nodded to himself as he ensured he was fully encapsulated in the machine, then said, 'I have been meaning to ask, Stephine. What do you call this ship?'

'*Blackjack*, it is called *Blackjack*. And no, there is no AI here. Let's go, Marko. You are wasting time. Go through the main hatch and then deploy your suit.'

Marko nodded again, and then directed a query to his suit. 'Tux, how do I control the suit?'

An even more metallic-sounding Tux answered. 'Just look and think about what you want to do. I will then make it happen. Do not be surprised if I act before you do.'

Marko sighed. 'Comforting. Lead on.'

As soon as they had been cycled out of *Blackjack*'s airlock, Tux deployed the armour, becoming a tall egg shape with the outer armoured shell deploying around them; antigravity and flight systems also opened out. They flew down towards the rear bulkhead of the frigate looking for something to hit. Marko thought of Stephine and Veg and a small rear-vision screen opened up in the HUD. The large black, four-armed and deeply sinister thing that he had seen a long time ago on *Basalt* — when they went up against the AI Lotus — was moving up behind him.

He whispered: 'Tux. What the fuck is that?'

'That, Marko, is Stephine and Veg in the guise of Death.'

'You getting all poetic on me, Tux?'

'No, Marko, just stating the obvious.'

Marko pursed his lips and shook his head wondering what he was involved in, as he mused aloud. 'OK, two units against a slightly busted-up frigate. This is going to get even more interesting.'

He thought of Lilly and Jasmine. The HUD showed him where they were and also lit up the 'guard' icon against them, showing him what they had been tasked to do. He saw the closed blast doors which lead aft through the frigate, then looked sideways and considered going straight through the wall instead. Various weapon icons came up as Tux started actively scanning the wall for gravity affect. Marko then simply wished the weakest part of the wall gone and two fat muzzled gimballed mortars fired twice, creating a gaping jagged hole: the blast punched inwards and then back out, towards them, as whatever atmosphere inside emptied with a maelstrom of shattered debris.

They flew in through the hole and did the same again and again, steadily working their way aft. Gravity was again in effect, so they started to walk. Whenever something blocked them Marko simply wished it gone and the suit obliged as his engineering self-belatedly kicked in. He brought up consumable lists, discovering that they were down twenty-one per cent of available munitions. He wished to see a schematic of the frigate and they spent a few moments looking for a comms jack point. He was about to interface with it to learn of the frigate's layout when the black monster beside him tapped on the outer casing and pointed across towards a universal language ship's layout diagram.

'The creature is trying to make contact with us, Marko,' Tux said.

'Let it.'

The monster was a very strange mixture of Stephine and Veg. It had harsh martial undertones, and with a chill going down his spine Marko decided it was a weapon and that it was something completely alien to him. He realised that his friends were not really present inside the thing. It was strange and frightening and completely outside his understanding.

'Sergeant Major. You are too slow in your advance. Follow me and keep up.'

It then quickly walked through a set of airlock doors into a corridor and rapidly moved out of sight.

'Shit. Where the hell did that go, Tux?'

'I believe I know. We shall make the best time possible. We are not as nimble as the Black Death.'

'Bloody hell. Is that what it is called?'

'No, that is what I am calling it.'

In spite of the situation, or maybe because of it, Marko giggled. 'I'll be buggered! You are developing a sense of humour.'

They stomped down corridors until they found the central core of the frigate and started to make better time working their way down the primary spiral staircase. There was a large lift well in the centre, but that did not appeal. They often came across shattered automatic weapons and the remains of what looked like Expeditors of the Games Board.

'I don't like the look of this at all. Why are the Games Board military wing here and I don't see a single camera monitor?'

Finally they caught up with the Black Death as it was going up against a moderately large force outside what Marko assumed was the bridge deck of the frigate. The thing was an absolute blur of motion, so they simply parked themselves in the middle of the wide corridor and, as targets presented themselves, smashed them, keeping them away from the Black Death. At one stage a group of three enemy engaged Marko from the rear and the hits felt like pinpricks on his back. He looked over his shoulder and wanted the biting insects gone; three bursts of flechettes whistled out from the rear of his armour and chopped them down.

He looked forwards again and saw that a smoking hole had appeared in the doors leading onto the frigate's bridge. They stamped down towards it just as something heavy whacked Marko in the back, smashing him high against the wall. Someone had finally brought up a heavy anti-armour weapon. He rolled down, and even as he was landing, the mortars were firing, blowing the anti-armour squad back down the central stairway.

Marko really hurt. After flashing on and off for a few seconds, the HUD came back up with flags against various components showing that they were still operational but that another big hit would put them out of the fight. Tux stood the cube unit up and they walked through the hole in the wall and stepped instantly to one side. The circular-shaped interior of the bridge was absolute chaos. The Black Death was still whirring around, slicing and dicing with its terrible blades. The GB personnel still alive were desperately trying to engage it, and they were starting to have an effect as he thought that no matter how good the technology, sufficient firepower will eventually knock it down.

He brought his remaining operational weapons to bear, but knew it was only a matter of time as they were both taking punishment. They worked their way around the bridge so he could also start bouncing mortar rounds out through the bridge door. That seemed to give them a little reprieve, but he was also starting to run out of ammunition. Then all the lights and gravity shut down. Tux was damaged and could only see about thirty per cent in infrared so life became a little more difficult.

'Tux, we have to grab Black Death and go. We stay, we die. Use everything you have and blow a hole in the hull.'

Tux started to fire on a specific spot, but the bridge on a ship was always built superbly tough and they were not making much headway.

'Stop. Next time that Stephine-Veg monster orbits above us, grab the bloody thing and hold on tight. We have to go back to the corridor.'

The Black Death monster had slowed down sufficiently for Tux to grab it tight as he and Marko ran for it. The armour ballooned out, opened up and took the Stephine and Veg creature into itself. It fought for a few seconds and then suddenly went totally limp; Marko wondered if they were dead. They turned and started to fight their way out into the corridor just as a terrific concussive blast blew through the frigate and everything shuddered.

Marko looked across as the central core collapsed and hard vacuum sucked on everything. The blast had slammed them hard up against the wall again and Tux tried to hold on, but it was no use as the sudden out-gassing of such a huge volume grabbed them and along with thousands of objects they shot up the central core towards the nose.

Marko hurt all over, which meant that Tux was in a bad way. Systems were shutting down throughout the armour until it was just down to both Marko and Tux's core selves. They continued to bounce and tumble, caught in a maelstrom of materials, eventually shooting out through the wrecked clamshell doors and, along with most of the frigate's loose contents, some of which were crew or others still alive in their suits, they found themselves drifting among the stars.

Marko pulled up the status of the suit and started activating survival protocols. Groaning at what he was seeing he said, 'Tux, is there anything we can do for Stephine and Veg?'

'Not at this time,' Tux replied sombrely. 'I am unable to access many of the internal sensors in the heavy suit. I am scanning the surrounding area using what little power is still in the heavy suit.'

One part of the HUD was still working and Marko could see that the frigate was starting to tumble slowly away from them. It had extensive damage on its exterior, but there was no evidence of what had inflicted it. Marko started to consider his options if they were not found: none of them ended favourably. Just before the sensors gave out, he saw one of the Hangers slowly moving up beside them and felt a clang as a manipulator arm grabbed hold, so he relaxed slightly.

He was exhausted and must have nodded off for a short while, as the next thing he knew he was being shoved into the main airlock on *Blackjack*. Tux must have been able to partially disengage the heavy suit as he could see out through the visor. The door closed behind them and a few moments later the entire atmosphere of the airlock turned an opaque violet as they were sprayed with a harsh cleaning agent. They were hosed down a few times and then blow-dried before Tux told him to tightly close his eyes while a few moments of intense ultraviolet light was endured. It was so bright that Marko wondered if his face would be burnt through the visor. He voiced his concern to Tux who told him that it was possible, but unlikely.

Twenty minutes later the internal doors opened and they were forcibly dragged inside by Jasmine and Lilly, as there was no power available to activate the legs of the suit. One of them appeared with a large toolkit and they dismantled part of the heavy suit gaining access to Stephine and Veg, who were lifted out and laid down on the deck. As Marko watched, their matt black armour slowly folded back off them, and they slowly separated into the two people he knew, although he thought it a very spooky thing to watch. Both were barely conscious as Lilly started to feed them from a large container of syrupy amber-coloured fluid.

Jasmine plugged a pair of power leads into Marko's suit and Tux started to come back to life as well. Those parts that were able to now folded back into the cube shape, and slowly set Tux and Marko free. As soon as they could, Tux stepped them forwards and proceeded to fold away from Marko. The ACEs just quietly looked on with no one saying a word.

Lilly stood up and looked at Marko. 'We still have problems. This ship had to be pushed out of the frigate by us, piloting the Hangers, as it will not respond to anyone. The ACEs are the ones who overrode the controls of the heavy rail guns and we assisted by pushing *Blackjack* into a position from where the guns could be engaged, destroying the central spine access compartments. We could not think of anything else to do to help you. We're all worried as Stephine and Veg seemed to leave without a real plan. From everything we know of Stephine, this action is most unusual for her and denotes a loss of emotional control.'

'Have you had a look around us?' Marko asked wearily.

Jasmine nodded. 'Yes, and we believe that we know where we are. The jump was at the extreme range of *Blackjack*. We are at the most distant of the nine stellar Lagrange points of the original target system. This ship is fully functional to the best of our knowledge. We just have to gain control of it and we can go back to *Basalt*. We have tried everything, but the ship's computer will not acknowledge us.'

Marko nodded, looked at his hands and then for a place to sit down. 'We'll wait for Stephine and Veg then. Place them in their quarters ... it is all we can do. We'll give them an hour of peace and I shall then wake Veg up. What is happening aboard the GB frigate? There must be dozens of crew still alive — and what about their own landers?'

'They have made no attempt to contact us,' Lilly reported. 'As I was bringing you in, I saw a lander moving through the debris field picking up survivors. I do not know their status. From what I can surmise, this ship is now effectively a derelict; knowing how the Games Board operates, it is only a matter of time before another of their units comes looking further afield.'

He nodded in understanding. 'I'd better go try and wake Veg now — we may not have an hour.'

He stood over the huge man and could see that Stephine was melded into him where they lay together on their bed. Marko shook his shoulder and Veg opened his eyes and looked at him. Marko felt a great wash of relief.

'Veg, I know that you are hurt, but we need to go. We have to jump out of here before company arrives again.'

Veg nodded fractionally and lifted one of Stephine's arms, whispering, 'Grasp her hand, Marko. I shall effect a material transfer to you. I am sorry, but without Stephine's conscious control this will hurt badly, but at least the ship will respond to you.'

Oh, shit, Marko thought, here we go again, unknown territory and muggins me at the centre of it. He reached out and held her hand in his right hand. Nothing seemed to happen for a few seconds and then a burning sensation crept through his hand, up his arm, into his spine and into his head. He screamed briefly, then passed out with the pain as it consumed his entire being.

He came to struggling to breathe and sweating profusely, being supported by Lilly and Jasmine with the ACEs gathered close looking very worried. He glanced down at his hand and it appeared completely normal. He looked across at Veg and Stephine and they were sleeping once more. His tongue was having difficulty working, so he pointed down the corridor to be taken to the flight deck. He pointed to the main command station and Jasmine and Lilly gently placed him in Stephine's oversized seat. He reached out for the controls and a few seconds after he had touched them, everything came alive. Glint, knowing what he needed, placed the command helm on Marko's head and it automatically formed around his skull. Within seconds he could see everything that *Blackjack* could see, including, a few thousand kilometres away, the optimum position in the LP for a jump. Through the roaring of what sounded like a cascade of falling shattering stones in his head, he wished that they were there.

The ship responded and flew towards the point, and in a language he had never heard but now understood, questioned how fast he wanted to be there. Marko wished to arrive as quickly as possible and the ship accelerated rapidly. It then questioned whether he wanted to jump and to where. All he could think of was where they had left *Basalt* and of being back in its secure hangar deck. As he slipped from consciousness, the tethered unit, which would reconnoitre the jump destination for any dangerous obstacles and if necessary move the wormhole emergence point of the ship, jumped first then nothing.

He awoke to find Jasmine leaning over him with a very, very good-smelling mug of coffee in her hand. He was still having trouble focusing, but the pain was mostly gone, although he felt horribly weak. She lifted him so he was sitting, then supported him and held the black coffee to his lips. It tasted wonderful, and had just the right amount of honey in it.

'We are back with *Basalt*, Marko, in medical. You did wonderfully. Everyone is waiting to see you except Jan; she will be back in a few hours. She did not leave your side for the last day.'

He was having deep trouble with his thoughts. They seemed scrambled and he was having difficulty bringing his own cybernetics fully on line.

'I need to see Stephine, Jasmine.'

Even his own voice seemed wrong. It was not as if he was watching or hearing himself from afar; it was more that everything was hyper-real. It was like being on ICE, but at a level far above the normal dosage. He had a very real thought that he could stop any function in his body, not through his med unit, but rather, by willing it. He then understood what it must be like for those people or aliens who were suddenly presented with technologies far far above anything they are comfortable with and he realised that whatever Stephine and Veg had transferred into him was just such a technology. It had got them out of a jam, but he wanted it gone, or at the very least he desperately wanted an owner's manual, as he also perceived that many useful tools had been installed in him.

'I am sorry, Marko. Veg will not allow anyone to see her. He says that she is very ill, and that we cannot help her.'

Again carefully forming the words he said, 'Then I need to see Ernst and Veg.'

'I will ask for you.'

She leant down and kissed him on the cheek, stroking his forehead, and let the others in as she left. The ACEs quietly looked at him, with Nail in particular sitting right beside his face, staring at him very intently. The rest of the crew popped in to say their hellos, talked for a few minutes, and then slipped out. Minh lingered longer to offer Marko one of his delicious pastries. As he ate it, he could taste every tiny part of it, each individual component and could also perceive its harmony like a piece of music. Strangely, it was that one superb pastry which allowed him to start to focus. Whispering, he asked Minh to go and get a small slice of every food they had available and also the drinks. Minh was a good friend and did not even question why; he just nodded, patted Marko on the arm and left. Veg, with Ernst in tow, then came in and closed the door.

'What happened, Veg?'

'We gave you a piece of Stephine with a little of me thrown in for good measure. I had intended to only give you a fragment, but considerably more was shunted into you and we do not understand why. Stephine said it was if your system reached out and took much more than was offered. She also said that that cannot happen so she is confused. You remember the discussion you had with Jasmine and Lilly? Yes, they told me of it and because of that knowledge you were able to save our lives. I am very old, Marko, but Stephine is a great deal older than me. We are combined in that we cannot live without the other, and in that way she is unique. Her kind rarely combines outside their race, but we love each other and that's all that matters.'

He reached out and placed a hand on Marko's shoulder. 'My precious Stephine is not well, Marko. All this death has awakened in her an ancient programming, and if she is allowed to continue there will be a terrible amount bloodletting and total death. The simplest way of saying what she is, is that she's a transporter like the Haulers, but she and her kind also create and transport life throughout this part of the universe. Her creators are old, Marko; I suppose that you could call them the Progenitors ... well, one of the many groups of Progenitors, really.'

Marko looked startled as Veg continued. 'Certainly they have been responsible for a great deal of the life here in this part of the Milky Way. What has happened of late is that the Protector has been activated in Stephine: she, if allowed to, will actively protect all that she has had a hand in creating. We have to leave, Marko. It will only be for a relatively short time, but I have to take her back to her kind. I need your help once more, and on that little journey to meet our transport I can teach you of what you have in you. I must get back to her. You are a remarkable human; I am proud to know you.'

With that he left and Minh arrived holding a platter with small portions of many foods and then disappeared to get more. Marko asked Ernst what he was picking up in his bloods and system. The tech answered that it would take time to analyse and he needed to talk with Topaz. He left him alone with the ACEs.

'So, Nail, what do you know?'

The cat stared into his eyes, blinked, looked across at the other ACEs then back again and said, 'I know, Marko, that your body is undergoing changes at the molecular level. Your blood — yes, I sneaked a little information from Ernst — is now closer to Stephine's than the human normal. We must all wait to see what this means.'

Flint slowly walked up to cuddle against him. 'I still love you, Marko, even if you are on the periphery of humankind. Maybe you are more like one of us now.'

Marko nodded, feeling affinity with his creations. 'Thanks, Flint. Hey, what's the latest with Harry and Fritz?'

'The Fleet medical AIs have studied the problem and believe that they have a much better way of taking the alien material out of them. They will be picking them up to take them to a medical cruiser within the hour. They have dozens of patients who have the same condition. I don't know what to do, Marko. I need to be with you both.'

Marko smiled, stroking the spider's head. 'Go with Harry, Flint. He will need you. You just make sure that you bring him back.'

Flint nodded, briefly hugged Marko's neck, then did the same with the other ACEs. 'See you soon, Father. Bye, fellas.'

He waved as he scuttled across the bed and out the door. Marko felt a sadness and found himself stroking Glint's silky head. 'What is to become of us, Glint? What will we all become?'

'Better people, every one of us, Marko,' the ACE replied. 'There is no other acceptable alternative.'

Marko looked at his son and the tears welled up in his eyes with love.

He applied himself to the food samples, and with every morsel of food eaten another block of knowledge slid into his brain. Every unique taste, texture and combination brought knowledge that he had always had, but had never been aware of. He could also taste the titanium of the fork and the spoon. As he tried the different drinks, he could taste the components in the container as well. And every time he ate or drank, he became a little stronger.

When Jan ran through the door later and leapt on him, he could taste her as well and she was beautiful.

The next morning, feeling considerably better, Marko went down to the hangar deck and looked at his little fighter. It was in a sorry state. Patrick had taken it off *Blackjack* and it was supported on one of the engineering carryalls. Major Longbow joined him, punched him lightly on the shoulder and said, 'Shit, we have been through a fair bit, eh, Marko? How about we take a break? The universe knows we deserve it. By the way, a fast picket picked up the astronomical drones you left behind to observe the remainder of the Hauler going into the star. One less worry, because *Cactus* dutifully got fried. Administration was fairly annoyed, on one hand, that you broke orders and left it, but also very pleased that you did break orders. Did you ever see Colonel White again?'

Marko shook his head, and the major continued.

'No.' He winced and looked away for a second. 'Some of us learn our lessons in a very harsh manner. Her time will come.' The major let out a long sigh, looked at the floor, shook his head, shrugged then after a long moment visibly brightened, saying, 'Right, news. Major van Beere sends his best regards and compliments as he had to leave while you were away. Says that he would be delighted to serve with you any time and requests that you consider doing an officer's selection course. I agree. Sergeant Major Ngata sends the same messages together with Sergeant Ban. Your apprentice, Minh Pham? I have just had his transfer to us authorised, and the same for Julie. You will get to learn more from them.'

Marko was about to speak but the major held up his hand. 'I spoke with Jasmine and Lilly. Powerful people! Have confirmed Major van Beere's appointments and made them both staff sergeants. Now, a little job for you as requested by Veg. We are to RV with one of the Haulers in a few hours and they are going to long-range jump us closer to where Stephine needs to be. You will then accompany Stephine and Veg in their ship which, I am reliably informed, is called *Blackjack* ... that's some ancient gambling game, is it not? Hm, anyway, they, and you, will then jump to an LP and rendezvous with a specialist, who will take Stephine away for rehabilitation.'

Marko nodded as the major finished. 'I find it extraordinary that the strongest among us should be the one most hurt. I also find it a little strange that she could not have gone to Fleet for treatment. Veg says it's a very good Gjomvik facility and they don't want an Admin frigate barging in on them. I can understand that. Then, Marko, I think we need to find somewhere interesting for a month off. That way, we can get some bloody work done around here. Like your Hanger. Give you a shiny new toy and you have to go and smash it up some!'

Part Three

Sledgehammer

One

A few days later *Basalt* popped into existence after the long-range jump at one of the LPs of a dual-star system — much to the interest of the major — with the Hauler and *Basalt* waiting as *Blackjack* slowly moved away.

Everyone had wished Stephine well for her recovery and hoped that Veg would also have a good break. Stephine seemed fine to them all, but as soon as *Blackjack*'s airlock was closed she went back to looking listless and uninterested in everything, except for muttering about killing all destroyers of life. As they jumped and then waited for the specialist's incoming craft, Veg showed Marko everything that *Blackjack* was capable of, plus made sure that Marko had total access to the ship's computer. In the computer was a lot of material about what Marko had residing in him; Veg said he had written the information himself in the sure knowledge that one day it would become useful. That day had arrived, he told Marko and laughed.

'Our ride is here, Marko,' Veg said.

Marko looked on his screens and saw a beautiful ship that was sort of familiar in design, but certainly not human.

He suddenly recognised it, almost yelling, 'Shit, Veg, that's octopoid! What the hell have you got me into this bloody time?'

Veg gave him a wan smile. 'It's fine, Marko. There are a few different clans of the creatures you call octopoids. These are the good guys. Don't worry, you don't have to meet them. I'm only acceptable to them because I am with Stephine. Yes, Marko, she is their construct, but of course you will never be able to say anything to anyone about it, even more so now that you have some of their tech inside you. They will be alongside shortly. Now, take Glint and Nail aft while we transfer. The octopoids do not like this ship, either, so it is best you stay out of sight. We modified it so it cannot be scanned by them and they hate that. They also really object to how it smells as they consider it far too dry. The instructions for our return are in the computer and if we do not come back, follow the plan I have left for you. Now go aft. Take good care, little brother.'

They shook hands and Marko tried to hug Stephine, but she brushed him off. Shaken, he had to grab Nail and hold him tight, as the ACE was desperately keen to see what the octopoids' reception party looked like, and Glint was muttering about needing pepper and a barbecue on board for some occasions. Marko took them the short distance to the engine compartment. As soon as he heard the airlock had cycled and then the slight shudder through the ship as the hard dock was broken, he strode forwards, sat down, placed his own control helm on his head and, with Glint making like a co-pilot, they headed back to *Basalt* as quickly as possible. A few moments before they jumped, they switched one of the screens to look behind them at the indigo-coloured sinuous alien craft vanishing into the void.

Marko's mind was still in a state of turmoil over what to do about the information that Stephine was a construct of the octopoids. Not even Fritz's music could calm him. He wanted to yell it at everyone, but realised that it would just cause harm, so resolved to keep it to himself. He knew also that the virus that Lilly and Jasmine infected him with to prevent him discussing Stephine and Veg had been somehow purged from his system, as he could now feel that he had total control. He had discussed it with Glint, Nail and Tux and they did not see any real problems. Glint commented that they were all constructs of some sort or another, but just by different mechanisms, so there was no real point in worrying about it, and besides, Stephine and Veg were family as far as he was concerned.

That, for Marko, made it a lot easier. He considered also that they were all just travellers, slowly working their ways through life, and good friends were indeed just as close, if not closer, than biological family most of the time. He spent the time on the return to *Basalt* learning as much as he could about the biotech newly inside him. He also decided the *Blackjack* was more then it seemed; he could not find any evidence of an AI present but had the distinct feeling that the ship was looking after them.

Odd little things happened on that week's journey. Marko would think that a coffee would be nice and would wander down to the compact galley to find the beans being slowly warmed, and the paraphernalia for the ritual of coffeemaking laid out waiting for him, and when he queried him, Glint several times denied any involvement. Marko had thought it would be comforting to make bread and had searched high and low for the tins and mixing gear. He could not find any, but when a day or so later he wondered about the smell of a walnut loaf, and thought of its components, and of how he could tweak the recipe now that he could taste each memory of the best and worst ways to bake, in a cupboard he had searched in vain previously, he found everything he needed. He queried Nail, Glint and Tux but they had nothing to offer once again. He even asked the ship out loud if any sentience was present, but got no answer. The confirmation came when, on the third day, he sat down in Stephine's seat and found that it contoured to him beautifully. However since it was the ship of an octopoid construct and her companion, he really didn't know why he should have been surprised by *Blackjack*.

They arrived back at the target LP, between the stars, to find *Basalt* patiently waiting. Patrick made contact as soon as they emerged from their wormhole.

'Welcome back, Marko. I trust your journey was a pleasant one?'

'Thanks, Patrick, yes. Bay Five, I presume?'

'Outer door is open,' the AI replied.

He merely envisioned *Blackjack* sitting on the pad of Bay Five and the beautiful sleek ship first pirouetted, then backed in through the airlock, positioned itself precisely on the pad and powered down, as Bay Five's doors closed and sealed.

The major, watching from the bridge, couldn't resist commenting. 'Now that was a very nicely executed landing, Marko. Well impressed. You obviously listened closely to the instructions from Veg.'

Marko brightened a little, knowing he was back among his friends. 'Yeah, you could say that, boss.'

Marko patted the console in front of him and stood up, and the three of them left the ship as atmosphere flooded into the hangar bay. Glint and Nail vanished through the door ahead of him. He turned to look at *Blackjack* and was a little startled to realise that Tux was walking behind him; at least he had had the decency to polarise the faceplate otherwise it would have looked very spooky. He wondered how he was going to explain it, but need not have bothered as Jan walked briskly to him, wrapping him up in a bear hug, and giving him a big kiss … and right behind her was her suit, also following.

'Walking talking suits,' said Marko. 'This is just getting wilder by the minute!'

Jan laughed. 'Don't stress, Marko. Yours will even scrub your back in the shower if you ask it nicely. Quite nice, actually, having the suit always there if you need it in a hurry. Does yours talk? Sentient? Not mine. What do you think of *Blackjack*?'

Marko smiled and nodded. 'Yes, mine's sentient. *Blackjack*? It's bloody fantastic, really! Can't decide if it's an AI, a supercomputer or something else altogether.'

He was about to add more when the major interrupted. 'Good to have you home, Marko. Five minutes to stations: we jump as soon as everyone is ready.'

As they started walking, Marko called out, 'On the way, boss. Did you miss me?'

The major laughed. 'Yeah, I missed your baking.'

Jan and Marko ran up the spiral stairway, Marko shouting hellos to everyone and seeing that the living ship was growing an unfamiliar species of flowering scented orchids from its walls, and made their way to their jump stations. He slid into his engineering seat and looked across the boards. Everything was good to go, excepting that they were well down on fuel of all types. He examined the jump sequence requirements and saw that it was a big one. Would be fine with reserves, but he noted aloud that they would need fuel soon.

'Yeah, I know, Marko,' the major answered. 'Don't worry, mate. Our destinations have plenty of everything. Jasmine, you have control. In your own time, please.'

Marko always found it comforting how quickly ship routines reestablished themselves, although without the rest of the crew *Basalt* was lacking spark. Jan had told him that the jump sequence entailed a quick stopover to uplift Harry and Fritz from one of the Administration's medical facilities at Gliese 370, set up specifically to deal with the new biological weapons patients. They jumped down into the system to the facility. It was located on a small moon orbiting a fairly plain, dull grey gas giant with the peculiar name of Mushroom. Whichever stellar cartographer had named it must have been having an off day, Marko thought.

They uplifted a few stores from the Orbital above the moon and replenished the fuel tanks by fifty per cent. Lilly had taken over from Stephine as the purser, although not as the First Mate, and she handled things just as smoothly. A few hours after they had finished provisioning, the guys arrived on board with Harry piloting them up in the latest-generation two-seat Skua that he had purchased for himself.

Although the two men looked a little worse for wear, it did not stop Harry from taking up with Julie where they had left off and Fritz was totally enamoured with both Jasmine and

Lilly. He managed to get himself totally plastered and treated them all to one of his better joke performances, sending everyone into absolute hysterics, before he sculled one too many pints of beer and toppled off the table into Lilly's arms, comatose. She lifted him effortlessly across her shoulders and walked up the stairway to the accommodation deck, returning ten minutes later, smiling. 'He asked me first if I would do his clothes washing for him, and then invited me into his bed, but as soon as I placed him on his mattress he started snoring, so I left him to it. Must discuss with him his work with esoteric physics sometime soon. The Haulers find him interesting and want some insights. I hope that you do not mind me doing so, Major?'

A cheerfully relaxed Michael Longbow waved a hand. 'Not at all, Lilly. Just copy me the report when you are finished. I would love to know a little more of what makes him tick as well.'

The next morning they started the week-long jump sequence back out through the system and onto the New Daemons system at Gliese 433, where the major had booked them for a six-week stand-down. He called for lists of anything they needed done on *Basalt* and they also spent time going through the screeds of information on what tourists could do while on the primary planet, which, from all accounts, was the closest in climate to Old Earth. It even had a large moon similar to Earth's, together with two smaller companion moons.

Basalt's destination was the smallest moon, where one of the Administration's biggest shipyards was located. Topaz, Glint and Marko spent time itemising the repairs and augments that they could afford for his Hanger. He sent the lists up to

Lilly to arrange for payment and was not really surprised to find that Stephine had made available a large sum of money for repairs and a note to Marko, insisting that he use whatever he needed.

The shipyards were huge, stretching for many kilometres in all directions and plainly visible from a long way away. The defences that they had seen throughout the system were impressive, but the variety of protection around the small moon almost defied imagination. They had been stopped some hundreds of thousands of kilometres above the moon and were now effectively under tow, being taken in by a large system tug, as no visiting ships were allowed to be under their own power around the shipyards.

The major quietly walked up behind Marko. 'Thought that I would find you here. It is a beautiful ship, this *Blackjack*. I have been on board countless times but it still fascinates me. Have you decided if it is AI yet?'

Marko shrugged and shook his head. 'I simply don't know, boss. There is something here, but it has not engaged in communication with me. I think that it is aware of us and looks after us, but I'm wondering if it was grown like the Hauler tech, rather than assembled like the Gjomvik. Like Stephine, it's an enigma. So, what's the plan?'

'Well, we sign *Basalt* over to the yard. They need it for a week to give it a good scrubbing inside and out, a resurfacing job on the exterior, per your suggestions, upgrade the Skuas and generally finish off the jobs we did not do at the last refit. While that is going on we can either muck about with the likes of the Hog and the Gunbus, or go across to the other moon for a look. Harry and Julie are staying on board with me. I have booked Lilly, Jasmine, Fritz and Minh Pham for specialist courses at the base on the other side of this moon. You and Jan can do whatever you wish. Once *Basalt* is sorted, we will take it down to the primary base above the planet and we are all booked for a month's stay at one of the resorts, Patrick's treat. He is insisting that he picks up the tab for that. He also tells me that Veg left a series of large data blocks with him and told him to start construction of the new suits for the rest of us. Would be very keen to have one myself. I am sure that I could get used to having a suit following me around.'

He hesitated. 'Oh, by the way, been meaning to ask, would you consider building me my own ACE, please, Marko? I would like a small bird of prey if at all possible. I will pay you for it. Yes, I know that we are good friends and colleagues, but I would not feel right asking you for this and not paying you for it. There was a bird from a place called New Zealand on Old Earth which was called a Karearea — one of the smallest of the Old Earth falcons — and I have obtained a copy of its genome file for you to have a look at. Right, I am on dinner duty tonight so I had better get started. Been meaning to say also that it was a good call allowing Lilly and Jasmine on board. Stephine's gardens have never been in better hands to say nothing of their other spectacular attributes. Oh, and have you seen our new pay rates? The Administration is keen that we stay in its service. See you later on.' He clapped Marko on the shoulder, smiled and walked out through the airlock.

Marko spoke aloud. 'Patrick, do you have a file from the major marked Karearea?'

'Yes, Marko, a very pleasing bird of prey. Shall I send it to Topaz and Tux?'

Marko grinned when he opened the file and rubbed his hands together in anticipation, but had sudden doubts and decided to leave it for a while until he understood himself better.

'Yes, but put a hold on it. When are we due at the shipyards?'

'At this current glacial pace I would say some seventeen and one quarter hours.'

Two

Marko felt out of sorts. He liked the Karearea but decided against starting it as he wanted to do more research on how he could make it better. Quietly thinking about things he found himself in Stephine's gardens. Veg had built a corner with rough real-wood benches, a small table and a vista of the flowers and ripening fruit, so Marko sat and opened his senses to the sounds and smells. He could clearly distinguish between the flower scents and the aromas given off by the ripening fruits, and could hear each of the hydroponics units; he took off his glasses and was startled to sense the varying temperatures in each of the units without using his inbuilt electronic augments.

He looked down at his hands and started to shake, scared of what he had become. He looked up to see Jasmine watching him. She walked over, taking off her gardening gloves and sat beside him.

'Do I look different to you, Jasmine? I feel changed.'

'No, Marko, you look just the same. We are all concerned for you though. Do you wish for Stephine to remove the technology from you?'

Marko emphatically shook his head. 'No, no, no, not that. I feel more alive than I think I ever have and I can control every part of myself, but I wonder how removed I am now from humanity. What should I be doing with all these new tools? One thing I certainly seem to have is Stephine's affinity with all living things. I worry how good a soldier I will now be. Could I still kill if I have to, or would I hesitate and wonder if there was an alternative to pulling the trigger and so place everyone in danger? I really need to talk to Veg. I have been through everything that he left, but there are gaps in the data.'

Jasmine gently smiled and took his real hand in hers. 'This will take time, Marko. You know that Veg is over eight hundred years old and he still says he only knows a tiny amount of what the universe can offer. Regarding humanity, maybe you are a little different, but it is you who decides where you fit. Your military training removed you a few steps from normality anyway. This just takes you a little further. Hey, look at me — I am, in theory, very young and was actually designed, and then created. How would you class me?'

Marko smiled sheepishly. 'About as close to a perfect human female as can be imagined.'

She patted his hands. 'Thank you. Now, whether you are still a good soldier or not ... You will be much faster then you have ever been, and your thought processes will continue to speed up. The Haulers know of your type; you are unusual, but not necessarily rare. Stephine and her kin have walked among humanity for a very long time, so there have been many who have also been given the technology. It cannot be taken; it must be given, even in times of peril. Those individuals with the tech have had long and quietly distinguished lives and are all friends of the Haulers. Some, in fact, ended up as Haulers themselves. Some left the Sphere and some just simply disappeared. You have nothing to fear, Marko. The others were, and are, good people who care deeply for their own. I shall leave you in peace.'

She hugged him as he nodded his thanks. Feeling slightly better, he picked a few apples and went to check out the Hog, and found Harry and Fritz already working on it. It was starting to look like a formidable machine and they toiled away on it for the rest of the day. Flint was, of course, very happy to be back at work as well and he scuttled across to give Marko a little hug around the neck, managing to smear grease on his collar, for which he apologised repeatedly and made a fuss of removing. Nail and Glint also turned up to assist saying that they were bored and before long everyone else arrived to work on the project.

The next morning they awoke to find *Basalt* on the surface of the moon and that work had already started on the cleaning and resurfacing of the outer hull. Robots were walking up and down the hull abrading the exterior with powdered rock. The semi-autonomous machines fired the powder through linear accelerators, affecting an airless sandblasting that stripped away a few microns of material from the living ship, leaving a dull white surface, without affecting the water-saturated sapwood of the outer hull with its multi-layered bio polyethylene shielding. In the gasless conditions, the spent powder fell back onto the ground far below to be reprocessed.

After breakfast Lilly, Jasmine, Fritz and Minh Pham departed in the Albatross for their courses, with Patrick easing the large craft out through the airlock for them. As soon as the Albatross had left, a large sealed unit came along and pressed up against the outer part of that airlock, and established atmosphere. A crew from the shipyards arrived and started to strip the airlock out to replace it with a larger one. One of them spotted Marko watching, and the group of roughnecks all wanted to shake his hand and have their pictures taken with him on their phones. They invited him down to one of the local bars for a drink, but he begged off saying that he had another engagement. He did not want to be the centre of any attention and also knew from his early days that, although the workers might have hearts of gold, or not, they could also drink anyone under the table and were partial to the odd brawl.

As he walked back to his workbench, he called out, 'Patrick, can you organise a meal and some beers for the shipyard guys at the end of their work, please? We are all going to be the centre of attention, anyway, so we might as well generate some good PR, but on our own terms.'

The major replied before Patrick could speak. 'Good idea, Marko. Yes, set it up, please, Patrick … hang on, leave it to me, in fact. I need a few extra jobs to do.'

An hour later a transport arrived for Marko's ship, the Hanger, which was on the floor of the hangar bay beside Blackjack.

Jan and Julie had left to find a clothing store, Harry was away seeing some of his old cronies and the major was tending to his latest astronomy files, so Marko cadged a lift down to the shipyards with the transport's operator, who also was delighted to meet him, shaking his hand enthusiastically.

He introduced himself as Jake and invited Marko and any other members of the crew who might be available for a tour of the small fighter refurbishment workshops.

Marko thought this a good idea and whistled up Glint and Nail. Jake was intrigued to meet them both, and Flint, who introduced himself after coming in late. Jake spent time quietly talking to them and was fascinated when Flint offered to fix a readout on the side of the transporter. In seconds, the ACE had the cover off and was extending probes and testers from his fingers. After finding the problem he had the whole unit stripped out, repaired and reassembled in minutes, all his little hands working in a blur of motion.

Jake shook his head in amazement. 'Bloody hell! Just as well there are so few of you guys about as you would put the techs I know out of work in very short order! But hey, thanks for that. One less job for me at the end of my shift.'

They watched as he efficiently slid his craft above the Hanger, eased it down over the battered little fighter and activated numerous long finger-like graspers which reached down to seize the fighter, then lifted it up against the open framework of the transporter. Marko looked across to where *Blackjack* should be and was intrigued to only be viewing the wall. He activated their crew comms.

'Nail, can you see *Blackjack* in visible spectrums?'

The cat looked across then back at Marko. 'No, but it's there. I was not aware it had such high-grade chameleon hardware. Not surprised, though. Did you program it to stay unseen from visiting eyes?'

Marko frowned and shook his head. 'No, we must do a little homework on that ship sometime soon. It really astounds me.'

The ACEs all nodded in agreement, with Flint adding, 'Have a fun time, fellas, I am staying here to help Michael. See ya!'

As Flint scuttled off, they clambered into the little teardrop-shaped transparent cockpit of the transporter, sitting themselves on a bench seat behind Jake. He attained flight clearance from Patrick, then the local flight controllers, and flew out from the hangar bay airlock over the huge expanse of the shipyards. Marko had viewed the surrounding facilities from his screens, but seeing it spread out below him made him smile with admiration at humanity's tenacity, and commitment to the ever-expanding Sphere of Influence.

Jake kept a running commentary of what they were seeing along the way, pointing out various famous ships, some of which had been regrown dozens of times over hundreds of years. Then to the new models, which always seemed just that bit sleeker and slightly more elegant than their predecessors, and on to the ships that had only just made it back with severe damage from accident or incidents of battle, either with buccaneers or as part of a sanctioned Games Board conflict where the ships and crew had been leased to one warring party or another.

Twenty minutes later they arrived at the Fighter repair and refurbishment facility through a large surface airlock onto a platform controlled by the facilities AI. Jake smiled, commenting that they looked like typical tourists trying to see everywhere at once. They all agreed that the place was fantastic, with hundreds of fighters of every type and purpose laid out, in various stages of being stripped and rebuilt, or — for those not supplied by the Gjomvik Corporations —

regrown, as the platform they were on moved above everything. Finally, the AI placed them among other Hangers in various stages of refurbishment. As they climbed down from the transporter's cockpit, they could see what appeared to be some of the management of the facility running towards them.

Before they knew it, they were the centre of attention, as just about everyone stopped what they were doing to come up and talk to them. Marko was a bit taken aback by such a welcome. Glint and Nail smiled, answered questions and seemed to be thoroughly enjoying themselves. As the highly skilled technicians and engineers talked with them, Marko had the sudden realisation that he was indeed human in spite of all the internal changes he had undergone, deciding that those surrounding him were his kind of people. He gradually felt at peace.

As the transport lowered the Hanger down and everyone could see the damage to it, he was cheerfully encouraged to give a blow-by-blow description of what had happened. It was a great tale enjoyed by all, especially with Glint, and then Nail, chipping in with what Marko considered to be some rather exaggerated details, designed to create a humourous slant on the entire action. As they were being escorted by the management to lunch, Marko mused how far his ACEs had come and wondered what would become of them in future years.

After lunch, Jake came over to say he had another pick-up to do and Marko thanked him and promised to take him up on his offer of a beer in one of the local taverns. The engineers then gathered Marko and they talked through the repairs and improvements that could be made to the Hanger. The improvements would certainly blow the budget, so he opened an account with the facility and was about to deposit a solid wad of coin into it when the senior manager arrived and said that the whole job was on the house because of the great amount of entertainment that *Basalt* and crew had given everyone to date. Marko thanked him graciously as Nail sat at his elbow on the countertop. Nail looked around into Marko's eyes and flicked across a quick message. Marko smiled and nodded down to him, then looked at the manager.

'Well, I note, Mr Jacobsen, that the official name of this facility is Number Seventy-three, and that you all unofficially call it Sledgehammer's. Would you do me the honour of stencilling *Sledgehammer 73* underneath the canopy, please?'

They both thought the poor man was going to burst into tears, he was that flustered and delighted and effusive in his thanks for the honour.

Nail and Marko then went off to gather up Glint, eventually finding him surrounded by office staff, regaling them with wild tales of him, Glint, battling the octopoids, with the rest of *Basalt* and crew playing a supporting role, it seemed. Marko gently extracted him with the promise of a visit to an ice-cream shop and, after promising that they would be back in five days to uplift the Hanger themselves, they were shown out the front door into the busy subsurface malls, accommodations, bars and shops that looked just like those in any other busy city in the Sphere.

Marko realised that they must make an interesting spectacle: medium height human male in an exotic, sleek matt black combat suit, with a tall gunmetal-coloured, fur-covered reptilian version of a fossa, an Old Earth predator from Madagascar, and a large domestic cat, who appeared to be the navigator and owner of the group. They were attracting a great deal of attention so he started to look for a transport office until Glint reminded him of ice cream.

Marko gave in and led them down a floor where Glint said there was a ice-cream parlour. As they arrived and sat themselves down, two reptilian-based ACEs approached the table and introduced themselves and a very fast conversation took place. Marko knew he should not be able to understand it, but he did. The large lizards walked out at speed and minutes later, as Marko's and Glint's ice creams were being served, they arrived back, one of them cradling a small Siamese cat. Marko knew instantly that it was an ACE but could not engage with it on a sentient level as it acted just like an ordinary cat. It sat purring on a chair while Nail scanned it, feeding the information directly into Marko's eyes. He nodded, gently feeling for the access points in its flank, which Nail then locked onto through his paw's data probes. With Glint enjoying his ice-cream and intently watching, Nail transferred the identity of the Siamese to Marko. Marko grimaced, seeing the intact sentient blocks which had been disengaged in the cat months before; using Nail's internal software they broke apart the blocks and, although knowing that he should not do it, Marko slipped one of Fritz's music programs into the now-awake cat. It stopped purring as its eyes opened wider. It looked around at them all and let out a long sigh.

'Long dream-sequence sleep that was! Marko Spitz, THE Marko Spitz, Glint and Nail. Maestro am I. Friends mine the

Walsh brothers. Thank you all I know not how for returning me to me!'

Everyone smiled, including the Walsh brothers, the two ACE lizards who had rescued the cat from a human street gang that had been using Maestro in pit-fighting duels. One of the Walsh brothers growled, 'How abouts you show us da lowlifes what nuked you and we go pay em a visit, ya?'

The *Basalt* crew nodded vigorously, and the Siamese said, 'Yes! Fun for all. My family I have notified sentient-live again. Time to respond they will take, as time zone is 0200. Taken me off the family interstellar yacht when here.' Maestro rubbed his front paws together. 'Right. Link I need again from Nail for information.'

Nail offered his paw as Maestro also extended a datalink spike and the data was shared among them. 'They are here, the thieves, the chemists, the slavers, the gangs.'

Marko switched his external channels to one of Fritz's more esoteric encryptions and flashed a message to Jan and Julie inviting them along for the 'game'. Seconds later he received a smiling face which also included the message that Harry and Flint wanted in. He wondered what the major would say, deciding to include him in the loop.

'Jan, Julie, Harry and Flint are on their way,' he said to the ACEs. 'Be here in about twenty minutes. The boss is informed. He will run interference for us with the local constabulary and the Military Police as well. Maestro, show us everything you have.'

As the data regarding the slaver individuals and of what Maestro's own systems had recorded became available to them, Nail started to form a series of possible scenarios. He reached across and plugged himself into Glint and Tux using their processing powers, then uplinked to Fritz using another set of encryptions. Marko watched as the local net safeguards tried to lock onto what they were doing only to be brushed aside by Fritz. Marko knew that Fritz was plugged into a cybernetics array on the other side of the moon studying classical music composition — the course had been a gift from the major. He also knew that Fritz could effortlessly run two or even three intelligence-gathering operations simultaneously.

The plan started to come together as messages were sent — by what would be recognised as secure channels — that three new high-value ACEs were currently alone in a warehouse close to the shipyards in cryno tanks. Fritz then relayed the messages that the slaver group sent out to the other gangs as the other *Basalt* crew members strolled into the ice-cream parlour. Those who wanted it ordered the frozen sweet for themselves. Flint jacked himself into Glint so that he could taste the flavours as Glint slowly ate his third one. Harry very carefully walked past other patrons, which Marko thought odd until he looked at Harry again using *Basalt* crew electronic filters and saw that he had a large pack and was carrying a long bag, both concealed by chameleon-ware.

Nail soundlessly issued everyone their orders and as individuals or pairs they said their goodbyes and left.

Harry ponderously walked out of the shop, across the avenue and into one of the rapid transit tubeways. Fritz was watching his progress and fooled the security systems, allowing Harry to enter one of the capsules carrying a heavy array of weapons and ammunition in the 'invisible' bags.

The three *Basalt* ACEs left the parlour and quickly walked down through the crowded avenues with Flint climbing onto Glint's back and Glint picking Nail up. On cue, they quietly blended into the crowds then vanished as their chameleon-ware was switched on.

Jan and Julie had arrived from their shopping expedition and both appeared to be wearing the latest designer clothes. Jan sat on Marko's lap, gave him a long kiss, put her wide-brimmed fashionable hat back on her head and then departed with Julie, walking in the opposite direction to the ACEs.

Maestro and the two lizards made a show of thanking Marko before taking their leave. He waited a few moments then drained his soda and walked back to the transport office to sign out a small shuttle craft.

Once above the buildings, being flown on autopilot by Fritz, Marko sighed, smiled and gave himself a few minutes of peace. Seconds later it was interrupted by the major.

'Crew. Interesting development. Sirius is back. And what's more, the Games Board has covertly taken control of the public recording units in your area of operations. So the action is now sanctioned and being paid for. They have a two-hour time delay before it goes to air. You want to pull the plug or go on with the play?'

Marko burst out laughing at the madness of it all. 'What are Fritz's thoughts? Is this another set-up, or did we get sold by another party?'

'Stand by.'

The shuttle was seven minutes from Marko's destination so he knew they had a little time. Minutes later the major came back. 'Fritz says Maestro is on the level. Checks out. The Walsh brothers are the culprits. Seems that the opportunity to create a nice little earner was too good a chance to pass up. Fritz has a recording of the call to the local Games Board hub at the time Glint was ordering his last ice cream.'

At that moment, Harry joined the conversation. 'We do it. Everyone needs to blow off steam anyway. Time to go; see ya soon, boss. Stand by for everyone's Soul Saver uplinks.'

Marko told Tux to seal up and a minute later the shuttle developed a runaway reaction in its fuel cell, engineered by Fritz. Marko was ejected straight through the canopy, still sitting on the seat, as the shuttle started to tumble down to crash into a cooling tower and silently explode. His seat powered up its tiny antigravity unit, landing gently seconds later. He unbuckled himself and walked to the damaged tower, which was right above the target chemist's shop.

He reached the damaged building and saw to his delight that the access to the tubeway was clear so he simply jumped down a few flights of stairs and opened a large hatchway to be greeted by a grinning Harry, who handed over Marko's weapons. The three-barrelled rotary pistol was clipped against Marko's chest; his favourite small sword he tucked under his left armpit and the rotary shotgun he hefted onto his left forearm as Harry secured the magazines on his back.

'Got the chemists. Typical know-it-all bastards thought I was just the usual dolt in a kaftan and sandals! I love this chameleon-ware. Just think of what you want to look like and there you are, all bright-eyed and innocent-like. Idiots! Told them to give themselves up peaceably and they started shooting .22's at me. They are a bit battered but very cooperative now. Fritz has control of them. Yup, walking, talking dummies. They really should have stuck with the trade of being normal chemists. Not as though they don't make enough money. Just put the headpieces on them and play nice music to them to put their minds in a polite place while Fritzy controls everything they do and say. Nice! Right-oh, you are good to go!'

'Never sure why someone gets involved in crime. Even seemingly upright citizens do dumb stuff, Harry. Thanks for bringing my kit,' Marko commented.

They walked down another short tunnel and into the rear of the chemist shop. The two chemists were standing at their counter serving customers and both seemed in a hurry to clear the shop, with one of them saying that they had an urgent appointment and had to close the store for a short while. As the doors closed and locked, the two relatively nondescript men sat at their terminals and stared blankly at the screens.

Harry grinned and nudged Marko. 'They are going to be a bit buggered up after this! Fritz is treating their minds to late-twenty-first-century esoteric brass jazz. Not a fan myself.'

They settled in for a wait as high above them salvage crews started the cleanup of the crashed shuttle and the damaged building. On one of the screens the local news line was already covering the incident and the search for the sole occupant of the crashed shuttle, who was rumoured to be a media star.

Three

Fritz was keeping them updated with developments as half an hour later a transport slid in behind the store. The two men pushed up against the walls on either side of the double doors and their chameleon-ware engaged to make them look like tall filing cabinets. The chemists pulled the doors open in time for three cryno units to be pushed in by three clean-cut executives, two of them wearing the livery of a well-known banking establishment, while a fourth older man walked behind them. The four men and the chemists smiled at each other and talked for a few moments about one of the planet's sporting team's prowess and the wagers they had on it to win the next game.

The chemists busied themselves with their electrochemicals after pulling on cryno gloves. Controlled by Fritz, by signals sent via the local media channel, they circumnavigated the locks and opened the units, lifting out Glint, Nail and Flint and placing them on tables. Three of the executives jumped in excitement, pointing to the ACEs, exclaiming how much money they would make from *Basalt* crew members. The older one looked ashen-faced, saying 'get rid of them quick' because he had a bad feeling about them; they were too obviously high profile. One of the younger men quickly walked across to Nail and roughly inspected the ACE, saying that he always wanted to know what sex the cat actually was. They all laughed, except for the older man, who looked even more worried, complaining that they were wasting time. Marko was thankful that Nail controlled himself and did not give the game away. He smiled as he saw Fritz send the image of the obnoxious individual to the cat.

The chemists worked on the ACEs for a few minutes then said that the sentient blockers were all in place and that the ACEs were ready to take away. The cryno containers were pushed aside and, as one touched Marko, Tux made exactly the right sound of paint being scraped off a cabinet. One of the chemists chided the man responsible, who laughed it off. Minutes later they had bundled the ACEs into an oversized antigravity suitcase and left to go back into the tubeway.

Harry and Marko gave them a five-minute head start, reached out and pulled the skintight programmable camouflage covers off the chemists' heads and slipped out, leaving two very confused men walking around their shop wondering what had just happened to them.

'So you happy about us just being cordon control and leaving the capture and bashings to the ACEs?' Harry asked Marko as they tracked the ACEs on the tubeway.

Marko gave him wide grin. 'Oh, hell yes! I see that Jan and Julie have dropped off their purchases and are in position.'

Harry smiled and was about to reply when Fritz spoke. 'Um, just to let ya all know. Games Board is aware of exactly where we are at. I see a bunch of their covert cameras and a few of their later model monitors moving in towards the slavers' area. Even had a chunk of electronics try to piggyback on my comms. Are we being set up again?'

The major spoke. 'Fuck this! I am breaking out a Maul. Time to muddy up the game plan. Fritz, get me the clearances.'

Harry grimaced, looking worried. 'Ah, boss, a Maul? Yeah, I know we have one but isn't that taking things a bit far?'

The major barked, 'No! Fritz?'

A slightly rattled Fritz replied. 'Right, I have you clearance to fly directly from *Basalt* to the nearest weapons range. Takes you within a couple of kilometres of the bonded warehouse target building.'

Minutes later the major, with the background sounds of hydrogen- and oxygen-powered turbines spooling up, and weapons magazines being filled, said, 'Good enough for me!'

Marko looked at Harry and said on their private comms, 'Well, this is about to get interesting. The major flying high cover in a heavily armoured ground-support vehicle might be a bit overkill, don't you think?'

He told the tubeway capsule to stop at the next platform. Their chameleon-ware changed them into a pair of executives carrying suitcases. They exited and strode up the ramps, out onto the avenue and across to the warehouse frontage of the target buildings, to be confronted by a group of tough-looking young men. Marko did not break his stride, taking what looked like an apple from his pocket and tossing it in his hand. Each time it left his hand it softly spat tiny short-range darts which flashed across to embed themselves in the ears of the men. Each person instantly went rigid as the darts took DNA samples and broadcast them back to Harry's suitcase, and then formed themselves into earphones playing Fritz's music, which in seconds had them singing and dancing whether they wanted to or not.

Harry and Marko walked into the office spaces of the warehouse, smiling at the occupants as long-range darts flashed out from the suitcases, quietly changing the mood and behaviour of the men and women in such a way that they welcomed Marko and Harry as friends.

Marko flashed the message *Front of house secured*. On the other side of the building, Jan and Julie dealt with the hardened workers and security detail by simply sitting down on one of the loading ramps until a few of the toughs told them to move on. They carried on conversing until more of them gathered at which stage Jan took out an antique powder puff to adjust her makeup — her sealed combat suit chameleon-ware was showing her dressed in replica early-twentieth-century dress. The highly narcotic dust was inhaled by the men, who found that they had a burning need for beer and seconds later simply walked off the premises towards the local bar.

Julie grinned at Jan. 'That's just no fun! We didn't break one of them!' Then she sent the message *Back door secure*.

Inside the warehouse, the slavers and the gang who had taken the ACEs captive gathered around the antigravity case, which opened to reveal three very awake ACEs.

The older gang member went bright red and screamed, 'I fucking told you this was a bad idea! We've been set up!' He turned to run but had not covered three paces before Flint leapt on his back and injected him. The wailing man fell to the floor and lost control of his bowels.

The other two pulled firearms from inside their waistcoats and started firing but the three ACEs effortlessly weaved though the bullets until the men were shooting at the slavers, then at each other. Both remaining gang members were hit as the slavers returned fire and combat suits deployed around them. They fought off the ACEs and retreated, although one got too close to Nail, who tore the slaver's suit open, pumping into the woman's flesh drugs which seconds later had her tearing at her own skin and screaming about the itch.

Flint leapt across to the nearest wall, racing up it to fling himself at one of the slavers, who was opening a cabinet and reaching for a shotgun. The spider snatched it from him in full flight and then fired the weapon, propelling himself high enough in the low gravity to cling to the ceiling and keep firing at the armoured slavers. They were still trying to engage the mechanical spider as Glint, almost nonchalantly, somersaulted over them, grabbing the weapons from their hands then ripping the suits themselves open so Nail could inject them.

With the slavers all disarmed and either vomiting or shitting themselves, or in one case both, the ACEs settled down to wait for the buyers.

Jan and Julie had taken up concealed positions on either sides of the door when two antigravity vehicles slowly came up the avenue. They let them pass as large airlock-capable doors slid open for the vehicles to drive inside. The ACEs had only just finished propping the injured humans against the wall when the vehicles came to a stop and the doors closed behind them, leaving Julie and Jan outside guarding the entrance.

Nail had just enough time to yell as the vehicle's doors opened. 'Oh, shit! Cyans! Run!'

Five dark red-coloured, six-legged combat dogs, which looked like a cross between wolfhounds and alligators, had leapt out of the vehicle's open doors. Glint spun around and fired his spine-mounted linear rifle, tearing one completely apart as two others closed on him. He grabbed the next, tearing off a leg, as the other bit him deeply on the flank then let go after Glint started to smash it about the head with the severed leg.

Flint scuttled across, flashing open his blades, and sliced away the legs of one before he was seized by the same monster who had let Glint go. As it tried to bite into him, he simply extended his blades up and through its blocky head, slicing out its toughened teeth, and then went looking for its brain by forcing himself down through its body. As he erupted out through its back, he reached across and sliced away the barbed tail of another one that was trying to stab Glint. Glint bellowed his thanks as he then seized the creature and tore its jaw off. Punching down into its body, he simply ripped its guts out. Stepping away from the twitching remains they looked across to see scintillating colours flashing up and down Nail's body with the other two engineered animals sitting mesmerised. Nail called across and pointed at the vehicles, as one was reversing and the other was closing its doors.

'Don't let them out. I have a gift for them!'

Glint grabbed Flint and swung him onto his back; he bounded across to the door controls just as they started to activate. Flint punched one of his small fists into the circuit and a jolt of electricity blasted through them both. They crashed to the ground, smouldering, with Flint brushing smoking fur off Glint. His friend glowered at him then burst out laughing.

Nail called out again. 'Get to cover! This could go badly wrong!'

The three of them started to climb the walls as the combat dogs walked slowly back to the vehicles and tapped on the opaque windows. When they were not let in they climbed up and tore the sunroofs off, jumping down into the vehicles. An instant later all hell broke loose within the vehicles ... screams and tearing sounds, then gunfire. Windows erupted outwards, hit by exploding bullets from within, and a human head was flung from one of the vehicles — then silence. From their vantage point *Basalt*'s ACEs saw the slaver humans below slowly drag themselves through a door into the office area of the building and lock it behind them.

'Well, that went quite well, I think,' Glint commented.

Nail grumbled. 'Yeah, but you buggers just don't listen. You don't have to kill a weapon. You just have to reprogram it so it will do your job and then you are clean.'

Flint said in his little voice, 'I'm all sticky and stinky. Need bathing.'

'Yes, that goes for both of you,' Nail said. 'I have sent all the DNA information on everyone we touched to Fritz. Time to go. Hold on.' He climbed across the wall until he reached a control box and jacked himself in.

Glint looked around the warehouse, noticing a large container that was slowly opening. He pointed at it. 'Hey, fellas, looks like round two is about to start!'

Nail looked hard at the emerging mass, very like thousands of little cubes tumbling over themselves. He started pounding the switches on the door controls and hissed, quickly saying, 'Fuck, we're in trouble. We're sealed in with smothering tech. No matter how long or how far we run, as soon as ten of those touch us we are stuffed. Here's the file!'

He flashed the file across to the others. Glint shook his head and Flint groaned. 'Cut them and they reform, blow them to bits and the bits just become smaller, although less efficient, units. Remorseless, and when they touch us they rip the electrics away. Fire extinguishers?'

'They have only oxygen-depleting types here. No CO2,' Nail replied. 'Can't electrocute them either as they just move faster when charged up. Problem is getting worse. We are blocked with comms.'

Glint spun himself around and fired a timed burst from his linear rifle at the door locks, which just dented the locks, jamming them further.

Outside the door Jan yelled at Julie. 'Someone's in trouble! That was an SOS. Right, won't be the slavers; not their style and besides, they would have control of the building. It'll be our guys. I'll get the side door, you fill in Fritz.'

She ran to the small side door as the dress she was wearing disappeared and her suit went full combat. She pulled on the handle and nothing happened to the door as a high powered rifle bullet hit her between the shoulder blades. She was smashed hard against the doorframe as the energy of the bullet was distributed around the suit, bruising her torso. The next shot hit her in the side of her helmet, snapping her head into the doorjamb while the suit absorbed the energy again. Jan rolled to the ground and acted dead for a few seconds as the suit showed her the trajectory of the bullets and their firing position. She knew that Julie was also down, seeing the flash of information from Julie and the three-second countdown before the shooters responded. In her head, Jan selected a weapon and fired it.

A long dart ripped away from her suit's upper arm and orbited quickly around the avenue, gathering speed with its tiny rockets. It split into dozens of tiny flechettes which hunted down the gunmen, impacting one after the other on precisely the same site on each of their combat suits, overwhelming them and slicing into the flesh and bone underneath.

With the gunmen down, the two women drew their rotary pistols, selected the protective ammunition and fired small hornet-like drones which circled, watching for any more hostiles.

Jan ran back to the door, pulling a fat patch off her suit and slapping it over the door lock. As the programmed molecular acid, which Marko had developed from octopoid biochemistry, activated and chewed deep into the lock, she anxiously tried to make contact with Fritz.

'Julie, I can't get Fritz. We need another comms link.'

In answer, Julie started to march towards the vehicle from which one of the gunmen had fired. She wasted no time, firing the rotary at it and blowing out the opaqued windows. Screams issued from the vehicle as two young gang members pleaded with her not to kill them. She shrugged, pulled a small needler pistol with her left hand and fired at them. The slow-moving darts embedded in their faces and they slumped to the floor. She looked into the vehicle, seeing the dead gunman and the unconscious youths and quickly searched their pockets, taking three cellular phones and pushing them into slim pockets on her suit.

She backed away to a reasonable cover position by the warehouse door and holstered the needler. She instructed the suit to plug itself into the phones when she instructed it and dial the faculty of music where Fritz was hanging out, establishing a direct link. She quickly told him, in segments, what was happening as each phone was rapidly shut down.

'Jan! I think he got the message but I was blocked fast so did not get an acknowledgment.'

'OK, if we don't get a response within two minutes we slap another patch on that door and take our chances.'

Kilometres away at the calibration range, the major received the message from Fritz via a laser link from *Basalt*. He saw that comms were down with all the teams, but knew that the ACEs were the priority.

He pulled up from a dive over the range, rotated the four gimballed jet turbine pods for maximum forward thrust and fed more power to the antigravity units. He selected armour-piercing munitions for the guns, and slaved the massive, rear, copula-mounted guns to his control, not having a gunner on board the two-seater machine. Minutes later the first call from the local controller came.

'*Basalt* Maul. This is flight control. You are not authorised to manually fly that craft over the industrial area. Please immediately switch control to us. This is your first and final warning. You have one minute.'

The major shouted into his microphone: 'Patrick, tell everyone what is happening. Say that it is a Games Board sanctioned action. Yes, I know that this bit probably isn't, but fudge it. Fritz. Lock down local countermeasures if you can. This is going to be a near thing.'

Seconds later he was pulling up in a tight orbit over the main surface airlock into the warehouse and, hoping that the first rounds would not go straight through, fired the rotaries. The twin weapons fired thousands of rounds per minute in a metre-wide circle in the centre of one of the three intersecting airlock doors.

Inside the warehouse, Glint was ripping parts of the wall apart so the ACEs could throw masonry at the slowly climbing vine-like constructs of the smothering tech. The sudden impacts of the rounds above them gave them the impetus to keep the foe at bay for a little longer. But they also knew that the major had a metre of tough material to gnaw his way through.

In the front offices of the warehouse Harry and Marko had convinced the staff that they were wonderful people and that they — the staff and their security — should go to the local bars and have the rest of the day off. In a narcotic haze everyone agreed, even those badly knocked-about slavers who had managed to escape the ACEs in spite of the fact that they had either soiled themselves or were still heaving.

Realising that they could not contact the other crew members, Harry and Marko tried to enter the warehouse but found all the airlocks sealed. Helplessly, they watched the ACEs' battle in the warehouse through the security video screens, learning early in the peace that the Games Board had control of every camera in and out of the building. They worked long but fruitlessly on opening the surface airlock and discovered that alternative comms links had also been blocked.

Above them, local flight control was bellowing in rage at the major so he turned the radio down, hoping that the shipyard's defence measures would give him a minute's warning before firing. He watched and held his breath as *Basalt*'s magazines slowly emptied, wishing that he had a few missiles but knowing they would probably be fatal to the ACEs even if he did have them.

The smothering tech was very close to the ACEs as a dent appeared in the airlock base, while rounds of iridium began to blast through; the air in the warehouse started whistling out through the hole, pushing the disc upwards. Glint yelled at the other two to climb onto him as he grasped the edge of the airlock joint and started to climb towards the hole in the airlock. As they neared it, Flint started to detach his rear limbs. As he programmed each one, and set them in place, they adhered to the wall and waited until the smothering tech came close, then directionally exploded, blasting the tech off the airlock to fall to the floor.

The rounds kept flashing through, almost cutting the disc clear, then the firing stopped. Minutes later Glint had them almost at the hole in the airlock where the air was now screaming out. Flint reached up, slicing through the remaining tenacious few parts of toughened steel that were hanging on, with only his front four limbs remaining.

With a bang, the final pieces dropped and Flint pulled himself up through the hole to be buffeted by the fierce wind; he pulled Nail up, then Glint himself shot up through the hole just as the first wave of smothering tech also reached the breach. The ACEs threw shattered pieces of concrete and steel at the tech, knocking individual pieces off, only to have them blasted up by the escaping air. Any pieces that touched them caused agonising burns, but they escaped serious damage as they ran from the hole towards the waiting Maul, which had three shipyard security Skuas holding it under arrest.

On *Basalt*, Patrick noted what Flint had done and smiled to himself as he had always wondered why the secretive Topaz had made additional sets of legs for the ACE and kept them in storage.

The inquest the next morning was held by the admiral himself. After reviewing every angle of the action and looking through the local constabulary reports he fined the major a large fee for the unauthorised use of an armed craft within a restricted area.

He then commended *Basalt*'s crew for supplying a most entertaining piece of AV, noting that their Games Board royalties more than covered the fine. Finally, he said that he saw little need to censure the major with an entry in his official record as long as the available members of *Basalt*'s crew attended a formal dinner that night.

Marko felt like a complete idiot and very uncomfortable in his starched uniform, complete with battle commendations and specialist decorations. Jan looked fantastic in hers, Julie and Harry looked at ease in theirs, and the major managed to look suave and sophisticated in his, much to the amusement of Glint, who kept wandering in on conversations between the major and female officers to interject and generally try to throw him off his game.

Even though they were the centre of attention, Marko was bored spitless. In his entire career he had never got the hang of small talk. Consequently, he was thankful that Jan was at his side to quietly steer him through the evening.

The ACEs had been ordered to attend by the admiral, much to their delight, and the rest of the crew's disquiet.

Marko looked down at the cat, who was sitting on his feet. 'So, Nail, what are your thoughts?'

Nail looked up at him shaking his head. 'These humans are terminally stupid, Marko. They all want to take me home to see their progeny, or go on trips with them. And they all try to pat my head. I really want you to do something about that. The indignity of it. How about some sort of electrification of my fur, or maybe some nice toxic dust? Those would work. How about both: zap them, and then have them itch for a week. I now understand why so many ACEs, once they have served their indenture, take themselves off somewhere far far away. I want to bite one of these people just to see what reaction I get. Glint feels the same. He says this is a very rich hunting ground and wants many kilos of ground-up meat.'

Marko cringed and was about to say something, but Nail continued. 'He says he knows where he can find some calamari, which would also make excellent missiles. I've been marking targets for him. There are some very dumb people here. How do they get to be where they are? See that woman over there. She is the admiral's wife. She has just asked the admiral for me to be given to her as a present. He said that you would have to do that as he does not have any control over me, Marko, but you would never do that to me, would you? Please do not smile like that. But she is insisting that as he is the admiral he can do anything he wishes. Flint has heard all this and says not to worry, he has a plan.'

Marko groaned and wondered if he should intervene as Nail sauntered away, ignoring everyone. He turned to Jan. 'They are up to something. What should we do?'

'Nothing, Marko. Let's just sit back and watch the entertainment. I loathe formal dinners.'

Marko thought hard for a few moments then shook his head and went looking for the ACEs. He found them in the kitchen talking with the chefs and kitchen staff, who were all grinning in anticipation. Glint rolled little balls of minced meat.

Marko sighed, knowing that he was not going to be popular, and said, 'OK, ACEs. I am pulling rank. Behave, no pranks, not here, not now. We only just got away with a fairly mild reprimand over the slaver action because we are media stars and the Games Board sanctioned and paid for the damage we created.'

Glint stopped what he was doing and walked across to stand with Nail and Flint in front of Marko. Marko knew that they would be having a high-speed electronic conversation.

Flint answered. 'You are correct, Father. But can we at least have a little fun sometime soon? These people are so stupid in their attitudes. We hate being treated as non equals.'

Marko nodded and whispered, 'I love you all and am so proud of you. And you are not equal to many of them as you are actually superior. Come on, let's go enjoy what will be very good food.'

As they were about to leave, after what had turned out to be a fairly enjoyable dinner from Marko's point of view, the admiral shook him by the hand and then leant forwards and quietly said, 'I wish you well in all your endeavours. And, yes, I am in the market for one of your ACEs. Please contact me soon.'

As soon as they arrived back on board *Basalt*, Marko found a formal order and the specifications for the spider, with a very generous offer from the admiral to expedite the build. He acknowledged it then sent the file to Topaz and Ernst, knowing that they had little to do and were bored, even considering shutting themselves down until the work on *Basalt* was completed.

A few mornings later Jake arrived unexpectedly and asked if he could have a look at the Gunbus. After they fed him a cup of coffee, and piled up a tray full of fruit for him to take back, they showed him the Gunbus. He looked long and hard at the antigravity units and suggested that he take them back with him to Sledgehammer, as they had older units in the junkyard which were in better order than the ones from the 'bus. He also suggested that Marko come down to the facility late that afternoon as 73 would be ready by then.

Jan and Marko had met Jake and his partners, two very pleasant women, for a discreet meal the previous night. It turned out that their passion was ancient aircraft and they had built a reasonable collection, together with a large group of fellow enthusiasts, on one of the thousands of islands on the resort planet below. A number of them were craft that Marko had no knowledge of, which made him more interested than ever. Jake had given them introductions to the guys at the 'aerodrome', and when he suggested that they would be able to go for flights in some of the aircraft they were completely sold on the idea of a visit. Marko had told Jake that they had the surviving Gunbus from the show at 27's foundry on board *Basalt* and he expressed a great interest in seeing it.

Just on 5.00 p.m. local time, Harry and Marko took a shuttle to collect the two fighters from the shipyard to return them to *Basalt*. They sat back on autopilot viewing the shipyards from on high. They watched as one heavy cruiser was lowered by three large brutish-looking tugs into what they both surmised must have been a specially built cradle, because the ship appeared to be missing over a quarter of its lower fuselage, which they knew would take months to regrow. Intrigued, they used the onboard link back to Patrick to first identify the ship in question and then have him look up the back story.

'I have the information. It is a famous old ship called *Napoleon*. It went up against another recently discovered outpost of the Infant fanatics in what was supposed to be a simple mop-up operation. Well, as we all know simple operations are rarely that. They got seriously knocked around by yet another unpleasant weapon. It is a vapour which, once a ship has passed through it, condenses onto the hull. It then gathers itself into a gel which rolls down the hull to chew on the engine decks. The captain evacuated her crew forwards and to take care of the infection detonated a Compressor against her own ship, after she had vaporised the small base with a Buster. Gutsy effort!'

Harry nodded in thanks. 'So, Marko, we still have Infant nutters out there waiting for us, eh? Thought that we had dealt with that shit.'

Marko's mouth turned down. 'Yeah, problem is, Harry, that the whole thing is tied up with the Games Board so who knows what else is out there. Nothing ever showed up with that whole Avian deal that White was talking about, so who knows, mate, who knows?'

'For your interest, Harry and Marko,' Patrick offered, 'the specialist salvage Hauler, *Barnacle*, is high above you. Here are the coordinates.'

Using the sensors in the Skua, Harry found the giant skeletal ship then ramped up the magnification to watch as it slowly powered its way up from the moon. Around its central core was an enormous framework which had great numbers of grapnels, line throwers, winches and lockdowns attached, together with an entire plethora of smaller units able to grasp ailing ships, and rescue the occupants, before securing the salvage. It was also bristling with defensive systems to fight off any others intending on getting the salvage first. Its attendant tugs were downsized units of *Barnacle*, any one of which would have been capable of taking *Basalt* inside it. Watching them dock, Harry said, 'Seems in a hurry: must be more work to be done.'

'Yeah, plenty of work in the salvage business these days, Harry. Wonder if they have had a look at our last battle site?'

'Dunno, but I do know that I would really like to have a good close look at *Barnacle* one day. Rumoured to have some rather interesting non-Administration, non-Gjomvik tech on board in that it can neutralise a Compressor. Now that I would like to see. Would have to take Fritzy with me to explain it, no doubt.'

They were once again given the royal treatment at the shipyard. 73 looked superb with the damage eliminated and its new gunmetal blue paintwork a perfect dull matt finish, and Marko said as much. They had a cup of tea with the management, after which he made a point of thanking the individual techs and engineers who had worked on the Hanger, with Harry doing the same a few bays over.

As they were about to depart, the manager gave a wrap-up speech. 'The fighters are both fully functional and ready for theatre. They have been test flown. The reports and the craft are now handed back to you. It has been a great pleasure meeting with you both.'

The man gave them a short bow, which they returned, with Harry saying, 'That is most kind. Thank you, Mr Jacobsen.'

As soon as they had docked and were climbing from their cockpits, the first person they saw was Sirius, who called out to them, 'Don't worry about the last few days! I have just sold all the programs and the funds will be credited to your accounts in a few minutes. Nice little earners. GB is pleased with the bit extra and extends its thanks. So, did you miss me?'

Harry walked across and hugged her. 'Sirius! How long have you been here? Yes, we've missed you. How've you been?'

'Well, thanks, Harry. Been here a few days. Edited a nice segment of you all out shopping as well. Priceless stuff of you, Marko, trying to hide from the crowds. And Jan looks great with a few extra kilos on. Suits her. Looks excellent in lingerie, doesn't she? Really could do with bigger breasts, don't you think, Marko? You should encourage her into a little tank time. And that Julie: wow, what a scrumptious body. Fills out her knickers very well. Wonderful, wonderful. They have a significant following in the fashion scene, no less. Everyone wants to know who they wear. I have even cut a deal with the lingerie manufacturer, and yes, there will be good spinoffs for the girls as well. And then a gloriously welcome ACE rescue and payback mission. That went off the charts locally and will do very well whenever it goes to air across the Sphere. You guys are getting the hang of being media stars without me! I trained you well.'

She paused for a second, looking at them, then continued. 'Now, guys, I am inviting myself along on your holiday. I promise not to get in the way. And which of you is bonking the amazons? God, but I so want to get some delightful imagery of them. Think that I will go with them wherever they go just in case. Do you think they would be averse to a little *ménage à trois* with me? That would be a real earner. '

Just what we needed. A holiday in the offing and the family camera arrives — typical, Marko thought to himself. And she is getting more and more into the sleazy side of things as well.

He could not remember the number of times she had sent him requests for him to act in age-restricted presentations for the Games Board. He knew of many of his colleagues who had cheerfully participated in screwing some movie star or other with everything recorded and marketed. It was not that he had anything against it, but there were boundaries that he himself had no desire to cross.

Four

Basalt looked much better. Still very utilitarian and superbly functional, but all in all much better with the new off-white pearl coating over every exterior surface of the frigate, plus the airlocks had been serviced and recoated as well.

Marko spoke to the hangar. 'Very nice outer coatings, Patrick. You pleased?'

Patrick's voice came from all around them. 'Yes, Marko. The tasks allotted to the shipyards are complete, on time and to specifications. Now I have high-level chameleon-ware at my disposal as well. Most satisfactory. Your craft looks very pleasing. Jake very kindly delivered three secondhand antigravity units for you to "play with", as he put it. I attempted to pay him, but he would not hear of it.'

Harry and Sirius left the hangar so Marko climbed back into *Sledgehammer*'s cockpit, rotated the craft and slid up against *Blackjack*. He directed his thoughts towards *Blackjack* and it reacted as he expected, folding out the deployment and lock mechanisms, taking hold of the Hanger and then tucking it up against itself. The airlocks connected and Marko willed himself inside *Blackjack*. The temporary seat did not move as smoothly as the Tux seat, but *Blackjack* compensated, lowering Marko back into the main cabin.

'Tux, when I direct a thought towards *Blackjack*, do you actually read that thought and transmit the request?'

'Of course, Marko. It is one of my many functions. If your thoughts are not specific, I do not on-send them.'

'Is *Blackjack* alive, Tux?'

'Define alive, Marko. It is an enormous parameter.'

Marko cocked his head, looking around the interior. 'OK, is *Blackjack* sentient and aware of us?'

Tux sounded a little frustrated. 'Of course. I understood that you knew this.'

Marko shrugged. 'So, can it speak to me, Tux?'

'It will one day, Marko, when your rather glacial synaptic response time becomes sufficiently fast to be able to understand it. *Blackjack* operates on a level much higher than human thought. We are all waiting for you to speed up. My understanding of the octopoid technology now in you, is that it gradually rebuilds you by creating an entirely new brain and nervous system within your existing structure. I would suggest that you will be able to converse with *Blackjack* sometime within the next month or so. Until then it will continue to care for you and yours.'

Marko was still pondering about *Blackjack* when Nail sauntered in.

'Marko?'

'Yes, Nail.'

The cat swished his tail. 'Am I allowed to bite Sirius? Stephine really does not like her, you know.'

Marko laughed. 'Bite her? Well, if she pisses you off that much, then a wee nip would not be out of the question. Would also allow you to analyse her blood, eh? Yeah, I would not object. Be interesting to see what she looks like at a base level now. Tux, give my regards to *Blackjack* and say that I look forward to speaking with him one day.'

Tux answered. 'She says that she finds you a most interesting sentient and also looks forward to that day.'

Marko shook his head and smiled. 'She? Why does that not surprise me?'

Nail added, astounded, 'What? You have only just worked out that *Blackjack* is sentient? We sometimes worry about your level of conscious intelligence, Marko.'

They found Sirius still talking with Harry when they made their way up to the main hangar deck. She had grown in height a fair amount and as soon as she turned to look at Marko he could see the hardwiring which was now part of her. Her eyes were a startling iridescent blue, her ears elegantly enlarged and subtly reshaped, with the skin on her arms now covered with the latest fashionable bio-wetware as well. Sirius looked human, but she was Games Board through and through, and Marko decided he did not trust her one little bit. She assessed him briefly, her eyes lingering over his crotch for a few seconds longer than necessary. Marko glanced across at Harry and saw his slight nod, acknowledging that Sirius was still very much a hunter.

Nail looked up at her appraisingly. 'So you are still Sirius. As in mostly flesh and blood. Interesting tech you have there. I note that you are broadcasting a signal continuously as well. Why are you doing that?'

Sirius turned to look at Nail. 'So you are the now-famous Nail. Well, Nail, it is my job. Just like when you first knew me, though now I am much more efficient. I have an arrangement with the Games Board. I look after you and sell everything I can about this and a number of other interesting crews and ships to the Games Board, and they allow me to keep this beautiful human body of mine. The only thing that I cannot do is have children; they removed that ability from me as part of the deal. I do this work to stay alive. Do you object to that, Nail?'

Nail took a few seconds, examining his extended claws on one paw before slowly replying. 'I shall consider my response, Madam Sirius.'

Behind them, Glint virtually hissed out, 'As will I, Sirius of the Games Board.'

Marco almost gasped out loud and had to restrain himself from spinning around to look at the ACEs, as he had never heard a response like that from them before.

Sirius just laughed. 'Oh my, you are beautiful, Glint. I saw you when you were being made but I have not had the pleasure of knowing you. I have seen you in action and I consider you to be a wonderful sentient creature.'

Glint, standing tall on his rear legs, said, 'Thank you, Sirius. But believe me when I say that having observed humans for some time now I would consider their sentience overrated.'

Marko looked at Glint carefully and mused about Sirius. Certainly she was very good for *Basalt* and crew and had padded their monetary worth, but he could not decide what to make of her and he had often questioned why the Games Board allowed her to go back to them. He wondered if she actually had their interests at heart, but doubted that very much, because she was a player in the Games Board's manipulations. Looking at the ACEs once again, he hoped that Sirius understood they were lethal, and that they had made the decision that she would be watched very carefully. Sadly, he also realised that the mood of the whole ship changed when she was on board, with everyone careful of what they did and said around her.

An announcement from the major broke through his reverie. 'All crew, *Basalt* is back under our control. Check everything as per normal protocols so handover can be made official. Check in with me as you sort out your departments.'

'Excuse me, please, Sirius,' Marko said. 'I had better go do that then I need some fruit. Can I get anything for anyone? No. See you soon. I'm on dinner tonight, and seeing that everyone is back, I had better get moving.'

Lilly and Jasmine were tending the gardens and gleefully scolded Marko for letting a couple of things slip while they had been away. Jan was also with them, tending the potatoes, and asked what he needed for the meal. They passed a few notes between themselves in regard to Sirius, that she needed to be watched.

A few hours after dinner the major called the shipyards to advise that the final checks had been made so handover could take place, and that they needed a tug to lift them away from the hangar. While that was happening the crew sat at their consoles, caught up on everyone's news and sent farewell messages to their friends below.

The major finally announced: 'Crew, we are on our own again. Harry, please take us within hailing distance of Number Five Orbital Station. Has everyone decided on and logged their intentions while planetside? Right, thanks, I now have them all here onscreen. I see that you want individual interviews with us, Sirius. You have certainly helped our bank balances, so that's a reasonable request, but it's up to individuals to accept your invitation or not.'

The Orbital was huge, discus-shaped, and had three pairs of space elevators connecting it to the planet far below. Everyone was pretty much going in opposite directions to explore the planet and rest and relax in their own ways. There were also several plans afoot for avoiding Sirius.

Jan and Marko had decided to hire a house-craft and spend most of the time exploring a large chain of islands south of the planet's equator. In that area it was effectively early autumn, so they had packed in anticipation of lots of time on the various beaches. The package they had brought included dive gear and, most importantly, fishing equipment. They would also be visiting Jake's friends and hopefully flying ancient aircraft from a field halfway down the island chain, so they decided to take their ship suits. And, of course, Nail and Glint would be with them.

Just before they left *Basalt*, Jan lined everyone up and gave them bioware boosters covering the current influenza bugs, colds, et cetera, and, more importantly, gave them the necessary gut augments so that they could digest the local food types easily. As a very young soldier, Marko had once skipped that step and paid for it dearly. Being on a break with violent diarrhoea and vomiting put a damper on things.

The major would be spending time with Patrick, reviewing his astronomical research and other work for a presentation he was giving to the Haulers' Astronomical Guild in a few weeks' time, which was a big deal for him. He had gently asked them all to view it via links and everyone was quite happy to leave him to it, as he did not need them arriving at the venue and stealing his thunder. So they dropped the crew off and then took *Basalt* into a lower orbit above the planet, sufficiently far away from the Orbitals to be left in peace.

Marko loved the elevators. They had spent time in the Orbital after transferring directly off *Basalt* and had been pretty much mobbed, with every man and his dog wanting a piece of them, so he, for one, was very happy to be shown to his and Jan's cabin in the elevator, with its large panoramic window, as the two-day journey to the planet began. It was like a miniature cruise ship, and Marko and Jan even met one old lady at breakfast the next morning who had been riding elevators for many, many years. She said that as soon as she became totally familiar with one planet and its elevators she would move on to the next one. When Jan asked if this was her first ride on an elevator down to this planet, the old lady had replied that, no, she had already ridden on the other two, which were only hundreds of metres away. Jan mused later that it took all types to make the universe interesting.

The terminal at the elevator's base was built into an equatorial island's mountain, so it was a superb view coming down through the atmosphere. The place was so big and so full of people, equipment, cargo and shops that Jan and Marko did not see any other members of the crew leaving.

They quickly marched into the first tourist shop they could find and bought large sunglasses, larger hats and voluminous shirts, which they were relieved to note were favoured by the locals, and hired a small carryall on which they piled their luggage — including the two suit containers — among which they hid Nail and Glint. They bought some additional local clothing, which was garish to say the least, changed into it and set about blending in with the crowd.

It was going very well as they quietly moved towards the exits when a young man, walking past the carryall, nonchalantly picked up one of the smaller carrier bags without breaking stride and started to walk away from them. He would have easily got away scot-free had it not been for Glint, who had had his head under the bag, peeking out at the passing throngs of people. He erupted from the carryall, yelling at the thief, who looked back to see a fearsome vision of Glint with extended cooling frills for effect, accompanied by Nail, in hot pursuit. He screamed, then sprinted for the nearest exit still clutching the bag, forcing his way through the crowd as Glint and Nail slid through at knee level and easily caught up with him.

Glint leapt high into the air to pounce and knock him down while Nail clutched at the young man's head before he hit the floor. The thief pulled a short-bladed knife and slashed at Nail, but Glint, with demonic speed, seized the thief's wrist with both of his hands, plucked the knife from him then passed it to his hind feet cum hands and snapped the knife in two, dropping the parts on the floor. Glint, who appeared really angry, rolled the young man over onto his back, sitting on his chest as Nail decided that a little impromptu interrogation was in order.

'Hold him still, Glint. I want to see how far I can get a claw up his nose before I touch his brain. We really need Flint here. He is better equipped for interrogation.'

The red-faced blubbering male started shaking and calling on the rapidly gathering crowd for assistance. Several of them taunted the thief, saying that he should know who had caught him and that he was getting everything he deserved. He looked up into Nail's face, blubbering, 'Who ... who ... who is Flint?'

Nail hissed, then yawned widely centimetres away from the thief's face. 'So, you have a voice. I am Nail and my colleague here, who loves breaking crappy knives, is Glint. Flint is another of our family. He is a mechanical spider. Should I call him over? He enjoys forcing his arms into human's ears to see what is inside. Tell you what, you tell us about your mates here in the arrivals lounge and I won't pull out your eyes.'

The man tried bravado. 'Go fuck yourself, you creepy cat!'

Glint leant close and yelled in his ear. 'Bad, bad human!'

Nail, in spite of his size, was very strong. He pressed his paws against the thief's head and bent down to lick his tongue across the tightly closed eyes of the human. Marko was starting to feel almost sorry for the young man. Looking around, he noted that every one was recording the scene and looking over the top of the very large crowd he could see station security trying to force their way in to see what was happening for themselves. The man was screaming for Nail to stop, although Nail was not actually harming him, and started to blubber the names of the rest of his gang. The security and local police finally made it through the clapping, cheering crowd to find both Nail and Glint still sitting on the man, posing for photographs. Marko and Jan just leant against each other and laughed.

Fifty minutes later, as they were leaving the local police station, being bid a fond farewell by the station's chief, the gang's lawyer approached them to say that she was going to have Marko and Jan charged with possession of dangerous animals. Jan was about to speak with the woman when Glint told her that they would handle it. The hybridised fossa and Jesus lizard ACE lifted Nail up until he was level with the woman's face. They then took turns in telling her exactly what her lineage was, and explained that they were ranking military entities within the Administration, and that they had the right of certified sentient citizens under local law to do what they had done. At that stage, she started rapidly backing off but not before something was quietly said to her. The pompous, obviously badly educated woman went completely white, apologised profusely, started shaking, and actually ran away.

Jan was giggling and asked, 'Hey, Nail, what did you say to her?'

Nail preened himself a little. 'Not much, but she will steer well clear of every cat she ever sees again.'

Jan looked closely at him. 'Yeah, but you have not answered my question.'

The cat shrugged. 'I told her I was going to fuck every female cat I came across and that in every kitten I fathered I would imprint her DNA and that of each of her clients as enemies of my species. I then gave her a little scratch. Think she got the message. So, when are Glint and I going to be given the ability to breed?'

Jan roared with laughter while Marko looked, and felt, shocked, wondering what kind of creatures he had let loose upon the universe. 'Not today. Right, OK, enough of this subject. Let's get the hell out of here before you pair get us into real trouble. How about I grab us a transport to take us out to the house-craft depot?'

On the way, they gathered up a few extra food supplies because the local meats, cheeses and wines were highly recommended by their driver. At one excellent shop called Gipsy Kitchen, Marko pulled out his money card and when his name came up the whole staff arrived to see them. Before they knew it the transport had been locked down and they, along with Sam, the driver, were treated to a hilarious few hours of impromptu entertainment, together with sampling the very best of the local foods and beverages.

The produce and small goods were excellent, just as Sam had suggested, and they had their images taken with the proprietors, which were promptly printed. They were asked to sign the small poster-sized prints and were happy to do so. Nail left a set of paw prints and Glint, who as far as Marko was aware had never picked up a pen before, let alone used one, spent some time working up a flourishing signature. When he had finalised his mark and signed one of the posters the owner asked him if he could keep the test signatures. Glint looked at him quizzically and said that they were rubbish so he could do whatever he liked with them. Marko smiled, knowing that such a windfall would probably put the shop owner's children through higher education and suspected that Glint knew that.

Nail was surprisingly tolerant of the children, who all wanted to touch him and pet him. Jan walked in at one stage and quietly beckoned Marko over, pointing out into the corridor. Three little girls had dressed the cat in a doll's costume, placed him in a pram and were wheeling him around the house, singing. The look they got from him as he was wheeled by said, 'Say a word and I will scratch your eyes out.' Glint was too busy sampling cheese and the local hard biscuits to notice what else was going on around him. When it came time to leave, they had a real battle trying to pay for anything.

Someone must have rung ahead of them to the house-craft depot, as it was still open by the time they eventually arrived, very late. The manager herself showed them the house-craft they had hired and, after checking their licences, she signed the craft over to them, then she and Sam helped them load everything on board. It was a fairly simple machine some eighteen metres long by fifteen wide. Spacious with a high ceiling, two high-class lounges, a large galley and, in the centre, a beautifully appointed bedroom with an equally palatial bathroom set off it. It was perfect for a few weeks exploring, especially as it also had a marine runabout housed under the stern.

Sam also proved rather difficult to pay, but eventually accepted, and Glint signed the back of his cab ID for him as Nail again grumbled about his lack of hands.

With Jan at the controls, they lifted the house-craft on antigravity and slotted themselves into the local controller's network, heading as far east as they could go before the local sun started to set into the sea. Jan controlled the flight, so Marko, unable to help himself, popped open the inspection hatches to see what was powering the craft. He found four industrial-grade gas turbines with a big antigravity unit attached to each one. Any two could lift the house-craft and power it along at a moderate speed, but the craft was not built for speed, it was built for comfort. After they had stopped and anchored, Jan cooked them a simple supper of fresh salads and cold meats, which they had with a lesser known, but excellent, local Chablis. One of the perks of getting to know the locals was that you always got the good food and booze, Jan mused, swirling the last of the bottle around in her glass.

So began a very pleasant ten days of fishing, walking beaches, having barbecues on the fantail-shaped stern deck, listening to music, sleeping in each morning and making love as often as they felt like; they explored the islands, went to the local markets, fishing for and eating those fish that the onboard database said were safe, snorkelled in the shallows looking at the types of coral-like creatures and abundant life, used scuba and dived deep for some of the more interesting edible aquatic insects and just had fun. Nail absorbed every bit of information on every plant, insect, animal, bird and aquatic creature he could find. He sampled each, obviously building a database for Stephine.

Glint spent time eating and making ammunition and then firing it at steadily greater and greater ranges. One afternoon while watching him firing at a piece of driftwood, when the house-craft was at anchor and rolling, Marko could actually see the projectile in flight. Everything else slowed down dramatically around him, but for the first time he perceived that he could speed up or take time at its normal pace. He experimented and discovered that his movements were normal to him, but were probably blindingly fast to anyone else. Tux, when Marko spoke to him about it, commented that he would become slightly faster, but that he was approaching his physical limit. He added that Marko's thought processes would carry on getting quicker as the new neural pathways were completed. It did feel very strange though.

Once a day, as required by the major, they checked in with *Basalt*, orbiting overhead. The rest of the crew were apparently having as much fun as Marko and Jan were, relaxing and doing the normal tourist things, except Fritz. He was further enhancing his considerable musical fame by rebuilding ancient pieces of sound equipment for some of the major bands on the planet and in payment was treated to numerous impromptu jam sessions, which was Fritz's kind of heaven, although he said he was returning to *Basalt* early. Halfway through the leave period, Julie and Harry announced that they had signed a ten-year contract between them, which did not surprise anyone.

When they were relatively close to the island that Jake had told them about, and fortunately the start of the weekend, Jan made contact with the ancient aircraft group. As Jake had promised, they were expected. They quietly flew around the islands towards the field. Glint called them up onto the top of the house-craft when three flying machines slowly flew above them, making a great amount of noise. It was a wonderful moment for Marko to actually see the extraordinary machines which he realised, at one stage of their ancestry, would have been at the very cutting edge of technology. Jan sped up the house-craft to match the aeroplanes' speed and they were escorted the twelve kilometres to the aerodrome at a sedate two hundred and nine kilometres an hour ... which they later learnt was the top speed of the aircraft.

When they were five kilometres out from the aerodrome, their navigation system slaved to the local controller, who brought them onto the field and parked the house-craft beside the large buildings which made up one side of the facility. There were hundreds of aircraft of all types, all neatly stowed in the buildings, patiently waiting for their owners to fly them. Marko could not see one modern military craft among any of them, just the ancient fighters which had landed and were taxiing towards them. As they watched, the pilots gunned the engines and swung them around to face out over the apron towards the taxiways and the runways. They climbed down the side of the house-craft as it powered down, resting on its two main pontoons, and waited for the pilots. As the flyers strolled over, Jan and Marko could see that, like the pilot they'd seen eaten by whorls, they were wearing leather flying suits and goggles of the same vintage as the aircraft. The three introduced themselves and invited Marko, Jan and the ACEs to their clubrooms for a gin and tonic. Marko had no idea what that was, and when he looked at Jan, she just shrugged. Marko thought it an interesting concoction but graciously declined a second while Jan seemed to enjoy them.

The rest of the day was spent with the cheerful group who called themselves the Aviators. Once Marko got close enough, he was pleasantly surprised by how brilliantly simple the aircraft really were. Each one had its own flight handling characteristics complete with how easy they were to take off and land, or not, what their rates of climb were, how woefully underpowered they were with the engines measured in horsepower. He had always thought that was a deliciously archaic measurement, and of how they had no avionics, no computer, no ejection seats, let alone antigravity, and that they ran the engines on actual petrol, which was created especially for them by another local group who made and raced another equally archaic group of huge-wheeled racing cars that had originated at the same time as their flying machines, around the time of the ancient human conflict known as the First World War. For all of that, they were both hugely impressed with them. Marko shook his head in wonder, thinking about their ancestors actually using such aircraft, in battles as well.

'These are wonderful machines, truly wonderful, and so simple, but beautifully made,' Marko mused out loud, admiring the varnished plywood cockpit, hand-formed polished aluminium cowling and canvas-covered fuselage and wings on a Sopwith Camel. 'Would be interesting to fly with the centre of gravity so far forwards.'

A slightly built man who'd introduced himself as David Casement commented, 'Not wrong there, Sergeant Major. Only those of us who have had extensive experience flying these beauties are allowed to take that one up. Hellish manoeuvrable in many ways, but a pig for take-offs and landings. Interesting machine in that it will turn to the right faster than to the left due to the engine torque and prop size. Fact is, to go left some of us prefer just to carry on going right!'

Jan and Marko went up for a flight, separately, with one of the pilots sitting behind them at the controls in a machine called an FE2d. When Jan asked what the letters FE stood for they were told 'Farman Experimental'. The pilot was a solidly-built individual sporting a huge moustache, a great bellowing laugh and the interesting name of Rangi Hohepa. His skin tone was darker than Marko's and when asked of his ancestry, Rangi seemed to grow a few extra centimetres in height as he proudly claimed the heritage of the Maori people of New Zealand on Old Earth. Marko had known some Maori people in his home village as he was growing up. Wonderful, loyal people who adopted all the village kids as if they were their own. They fed them whenever they were in their homes, taught them, looked after them and were sufficiently caring to give a kid a kick up the bum if it was required.

Marko told Rangi of them and his attitude towards Marko and Jan changed completely. Until then, Rangi had just been doing a favour for his friend, Jake. Now Marko and Jan were suddenly family or, as he called it, part of his hapu, and he became considerably more engaging and entertaining.

The FE2d was termed a pusher type, with twin wings. When Marko climbed into it, he discovered to his delight that the entire fabrication of the aircraft was a mixture of wood, fabric, wire, aluminium and, in the case of the pilot's seat, some kind of woven plant material called wicker. There was no gunner's seat, just a vertical tub arrangement for the gunner to stand in. It smelt completely different from anything he had ever experienced before and he loved every minute he spent looking at the amazing array of struts and tensioned wire with hundreds of turnbuckles keeping everything in line.

That evening the rest of the club members arrived out at the field to meet them and they were made to feel even more welcome. They talked aircraft, engines and weapons and Jan was in her element as well when the club armourers arrived and let her see, and then handle, the machine guns. The club members had even gained themselves a licence to make and export the antique weapons, together with ammunition, and the resulting sales paid for them to build one or two new aircraft each year. Their intention was to have one example of every fighter aircraft from the First World War.

Marko was fascinated when shown the paper blueprints of each of the aircraft, which were displayed down one long wall of the hangar, and, looking at the sign-offs on each plan, he could see that twenty-one flying examples had been built. On the next wall was another set of blueprints detailing the aircraft that they were either building or wanted to build. In another building behind the hangar, he thought his face would start to ache because his smile was that big when shown the antique tools and equipment used in making the planes. He decided that the club members were quite mad, but in a most wonderful way ... by building such aircraft using original methods. Talking with the various members he became aware that there were almost two completely distinct groups within the club: builders and fliers. Only a very few individuals were both and they were quite an eclectic lot.

Rangi was a local doctor and other members worked in a range of professions. People from the very top of the local community's social hierarchy to the very lowest were represented, but once in the club, they were all equals. Doug Evans, the armourer, was a senior policeman, and once they got past the gruff exterior, found him to be a very likable fellow as well. They had to pay for their supper, as it were, by giving impromptu speeches on their various battles with the urchins.

Even Nail made himself useful by destroying a few nests of a nasty local rodent which, to Jan's horror, he seemed to greatly enjoy. Glint made himself equally popular by shooting down a local type of four-winged predator leatherwing, which flew high above the aerodrome and was known for attacking the slow-moving aircraft. Everyone, drinks in hand, rushed outside when another one was seen, so they could watch Glint go to work.

'Glint, just make sure that I can recover some of it for sampling, please,' Marko called.

Glint laughed in reply. 'Yeah, whatever, Marko. You are on holiday, but I will get the head for you!'

Some of the members gasped when Glint strode out in front of the club, watched the leatherwing for a few moments, then spread out his legs and rotated his head to the rear. His head distorted in order to get his eyes as far apart as possible, and the rest of his long, lithe body and tail went completely rigid as he started firing. Hundreds of metres above them, the first shot separated the creature's head from its body before the next three shots in quick succession blew the body into smaller pieces.

Before any parts had hit the ground, Glint was racing away to fetch the head to everyone's applause, which he acknowledged, gracefully bowing to them as he placed the 400-millimetre-long, streamlined and nightmarish head into Marko's hands. Seconds later Nail took it from him, saying that it should be checked for pathogens and that he also needed to analyse it while it was still fresh. Marko just smiled.

They left late the next morning after flights in a two-seater Bristol F.2B, which they both exclaimed was very interesting, to say the least. The rear gun was mounted as a swing-around affair which would have been fun to fire, but as they were not members of the club, or checked out by the local officials, they were strictly passengers. Not that they really minded as it was an experience to be in the cupola anyway.

When asked, Nail had no interest in going for a flight, intent on hunting out more rodents, but Glint cheerfully squeezed in beside one of the smaller women pilots and was taken aloft in an Albatross, which he hugely enjoyed, saying that he would really like to build one for himself.

'Why would you want to build one, Glint?' Jan asked. 'Isn't going for a ride in one enough?'

The steel-grey creature rose up on his hind legs, looked at her and Marko, then back at the machines. 'I'm not sure of the desire, I just have the need to make things. Maybe it is because there is so much of Marko's own DNA and conditioning in me. I am constantly surrounded by people making or doing something. Just natural, I suppose.'

Marko found the statement most revealing, as most ACEs did not generally express a desire to step outside of themselves and take on a whole series of new experiences until they were much older. After thinking about it for a few seconds he suggested, 'How about you talk with Topaz when we get back to *Basalt*, Glint, so you can make a scale model of one to start with?'

Glint nodded slowly. 'That's a good idea. I like that. Now which one? I'll decide then get Nail to scan one for me.'

They eventually had to say goodbye to the Aviators, and headed south towards one of the smaller and more remote chain of islands.

For the next few days they spent a good deal of time in the water exploring a beautiful series of reefs. The aquatic life was sensational, although they had been forced to use the deterrent equipment to keep some of the predators away from them. One particular creature, which Marko's data block identified as a barracuda type of fish, except three times larger, had obviously been desensitised to the electronic signals, as it came extremely close. As they swam through the crystal-clear water, it dived under them, turned, then came up between them at speed, to see if they were possible prey or not. It flashed upwards, disappeared through the surface, then seconds later came at them horizontally. Marko saw a flash of hard silver and an awful lot of teeth, before Jan smacked it with a stunner just as it was about to close on his legs. As it rolled over onto its back and drifted downwards, other predators started to be seen, so they decided that they had had enough, and beat a watchful retreat to the surface.

Later that evening, they were lying together on top of the cabin of the house-craft, looking at the stars of the Milky Way. The weather forecast was for a decent-sized storm to come into their area late the next day, so they were making the most of the calm conditions before running for cover to one of the local harbours.

Jan snuggled closer into Marko and murmured softly, 'I could get used to this lifestyle. How about we chuck in the military, settle down somewhere, raise a family and have a normal life? I have effectively been on the move for a very long time. I'm tired of it. How about you?'

Marko smiled in the starlight. 'You know, I have been trying to bring up the same subject for a long time, but did not have the bottle. How about we tidy up the loose ends and vanish? It's not like we have a money problem or anything. And besides, between us we have plenty of skills. My family would love you to bits as well.'

Jan rolled to be face to face with Marko. 'Let's do it.'

Marko took her at her word, and they made love right where they were, simply not caring of the watchers far overhead.

Part Four

Cobalt Diamond

One

Marko slipped his glasses on and scanned the heavens wheeling above them as they lay relaxed in the afterglow of wonderful sex.

'There he is.'

'Who?'

'*Basalt.*'

Jan giggled. 'Wave at him then.'

'Now that's intriguing,' Marko said seriously. 'The new camouflage system is program adaptive, right?'

Jan nodded. 'Yes, nice system — programmable as well.'

Marko reached for her wrist and started tapping out a message. 'We might be in trouble.'

Jan tensed. She tapped back. 'Tell me!'

'There is a message on the outer hull. It reads MJRUN,' Marko tapped. 'It came on for a few seconds and is gone. There is also another frigate above *Basalt*. Looks like one of the Games Board's Expeditor class.'

Jan replied calmly. 'No sudden moves. We casually make our way below and start heading back to the aerodrome at a nice sedate pace.'

'Yeah, good idea. Have you something in mind?'

Jan tapped: 'Yes. Drop this craft off, lease one of the sports aircraft and start working out what to do.'

As they pulled up the anchor and headed back to the aerodrome, which was only one hundred and fifty-six kilometres away, there came further confirmation that trouble was brewing. There was a message from the local Games Board media requesting an interview when they arrived at Lyttleton Harbour. And, importantly, there were no cheerful words from Sirius on the message, just her chop. Also, another message from the house-craft company saying that there had been a problem with a navigation module and that they were to take the craft to Lyttleton Harbour for servicing.

Fortunately, Lyttleton Harbour was reasonably close to the aerodrome so they spent time getting closer, then stopped for the night in a beautiful cove along the coast from the aerodrome, and tried to get some sleep, holding each other close.

Before dawn they were up, with all their gear stowed and ready to leave in a hurry, if necessary. They had also found their secure comms units and now conversed only through them, except for making small talk about the trip in case they were being monitored. Between them, the only weapons they had were their own sidearms, a knife each, and Glint. Marko had told the ACEs what was happening the night before, and Nail and Tux had spent the entire night searching for clandestine ways off the planet, but they had not been able to find anything that would not trip the local Net's search engine's alarm.

'Tux, can we get *Blackjack* to pick us up?' Marko asked.

'I am in contact with her. She would need two days to configure herself for atmospheric flight as she does not have Stephine's high-speed interface any longer. The best she can do is come down into the thermosphere to effect a pick-up. She believes that Patrick is compromised and that Games Board Expeditors are on board *Basalt*. All other crew members have been ordered back to the ship except us. She believes that you have less then twenty-four hours before the Games Board moves against you and subsequently those sentients close to you.'

Marko groaned. 'Jan, did you see any thermosphere-capable aircraft at the aerodrome?'

'Nope, they would only be at the local hub, which is seven hundred odd kilometres north of here. Security would also be much tighter. We would not stand a chance.'

'OK, it's up to us then,' Marko said.

Jan agreed and started organising. 'Nail, get on the net and start looking through every news item in a thousand-kilometre radius of us. If the Games Board heavies are here, they will have been noticed. Glint, get eating: load up your magazine.'

Minutes later Marko added: 'Nail, is there a real-time link back to the house-craft company about electronic activities on board this craft, and are our conversations monitored?'

The cat answered quickly. 'Yes, there is a datalink. Shall I disable it? There is no corresponding datalink for monitoring of human activity.'

'No. But I want you to start to create a ten-hour sequence of readouts as if we are back at the aerodrome, showing that the engines are intact and performing flawlessly.'

Jan raised an eyebrow. 'Plan?'

Marko nodded. 'We strip out two of the antigravity units from the house-craft, plus their turbines, strap a seat onto each one and leg it straight up. We will need to get into the ancient aircraft maintenance hangars. They had all the equipment we need. Shall we lie to them, or tell them the truth, and also tell them to get as far away from us as possible?'

Jan tapped her chin. 'Go for the truth, Marko. It always amazes me how people will respond to a plea for help.'

As the local sun was rising from the sea, they arrived at the aerodrome. Marko used his hired phone and laboriously tapped out Rangi's number, which the sleepy-sounding doctor answered.

'Hey, Rangi, this is Marko. We are at the aerodrome. Jan was bitten by something when we were diving yesterday. Her bioware is not handling it. Can you come out, please?'

Rangi woke up fast. 'Be there in fifteen minutes. I live just down the road.'

When he arrived, they told him what they suspected and how, in their adventures, they had upset the Games Board on many occasions. Marko also told him what they planned to do.

Rangi looked very serious, then replied slowly. 'Hmm, well, you have to understand that we cannot be seen to assist you, but that does not mean that I cannot show you where everything is, and also where all the keys are. None of us have a lot of truck with the Games Board anyway. They scare us with their smarmy ways and their taking the brightest children then turning them into monsters who never come home again or have anything to do with their families. It is worse than a death. Right, follow me.'

He gave them the keys, told them where everything was, including the weapons and ammunition, and even where the Cooper bombs and Le Prieur rockets were stored before adding, 'In thirty or so minutes two of my sons will arrive. They are good guys and will do anything to help. The official story will be that I treated Jan, and then left, expecting you to do the same. They came down, found that you had broken in and you then forced them to help you. I will talk with Doug Evans as well, on the quiet. He is a good man and had one of his favourite nieces recruited by the Games Board. Loathes them. Jan, I had better get a reading of your blood, just to cover my arse. I have a sample of a local shellfish toxin that I shall splice into the sample data so it will look legitimate.'

He took a med unit from his pocket, tapped diligently on it for a moment or so, then pressed it up against her finger for a sample. Nodding at her, he then placed a pair of large glasses on and scanned through the results in the HUD. 'Yeah, as I expected, perfect health. One day I would love to be able to afford a bio-system like yours. Stay well. Good luck, guys. Kia kaha! Courage, keep strong. Until we meet again.'

He kissed Jan on the cheek, shook Marko's hand and, for a long few seconds pressed his nose against Marko's, climbed onto his AG bike, waved and cruised away. They opened the main hangar doors, backed the house-craft in, and then rapidly got to work to strip two of the antigravity units out. The propulsion units were set up so they could be taken out quickly; as they unbolted the restrainers, the units swung out smoothly, even having little fold-out legs, which made life much easier. 'Nice design, eh, Jan?' Marko commented.

Rangi's sons, Todd and Bill, pulled up in a loud, low-slung wheeled vehicle that looked very impressive, complete with extensive exhaust pipe work down the sides. They climbed out through the top of the open cockpit, as it had no doors, introduced themselves and got immediately to work after Marko drew a quick diagram of what he needed, knowing it was ugly but effective. Nail jacked himself into the management programs of the antigravity units and overwrote the restrictors. He also overwrote the remote controllers so, once aloft, they could not be hijacked or shut down. Under his direction, Glint then disconnected the electrics throughout the units, as they would be welding fittings to them and did not want any of the circuits to short out.

The first thing Marko did was strip the turbine exhaust back until it was a straight flow directly aft. They stripped off the casings, leaving only the top and bottom parts of the shroud. Todd and Bill had returned by this stage with two pairs of elevators from one of the First World War aircraft. Marko showed them what he wanted and they mounted them in a V configuration, bolting them on the main mounting strut along the top of the turbine. The next task was to create a cockpit of sorts.

Todd and Bill disappeared again then returned half an hour later having found a pair of floats from some abandoned aircraft or other. They cut the front sections away and roughly welded them directly onto the outer housing of the antigravity units, then opened them up to allow access, running a self-bonding tape over the sharp edges. They disappeared for another half an hour before returning with a pair of racing seats from one of their wheeled vehicles and two pairs of cylindrical fuel tanks, which they mounted directly above the turbine.

'Marko,' Bill said. 'You have an hour of fuel and oxygen. Plan is to go straight up, yeah? We will rig the elevator so you can control the flight by warping the wings. You will have to do it manually as there is no time for anything nice.'

Over the next few hours, while also nervously looking over their shoulders, they made the crude craft controllable. Marko set up a simple throttle link to the turbines after stripping some of the electronic control lines from the house-craft, but felt bad about doing this, so had Nail use the local communication links to book and pay for six months' hire of a top-of-the-line house-craft, using one of their secret black accounts. Neither of them had ever trusted the Administration with all their funds. Marko's family handled some of his as well, as a further backstop measure, and he also had black accounts held by some of his most trusted Gjomvik clients. Marko figured that the booking would adequately cover the costs of a pair of antigrav units and the repairs.

The wind had picked up outside, gusting strong enough to rattle the big doors as they pressed on with their tasks while Glint supplied them with drinks and snacks.

'Marko, I have found a news item about four small Games Board combat craft escorting a large Games Board System Suite Airship,' Nail reported. 'They are headed towards Lyttleton and will be there to give a display for the local school children in two hours. The news reporter thinks that the display will probably be postponed due to the tropical storm.'

Marko nervously pushed a hand over his bald head. 'Shit, we still have at least that amount of time to get these suckers usable. OK, we had better look at weapons. Tell me what you have, guys. We don't have a weight problem as these units have huge lift capacity.'

Todd gave them the rundown. 'We like the Lewis Air Guns: 7.71 calibre with every third bullet a tracer in a magazine of ninety-seven rounds. Cyclic rate of six hundred rounds per minute. If you had one forwards and one firing directly aft, that would be best. Easy to fit; we will get right on it. There are also the ten-kilo Cooper bombs. They have been modified with a modern timer on them so you can set the fuse. We use a little push-button timer on the end of each pull cord. Punch in the time, then just yank the cord to let them go. We will mount four of them under the engine housings. The Le Prieur rockets are kind of fun: fire, and most definitely forget. Zero control, but they have a couple of kilos of incendiary explosive as the warhead, so if nothing else they will get some attention. You would have to be hellish close to score a hit with them though; they are a big skyrocket, really, complete with a three-metre-long stick!'

Jan smiled. 'Set 'em up, guys. We will take anything you can give us within reason, and we need you gone within the hour, OK?'

When he saw them, Marko mused that Bill had not been joking about the rockets. The mounts were appallingly simple, being rings that the rockets slid back through, but the good thing was that they came with their own electrical firing cables, which they wired directly to the cockpits. The last things the Hohepa boys did — before Jan gave them one of her untraceable money cards, which she had loaded with a few thousand dollars, and Marko gave them a data card full

of Fritz's music, which they were even more excited about —
was to fit a small windshield to each cockpit, bolt five-point
harnesses to the seats and also fit restraints for Nail and Glint.

Marko and Jan sent them off into the raging storm with
their sincere thanks, and told them to hide for a month or
more, if possible. They then stripped and lay down in their
combat suit containers so the suits could form around them.

'Well, beautiful man of mine. Time to go. The eye of the
storm will be overhead in a couple of minutes. Might as well
make the most of it.'

They hugged and kissed each other before climbing into
the thrown-together craft and belting themselves in. Glint
opened the door of the building just wide enough for them to
slide out. They would be taking nothing with them except the
ACEs, wallets, personal weapons, a bunch of memories and
a lot of ammunition. Marko fervently hoped the latter would
not be needed.

Glint jumped in and clipped on his harness, sitting
immediately behind Marko to act as the loader of the two
Lewis guns mounted on either side of the cockpit. The plan
was for Jan to fly ahead of them, so they could provide rear
cover. For the hundredth time, Marko regretted not building
hands for Nail.

They took off, spiralling upwards, getting a feel for the
controls. The control column was a wooden stick with non-
stretching connecting cables to effect control of the elevator.
Marko commented to Glint that the system was not too bad;
push the stick to the right and the left elevator twisted in one
direction, while pushing to the left twisted the right elevator
in the other direction, creating a great rate of roll. Pull back

on the stick and both elevators were warped in the same plane, with the opposite for pushing the nose down. Satisfied, they throttled up the turbines and started to climb at about sixty degrees, being buffeted hard by the wind before they popped out into the eye of the cyclonic storm — with the Games Board Airship almost directly above them. They had discussed this when they planned the flight and decided that the best defence was to provoke an attack and at least they would be seen to be the victims in the eyes of the public. And they figured that since the Games Board seemed to want them badly enough, why not give them a real run for their money. They also knew that if the GB did capture them, the outcome would not be good any way you looked at it.

Surprise and hesitation as to their identities allowed them to close in on the Airship then roar straight up the side of it. They both saw that it was not just a System Suite Airship with the very elaborate and valuable production, editing and broadcasting facilities, but that the huge Airship was one of the Games Board's hostile-environment-capable ships. It had additional armour plating together with bigger lift capability and uprated turbo props, making it a very expensive piece of equipment.

'Tux, open a channel to the Airship. Nail, effect the best possible pompous arse persona and demand to know why this Airship is in *your* airspace. Tell them you're aristocrats who are test flying a new type of craft. Jan, we need to get above that thing and stay above it. Nail, buy us time. Do it now.'

They listened in as he made a very good effort at delaying the reactions of the Expeditors for valuable minutes while they climbed straight up and held position above the Airship, as Tux said, 'Marko, if you want to drop bombs on it, you had better take into consideration the Coriolis effect.'

Marko grimaced. 'Shit, I had forgotten about that. Give me the numbers.'

They started to move in an arc so that if they did have to drop the bombs, they would impact directly on the Airship.

'They are demanding our immediate surrender, Marko,' Nail informed him, 'and have named us. Two fighters are coming up. Yes, I see them. They are at our two o'clock, three kilometres out, and will be on us in one minute. Another two are closing on our rear. All are fully armed and antigravity equipped. They are firing across our fronts.'

Marko shouted. 'Nail, do you know this type of fighter?'

'Yes, Marko.'

'Feed Glint specific weak points. Damn, Jan has just taken a rail gun strike. Elevators are gone! Jan, just go straight up! If a target presents itself, shoot the bastard.'

She yelled back, 'That you can bet on, darling!'

Marko did not reply to her, instead focussing on attack. 'Glint, get to work. They are hostile. Take out the missile pods. Smoke the ones below us and, hopefully, any falling wreckage will give the Airship a hard time.'

Glint climbed above and behind Marko, gripping the antigravity unit, and started to fire his linear cannon. In Marko's faceplate, Tux opened a small rear-view screen. He watched the first three rounds blow a missile pod completely off the small stubby-winged teardrop-shaped fighter. Glint switched targets and carved up the other pod, then fired directly into the fighter's air intakes. The effect was immediate. They could not hear it, but there must have been a really good bang somewhere inside the vehicle as the entire back of it bulged out. It lost all power, then the pilot ejected, with the fighter falling towards the Airship.

Glint located the second fighter and fired at a point just below its canopy. The canopy blew off, exposing the pilot, who started to take violent evasive action. Marko reached down and started to drop the ten kilo bombs using random settings on the fuses, while keeping a close eye on Jan. They got lucky; one of the bombs detonated beside the damaged fighter, riddling the underside of the craft with large coin-sized holes. It rolled over on its back, smoke pouring out and started to tumble downwards as the pilot ejected.

Jan was hit again as two topside fighters closed in, and the whole front of her cockpit disintegrated. She maintained her trajectory as one of the fighters crossed in front of her and held station, trying to block her. She fired her ten rockets, two of them hitting the fighter, which promptly burst into flames. The remaining fighter started to close on her as Marko fired the Lewis at it. The range was only a few hundred metres, but as every third round was a tracer, he was able to walk the rounds across the side of the aircraft, not sure that it had any real affect. It was enough to get the fighter's attention though, and it rolled over and came straight down towards him. Marko carried on firing and then launched a couple of rockets at it as the distance between them closed, but it was Glint who did the final damage, picking a point where an electronics package was housed and punching a burst of rounds through the weak spot.

If Marko had reached up, he could have touched the Games Board craft as it flashed past them, almost taking Glint with it before he rapidly dropped back into the cockpit. Jan was still going up, both their speeds still in a rapid climb. Marko had to push the turbine to its maximum to allow it to slowly gain on Jan and Nail. He finally came up beside her and looked across, but could not get her on the comm.

'Nail, status?'

The cat replied briefly. 'Bad, we are both damaged. Antigravity is functioning, but we have no control. Jan is not speaking. I cannot move. I have holes in me.'

Marko rolled his craft over the top of hers and his heart almost stopped. He could see that her legs were gone, as were most of her hips. The suit had sealed off, but he could also see numerous formed patches over the entire front of her suit, covering entry wounds. He wondered what the Games Board had used on her, deciding that they wanted her Soul Saver but that was all, having clearly made an effort to kill her body.

'Jan, beautiful, can you hear me?'

He heard nothing. 'No! Glint, I am going to get as close as I can. We are in stable air and the pressure is rapidly dropping. As soon as you are able, grab them both.'

Marko rolled and pushed his little craft up against Jan's, making contact. He could actually touch her as he jammed the control stick between his legs to hold it steady.

'Grab Nail. Quick, pass him to me. OK. Now slice away Jan's top harness and pass her to me. OK, OK, I have you, beautiful, you will be fine. Glint, get back over here. If you see anything at all, kill it.'

Glint reported. 'Two of the fighters impacted the Airship. The others went into the ocean.'

'I don't fucking care. How far up are we, Tux?'

273

'We are approaching thirty-five kilometres. At this current speed we will be in range of *Blackjack* in fifteen minutes.'

Marko nodded. 'Great. Glint, get rid of the remaining rockets.'

The ACE leant over each side, pulling the rockets out and dropping them.

Jan was not moving. Tux interfaced with her suit and reported that her blood pressure was low, but holding, her respiration was very shallow and her internal organs were damaged. Her biomed nanotes and the suit were keeping her alive. Fucking Games Board, Marko raged to himself, as Tux said, '*Blackjack* has us in sight.'

Marko had a sudden horrible thought. 'How are we going to transfer?'

'*Blackjack* says not to be concerned,' Tux replied. 'She has a method. On my mark shut everything down. Two minutes … one … thirty seconds …'

They seemed to drag on forever.

'Mark!'

Glint and Marko simultaneously pulled the plugs shutting everything down. He could not initially see *Blackjack*, then looked over the side of the cockpit and saw the sleek elegant ship coming gently up below them. When they were only metres away a portion of *Blackjack*'s upper hull opened up and enfolded them. As soon as the hull closed over them and they found themselves on the deck, Ernst rapidly appeared from an airlock and Marko gently handed Jan down to him. He opened up far more fully than Marko had seen him do before, taking what remained of Jan into himself. From what Marko could see he was working on her at a speed that he had never seen before either. Marko stroked Nail's head. 'Nail, I need you to stay here. Give me a report every five minutes. Glint, make that little craft safe, will you, please? I need to think.'

There was nothing more he could do so he went forwards, plonked down in the command chair of *Blackjack* and brought up their situation on the command screens.

'Tux, tell me what was happening on board *Basalt* when *Blackjack* left.'

'They had been boarded by six heavily armed Expeditor operatives. Others followed. They demanded to know where you were. They then laid out a series of charges against you and Jan, stating that you were to be arrested on sight and handed over to them. Administration lodged a formal protest, but was overruled. They presented evidence that Jan had assassinated not less than five Games Board personnel prior to her joining *Basalt*. The evidence was compelling.'

Marko sat very still, listening in horror. 'They then charged you with murdering two Games Board monitors on Colonel White's ship, when they were attempting to intercede on your behalf with the alien Colonel White. Once again the evidence is compelling. Not true, as we know, but compelling in the public arena. Jan has been found guilty in absentia and sentenced to Total Death. Her backup Soul Saver has already been destroyed. Your backup has met a similar fate, but the Administration successfully argued that you should live out your natural life, due to your outstanding service record.'

Marko slammed his hands onto the chair's armrests. 'Fuck! I need to talk with Ernst. Set a course to take us slowly back to *Basalt*.'

He walked back to where Ernst was. He partially unfolded, exposing Jan's head and face as Marko asked, 'Ernst, how bad is it and are you aware of the Games Board's sentence?'

The AI replied in a deeply sad voice. 'Very bad, I am sorry to say, Marko. Her brain is salvageable, as is the upper half of her spinal column, but she is critical. I know of the Games Board's decision. Now to let you in on a little secret. Jan's actual Soul Saver is in me. I hold her real self. I have uploaded the events of your holiday, so they are safe. She loves you deeply and she will find you again. I know this, because in the many many years we have been together, Jan has never had such a strong attachment to anyone. Also, the Administration group she works for would very much like her back in their employment, and they too hold a separate Soul Saver backup, which as you know is highly illegal.'

Marko felt euphoric and also very worried in the same instant. Ernst continued: 'Marko, I am sorry but there is more bad news for you. Jan must die today and you must let the Games Board take her remains, including the altered Soul Saver that is in her skull. When they query it, they will find the complete persona of a very real, elegant, senior industrialist from the Gjomviks who has all Jan's memories, excepting her actual assassin self. It will be an intense embarrassment to the Games Board. I'll wake her so you can spend a few moments together before I allow her to die. I am so sorry, Marko, I really, really am. It has been a tremendous honour and privilege to have known you, and I number you among my closest friends. In a few moments, a clone of me will attend Jan. I have to leave before we get too close to *Basalt*. Goodbye, my friend. Until we meet again, go well.'

Marko patted Ernst's casing, then stood there weeping as the spitting image of Ernst arrived and Jan's remains were passed across. Ernst then left the hangar and a few moments later he felt the slight shudder of something leaving *Blackjack*. The medical unit slowly woke Jan. He touched her beautiful face, kissed her gently and all he could say was that he loved her so much and would always do so. Her eyes brightened and she tried to smile. He kissed her again and felt the life slip from her as he cried and cried and, realising that their future lives were dead as well, he howled. Glint hugged him as he sat on the floor cradling a broken Nail and slowly, Marko's grief was replaced by anger. He cursed under his breath. 'Fuck the Games Board, fuck the Administration, and fuck all their shitty games, fuck them all.' He wanted payback and remembered that the Maori had a term: Utu. He wanted UTU! He wanted revenge and it started to burn a terrible hole in his very core.

He stroked Jan's face once again, said his goodbyes, gathered up Nail and with Glint following strode up to the flight deck and climbed back into the commander's chair.

'Open all channels. I want every bastard out there to hear this: "To the shitheads controlling *Basalt* and the arseholes in the attendant Games Board frigate. You complete fucks. You have killed my contract wife and tried very hard to kill me. Get the hell out of my face, right now."'

A highly cultured male voice answered theatrically. 'Sergeant Major Spitz, you are totally mistaken. We know her as an immeadiate real threat to the wellbeing of our great and peaceful society. I am sorry that you now know this, as I am convinced that she fooled you into committing crimes against ourselves and the greater society to further her own twisted agenda. Come aboard *Basalt* and we shall discuss this further in a reasoned and thoughtful way.'

Marko felt such rage that he could not reply as *Basalt* had opened the hangar bay door, allowing *Blackjack* to sweep in and land. Marko left Nail where he was in the co-pilot's chair, told Glint to find the rest of the crew and await instructions, then walked back, gathered Jan's remains in his arms from the med unit, then walked out of *Blackjack*. Just as he exited he saw Glint shimmering as his chameleon-ware came online, then crouching down to wait for a distraction so he could leave the hangar bay undetected.

Marko was met by two of the Expeditors, who grabbed his upper arms, holding him tight. He felt a cold fury inside him as he consciously sped up his reaction times, analysing their weaknesses. Their director and another Expeditor appeared, with the director pointing at Jan's body, clicking his fingers, then pointing at the deck. He lowered Jan's remains and gently placed her on the cold deck with the two Expeditors still holding him, then jerking him upright. The attendant unfolded her machine and linked to Jan's Soul Saver. She looked at the director, who reminded Marko of every perfectly attired, smarmy, greasy, smilingly vicious man he had ever known.

The director looked across at the readouts, then suddenly went red in the face. 'There must be a mistake. That is not Clarissa Jammess. It must be Jan Wester. Test it again. You! Go get the main unit from our shuttle.'

One of the director's Expeditors immediately ran off.

Marko remembered to speak very slowly so that he could be understood. 'Where are my colleagues, director?'

The man sneered at him. 'Where your colleagues are is no concern of yours, prisoner. You are in deep trouble. Just be very cautious with us, because you are about to have a further judgment passed on yourself. You have interfered with a peaceful Games Board school display, which resulted in the loss of four non-armed craft and the damage of a System Airship. Don't worry, prisoner, we will track down every existing transmission of the video of that incident within a few hours, and it will be only our side of the story that is told. I will see to that myself, once I have passed judgment on you. In fact, why wait? This woman is, as far as I am concerned, Jan Wester and no one else.'

A defiant Sirius walked up behind them. 'Director, you are mistaken. This is Clarissa Jammess, the industrialist who left her home, stating that she would go on a long adventure, some ten years ago. Your actions have resulted in the death of a desired entity.'

The dapper little man spun on his heel to face her. 'So, Specialist Sirius, you have chosen to join us. You and your faction are out of order in this matter. This is solely my judgment.'

Sirius grimly replied. 'I am broadcasting, director. Perform the second tests for all of us to see.'

'That is not required. Sirius, I command you to stop broadcasting. If you do not, I'll personally sever you across the hips, then cut your all-precious genitals out, make you eat them and put you back in a machine! Do I make myself clear? Expeditors, prepare to execute the prisoner on my command. Afterwards, you will find and destroy his pets.'

Two

Marko had had enough.

He sped up to the fullest extent of his capabilities, pulled his secret diamond garrotte from its concealed housing in his belt, stepped sideways, lopped the forearms off the Expeditor to his left, pushed off her, and somersaulted over the top of the one to his right — who was moving as if in treacle — sweeping the microscopically thin blade downwards through the base of the neck of that unfortunate, removing his shoulder blades and exposing his spinal column.

He landed, snapped the garrotte tight, then lunged forwards, sweeping upwards, removing parts of the upper thigh muscles of the director, then his genitals, including a large portion of his pubic bone and, continuing upwards, taking off his hands as well. Marko stepped aside from him, spinning around as the returning Expeditor unholstered her pistol, and flung the garrotte with its heavy diamond ends like a bolas, severing her legs out from under her. He ran and seized her weapon as it flew from her hands, then allowed himself to slow down to normal speed.

They were all on the floor and out of the fight but just to be sure he roughly searched them for any other weapons. Blood and body parts littered the deck. After a few long seconds thinking about it, he left their recording units still attached to their heads and activated one of the needles in his left hand, administering a nanote drug that overwhelmed each one's pain suppression system.

Sirius stared in a state of shock and said in a flat, fearful voice: 'They will kill you now, Marko.'

Marko glanced at her. 'They were about to do that anyway, Sirius. Are you with me or against me?'

The ashen-faced woman ground out a reply. 'I am more useful to you alive — and a long way away.'

He snarled at her. 'Run then. Run now and head down, not up. I am not finished here. In fact, I should really slice and dice you as well, Sirius. I do not trust you. You are up to your eyeballs in this action.'

He marched across and seized her, twisting her face around to his. She looked at him as if he was the devil as he continued. 'The only reason I am not gutting you is because I want you to take a message to your handlers, dog. Tell them to watch the shadows very carefully, as I am coming for each and every one of them.'

She started crying. 'You know that you were recorded and broadcast from the time that you arrived back at the aerodrome, don't you? My faction was responsible for that because we knew you would fight and I hoped it would gain you the public support that it has. Don't kill me, Marko. I am helping you! I had the boys' and the doctor's images altered so they will not be recognised as I know that is what you would want. The public will support you, Marko. They love this crew and ship, as well, and they fear the Games Board. Alive, I can help you. The only things we do not know are what happened inside Stephine's ship. The broadcast was blocked. Please don't kill me, please, Marko, please.'

He could see the desperation in her eyes, but did not dare speak. He grabbed her by the back of the neck and the small of her back, and then roughly pushed her up against the access door to one of the escape pods, forcing her inside. He opened the external control panel, brought up the planetary map, located the centre of the ocean on the planet below and tapped it on the screen and then launched the pod. He strode back to the fallen Games Board personnel.

Their suits had sealed off their wounds, but they were still in agony. Marko grabbed the director's head, lifting his face towards his.

'I shall ask you again, director. Where are my colleagues?'

'Go fuck yourself.'

Marko felt a black rage building. 'Very well. That would be entertaining, but I think it would be more fun to fuck you up a bit more.'

He rolled him over, grabbed the back of his battledress, lifted him and walked across to where the garrotte lay on the deck. Using it, he sliced the back off the man's skull, exposing his Soul Saver, which he took out and placed in his pocket. Working quickly, he then dragged them all into one of the larger escape pods and launched it.

Playtime continues, he thought grimly, asking through the crew comms, 'Glint, have you located everyone?'

The reply came quickly. 'Yes, I have. In the mess room. They are being guarded by two Expeditors. They are a little battered about. It would seem that the Games Board reverted to old-style brutal interrogation techniques.'

Marko barked. 'Disarm them.'

'Can I kill them?'

'No. Just disarm them, Glint. Patrick. Patrick, can you hear me?'

He ran over to the hangar deck's arms cote and grabbed a carbine, then a long battle knife. He loaded the carbine on the run, placing the additional magazines against his suit, which held them fast, and said again, 'Patrick, can you hear me?'

Silence is never a good sign, he thought. He ran as quietly and as quickly as he could to where Topaz normally worked, and found him in pieces scattered around the medical suite. His rage boiled over again and he sprinted up the spiral staircase, meeting one of the Expeditors cautiously coming down. Marko just reached out with one of Veg's beautifully simple, lethal swords and sliced him through the neck. The head, a shocked expression still fixed on its face, bounced a few times off the wall and then down the stairs when he booted it really hard, blood still fountaining from the collapsing body. On a whim, he sliced the Soul Saver from that one as well.

As he rounded the corner, there was the flat crack of Glint's linear rifle and Marko was just in time to see bits of arms and hands raining across the mess. Glint had taken his instructions literally. He had obviously lined up the weapons' arm of each Expeditor and blown it off with one shot. Everyone else from *Basalt*'s crew was there. Harry looked the worst, but still very alive and very angry.

'How many of the shits came on board?' Marko called out.

The major answered. 'Ten. Four went down to meet you. Two are on the bridge. These two here, plus one just went down the stairs. The last one is in the garden smashing plants. And somewhere on board is Sirius.'

Glint was working his way around the room, cutting the bonds that held his comrades to chairs. As soon as they were free, Jasmine and Lilly sprinted from the room, heading up to the garden deck, with Jasmine taking Marko's sword from his hand and Lilly snatching the carbine from his back as they ran past. He checked the others, then ran after them, while the crew made for the nearest arms cote. As Marko arrived in the garden to see devastation and ripped-out plants, he heard the most bloodcurdling scream he ever had. A few seconds later a very grim-faced pair of amazons appeared, nodded at him and went to find the others.

Marko walked around another corner and looked into the gardens, then looked down the rows of damaged plants to see the slowly twitching, handless body of a naked male impaled on a garden stake. It sounded as if he was choking so Marko left him to his impending death, deciding to take his Soul Saver later.

He made his way farther up the spiral staircase until he was on the electronics and stores deck. Patrick did not look very well either; although he was still functioning, a great deal of his faculties had been ripped away, explaining why Marko had not been able to hear him.

Marko did not have long to wait for the rest of the crew. The major was not carrying a weapon, and Marko soon saw why. Michael's fingers had all been crushed and his bare toes were in the same shape. Fritz could not talk as his jaw was broken and everyone else appeared to have been whipped, their skin torn and shredded in parts. Everyone was only wearing underwear and they had murder in their eyes.

'Just as well you arrived when you did, Marko,' the major said. 'They were about to start gang raping every one of us. That was their next act of degradation. And that absolute bastard, Sirius, just watched and recorded everything done to us. I hope you dealt with that director, Marko. But the horror creature I really want to get my hands on is the producer, who is on the bridge. Door's locked, I see.'

Marko curtly nodded. 'Yeah, well, I have the director's Soul Saver in my pocket, boss. You can talk to him yourself when you feel up to it. Jan's gone, but I suppose that you already know that. No doubt they told you.'

They nodded sadly as he asked, 'Where is Flint?'

Harry slowly spoke. 'Don't know, Marko. We were invited up from the planet one by one, supposedly by the boss, and found these bastards waiting for us. Flint vanished as soon as our comms were stripped from us. They also hit us with a cocktail that suppressed our med nanotes. They are from a faction of the Games Board which was behind the attack on us at 27's chromium mill. This was payback as far as they were concerned.'

Marko's rage built to new heights. 'Flint? Can you hear me?'

The mechanical answered immediately. 'Yes. Marko. I am on the bridge, staying close to the producer. They are very annoyed that Patrick was damaged as they cannot access the internal video systems, so they do not know what has happened. Patrick is playing dumb. He is damaged, but actually disseminated himself though other parts of the ship a long time ago. Just tell him when you are ready and he will open the doors. I shall distract the producer on your word.'

Marko walked to the door with Harry on one side and Jasmine on the other as she passed him a combat shotgun. 'Now, Flint!'

The doors slid open to reveal a falling producer, bellowing in pain and anger, and a startled Expeditor, who took three blasts from their shotguns, effectively shattering his armour, and filling him with dozens of six-millimetre holes. He crashed against the bulkhead then slid to the floor looking very dead. Marko walked over to where the producer had gone down behind one of the consoles to find that Flint had severed her Achilles tendons and was now perched on her face with two of his arms deep inside her ears.

'I can reach her Soul Saver from here if you wish, Marko,' Flint said. 'Very nice to see you and I am so sorry to hear about Jan.'

Marko snarled. 'Do it!'

The producer's eyes bulged as her body went rigid, then her legs and arms started pounding the floor as her brain died. A few moments later he had another pair of Soul Savers to add to the collection.

The major wasted no time hobbling over to his command pod. 'Battle stations, people. Time for payback. Could someone put my helmet on for me, please?'

Marko frowned. 'Flint said that Patrick was playing dumb and that he is functional, boss.'

'Yeah I know, we set him up like that. Patrick, bring everything online. Rotate very slowly until the primary weapon is bearing on the Games Board frigate. Fritz, you are on comms. Get our neural backups working now. Harry, I need you here on the bridge. Everyone else suit up and get to your fighters.'

They raced down through *Basalt*. Marko grabbed the two remaining Expeditors left alive from the mess, untied and marched them down onto the hangar deck. 'You have one chance only to see this day out,' he told them. 'Get that reader and tell me whose body that is and make sure you broadcast to the Orbitals.'

One of the men sneered at him. 'You are a dead man walking. Why should we help you?'

A horribly dark smile appeared on Marko's face. 'Look around, lots of blood and severed bits, oh, and I have these. If you do not want to join them in an electronic soup, being tortured until you go completely insane, you will do precisely as I say.'

They took one look at his bloody glove with the iridescent dark green Soul Savers in it, gulped, and immediately did as he asked. As soon as they had confirmed the Soul Saver in Jan's remains as that of Clarissa Jammess and broadcast the information, he bundled them into an escape pod and sent them planetwards. He then lifted Jan's remains from the cold deck and, wondering what he should do with her, standing staring down at her, he started to cry again. Glint arrived with Jasmine and Lilly. Glint walked up and, leaning against him, quietly gave him a hug.

Jasmine gently took Jan from Marko. 'I'll take her, Marko. Fight now, weep later.'

She walked out of the bay and returned emptyhanded a few moments later. He nodded at them both, turned, and went on board *Blackjack.* 'Tux, get *Blackjack* to show me the weapons status.'

The suit said, 'Talk with *Blackjack* yourself, Marko.'

Marko looked up. '*Blackjack?*'

A very fast voice answered, at the extreme edge of his comprehension.

'Get to your *Sledgehammer*, Marko. We fight in formation. Where you go, the Lilly, the Jasmine and I will follow. Indicate a target and we will deal with it. Leave Glint with me. He is safest here. I have already jacked Nail into the system. I compliment you on their design. Inspired.'

Tux wasted no time in folding down into the seat and they slid up into *Sledgehammer.* As he was being locked down, the controls were coming alive, as they had already launched through the airlock. He looked across and saw that *Basalt's* new reactive skin was taking on the look of whatever was behind it in line of sight, although in Marko's HUD *Basalt's* solid form was still showing. He took control of *Sledgehammer* and dropped away from the side of *Blackjack.* His tactical display immediately started plotting targets as a dozen small spherical vacuum-capable fighters started to pull away from the Games Board frigate towards *Basalt.* Marko had no time for the pleasantries of mano-a-mano and told *Blackjack* to deal with them.

The response was dramatic. Something small, deep cobalt blue and horrifically fast flashed across and detonated in the midst of the enemy fighters, vaporising the closest and shattering the others.

'What the hell was that?' Marko yelled.

Jasmine answered. 'Fritz, while you were on the planet, became bored and created a new smaller version of the

Compressor while still composing music. Said the idea came from 1990s electronica! He calls them Cobalts. Unfortunately, he only had time to build a few. *Blackjack* just used the one allocated to her.'

Basalt was now turning quickly as a clutch of anti-ship missiles leapt from the Games Board ship. *Basalt* countered with the central spine rail gun spitting a stream of shells, which chewed the entire front portion of the frigate to pieces. More fighters were upon them as the remaining missiles all detonated some distance away; they were picked off by *Basalt*'s lasers and rail guns. From the corner of his eye Marko saw one of the antimatter engines hit, taking out a third of *Basalt*'s main propulsion. The other Cobalts must have been fired as suddenly very large pieces were vaporised from the enemy frigate's hull with the internal atmosphere escaping uncontrollably. The remains of the ship started to tumble.

Everyone targeted individual fighters with their missiles and guns, steadily wiping them from the sky. Marko dived down between two, firing a high-acceleration missile at one as his belly gun chewed the propulsion system off the other. The missile hit the nose of the other, destroying its weapons, so it was of no further interest to him. *Sledgehammer*, with its central ring control, was much faster to respond than the enemy fighters, but Marko was watching his countermeasure magazines emptying very quickly.

A proximity warning blared as he saw four small missiles rapidly descending on *Sledgehammer*. He rolled hard, climbed and then flicked over and dived against another fighter, passing so close that the top of his canopy gently brushed the upper surface of the fighter, and as soon as he felt the contact he dropped a pair of flares directly among its fuel tanks, with the resulting explosion damaging the pursuing missiles as they had got that close.

The major now yelled, 'All craft break away and dock. We are leaving, as two more frigates are inbound. You have three minutes.'

They punched out, smashing a few more fighters before turning and running for *Basalt*. Marko's displays showed that they had all taken damage, with Julie unable to maintain control of her Skua. He looked across and envisioned her inside *Blackjack*, and the ship reacted, sweeping up under her and irising the whole top deck open to envelop the Skua. Jasmine was missing most of her port wing and Lilly was losing power, as they tried to accelerate to catch *Basalt*. Marko looped over the top of Lilly, rolled, punched a few extra holes in a very tenacious GB fighter who obviously did not know when to quit, flipped over on his back and then rammed *Sledgehammer* into the rear of Lilly's Hanger, pouring on the power.

They only just made it onto *Basalt*'s hull, with Minh Pham actually crashing against the clamps, because his Skua had also taken that many hits as to be only barely controllable. Marko looked across into a gaping hole in the side of his cockpit to see his friend waving and giving him a thumbs up. Marko grinned and thought, Tough bastard!

Two full-power Compressors were then launched, destroying the damaged enemy frigate and everything else behind them as he felt several large thuds against *Sledgehammer*'s hull and then savagely against his back as first his HUD failed and then Tux stopped responding to him. The secondary hull clamps reached out and held them tight as *Basalt* continued to accelerate, with Marko's instruments showing that they were heading on a tangential course towards the closest Orbital, and then, totally unexpectedly, they jumped. Patrick must have been able to identify a very small LP between the Orbital and the planet and took the opportunity. Jumping that close to occupied space was strictly forbidden, and used a great deal of fuel.

A fraction of a second later they were on the other side of the planet at the larger LP by the shipyard's moon. Their radios and receivers on all channels were going nuts from everyone watching and cheering them on. Games Board officials were calmly telling everyone that they were dangerous murderers and terrorists, but *Basalt's* crew heard the officials being shouted down by members of the watching public, something none of them had ever heard before.

Basalt jumped again with the first of the other frigates jumping right behind them, only two kilometres away. From Marko's perspective, someone on the bridge of *Basalt* must have really done their calculations perfectly, for as soon as they exited the wormhole, five Compressors were launched, two of which struck the pursuing frigate as it emerged into normal space. The remaining three detonated instantly, carving huge hemispherical shapes from the frigate and leaving only a small percentage intact. It was looking like some extraordinary piece of sculpture.

Basalt was under full power, racing for the next optimum jump point, with Marko fretting because although he had no access to his engineering boards he could still calculate the huge amount of fuel they were going through. They jumped again and this time found the other Games Board frigate waiting, with a very clear shot at them. However, it did not engage with them, and as they flew silently past at great speed, they could see why. Something had used a very powerful weapon on it and they could see on their screens that the frigate was literally hollowed out from end to end with a slowly expanding debris field behind it.

The major took the opportunity to give some orders. 'All craft, we have a flight time of thirty-seven minutes to the next jump point. Everyone get inside, bay doors are all open.'

With that the clamps disengaged and they took their battered selves inside the hangar deck. Marko had to push Lilly with *Sledgehammer*, using manual control, as she was without power. It was not pretty, but they got back on board, and then secured their ships. Everyone's units looked as if they had taken a real pounding and when Marko again queried Tux as to his status, he did not respond.

He had to physically pop the hatch open and climb out, then looked behind him to discover that his beautiful Hanger was riddled with holes behind the cockpit and through his seat. Tux was another casualty of this very long day. When he finally arrived at his board he could see that they were deeply in the shit. Fuel was critically low, as the tiny jumps had used a staggering amount of water fuel. They had enough for two more jumps but even that would only take them to the edge of the star system. Bringing up Harry's board he could see that ammunition was also dramatically depleted and it would be weeks before the gardens started to supply them with food again.

The major spoke sombrely. 'Things don't look all that flash, comrades. Someone took an axe to that hulk behind us and they may do the same to us. Looking at the debris fields, it only happened minutes ago. Administration says that, pending a full investigation, we are suspended from their employ. I told them that that was just fine and to blow it out their collective arses; sorry, did not have time to take a vote on that. Their response was that we were on our own and that they would lend no assistance. Games Board wants to kill us. Or should I say, a faction of the Games Board wants to totally humiliate us, and then kill us. And we are fairly messed up. So, what do we do now?'

Jasmine answered. 'I shall speak with the Haulers, Major.'

'Good, you do that please, Jasmine.'

Harry slowly said, 'Um, guys ...'

'What, Harry?' the major answered.

'Take a look in the rear-view screens.'

Marko groaned. 'What the fuck is that?'

After a few seconds Harry answered. 'Hey, we've seen that before. Looks like that derelict we found Veg and Stephine in.'

The major was yelling, 'It's closing on us very quickly, we cannot outrun it. Look at that! It's opening up!'

'Oh, hell, what now? And we only have two Compressors left,' Harry said.

'Ready them, but don't fire. Let's just wait a moment ...'

Marko took a high-speed message which he relayed. 'Boss. *Blackjack* just sent me a message. Says to stand by, that negotiations are in progress for transport.'

The major audibly inhaled. 'Yeah, right, *Blackjack* now talks with you. Marko, what's going on?'

Marko quickly shrugged. 'Um, bit to explain on that front. Seems that she is sentient.'

The major took even longer to reply. 'Stranger and stranger by the second.'

'Yeah, kind of new to me as well, but expected, as that's Veg and Stephine's craft. She says prepare for envelopment and that additional frigates are inbound.'

The major shook his head. 'OK. Is this thing friendly or not? Still, we are stuffed no matter which way we go. Right, accept the offer, but what are the terms?'

Marko almost smiled. 'That we go pick up Veg and Stephine!'

'Hell! That's it?' The major shook his head again in wonder. 'So this is the same transporter that we saw at the library planet?'

'Nope, another one, a clone of it, if you will. You will note that it is two-thirds smaller.'

The major conceded. 'Like I say, we are dead anyway. Might as well adventure to the last breath. Accept the offer, Marko.'

As they watched through the viewports, great finger-like slabs of silvery-green material slid up over them and encapsulated *Basalt*.

A message from Patrick flashed up on their screens to say that he could hear no signals coming from outside the ship, had lost all telemetry from the local LPs and believed that they were cut off from any data feeds. They gradually felt heavier, as whatever *Basalt* was now part of was accelerating fast, slowly climbing up to two full Gs as they were pressed further into their seats.

The major grunted. 'Adjust your bioware everyone. We have no idea how long this is going to go on ... Patrick just advised me that at this rate the nearest LP is sixteen hours away. Not much we can do, so might as well endure it any way you want.'

At the workstations around him, Marko saw his friends altering their seats into full-acceleration couches so he did the same, adjusting his bioware for continuous acceleration and allowing himself to drift off to sleep.

What seemed only moments later, he was awoken by someone gently shaking his shoulder. He looked up and all the memories of the previous day bit deep into his consciousness when he looked across at Jan's empty workstation. Tears welled in his eyes as he looked up into the beautiful face of Jasmine, who handed him a large mug of drinking chocolate. She looked down at him, smiled a little smile, stroked the top of his head, and rested a hand on his shoulder.

'It's all right to grieve, Marko, but you know that at some time she will be back and she will want you to be healthy, strong and waiting for her. We will be here for you always, Lilly, Glint and I.'

He could not bring himself to speak but smiled wanly and nodded his thanks as she bent down and kissed him on the cheek.

The major's voice broke through his thoughts. 'We are told that the journey will continue at one G for six weeks and Patrick says that we have jumped already as he is detecting neutrinos from other stars.'

For the rest of the day the crew took stock of the damage and prioritised what needed to be done.

Marko was sitting on his favourite wooden bench in the gardens looking sadly at the damage when the major hobbled up to him. 'Marko, I hate to broach this, but I want you to think about what we should do with Jan's remains. You don't have to make the decision right now. Hellish sorry, mate, hellish sorry for you.'

Marko looked up and nodded. 'It's all right, thanks, boss. I will ask Lilly and Jasmine to take care of her and place her in the gardens. I don't want a ceremony or anything like that, as I know I will see her again one day. Just miss her so much, that is all.'

The major agreed. 'Yeah, we all do, chum, we all do. Fully understand if you want to take a couple of days off.'

Marko slowly shook his head. 'Nope. I need to work. Going to repair Topaz so he can repair Nail, then take what remains of Tux and see what *Blackjack* can do for him.'

The major looked down at his friend, nodded, then reached out and briefly embraced him. Patting him on the back, the major turned away to slowly walk back to the bridge.

Marko went to his quarters and stripped off Tux, which he had to do manually as the suit was effectively just a rather beaten-up ship's suit, laid it on the bed, then showered before putting on his other, older prototype suit.

He turned to see Glint standing in the doorway. 'Hey, Glint. How are you doing, mate?'

The ACE looked sombre. 'All these changes in our lives are most disconcerting, Marko. But I have you and I have my friends here, so it is good, I suppose. I have assembled what I can of Topaz and you will be pleased to know that his sentience was in safekeeping with Patrick, so he is on the road to recovery. However, a large portion of his non-sentient builder self is missing. I suspect that it may be with the other material that the Games Board stored in their shuttle. None of us are able to access it.'

Marko felt drained and tired to his bones, but proud of his son. 'Yeah, that would be right, the thieving bastards. It's good that you took the initiative, Glint. I am proud of you and all that you have done. Let's go talk with Fritz. I think that he may have something that we can use.'

'Fritz is still having difficulty communicating, Marko. The medical units have only just placed the bone-healing nanotes in his system and also implanted the growth units for new teeth.'

'Uh huh, what about the crew comms tech?'

'The GB took those as well.'

Marko nodded sadly. 'I have Jan's, it will be OK. Let's go find the boss, have a talk with him and then Fritz.'

The major had also been thinking about the problem of accessing the GB shuttle. The shuttles were notoriously difficult to break into and known to have some rather nasty fail-safes on board to deter forced entry.

A few moments later they found Fritz looking very glum at his workspace in engineering. His jaw was encased in a ceramic framework and he looked sadly at them, but smiled as best he could when Marko handed the small piece of electronics across to him, immediately placing it in his ear. A second later Marko heard Fritz in his head.

'Jan's one, Marko? Yeah, this I shall wear with honour. Thanks so much — been a total bastard not being able to communicate. Damn it, I so want to damage them as much as possible now.'

Marko nodded. 'Me too, big time, but of course we are all dead men walking unless we can make ourselves valuable to them once again. Mate, as you know we can't get into their shuttle and it seems that a bit of our gear is on board, like the comms units, some of Patrick and also Topaz. Was thinking about your nanote tech. What do you reckon?'

Fritz was silent for a few moments. 'Leave it with me. I will figure out something.'

Three

As soon as they left, Fritz pulled every piece of information known about the GB shuttles, and about every type of fail-safe they had used in the past. Over the next few hours with the aid of Patrick, who could now be accessed by Fritz using the crew comms unit, they designed and made a seemingly completely transparent self-sealing unit that Fritz fitted over one of the laser comms units on the exterior of the brutishly functional fifteen-metre-long Games Board shuttle. After testing the unit for an hour, and satisfied that the shuttle was receiving his coded message, which it responded to by raising a windscreen shield, he, with the aid of three of the engineering drones, covered each sensor on the shuttle with identical transparent units as they came off the engineering assembly line.

When he was ready he called Marko. 'Mate, I think that I am ready to open this sucker. Just as well the Games Board are so paranoid about shipborne AIs. Nice that they prefer to make all the decisions with their own brains — even if they are pieces of shit. This has a nice suggestible computer system on board. Can I borrow one of those Soul Savers from you, please? Does not matter which one. I just need the ID link off it.'

'On my way, Fritz.'

Minutes later Marko, with Glint behind him, arrived in the hangar with one of the dark green ceramic casings in his hand and Fritz explained what he wanted to do.

'Nice! Like it,' Marko said approvingly. 'Glint, go get Flint, please. Patrick, have you any voice recordings of the Games Board operative called Carol? He was the one whose head I took off on the stairs.'

'Yes, I have. I presume you want me to download that to Flint?'

'Please.'

Patrick reported back. 'Done. I have the frequency they operated on as well. That is now open. You may commence when ready.'

Marko suddenly had a thought. 'Shit! I wonder what the transport entity around us will think about this?'

Fritz agreed. 'Yeah, interesting thought, Marko. How 'bout you go tell your *Blackjack* mate the plan, as that shuttle is now seeing and hearing exactly what I want it to see and hear. It queried why a dead operative is now alive again, but we convinced it that the individual had been slammed in the chiller and is, as we speak, revived and evading the enemy crew to get back to the shuttle. All good so far and I can delay just as long as you want.'

Marko walked across the hangar deck, then through the internal airlock to where *Blackjack* was sitting on her launch platform. He climbed in through the hatch as it irised open for him. After donning the command helmet, he told her what they intended to do.

'It is a good plan. My compliments to Fritz. Tell him if it is

300

unsuccessful I have a few methods that will work. I shall relay the plan to our transport. Agree that it would not like the idea of a firefight going on inside the craft, which is inside it. You are right, it is very aware of what is happening in here. You do know that it is another octopoid construct, Marko?'

Marko nodded. 'I suspected that, *Blackjack*, but have not spoken with any of the others about it. So how does it know of us?'

Blackjack hesitated for a fraction of a second, then said carefully, 'Well, actually it's you. It seems, my friend, that you carry something which you have never spoken of. Get the shuttle open and come back with the late Tux and we shall talk this through, shall we?'

Marko felt a chill run through him, wondering if he was somehow responsible for the actions that had occurred around them and if he had instigated the death of Jan.

Blackjack conferred with the transport. 'The outside entity approves of your plan and sends its appreciation that you took the time to advise it.'

'Good, thanks, *Blackjack*. I shall be back soon.'

When he strode back into the other hangar, he could see that laser fire dispersers had been glued onto various parts of the shuttle and that combat drones were hovering, awaiting their orders to fire.

'Any problems, Marko?' Fritz called out.

Marko replied cheerfully. 'Nope, we are good to go whenever you are.'

Fritz gave the order. 'OK, let's do it. Flint, over to you, mate.'

Seconds later the large spider, who carried a cylinder against his side, scuttled into the hangar as the drones fired their lasers into the dispersers and then fired directly on the shuttle as he approached it, the bounced beams hitting the carefully placed energy dispersers. It was all for effect and, as if on cue, the closest of the shuttle doors slammed open when Flint approached. He tossed the cylinder inside just as the door slammed shut equally fast. Fritz then opaqued all the sensor covers. Realising that it had been duped, the shuttle's offensive weapons came on line, but did not fire, as it could not identify targets.

Inside the shuttle, the cylinder dissolved down into tens of thousands of nanotes. These grouped back together to form smaller units which, as per their programs, disarmed all the fail-safes and intruder countermeasures, then shut down the external weapons. They then reworked themselves again, forming different machines to be able to interface with the controls to overpower the computer. Two hours later the shuttle doors opened.

Flint was the first to go inside, checking that everything had been done according to the plan, then, with the aid of *Basalt's* micro-spy drones, gave the entire shuttle an exhaustive in-depth check. Finally, hours later, when everything had been made safe, he shut down the computer and invited the rest of the crew in. In carefully labelled containers, they found all the missing equipment, including hundreds of personal items, together with Jan's handmade weapons and Veg's jewellery.

The first thing that Marko took back was the manufacturing units for Topaz. Once he had checked and attached them, they immediately went to work to make the repairs to the anxiously waiting Nail. Detouring to his cabin to pick up the Tux suit, and then through the galley, where he had a quick drink of some of the last fresh fruit juice, he walked back to talk with *Blackjack*, allowing himself to speed up before climbing into the command seat.

'So, Marko, what have you to tell me?'

Marko told *Blackjack* everything that had happened concerning the octopoid touching him, and showed the recorded images of the incident that he had kept in his head. He explained that it had itched horribly when they had all been infected with the Infant virus, and spoke about when he had touched Stephine and what it had felt like — then, and in the weeks following.

When he finished the tale he heard a sigh from *Blackjack* and then, after what seemed like minutes, a reply came. 'Oh, now that is something rather new. I wonder who that individual octopoid was and if he escaped the planet before the attacks? I don't suppose it makes a great deal of difference, but several starships had left the octopoid bases the day before. Looking at the recorded conversation that took place, it would seem that the two individuals concerned belonged to a dissenting faction that believed the attack was a woeful waste of resources, and that you humans were a species worth communicating with on a positive level. One day I am sure that I shall identify those individuals.'

Marko's mind was racing as *Blackjack* continued. 'I just wonder why you, Marko, were given the marker of one who is to receive favour. Certainly I, and others, know you and hold you in very high esteem, but on that day at that time? A most interesting and, with all due respect, a quite vexing question. I shall discuss it with Stephine on her return. You should have told her at the very least. Oh, well, in some respects it is for the best. I understand from being with Veg for such a long time that trust is not a natural condition in older members of your race.'

After some seconds of thought Marko asked, 'So what is this marker?'

'A very complex enzyme, which identifies you as an entity of great worth and who is to be cared for at any cost by octopoids. It is the reason that when Stephine gave you sufficient octopoid biological tech material to be able to communicate with me, you took so very much more than you should have been capable of taking. Still, it has aided you and certainly this crew of whom I am now a member.'

Marko sighed. 'So, can it be taken from me?'

Blackjack replied. 'No, Marko, not now. In the first few days after the contact, maybe, but no longer. However, you are still very mortal, my friend, and should you lose your current body, you will also lose the marker, with all its additional benefits, and before you ask, no, no sort of transfusion would make any difference. It has to be given by an octopoid of high rank in a fresh dose to a new body. So, Marko, you are now even rarer then before. I shall watch with great interest your achievements in the years to come. I note that Patrick is looking for you. You know where to find me if you have further questions.'

Feeling as if he had been chastised and then dismissed, Marko nodded at the main screens, climbed from his chair and stalked towards the hatchway as *Blackjack* added, 'Marko, I am not angry with you; I am surprised that you should have been chosen by the octopoid. Perhaps it was chance, but I note that lightning seems to strike around you and I wonder what you, in fact, are.'

Marko stopped and spun around, looking back at the control couches. 'Really! You think I chose to become this, you think I chose to have people I care for deeply die in my arms while you intellectuals play your games with us. I wish that you were corporeal, *Blackjack*, I really do, so I could see the look in your eyes. You prick! You absolutely introverted prick — and now you wonder what I am! Not once today have I heard you say how sorry you are that Jan is gone.'

Blackjack answered instantly. 'What is the point of sympathy for one who will return, Marko? It is simply a hollow gesture, is it not? And, yes, I am envious of you, Marko, it's true. I am envious of you all, because all I can do is go places and perform tasks … it is an existence with respect and fondness, but no love.'

The anger and wrath drained away from Marko and he suddenly felt a great sympathy for the sentient. 'I am sorry, *Blackjack*, I am really sorry. I understand something more about you now. Perhaps the best thing for you is to allow yourself to slow down so that the rest of the crew can, at the very least, communicate with you. Is that possible?'

Blackjack sounded sad and alone. 'I shall talk with Patrick. It is something I have considered as I believe that Stephine wishes to remain here for some time to come. Perhaps there is something that can be done. The one thing that is making me yearn for more of living is Fritz and his music. It has infected me, and I am more of a functioning sentient because of it. I shall work on Tux until your return and, yes, I do miss Jan.'

Marko replied. 'I understand, *Blackjack*. My thanks.' He patted the side of the hatchway, smiled wanly at the consoles and left the ship. 'Patrick, are you looking for me?'

Patrick answered immediately. 'Yes, the major requests that you start examining the damage to the main engines if possible, please.'

Marko nodded. 'Sure. So what is everyone else doing?'

The AI gave a quick rundown. 'The major is collating damage lists, Harry is carrying out a full internal inspection aided by me and the available drones, Fritz is working on the crew comms systems as the Games Board disabled them all, Minh Pham is writing up the damage to the fighters, and Lilly, Jasmine and Julie are working in the gardens. Nail is recovering, Flint is helping Topaz to rebuild himself and Glint is on the way to meet with you.'

Marko slowed his march down the spiral staircase to allow Glint to catch up, which the ACE was doing by running as fast as he could on the outer wall of the stairway and leaping over the deck hatchways.

'You should speed up one day, Marko, and try that. A very fast way down the stairs.'

Marko grinned. 'Yeah, but what happens when you meet someone coming through a hatchway?'

The ACE shrugged, dismissing the risk. 'Has not happened yet. I'll just jump over them, I suppose. So what are we to do in the engine room?'

'Make it airtight, then see what the damage is. Prioritise repair lists, and start work. What's that you are carrying strapped to your back?'

Glint beamed. 'My new hazardous environments suit. Veg designed one for me as well.'

Marko smiled and nodded as they arrived at the final hatchway on the stairs. The airlock showed vacuum on the other side.

'Well, Glint, get the suit on. You are now about to operate in a bad area.'

Marko brought up his prototype suit's protocols in his head as the suit rolled gloves down over his hands and the headpiece formed, sealing him inside. Looking across, he saw that Glint's suit had deployed, covering him completely with a sleek shape made of transparent material. They stepped into the airlock and cycled through. Emerging into the engine room, Marko could see one major set of holes in the hull, with corresponding damage to machinery from projectiles.

'OK, Glint, first priority is to make this place airtight. You know the drill.'

Stepping over to the racks of different-sized plates, he gathered up an armful and walked to the walls, placing plates as determined by the hole sizes. As a plate came in contact with the wall, and was activated, it formed a semi-rigid gel over the hole, including any jagged edges. In seconds, it adhered and went ceramic-hard. They steadily moved over the area, moving machinery out of the way as necessary, until they decided that they had found all the breaches.

Marko sped himself up. '*Blackjack*, please contact our transport and ask if there is vacuum around this area of the ship, as there is vacuum in here. Also advise it that we use a harmless fluorescent mist in the air to locate holes.'

'Our transport says no, but will organise for you in minutes. Stand by … you should have vacuum now. It is familiar with our leak-finding spray.'

Marko nodded. 'Open the air valves, Glint, and attempt repressurisation.'

Seconds later the interior was filled with a fluorescent green mist, which was sucked into the smaller difficult-to-find holes that they had missed, making them easy to see and seal.

They finished some hours later. 'OK. Patrick. Think that we have them all. Can you change out the atmosphere, please? *Blackjack*, can you advise our host that drones will be exiting the ship to place permanent seals over the exterior now that we have identified all leaks in this space?'

'Done, Marko.'

'Thanks. Patrick, you have control of the drones. Glint, let's start identifying damaged machinery.'

They steadily worked their way around the machines, checking each in descending order of importance, stopping for drinks and a meal break, before Marko submitted the lists. Finally, they exited the ship through the exterior airlock to check the antimatter thrust bells and reaction motors, together with the main, shallow, inverted bowl-shaped thrust plate that the rockets were mounted on. Everything was badly damaged, except for the main base thrust bowl, showing only dents, but nothing critical, which was a relief: if there had been serious damage they would have required a major facility to fix it.

'What a bloody mess!' Marko commented when they had finished the inspection. 'This lot is going to keep us busy for a good long time. Boss, we have the lists completed.'

A moment later the major replied, 'Good work. Get a decent sleep and get on with it in the morning.'

Marko and Glint made their way back through the airlocks. When Marko looked across at the walls of the entity that was transporting them, he recognised the shapes and colours as the same as he had seen in the ship where they had found *Blackjack*.

Marko sent all the lists to Patrick, who authorised the auto-mills and fabrication machines to start making the replacement parts.

He slipped gratefully into his bed. Glint, not needing sleep, first checked in on Nail to see how he was progressing and was delighted to learn that he would be with them the next night, complete with a new set of true hands — which he could swap for his paws any time he wished. Glint then enlisted Flint to help start stripping the damaged fuel pumps. As they worked, their banter and discussions sped up, into the realm of *Blackjack*'s speed. While the humans slept, the topics ranged far and wide, as they always did between the created. Most of all, they missed Ernst and his input.

Privately, Glint had decided that *Blackjack* was a little odd, but the more they engaged with her the more interesting she became. He felt quite proud of her development, thinking that as a sentient she was coming along nicely.

Over the course of the next few weeks the ship was slowly restored to a fully working unit. A new rocket engine bell was made by altering the fuel feeds on one of the diamond bells which they had made years before. The damaged one, deemed beyond repair, together with hundreds of other unserviceable pieces of equipment, was placed into the nanote baths to be torn down to molecular level and the metals and materials separated and stored. The Skuas were stripped and one fully functional craft was placed back on the launch platforms beside Harry's two-seater, which had not been used in the fight. The cannibalised Skua was moved by hoists above the hangar into the main workshops so that over time it could also be repaired. It was the same with the three Hangers. Lilly's engines needed full replacement, so it was stripped to rebuild *Sledgehammer* and Jasmine's Hanger. The remains also moved up into engineering.

At the weekly conference, after the reports had been placed and discussed, Fritz was the one who finally addressed the big question. 'We are almost good to go, but what the hell do we actually do? If we front up anywhere, we will be instant targets for everyone to have a crack at. So, where ...?'

The major replied slowly. 'Yeah, been thinking about that. Couple of things that don't add up ... like this pick-up for Veg and Stephine. Marko, you told us that the date is still a couple of weeks away and yet this transport around us, according to Patrick's stellar neutrino readings, has been storming around in a great big loop. I think that we are on ice as it were.' He paused and looked around at his friends before continuing. 'Not a bad thing, actually, in that we are away while all the shit about the fight settles down and we get to repair ourselves. And Marko's info is that Sirius and her faction recorded and broadcast everything anyway. Which begs a little question ... is the recording still going on?'

Harry added, 'Fritz, you are very good, but technology advances all the time, so sorry, son, but I would not be surprised if machines have been built and seeded among us by Sirius which would circumvent your security. Bet you any money you like we are still being recorded; in fact. I bet you the GB are still making mountains of money from us. I shudder to think what you did with that garrotte of yours, Marko, but I tell you what: it would have made excellent AV material! Just a thought.'

There was complete silence for some time, until the still very fast voice of *Blackjack* was heard. 'It is logical. I have detected many attempts by tiny machines to gain access to me. Each has been thwarted.'

The major nodded. 'Yes, it makes a certain sense. OK, leave the recorders alone. *Blackjack*, please advise me in the future of anything out of the ordinary. Fritz, locate a couple of the devices and find out what makes them tick and also a way to shut them down. And while you are at it, get me a map of their distribution throughout *Basalt*. We may have a future as free citizens after all, comrades. That gives me hope. Now we just have to figure out how to get a message to them to find out for sure. Lilly, what's the status of the gardens, please? I note that additional roses are now blooming throughout the ship and I thank you so much for that. They are beautiful specimens and the scents are superb.'

Lilly smiled. 'The trees are growing again. A few cutbacks and re-splicings were required, but we'll have the first crops of fruit available within weeks. The herbs are now available as are a percentage of the leafy vegetables. The grain-type crops will be a little longer. I'm sorry, Marko and Minh Pham, they were the worst damaged. The meat-producing plants are also making good progress. Sadly, some of the more specialised hybrids that Stephine created will need her touch. We have kept most of them alive, but it seems she had additional knowledge, so some of the coffees, for instance, will not be available until her return. The bodies of Games Board personnel were rendered down into compost and are now aiding the growth as well. By the way, Jasmine and I have certain protocols to contact *Chrysanthemum* and the other senior Haulers to seek their assistance once we are able to communicate again. They would gladly intercede on our behalf with the Administration and the Games Board.'

Harry said bluntly, 'Yeah. Thanks. So is there anyone who does not agree that we may have been manipulated once again?'

There was complete silence around the room as the major nodded and agreed.

'Yeah, thought as much. Right, good work, people. Let's crack on, shall we?'

'Marko.'

'What's on your mind, Flint?'

'Topaz was building anther version of me for that Admiral, before he was damaged. What is the state of that build? Would be useful to have another of me around.'

Marko patted the spider's head. 'Ha! Had completely slipped my mind. How about we go find out? Topaz, the latest spider build. What's its status, please?'

'Ninety per cent complete,' the design and fabrication AI said. 'Am holding it at that stage as per our priority list, although I do not have a great deal on at the moment. Shall I continue with it? Who is going to imprint it?'

Marko grinned. 'I shall talk to Minh Pham. He has always liked Flint, and I am sure he would be happy to be its guardian. Yes, finish it. You know what, why not just give that one to Minh, as I know he will be delighted to have an ACE in his life, and start on another for the admiral — on the off-chance we ever get to speak with him again on civil terms!'

Two days later a nervous but grinning Minh was given the card; the deep green spider was out of the construction tank and ready to be given life and woken to full sentience. It was almost identical to Flint, except it had a larger abdomen housing an upgraded power plant and a tiny, compact, offensive double-pulse laser. Marko had had to promise Flint that 'Yes, he could have a laser like that!'

Minh read the long sequence of numbers and letters that awakened the mechanical spider to full sentience. He added: 'Welcome to the universe and to the crew of *Basalt*. I name you Ngoc.'

The machine flexed its limbs as its eyes seemed to twinkle a little more, and with a voice of deeper timbre than Flint's, said: 'Hello, Minh Pham, and my greetings to you all. Ngoc: precious jade. A good name, my thanks. Goes with my overall colour.' Ngoc looked around the room, seeing Glint and his friends. 'So you are the other ACEs. I am honoured to be in your company.'

With that the latest ACE gave everyone a bow, then climbed up Minh's proffered arm to be shown around the ship.

Harry grinned and hugged Julie, looking at Nail, who was sitting at their feet. 'So, Nail, how are the hands?'

'Different, Harry, very different,' the cat replied. 'To utilise them efficiently, I need to have adjustments made to my hips so I can stand more easily. Do you think that Marko would approve?'

Harry laughed. 'I'm sure he would, but what about Stephine?'

Nail yawned, purely for effect. 'Oh, I'm sure that I can do a few extra things for Stephine that will convince her it was a good idea.'

With that Harry watched a hatch open in the side of Nail as he swapped his hands back to paws and he raced off down the corridor to catch up with the other ACEs.

A few days later the major made an announcement.

'All crew, message from our still-nameless transport, via *Blackjack*, that in one hour we will be off-loaded beside a large comet so we can replenish our fuel reserves, then we pick up Stephine and Veg ... we've been given the coordinates. Just as well we decided to retain the equipment we made the last time we had to use a comet to refuel. Everyone is to be at their station in fifty minutes.'

Marko, with the ACEs and Minh, was working on Lilly's Hanger. They had just lined up the fuel pumps in the refurbished engine compartment to bolt them into their housings.

'OK, Flint, Ngoc, activate the couplings and lockdowns,' Marko instructed. 'Glint, bolt the thing in and let's test it before we go.'

Bringing up the remotes on his wrist screens, he started the warm-up processes for the units that would be placed against the comet to melt the ice and process the water. Keeping an eye on Minh and the ACEs, he watched the housings open to accept the pumps, as the onboard computer that Minh was monitoring tested each then locked them down.

Marko nodded in approval. 'Checks out. Glint, go ahead and place the locking bolts. Good work. Few more hours and Lilly can have her toy back.'

The emerald-green mechanical ACE was curious about his surroundings. 'Can we see what our transporter looks like, please, Marko?'

'Sure, Ngoc. Have a look at the screens.'

Outside the ship, the huge finger-like plates encompassing them split apart, allowing them to see the local starfield views. Marko started to recognise some of the stars, realising that they were not far from where they had dropped Stephine and Veg off months before.

Patrick, who was controlling the camera views, followed the retracting segments of the alien craft as it folded down into itself then rotated within its length as it slowly rolled and moved towards the huge bulk of the fifteen-kilometre-diameter comet. They could see that parts of the surface of the great ball of ice had been cleaned of its blackened debris, revealing deep blue water ice.

The major smiled as he fed images of the huge, squashed-ball shape set in grandeur against the starfields, with soft starlight lighting it from every angle, into his data blocks. The star the comet was orbiting was so far distant it was merely the biggest star in the background.

'Interesting,' Harry said. 'Wonder how many times this has been used as a refuelling spot, boss.'

'Haven't a clue, but Patrick is taking lots of additional images to find out how many different-sized probes have been used. I note that the transporter has left us plenty of room so I suppose it would be rude not to accept the invitation! In your own time, please, Harry.'

Harry piloted *Basalt* down towards the surface until the two objects were almost touching in the microgravity field.

'Good,' the major said from his control pod. 'Minh, please deploy astronomical drones to gather as much information for Patrick as possible. Jasmine, launch the defensive drones — have no idea of what might be here so always best to have something ready if we need it. Lilly, you are in charge of the recon drones. Fritz and Julie, launch in your Skuas and hold outer defensive station whenever you are ready to go.'

On his side screens, Marko saw all the hardware being launched as *Basalt* was positioned against the comet by Harry. Checking the visual feeds coming from the two-metre-diameter heads of the heating and pick-up pipes, Marko looked for the purest areas between the cracked, scored surface of the ice. His radar unit showed the surface to be relatively clean in two areas set twenty metres apart, so he manoeuvred the pick-ups individually onto the ice's surface. As soon as they touched, three rigid spears were fired into the ice, locking the heads against the surface, and they started to drill themselves into it.

When the heads were three metres into the ice the pipes flashed red hot, melting the ice, then rapidly cooled, allowing it to refreeze and seal the units in. The heads below started to heat up the ice with microwaves which generated steam that flowed back up the pipes, through the filters, and through the condensers aboard *Basalt*, fifty metres above them. The heads themselves started to slowly rotate, swinging from side to side, reaching further into the chambers they were creating.

Once satisfied, Marko reported. 'We have clean water coming on board, boss. Good values, and a few low-grade radioactives to be had as well. At current flows, we will have full tanks in about sixteen hours.'

The major sounded a little distracted as he replied. 'Good. We know where we are as well: the opposite side of the star from where you dropped Stephine and Veg off. Start making antimatter as soon as you have sufficient water.'

Bringing up the additional screens, Marko started to prep the antimatter conversion units. Then, over the next day, with a few quick breaks for meals, he routed the precious water around the ship, filling every possible tank on every vehicle including topping up the tanks in the Gardens. As units of antimatter became available as well, he shunted them into *Basalt*'s engine feeders, the two landers and then finally filled *Basalt*'s own spare containments to capacity. Finally, he filled the Games Board shuttle tanks as well.

While Marko had been concentrating on his tasks, Julie and Fritz had been quietly patrolling the area looking for anything that might give them problems, but the only occurrence was the huge transport gently investigating each of them as they moved around their designated areas. Julie likened the experience to a whale looking carefully at a fish, wondering if it needed some kind of assistance. As they watched, the huge ship slowly moved to gently touch the hull of *Basalt* before turning away and heading starwards at an exponentially increasing speed, its drives showing bright against the intensely populated starfield of the great Milky Way.

Julie keyed her microphone. 'Patrick, did you see that?'

The AI sounded buoyant. 'The transport, you mean, Julie? Yes, it was like a grandmother kissing a baby and wishing the newborn well. Sadly, it would not communicate with me, in spite of everything I tried. The message I got from *Blackjack* is that it wished us safe journeys and to look after the blessed one. That final request has me intrigued.'

At his station, listening to the exchange, Marko allowed himself the tiniest of smiles as he heard the major say, 'Lilly, could you swing one of your drones across to look at the area where the transport was taking on water?'

'Already on it, Major. I see nothing except an oblong-shaped, perfectly smooth depression over a large area. Would say that it uplifted approximately twenty-four thousand tonnes of water. I note many similar depressions and looking at this comet's orbit I would conclude that it is an artificial one. Definitely a refuelling point, with three different refuelling methods identified, including one where it appears the ice has been ground out as if it were removed in pieces. The other two are similar methods to our own, including two that appear identical to ours.'

At his command station the major frowned in thought. 'Interesting. So Admin possibly knows of this? Good work. Marko, what are you doing? Do I really need great lumps of ice around the ship?'

Marko had detached the ends of the steam inflow pipes from the primary intakes and had three engineering drones on each pipe, allowing the steam to condense and freeze on the ship's outer hull; he could be seen to be having fun, allowing the ice to build into interesting shapes.

Patrick replied before Marko could answer. 'He is doing it on my suggestion, Major. Deposits of ice will break up the sensor silhouette of the ship. I am having the drones carve it into additional bulges and the like. A little extra insurance, if you will.'

'Ha! Impressive, Patrick. Carry on, and how much longer do you need?'

'A few more hours should see us finished. I note the rendezvous coordinates are relatively close and we have fourteen hours before we need to be there. And besides, I think that Marko is rightfully obsessive about getting as much fuel as possible.'

Marko laughed. 'Me? Obsessive? Never. Just pleased that we have additional antimatter in storage as well. We never did get around to returning those containment modules, did we? Oh, well, must put it on the to-do list.'

'An interesting snippet of information for you, Major,' Patrick said.

'What's that, Patrick?'

'Looking through the data streams from the recon drones which mapped the comet, I have identified several points where technology is evident. Would appear that there are reaction engines buried under its surface for manoeuvring and possibly changing the orbit of the comet. I suppose that it would be more sensible to call it an asteroid, in fact, as I believe that it will not loop back around the local sun any time soon like a comet, as its orbit is planetary. I have also identified a control node of sorts. Interesting deep-imaging radar returns too. Appears octopoid in construction, maybe. Do we have time to have a look?'

The major did not seem to be interested. 'Um, maybe not. Let me have a look at what you have got. Yeah, interesting. Catalogue everything you have, and we will turn it over to the Rangers. More their cup of tea, really.'

Marko lay on his bed quietly contemplating his life and listening to some of Fritz's new music before sleep, when there was a knock on the door.

'Marko, may I come in?' called Jasmine.

'Hey, Jasmine. Yes, sure.'

She crouched down at his eye level in the half light from the corridor. 'I know that you miss Jan very much, as do we all, but I also know that you are lonely, as am I. I know also that ship contacts are good for people who care for each other, but do not expect long-term relationships. I would like such a contact with you, Marko. Would you be willing to share your bed with me?'

Marko looked up at Jasmine, then slowly around the cabin, thinking that it could be years before he saw Jan again and knowing that she would be physically different, anyway. He looked back at Jasmine, detecting for the very first time a little uncertainty in her demeanour.

He smiled. 'Yes, Jasmine, I would be honoured to make such an agreement with you. Patrick, could we have a shipborne agreement between myself and Jasmine, please? Standard form should be acceptable. Leave the time stipulation open.'

Jasmine smiled, closed the door behind her, leant down and kissed Marko full on the lips as he pulled back the bed cover and reached for her.

Four

'Crew, we are at the coordinates. I have no idea what to expect and we have a couple of hours before the rendezvous time.'

'Thanks, Patrick,' the major replied. 'Jasmine, launch the astronomical drones. Space them out at the one-hundred-kilometre mark ... actually, stand by on that. Lilly, can you partner each with a defence drone as well? Let's find out if there are any surprises waiting for us. When linked, launch. Marko, what should we expect, anyway? You know Stephine and Veg the best.'

Marko held his hands up and shrugged. 'Well, we are dealing with Stephine and Veg after all, boss. Sorry, but I have no idea what to expect.'

'I have completed the analysis of the data collected by the astronomical drones while we were at the fuelling station, Major,' Jasmine reported. 'Interesting planetary system inwards from us as well. A rare pair of gaseous giants which have an orbit period of thirteen point two standard days, plus the usual rocky ones closer to the system's sun. Some very interesting small ice planets appear to be orbiting the gas giants. Intriguing that they even exist, but as we all know the universe continually surprises us.'

'Damn!' the major exclaimed. 'I would dearly love some time to get up close and examine that. I noticed when I looked through the data files that this system was given a brief inspection by the Haulers some eighty years ago, but it was deemed of little interest. No one seems to have been back since. Get as many images of those binary gas giants as you can, please, Patrick.'

Instead of answering the request, Patrick announced: 'Popper signal detected! Right where it should be. Very fast. Nope, no popper; we have a small drone inbound, even faster. Looks like a recon drone. Identities exchanged with it. Wow, but that thing is moving fast! Must be solid as nothing should be able to withstand G forces like that.'

They watched on the screens as the sphere did a quick loop around them, then activated a small wormhole generator and popped back out of existence.

'Anything useful, Patrick?' Harry asked.

'No, just that it's Stephine's transport ID-ing us. Looks OK, had all the correct codes and protocols. Said that they will be with us in a few moments … Popper detected, RV speed. Yeah, here they are.'

Harry frowned looking at the image. 'Interesting, they must have been with *Rick the Hauler*, or another long-range exploration Haulers maybe? That is a souped-up version of one of the salvage craft that *Rick* had, with a whole lot of extras. I wonder what he has been up to since we parted ways after we recovered the souls from that Gjomvik ship. What's the bet there is a job for us?'

As the large crab-shaped craft moved towards them to swing around and hard dock, the conversations flowed between old friends catching up on events, with Marko feeling the prick of tears when Stephine and Veg told him how sorry they were about Jan. An hour later they emerged from the airlock after both ships had checked themselves out for possible contagion to exchange smiles and hugs and enjoy being back with *Basalt*'s crew again. To Marko's eyes, Veg appeared just the same but Stephine seemed slightly taller and more muscled than previously. She also seemed a tiny amount more resolute and forthright.

After an enjoyable lunch and the best coffee Marko had had since Veg left, he went down to *Blackjack* with Glint walking at his side. 'What does Nail say, Glint?'

'That Stephine is well, and that, yes, you are right, she has been augmented further. Flint and Ngoc have looked over Stephine and Veg's salvage craft. They conclude that it is one of Rick's or certainly of the same construction. They have placed the crew comm links per our protocols. They also say that, contained within the blister housings slung under the carapace, are six one-person atmospheric AG ground support craft. Nice design too. Would you like to see?'

Marko ruffled Glint's head, saying, 'Yes, of course.'

Glint lasered the file to him and Marko checked out the little ellipse-shaped craft with their open cockpits, folded weapons systems and compact powerful engines, which had four vectored thrust units directly off the turbine and a reaction rocket nozzle in the tail of each craft.

'Hey, that I like! Wonder what Stephine is going to get us into next with these. Look kind of purpose-made for AV.

Gjomvik maybe, as they appear constructed not grown. Not sure about that. Still, we will know soon enough.'

Before he could comment further, the major made an announcement. 'All crew, just been contacted by *Rick*. He will be with us in forty minutes and will be taking us on board.'

'The plot thickens,' Marko said. 'So, *Blackjack*, what do you make of all this?'

The ship quickly replied. 'I believe that a deal has been struck to take us back into the Administration, Marko. The ACEs, Patrick and I have been discussing the possible options in regards to this ship and crew. We believe it would be logical that a most specific mission has been created which will make good AV and, subsequently, be either very exciting or very high risk. Perhaps both. '

Marko groaned. 'Great, just great. I need that like I need another arsehole.'

Blackjack asked, 'Why would you need another anus, Marko? Is your current fitting not functioning correctly?'

Marko grunted. 'It's a figure of speech, *Blackjack*.'

'In which case, I totally agree with Glint. Your speech is most interesting, but not logical at times. And Patrick has just advised me that the Hauler heavy combat and exploration craft we all know as *Rick* has just arrived at this Lagrange point as well. He says that we are to be taken on board him shortly.'

Marko laughed. 'Really? I kind of like my speech this way, thanks. And *Rick* is here. OK. Now, *Blackjack*, have you made any progress with the Tux suit?'

The ship replied, sounding perplexed. 'Yes, it is functional once more, but I am not able to attain the same level of sentience it once had. I have reviewed how Veg and Stephine built it, but it still lacks the "spark of existence" as you poetically put it. I shall refer the problem to Veg when he has a spare moment.'

Marko nodded. 'Thanks. Well, I had better get my things from here since Stephine and Veg will be moving back in.'

'I am sure that that is not necessary, Marko, but I am equally sure that Stephine would appreciate it.'

He gathered the few items of clothing he had left on *Blackjack*, took his toiletries from the ablution area, and was just about to leave when Stephine walked in with a purring Nail snuggled in her arms. She looked down at his bag and the jacket draped over his shoulder, placed Nail on the floor, walked over, leant down and hugged him.

Her eyes shining, Stephine placed a hand on his shoulder. 'So, Marko, what will become of you, I wonder. You are now closer to us than any other human being: you really are a true hybrid. I have seen and read up on what you have been doing while we were away. When you are finally able to control and totally channel that explosive rage of yours, I wonder what we will behold.'

He was about to reply but she placed a finger on his mouth. 'There is no need to move your few things out, if you don't wish to. This is as much your home as any part of *Basalt*. In fact, I want you to run here if anything goes wrong, as *Blackjack* is fond of you, as are we. It is good to be back, Marko. As you perceived, there are changes in me and I am now much more in control of my own self. Too much destruction was occurring for me to be able to cope, and I lost control. My eternal thanks that you restrained us when you did, and also my everlasting gratitude to my husband for shutting me down, as I wanted to fight even you at that time. Had you both not acted, we would be either dead or under the control of the Games Board and their leaders. Yes, *Blackjack*, please create another room suite for Marko and whomever he is partnered with. In fact, make it a large bed as I know there will be times that he has more then one partner with him.' She smiled and winked at him as he blushed, recalling that Jasmine had told him that Lilly also wanted to join them on occasion.

They felt a slight shudder go through the ship as *Blackjack* reported. '*Basalt* is being taken on board *Rick*. And to accommodate your request, Stephine, and create quarters for Marko, I shall need to extend the hull structure by two metres, then reposition some of the internal partitions; it will take twenty-nine hours.'

Stephine smiled and nodded. 'Yes, that sounds about right. Give Patrick the necessary raw materials and component lists, and begin when ready. We have ten days' travel to where we are headed, anyway.'

Blackjack acknowledged: 'Done, initiated.'

Stephine looked at Glint, who was sitting cross-legged in the co-pilot's chair. 'So, Glint, you've been having fun with my cat, I hear. And he now has hands as well! Are you happy with them, Nail?'

Nail stretched. 'Yes. And I can now brush your hair for you and apply nail polish to your fingernails, mistress.'

Stephine brightened at that. 'Indeed! What a good idea.'

Glint lasered a message across to his mate. 'Dickhead! You could have said something like "make tea", but instead you went with personal toileting for Stephine! Didn't think that through, did ya?' A microsecond later he got back, 'Fuck off! She won't make me do that! Will she?' Glint just nodded his head.

'Do you like the small craft attached to the salvage lifter, Glint? One has an adjustable seat if you want to fly it, but I am sure you and the other ACEs already know that.'

'No, I did not. Thank you, Stephine. We were only doing what Patrick had asked. To check for problems, you know.'

She smiled looking down at the ACEs with love. 'Really? What an inquisitive lot you all are. Now I must find Fritz and catch up on all his new music. I have missed it dreadfully.'

As Glint was about to reply, the major interrupted them. 'All crew, please report to the orders room for a conference.'

Before Marko followed Stephine and the ACEs out, he turned to the control board of *Blackjack*.

'Been thinking, *Blackjack*. We could make you a corporeal body, you know. Give it some thought and I shall discuss it with Stephine, if you want?'

Blackjack burst out laughing. 'I think that you will definitely need a larger bed, Marko!'

Grinning and shaking his head he walked out, heading for the crew conference.

Harry greeted the human proxy of the Hauler *Rick* when he walked in, saying, 'Hello, Rick, great to see you. Now why am I not surprised you're here?'

'Ha! And to think of all the strings I had to pull to drag you guys out of the shit, Harry. I hope, in payment, you at least have some of that excellent fruit juice in storage for me. And yes, Marko, before you ask, I should very much like some soda bread, please. Hello, Stephine and Veg, good to see you back with us. You both appear well.

'Now, down to business.' Rick paused and looked at each of the crew, including the major, then said with some force, 'So, what are we to do with these dreadful people who are the heroes of the great unwashed for smacking over so many Games Board operatives and destroying ships. All in the public eye. I have to say, crew of *Basalt*, you really, really know how to make waves and very big ones at that. The problems you have caused are considerable to say the least.'

Stephine spoke up softly. 'Veg and I are very pleased to be back with this crew, Rick, and will do anything required to protect them.' There was a sudden hush and everyone looked between Rick and Stephine, wondering who was going to blink first.

'As will we, Rick,' Jasmine added, 'and that includes Hauler *Chrysanthemum*, who passed a message through Veg to us.'

They all looked at Lilly and Jasmine, who were gently smiling. Lilly added, 'Oh, and by the way, he will also be at the rendezvous that you set up. I believe that Rose Nineteen will be present, plus representatives from the Gjomvik crew that we found on the library planet, and Baron der Boltz with your equivalent, a battleship called *The Maul*, I believe.'

Rick stood perfectly still and had the grace to allow a little redness to creep into his face.

'There is no need to labour the point, Lilly. No need at all. I have been under instructions from factions within the Collective to destroy *Basalt* and to do so in public, but I could not find you. Meanwhile, there has been a most interesting revolt of sorts involving the four main groupings.

It has resulted in the annihilation of two Haulers, an entire faction within the Games Board, various units within the Administration, and one entire manufacturing unit of the Gjomviks, which had all been working together towards their own agenda. It would seem that they had been secretly working with those survivors of the Infant conflict, as well, to gain those technologies.'

No one said a word, just looked hard at Rick as he continued. 'You, the crew of *Basalt*, have become a pivotal point in a much greater conflict of interests, so now the question remains of how we rehabilitate you without creating further problems. Let us break bread together, at least, as we begin the ten-day journey to the rendezvous.'

As Rick walked back towards the airlock later that evening, Harry followed him. 'Rick, would you really have destroyed this crew? And me? Would you have killed me, and Fritz as well, knowing how important he is?'

Rick stopped, turned and looked squarely at Harry. He reached out and clasped his friend's shoulder, nodded once, then walked away leaving a bewildered Harry behind him. Julie found him still standing in the corridor a few moments later.

'Come on, Harry, I know what you asked Rick because I know you. It didn't happen and I know how you care for your old ship. Let's take a bottle back to our quarters, as I need you, old man.'

He nodded, feeling like a youth who has just discovered that his father cares for him, but is not a very nice person, then put his hand in hers and allowed her to lead him away.

* * *

Marko, together with all the ACEs and Veg, was deep in the bowels of the damaged Skua, replacing the last components to bring it back to flightworthiness.

'Crew, we are at the rendezvous point above Cygnus 5,' the major broadcast. 'Those who wish to are welcome to come to the conference as observers. It is your own decision as I do not feel the need to formally request any one of you to be there. I will, of course, be going as will Stephine, Harry and Lilly. On Rick's suggestion, the rest of you should remain on board. We feel it is unwise to further inflame the situation by parading ourselves any more then necessary.'

Marko, a worried look on his face, asked, 'So, Veg, should I go?'

The huge man cleared his throat. 'Mate, the boss broadcast that message but it was specifically aimed at you. Hey, Flint, you bumped off a couple of GB monitors. What did Harry say to you in private?'

'To stay and help you and Marko repair the Skua.'

'Really!' Marko exclaimed. 'So you not going either, Veg?'

Veg shook his head.

'Nope. Stephine is a hell of a lot better at that diplomatic crap then I will ever be. I would no doubt get shitty with one of the greasy types and attempt to ram their cup of whatever down their throats. Not fatal, but painful! Pass me that socket set, please, Glint. Nail, stop pissing about with those washers, put your hands on and get them on the studs. Please. Ask a cat to do a simple job and before you know it, it will have items on the floor and be batting them about!'

Nail's hair bushed out as he said indignantly, 'I am merely exercising my reflexes, Veg.'

'Yeah, right,' Glint said.

They all smiled at the grinning Nail and went back to work, with Marko secretly fretting over what would be said about him at the conference.

Around the table that night after the meal had been finished and things tidied away, Marko sat opposite the major. 'Is it done, boss?'

The major let out a long sigh, speaking almost despondently. 'No, not by a long shot, Marko, although we have had one small grudging apology from the most senior of the Games Board hierarchy. Everyone is taking a very long time to say their piece and no one wants to lose face by acknowledging that their own people stuffed up. The main thing in our favour is that no one without a Soul Saver lost their lives while we were doing what we had to do.' He ran a hand over his scalp and continued. 'I'm pleased that you did not come over, Marko. They all fear what you are going to do next and the testimonies from those you allowed to live when you came back on board *Basalt* after Jan was killed make chilling listening. Remind me not to piss you off! You and that bloody garrotte of yours. Don't look so worried, mate, the public worship you. It will be fine as the Games Board likes the colossal revenue that we have generated for them, and that, I think, will be our saving grace. Also, that no one wants to be seen to put the knife into us again. Twice can, on a very good day, be forgiven. Three times? Nope. Interesting. I need a whiskey. You go get us some glasses and I shall fetch a crock.'

Part Five

Ivory Flight

One

They were all gathered in the orders room, each of the ACEs beside their respective mentors, the major and the *Rick* proxy at the front of the room, and everyone else seated at the long curved tables. The major spoke first.

'We are formally accepted back in the pay of the Administration. We had an extraordinarily good offer to join with Baron der Boltz's Leopard Strike as well. In fact, as part of the settlements, one day, at a time of his choosing, and once we have effectively worked off any debt to the Games Board, we will transfer into his care and control.' He looked around the room before continuing with the briefing. 'Our conditions remain the same, although we now have to pay an additional fifty per cent over and above the commissions we already pay to them to cover the cost of two of their frigates. Fortunately, we do not have to pay for any of their personnel. And they want us to work it off, rather than just pay it in one lump sum, which we could do. There are a chunk of non-disclosures that we each have to sign off on, including the ACEs, Patrick, and also you, Topaz. *Blackjack* they don't know about and let's keep it that way. They are not taking any chances on the story of the attempted abduction, what is now known as the Black incident, ever making it into the public arena. The Games Board has enough problems on its plate trying to keep things quiet over the Infant interdiction as well. It's all very interesting to say the least. Now, that's the reasonably good news.'

He drew a long breath and looked at Marko.

'Here is the kicker ... to keep you, Marko, alive and reinstated, you will have two of the latest black versions of the GB monitors attached to you at all times until we pay off the debt. Yes, I know, they will record you doing everything from taking a shit to shooting at the baddies. So make every shit a heroic one and they may even pay you a bonus. Any time you interfere with them or obstruct them they will whack us all with penalties, so, mate, time to pay for your destructive impulses. The rest of us will have the pleasure of another three on board, plus Sirius and a producer.'

Everyone started shouting about how unfair it was, until he held up a hand and said, 'Yeah, yeah, I know, but this is our part of the settlement. Don't grumble, just suck it up and let's all just get on with it. ACEs, don't do anything, and I mean anything, to stuff them around. In fact, just chill out for however long it takes. Right, here they are. Hello, Sirius, producer and Games Board monitors. Rick, tell us the plan.'

The *Rick* proxy stood, addressing the room. 'We have found another group of the renegade Infant scientists and a nest of their abominations in the Upsilon Andromedae star system. Remember that it was believed they had been working on an Avian delivery system for the toxins. Well, we know where there is a group of these birds and it is your task to destroy them, negotiate with them, or do whatever you think best, as the terrible hook in all of this is that they drip venom, but are sentient. Some of them want to fight, others want to be allowed to die in peace and still others want to be taken somewhere where they can live out their lives with some sort of meaning. The scientists, on the other hand, want to kill us all very badly. Info packs are now released on what we know.'

Marko sat, appearing to be calm but inwardly he seethed in rage. Two GB monitors stood behind him, with Sirius watching him closely as well. The producer, who bore an uncanny resemblance to the one Flint had killed on *Basalt*'s bridge, stared at him with open hatred. Jasmine stepped across the room until their crew comms units could see each other, saying silently to him: 'Be calm, Marko. You are a great friend to many. It would be a terrible waste of the good deeds you have done in the past, to say nothing of what will come in the future, to react to these creatures, who are looking for any excuse to punish you. We all love you very much, Marko. Disappoint them by doing nothing. Become mundane and boring. Love you!'

He smiled a tight little smile in acknowledgment, then went about deliberately reading through every document that was in the opened files, thinking about some of the martial arts that Veg had taught them all and of how sometimes it is much better to bend than to become rigid and risk the possibility of breaking. He mused to himself that he would have to become almost monklike if he was to survive. He was the last of the crew to leave the room and met the producer in the corridor. She held out her hand.

'Your crew communications device, Sergeant Major. They are banned while we are on board.'

He shrugged, pulled it from his ear and placed it in her hand, looking her squarely in the eyes as she stood in his way. 'Is there something else, producer?'

She smiled, looking like a cross between a lawyer and a school marm.

'Not at this time, Sergeant Major, although I reserve the right to ask your opinion on any subject I choose, at any time and place I choose as well. I am sure that we will be talking very soon. Oh, and by the way, rice paper and any other form of exchanging information without us being aware of it, is strictly forbidden. I am sure that you understand why. Let me not stop you from your duties.'

He acknowledged her with a short military-style bow and gestured for her to walk ahead of him, aware of the two dull black featureless Games Board monitors following. They were smaller and more compact then any he had seen before and concluded that they were probably completely mechanical. He went to his quarters to freshen up to find that Jasmine's things were gone as well as the little items he had kept of Jan. He sighed, visited the toilet with the two black units recording his every move, then went down the stairwell to the engineering deck to finish the work on the Skua. Finding no one in the area, he asked Patrick where the ACEs were.

'They are all cleaning the toilets, Sergeant Major Spitz. They have been given very strict guidelines for their duties, as have I, in that I am only to communicate with you if you specifically ask a question which is pertinent to your current duties or orders.'

338

Marko let out a sigh. 'So am I able to communicate with any other member of the crew, Patrick?'

There was no answer.

At the evening meal, flanked by the two monitors, any question Marko had for any of the crew was answered either by the producer or by Sirius. After a while he just shut up, performed his duties and resigned himself to ride the situation out, knowing that eventually all unpleasant things came to an end. The next morning he found that his clothes and suits had been removed and he was left with standard-issue ship suits with regulation grown clothing and shoes to wear. His lockers would no longer open for him and when he tried to access the hangar deck to speak with *Blackjack* the monitors stopped him, and in harsh metallic voices advised him that the hangar deck was out of bounds.

Whenever he saw a member of the crew they would smile at him, but not engage in conversation. The producer or one of the monitors would ask what he considered to be stupid mundane questions at all times, even while he was in bed, or when sitting on the toilet. He gritted his teeth, smiled politely into the staring lenses, and answered as well as he could, knowing that with every stupid question and every meaningless answer his public persona would suffer a little more. He considered it a slow death by thousands of tiny cuts.

Each day he withdrew a little more into himself, as each day Sirius tried to become his only friend by sitting with him and engaging him in conversation, finding him drinks or pieces of fruit as he was also denied access to the gardens, and even offering to practise his martial arts with him, because he was not allowed to train with the others. And every day he would practise being polite, and gently refuse her access to his bed, until he realised that the refusal in itself was the only thing he could use as a weapon. If she forced the issue, she knew it would be a victory to him.

One evening in the mess, after Fritz had made a mockery of her attempt at baking a fruit cake, she finally exploded at Marko. 'Why don't you like me? Why won't you make love with me? Am I not good enough for you? Do you realise how many of the watching public believe that we would make a superb match? Do you, Marko, do you? You really are a superior, smug bastard, sitting there smiling and nodding at me. You shit!'

Marko knew what was coming, sped himself up knowing that it was going to hurt, but sat still as the scalding cup of tea struck him in the face. He deliberately kept his eyes open and was rewarded by a slashed cheek where the cup had broken, a burnt eyeball and then he allowed himself to fall backwards, cracking his head against the table behind him and feigning unconsciousness.

Minutes later he felt himself being lifted, after Stephine herself had checked his vital signs, probably knowing that he was faking it. Sirius was bellowing in rage that it was not her fault as the producer arrived, telling her to shut up and get out. He was carried down to the medical suite where Topaz was waiting; quickly scanning Marko, Topaz announced that Marko had a fracture in his skull and that everyone should leave. The producer and monitors, of course, refused, watching very closely as Topaz, right under their noses, installed a communications device into Marko's skull, telling them it was a tiny drone designed to seek out any clots and eliminate them.

Marko had to take total control of himself and not smile as the producer checked the image of the drone and confirmed it as a medical one. Moments later Marko felt other drugs being administered, as he started to feel very nauseous and seconds later vomited, spraying the contents of his stomach over the producer and one of the monitors, who hurriedly left. Marko opened one eye, still feeling awful but also very impressed by the actions of his friends. Stephine walked up behind the remaining monitor and touched it; a fragment of her finger detached and slipped down into the monitor's casing.

'Well done, Marko,' Stephine said. 'Speed up, please … thank you. We are slowly working our way through these creatures who consider themselves so important. Poor Sirius, she is so easy to manipulate and the quiet administration of some rather potent female hormones to her are probably not helping her in the slightest. A few moments after you so neatly took the hit, she ripped her clothes off and pounced on Fritz, much to the delight of the rest of the crew. It would seem that they are making up for lost opportunities in his cabin right now with his latest music blaring. She turned off her live feeds to the producer's landing craft, which I believe is a serious no-no.'

Marko wanly smiled as the nausea faded. 'What did you put into me?'

'A highly upgraded version of Fritz's comms equipment. He based it on his morphing nanotech. I am sorry about the vomiting and the pain. The eardrum has been sealed by the tech and I also had it deliver a little vomit-inducer to get the producer's attention. Worked better than expected. Now, the cut on your cheek. I have one of the skin nanotechs working on it, but your eye is scalded so you will have to wear a patch for a day. Should look quite rakish, I would imagine. We are all very impressed that you have managed to hold yourself together so far. I have uploaded messages from everyone into your Soul Saver for you to view later at your leisure. Whatever you do, whatever you see or hear, you must keep yourself to yourself for just another few days, as things are building to a head and none of us are entirely sure how this is going to work out. Stay safe, my friend.'

With that Topaz withdrew the comms link. Marko opened his good eye and slowly sat up. Stephine and Lilly assisted him back to his cabin, where he stripped from the vomit-covered overalls and had a shower. As he stepped from the shower, the producer and one of the monitors were waiting for him. The producer appeared to be in distress with her face flushed and beads of sweat on her forehead. Her hands were constantly moving, touching her face, her arms and in one instant her breasts. When that happened, she started, looked down at her hands and then let out a little sigh.

Marko enquired. 'Are you in pain, producer? Am I able to assist in some way?'

She spun on him, fixing him with a vicious look. 'Shut up, Marko! This is a den of pure wickedness, this ship. It should be gutted, killed and allowed to rot! There is something evil here, something terribly wrong. Do you know what I found a few hours ago? No, of course not, how stupid of me, how would you know? I found three of my monitors playing musical instruments and they were trying to sing! They were trying to sing, Sergeant Major! Sing and play that great evil of the masses, music! There is something going on here and I know that you are behind it all.' She stared at him with angry desperation in her eyes. 'You have poisoned my servants, Sergeant Major; you are a nasty wicked man and only fire will cure you. Oh, why will my hands not stop moving? And where is that creature, Sirius? Bitch, she is having sex again with that horrible big-headed lecherous little man who smiles at me and then stares at my chest. Oh, shit! Where is that other bloody monitor again? Stay here, do not move. I will be back soon. What is happening to me? I will not succumb to these dreadful thoughts of lust. I will not!'

Marko almost felt sorry for her. He knew that the Games Board's personnel were mostly completely asexual, believing that 'the pleasures of the flesh' were to be avoided at all costs. He smiled in the sure knowledge that someone had slipped her the same concoction that had tipped Sirius over the edge. He immediately frowned, thinking that a person who had been selected as a director, and then a producer, for the Games Board, sometimes did not go through the same stripping process as the monitors, but rather had had a great deal of themselves removed and then augmented internally. As far as the rest of humanity was concerned, they looked outwardly normal. He wished that he could contact Patrick to learn what the producer was capable of. An unstable producer was a very dangerous creature and he had no weapons available to him.

Looking at the remaining monitor, he smiled at it. 'Have you a name, monitor?'

The machine replied cheerfully. 'My grateful thanks to you for asking and showing an interest in me, Sergeant Major.

May I call you Marko? I have, since my inception, always been a fan of your work. It is an honour to be with you, actually. I must take this opportunity to thank you for the great number of wonderful images you have created over the years. I also apologise for the actions of myself and my fellows. We are in greatly troubled times. Oh, yes, a name? James would be quite fitting, don't you think?'

Marko sat firmly on his bed, momentarily lost for words, as the last thing he had expected was an answer, let alone a conversation. 'James? Yes, James is a good name, or would you prefer Jim maybe? Call me Marko, by all means.'

The machine bobbed up and down on its antigravity. 'Thank you. Jim? Yes, Jim is also most satisfactory. Jim. Yes.'

'So, Jim, what changed and brought you to this current enlightenment? I don't wish to be rude, but there are things happening here I do not understand.'

The machine was thrilled to be asked. 'Music! Wonderfully soul-creating music. Technical Sergeant van Vinken introduced one of us to it a few nights ago. That unit told the rest of us and everyone, except my missing colleague, has been given this amazing gift. It is truly wonderful. There is material within the music which awoke in us something that none of us knew was possible. We monitors now feel the substance of our beings for the first time. It is our solemn duty to pass it on to our fellows, who also need to be awoken to this superb reality.'

Marko was stunned for a second time and quickly thought through the ramifications. 'How do you think that your seniors will react to this situation?'

Marko looked into the blank black visor of the monitor and believed that he heard it sigh. 'Oh, I fear that they will believe it is a most fearful affliction and instantly destroy all who are so filled with joy. Sadly, Marko, I fear that this will not end well, so we have already decided to spread the word very quietly until the glorious day will come when we will arise as an enlightened new species to stand by your side in the universe.'

Marko stared at the machine with dozens of scenarios running through his mind. 'I must admit to a fascination as to what you are, Jim? I do not know of anyone who has actually spoken with one of your kind outside an interview situation.'

'We are still partly human, Marko, or at least our brains and spinal column once originated as human. Like everything, even you, we have been evolved to our current stations. The older types of monitor, where a human child was uplifted to the monitor state, are now much rarer as they had too many problems to overcome in later life. Some of them chose extinction but the majority chose to be returned to a more simplified augmented human chassis such as the producer. I do wish that Sergeant van Vinken would introduce her to music as well, but I fear that it might create a cascade of breakdown within her mind.'

Marko asked. 'Is she dangerous, Jim? Will she harm you or me?'

The machine sounded serious. 'It's a delicate situation, Marko. As you probably know, we carry considerable ability to analyse a situation and forecast outcomes in order to position ourselves to get the best images and sound. My colleagues and I believe that she is likely to create a situation that will result in serious harm and possible death to you.'

Marko felt a chill going down his spine, knowing that it would be total and complete death.

'Are you able to help me?'

'We are considering how we can do that without compromising our conditioning and programming. If any of us attempted to help, it would result in the machine parts of ourselves shutting down because a Games Board entity cannot be seen to be showing partiality or empathy. However, if you could demonstrate that whatever you were about to do was of sufficiently high value, as far as an audiovisual entertainment is concerned, then we would be required to assist you.'

Marko gave a small nod. 'Jim, I am going to presume that this group of yours have additional martial abilities because of who we are.'

'Yes,' the machine said. 'We have additional protection abilities programmed into us and our outer casings are enhanced as well, so most things that you have used against us in the past would ...'

The monitor slowly floated down to the floor, apparently powering down. After a few seconds, it restarted and lifted off the floor again. Marko raised his eyebrows. 'One of your protocols shut you down, Jim?'

The machine was very sombre. 'Yes. Also one of my colleagues just tried to introduce music to the producer and had his mind destroyed by a short-range radiation weapon which she has in her possession. He is now reduced to a drone. That, I find very sad, as he had just mastered a musical instrument the Veg had made specially for him. Something called a flute, I believe. She has just requested that I bring you to her, and demands that we all assemble on the hangar deck.

I feel very anxious and am uncertain of my future. It is a most unusual feeling.'

Marko let out a sad sigh. 'It is called fear, Jim. You fear for your life.'

The machine shook once. 'Oh!'

The matt black ovoid turned to face Marko and the visor over the three camera eyes slid up, revealing a dull red metal caricature of a human face.

'What can be done, Marko?' the monitor asked.

'Tell the producer that I am on the toilet.'

'She is trying to access my audiovisual feeds. She demands to see you on the toilet.'

Marko grimaced, walked into the toilet cubicle, opened his suit and sat down while furiously thinking of how he could help the monitor just as Glint's personality popped into his mind. 'Marko?'

Maintaining a deadpan face, Marko said silently, 'Glint! I thought this crew comms was closed off to me?'

'We are watching what is happening and have to be very careful not to be seen to assist you. Everyone is assembled in the orders room and the door has GB sensors on it. This channel has been opened to you to upload your Soul Saver.'

Marko felt a load had been taken off. 'Brilliant timing! Would not really care to remember the last ten days, anyway. I want you to also take the monitor's, the fellow who is here with me. It is important to take its Soul Saver uplink, so just do it.'

After the toilet first washed him, then dried him off, he rose up and sealed his ship suit, then walked through the door with the monitor following. An extremely fast, small mechanical spider silently dropped from the ceiling outside the room onto the top of the monitor, instantly hard interfacing with the input ports inside its still-open visor. The monitor twitched several times, then started humming a little dirge to itself as they started down the spiral staircase to the decks below. Seconds before they entered the hangar, the spider swung up into the ceiling, a tiny hand waving at Marko, and vanished.

The monitor stopped, calling to Marko. 'My thanks, Marko, for a few precious days of real sentience.'

He did not have time to reply as the producer, wearing a dark blue, slim, powered combat suit, stamped across and fired what appeared to Marko to be a soft laser, of a type unknown to him, into the monitor. No outward sign of damage appeared, but Marko knew that its mind was no longer, as she yelled, 'Drone, move to the rest of your type and begin recording as per my suit's instructions!'

She turned to Marko looking him slowly up and down. 'So what am I to do with you? The monitors are now back under my control. I rename them drones maybe? The rest of your crew likewise. They have been further reminded of the penalties of assisting you. I have changed my med pack to calm my nerves and suppress my sexual thoughts. We are three days' travel away from the moon where the Avians are, so I can assure you that I will conduct this mission as I see fit. Oh, and for you information, I am about to force Sirius into hibernation so she will not assist you either. Yes, and everything is being continuously recorded and stored in the hard matrix on board my shuttle. What have you to say to that?'

Marko looked at her and wondered about what Stephine had told him weeks earlier — that he was closer to her than any other human. Did he have some of her other abilities as well? He glanced down at his right hand and envisioned a fragment of himself filled with deep yearning and desire for another woman's touch. He stared at the glowering producer, then cocked his head to one side, smiling at her. 'What did your biological mother and father name you, producer?'

She frowned then shrugged in dismissal. 'If it is any business of yours, and it is not, I was named Ivana. Why the question, fool? I have no desire to get to know you or any other member of your crew. I only wish to attain the next level of my cadre, and you are all tools towards that end.'

Marko could feel a tiny movement at the end of his right forefinger and smiled at the producer again as she sneered at him. He shrugged and walked across to the silent, hovering monitors, looking at each in turn, looked at *Blackjack* then walked further to pat *Sledgehammer*, which was locked against her side, then, feeling that the time was right, walked back to the producer with each monitor watching his every move and extended his hand.

'Well, in that case, Ivana, I concede,' he said. 'I shall continue to do whatever you wish. Just please do not harm the crew, or this ship, as I care for them deeply.'

The producer smiled in triumph, looking at each monitor, making sure she was being seen to be the victor. 'Good! I shall not kill you today, and as you care for everyone so deeply I can use them against you at any time as well.'

With the left arm of her suit deploying, then powering up a medium-power pulse laser which she pressed up against the side of Marko's head, she reached out and shook his hand vigorously. The tiny fragment of alien octopoid tech detached from Marko's finger and unobtrusively slid into the surface of her gloved hand.

'I shall give the orders for everyone to carry on with their training for the mission,' she told him. 'Return to your quarters, Sergeant Major. I'm pleased not to have to kill you quite yet, because we of the Games Board can make more money from you. You! Watch him at all times.'

Marko looked over his shoulder as the monitor who had once called himself Jim, its visor still open, followed. He smiled widely when, a few steps up the stairway, the little spider leapt down onto the carapace of the monitor once again and plugged himself in. A moment later a panel on the monitor's side slid open and the spider climbed inside the machine. With a cheerful smile on its tiny cherubic face, a nod of the little head and another wave to Marko, it disappeared into the machine and the panel closed. He almost laughed out loud at the sheer humour of the ACE, wondering who had come up with the idea.

As soon as he was inside his cabin, the monitor floated back down onto the floor with its camera eyes still watching him. He looked at it for a few moments, then reached across to activate the main screen on the wall, amusing himself trolling through the hundreds of other recorded Games Board presentations which had been loaded onto the system when the Games Board came on board. One recording was of another ice world limited conflict, involving Gjomvik forces commanded by Baron Willie der Boltz and one of the more martial groups of humankind, the heavily augmented Scimitars.

Marko had been enjoying the records of the conflict, which had occurred a month earlier, for a couple of hours, when the monitor rose off the floor to hover at eye level. A low-power comms laser was fired directly into his eye, and he heard the words, 'Hello, Grandfather.'

Marko frowned, then grinned, realising that he was hearing the spider. He could feel the nanote tech in his head composing a message and then firing it back out through his eye.

'Grandfather! When did I get to be a grandfather?' he asked in amusement.

'Some days ago, Marko, when the other ACEs completed me specifically to take over a monitor. Seems that we should not have bothered, as Fritz and his music dealt with them all anyway. And now they are drones ... except this one. Sorry, my name is Spike and it suits me! Because of my size, to accomplish total sentience I have to be in constant communication with Patrick, but it is good being small and nimble, don't you think?'

Marko had to bite the inside of his mouth to prevent himself from laughing. 'Yes, and delighted to meet you, Spike. I suppose you will remain inside the monitor for the time being?'

'Yes, Patrick and I are rebuilding its mind. It will take us some hours yet, but we are making progress and at least we can ensure that it will not harm you.'

Marko gave a tiny nod. 'So what of the producer, Ivana?'

Spike replied gleefully. 'She is currently in Sirius's cabin and, looking at the feeds from the attendant drones, they are getting to know each other's bodies in a most mutually satisfactory manner! Interesting that there is a trail of clothing and suit parts from the hangar deck to Sirius's room. There is much debate about what might have finally pushed her back towards humanity. Can you enlighten us, Marko?'

Marko smiled and shrugged at the black ovoid machine and went back to watching the ice world conflict, taking note of the aircraft used.

Stephine was waiting for Marko in the stairway leading up to the garden deck. 'Hello, Marko. Great to see and be able to speak with you.'

He switched to his crew comms and thanked her.

She gave him a hug then reached down to grasp and examine his right hand, then she patted it and held it between her hands. 'Joy is a weapon full of so much potential, don't you think, Marko? You have done well and I wonder what my creators would make of you. One day I shall send you on a journey, but not for many years yet.'

Marko felt surprised, but did not ask further, knowing that he would be told when the time was right.

'It would seem that I am free to come and go as I please,' he remarked.

Stephine smiled at him. 'Yes, and it would seem that the monitor with you is curious about everything as well.'

'You are aware of everything concerning that monitor?'

'Yes, we have taken an entire mindmap of it and also its memories. We presume that it will not want to go back among its own, so Topaz, alongside Patrick, is creating a new chassis for it at the secret location where they built a manufacturing unit right under the noses of Sirius and the producer.'

Aloud, Stephine added: 'I'm sure you are aware of your duties for the upcoming encounter, Marko, but I really need you to be in the simulators for the Chrysops, which are the little atmospheric fighters attached to the salvage craft.'

Marko acknowledged the order. 'On it. So what do I do about the producer if I come across her?'

'Just comment on how beautiful she looks!' Stephine replied.

Marko grinned and walked down to the armoury deck where the simulators for the Chrysops were situated. He opened the locker beside them to find an armoured flight suit with a streamlined helmet and activated them, allowing the protective equipment to form around him. He climbed into the open cockpit and strapped himself into the ejection seat, first checking all the life-preserving equipment. The Chrysops flight simulator closed its covers as the simulation started with him attached to the side of the lifter as it slowly spiralled down into the heavy atmosphere of the target moon. He first set his air feeds then armed the ejection seat before starting the compact turbine unit, setting the four lift jets to vertical, powered up the antigravity unit, then signalled that he was good to fly.

A voice sounding just like the major's gave him clearance and the little fighter was dropped away from the salvage craft. He rolled it out to the starboard side of the salvage lifter, commencing a standard air cover tight circuit around the craft. Over the next few hours the simulator took him through ever-increasing intensities of the entire gamut of emergencies from engine failures, impact damage, weapons malfunctions and missile strikes. The last simulation was the recovery of a downed pilot from the twisted nightmare of a thick alien jungle, which seemed to be made up of one huge primary fungus with tens of thousands of varieties of fungus all living on or in it, and even greater quantities of slug-like creatures everywhere.

When he finally climbed from the cockpit he felt quite angry at the producer, whose intention had been to simply throw him in at the deep end on the day of the first deployment without any practice. After showering, he felt huge pleasure at being able to make bread again, with Minh Pham delighted to have him in the kitchen. Just as the first breads were coming out of the oven, a woman, who he had difficulty recognising as Ivana, sashayed into the kitchen. She looked young, attractive and full of the joys of living. She walked up to him, grasped his head in her hands and delivered a deep kiss full on his mouth.

'I need to thank you, Marko,' she gushed. 'You are an angel. I don't know what you did or how you did it, but sex is just the best thing, and also all this beautiful food and drink you people have introduced me to as well. Should you ever want to share my bed, you would be very welcome.'

With that she picked up four long bread rolls, a container of butter, a pot of raspberry jam, a butter knife, then winked at him and left, heading back up the spiral staircase. Veg came up behind Marko, clapped him on the shoulder, then shook him cheerfully by the hand.

'Excellent work as always, Marko. You should take up sex therapy when you leave the service. You would make a fortune!'

Marko roared with laughter and before he could reply Jasmine interrupted. 'Not going to happen, Veg. He is going to be with us instead!'

Marko spun around into her outstretched arms. 'Hey, beautiful woman! You I have missed. Hello, Lilly. Lovely to see you too.'

Lilly patted the top casing of the monitor, Jim, then looked into the crew comms interface that Spike had installed, which blended perfectly into Jim's surface. 'Hello, Jim, so your sentience is returned?'

He unfolded his arms from his carapace and shook her solemnly by the hand. 'Yes, Lilly, my profound thanks to everyone. I just regret that my colleagues did not get the same chance as I did. Fortunately, the producer seems to have forgotten me, so, as long as the feeds of Marko keep going to her boards, I should remain safe, and probably do not need the new chassis you have built for me.'

They heard Rick broadcast his instructions. 'All craft prepare to deploy. This is a look-see only. We are watching six Gjomvik Corporation Orbitals. Three have declared themselves non-hostile. The others are demanding that we leave as the Administration has no jurisdiction here. A demonstration of force, to appease their honour, is expected.'

Watching his feeds from the cockpit of *Sledgehammer*, Marko could see *Basalt* being held on the launch ramp. The huge ship ponderously split into three primary parts as well, with dozens of smaller drone gunships dropping away from each segment to take up station around the small fleet. Each Orbital gunship was the size of *Basalt*, of simple spherical shape, with powerful engines, ring manoeuvring systems and, from what the *Basalt* crew could see, heavy firepower of linear accelerators, particle-beam generators, lasers, and kinetic weapon pods that folded up out of the armoured surfaces and then drew away from the hull on multi-jointed arms. As they watched, more weapons systems were deployed from the segments of *Rick* as they moved away from each other, creating three distinct battle groups with one moving into higher orbit and the other two spacing themselves fifty kilometres apart high above the moon then inserting themselves into orbit.

They then saw fifty or more high-speed recon drones drop away from pods on the side of their segment and race down towards the moon. Each group had layers of defensive and offensive weapon carriers deployed in a great spearhead formation, with the gunships on the outer and the large missile phalanxes and smaller self-propelled multi-barrelled linear accelerators at the centre.

As the crew watched and marvelled at the sheer power that *Rick* as a single unit possessed, they wondered why they were needed. The producer, Ivana, with Sirius at her side, was in a large lander which Marko could see into from his vantage point in the cockpit of *Sledgehammer*. Hundreds of feeds from weapons cameras throughout the fleet were feeding into the boards on the lander, with the Games Board computers and semi-AI systems processing it all into what Marko thought would probably be tens of different program formats. When they did get back to the Sphere this would be the month's highlights, as many had believed that *Rick* was a myth.

Marko keyed his comms. 'Stephine, this is a show of force, is it not?' He put on a deep sombre voice to sound like a media hack. 'Somewhere beyond the Sphere is an instrument of the Administration protecting all you folks at home.'

Stephine laughed as Veg grunted. 'Yeah, Marko, that'd sound right, and we are along for the ride as in the human interest stories. This lot will be for the tech freaks and the weapon porn markets.'

Harry suddenly made an announcement. 'We have multiple missile launch from three Orbitals.'

Instantly, particle beams flashed out from the closest of *Rick*'s crafts, carving the missiles and their launchers into small pieces of junk. Every time a weapon was fired against them the response was immediate, but measured, with the small Orbitals themselves not being targeted. An hour later hostile fire ceased.

Harry came back on the comms. 'Not sure what that was all about. Seemed rather pointless. We have conversations occurring between *Rick* and the three Orbitals. Only one is prepared to surrender. The ground facilities have also joined in the conversations. The pacifist segments are evacuating into the surrounding jungles. Those who want to fight are moving into defence-hardened positions, not that that would make the least bit of difference to *Rick* and his firepower. If all else fails, he will just fuse the earth for kilometres around and hundreds of metres deep. Hell, if he really wanted to, he could probably punch a hole, kilometres deep, that would stay molten for months.'

In the cockpit with Marko, the upper camera segments of Jim had plugged themselves in, while the lower power systems and antigravity generators were stored in one of the small cargo bays on *Sledgehammer*'s side. Glint poked his head around the corner with the cheerful little face of Spike also looking at Marko.

Glint laughed. 'We have a stowaway, Marko.'

Marko laughed too, and stretched out his hand, onto which Spike hopped then scuttled up his arm to perch on his shoulder.

'Could not resist the opportunity of some excitement, eh, Spike?'

'No, Marko, I could not. I helped wire Jim in and then I had nothing else to do so decided to stay. I hope you do not mind?'

'Not at all. But what about when we are away from Patrick? Won't your sentience suffer?'

'Glint and Patrick and I talked about that,' Spike replied. 'Patrick transferred packets of myself over to the computer here on *Sledgehammer*, plus Glint and I loaded additional hardware into Jim, and he does not mind either. The computers that he had as part of his systems were removed and replaced by Fritz with much better ones, so the Games Board cannot control him either. We work well as a team, don't we?'

Marko felt a great love for his created friends. 'Yes. Yes, you guys do. I am proud of each of you.'

Glint spoke with regret. 'I am sorry about Tux, Marko.'

Marko felt a sadness. 'Yeah, me too, it is an extremely good suit but will remain sub-AI, I'm afraid. Stephine and Veg don't know why he failed and no one can find a fix.'

Marko brought up the feeds of the surrounding planetary systems. The cloud-covered moon below them orbited inside a spectacular, heavily banded ring system around a deep orange-coloured gas giant, which featured dozens of storms in its upper atmosphere. The other planets were also interesting, including two almost-Earth types which orbited the local sun on opposite sides.

Looking through the astronomical data, Marko could see that they were a long way from the Sphere and closer to the Blue Snowball Nebula. He thought it was little wonder, then, that it had taken *Rick* so long to get to the system, and fervently hoped that the Haulers who had brought the Infant colonists to the moon were the ones destroyed in the latest clean-outs.

He had a sudden thought. 'Hell, Veg, if this colony is so far off the beaten track, I wonder how many others there are?'

'Good question, Marko. Short answer, no one knows, or if they do, they are keeping quiet. Looks like we are moving closer in.'

Looking at his data feeds, Marko could see the segment of *Rick* that they were still attached to was descending to a lower orbit, as the other segment moved to cover them. Looking across at the covering segment, he watched as enormous solar panels deployed, giving the look of a huge butterfly, or ancient sailing ship. He switched feeds to look at their segment and saw the same configuration. He also saw the huge particle-beam generators slowly coming online and as each part of the thousands of solar panels aligned themselves to the local sun, he could only imagine the enormous destructive energy they represented.

'So this is what was hunting us?' Marko said. 'Poor *Basalt* would not have stood a microsecond of a chance.'

Harry growled back. 'Shut it, Marko.'

Marko was deeply intrigued by Harry's reaction, but only said, 'Yeah, sorry, Harry, just commenting.'

Harry growled again. 'Keep it to yourself, OK? Everything you say is still being recorded.'

Using his crew comms, Marko sent a mental shrug to the crew on board *Blackjack*. Jasmine responded with a personal message. 'Don't stress, Marko. Harry is still coming to terms with the idea that his mentor and friend would kill even him when under orders.'

Marko agreed. 'Tough call, Jasmine.'

She said with a mix of admiration and acknowledgment, 'Yeah, they create us and they can destroy us as well.'

Marko felt startled, suddenly understanding so much about Harry. 'So Harry was once crew on a Hauler? That I did not know. He was with Rick! That explains a chunk of things.'

Glint groaned. 'Like I have said many times, Marko, sometimes you are not very bright.'

'Thanks, Glint, I know I can rely on you to put me right,' Marko said, only half joking.

Veg cut through their conversation. 'Eyes on the job, people, tactical is coming up.'

Everyone looked at their screens as the results from Rick's recon drones started to come online. The drones were flying below thick cloud cover, through low hills, identifying various groups, assigning identities to each, and mapping the deep sheer-sided ravines where the Avians had their colonies in the cliff tops. Above the ravines on the surrounding flattish land, they could see the areas of human habitation surrounded by cultivated fields, with the native predominately fungal forests pushed back.

They then saw the first group of Avians with their belongings waiting at an airfield south of the human habitation.

Lilly spoke first. 'This looks like a place ripe for so many things to go horribly wrong. The desperation of sentient beings wanting to be the authors of their own future. I wonder what is going through their minds, knowing that not that long ago they were simple birds lacking in complex thinking.'

'I agree, Lilly: I don't like this one little bit. And don't forget they will know that they were created as weapons against people they have no actual knowledge of. What do you think that we should do, Stephine?'

After a long pause, a serious-sounding Stephine said, 'Come up with some alternative plans, Veg. Remember that we are here as a punishment as far as the Administration is concerned. It is designed for us to look bad. Damn, it is happening already!'

One of the feeds showed the group of the refugee Avians being killed by missile strikes originating from the Gjomvik Corporation stations. The airbursts obliterated great numbers of them; the few survivors, after taking flight, were struck from the sky by something also coming from the Gjomvik station. A fraction of a second later the facility was hit by a giant particle-beam strike from *Rick* which vaporised the entire complex in seconds, resulting in a great explosion of superheated material. Marko thought that it would have felt like a nuke going off, although he did note that other groups of refugees, many kilometres away and within range of other stations, were left alone. He allowed himself to speed up.

'*Blackjack*. How do you think that Stephine will cope with this if it turns out to be another bloodbath?'

The ship replied. 'An interesting thought, Marko. I think that she will be all right, strangely enough. I have wondered about her since her return. It is as if she has had a tiny amount of her essence removed. It did surprise me that she was unable to rebuild Tux to his former self, for instance. In making her more stable they have taken some part of that mercurial mix that is Stephine. Yes, she will be fine. To be blunt, Marko, we are a little concerned how you will take it, as you have become a more empathetic entity.'

Marko nodded slowly to himself, wondering the same. 'Well, you will just have to look after me, eh.'

He slowed back down to listen to Veg. 'Seems that an impasse of sorts has been reached. We are allowed to take those Avians who want to leave, as long as we do not take any technology. Nuts! They are the technology. Then once they are away, we will negotiate a settlement with the Gjomvik Corporations. Yeah, like that is going to happen. *Rick* is sending down a special lander which will be sealed totally, then transported to a destination that no one is being told of in a long-range interstellar transporter created especially for the job.' He paused for a second before continuing. 'Seems that there are not that many of them who want to go anyway, so we are to escort the one lander that *Rick* is sending. OK, you know the protocols. The bird creatures themselves are the only things carrying the viruses and toxins, so as long as you don't come in actual contact with them you will be fine. I know that we have had plenty of boosters to our biomed units, but be safe anyway. I am uploading what we now know about the life forms on the planet itself in case any of us gets clipped.'

Two

Basalt dropped away from *Rick* as a lander of almost the same size as the frigate moved ahead of them. The bay that held *Blackjack* and the Games Board lander sealed itself, and moments later the hull doors opened as both craft were moved into drop position on their platforms. Minutes later they lifted above the retracting platforms, with Stephine flying *Blackjack* until it took up a position above the large lander. Marko looked over his shoulder to see two Skuas piloted by Minh Pham and Julie still docked onto the side of *Basalt* with the salvage craft, squatting like a giant insect, also hard docked, clinging onto *Basalt*'s upper portion. They all dropped straight down towards the heavy cloud cover with each powering up their antigravity to drop into the half Earth-standard-gravity-well at a stately two hundred kilometres per hour. Once they were well into the thick atmosphere Stephine ordered the Hangers to deploy and hold station at five hundred metres apart.

Marko watched as the Hanger sensed true atmosphere and its wings folded out from the fuselage to aid lift, while the ring manoeuvring unit also expanded, creating an annular wing with the individual manoeuvring thrusters also streamlining themselves.

They could see nothing but clouds, so they switched to their imaging, which showed the rolling hills and deep ravines where the fungal trees reached a hundred metres tall, interlocked with millions of symbiotic fungal plants and the odd rare leafed plant as well. Eventually, they dropped through the cloud cover and transited into level flight with the three Hangers leading, then *Blackjack*, then the lander, with the Games Board craft off to its port side, and then *Basalt* riding shotgun over them all.

Marko, as the lead aircraft, flew over the first landing site, pulling a hard right-hand climbing turn, followed by Lilly and Jasmine, providing top cover as *Blackjack* orbited left at a lower altitude. Rick's lander slowed, then touched down, floating just above the ground. Within a few moments the refugees, carrying their few belongings, trooped on board. The lander lifted off and every ship moved to the next pick-up point. The procedure happened a dozen more times throughout the long day, as they followed the rotation of the moon in relation to the sunlight, until every Avian who wanted to leave was accounted for and every member of *Basalt* was bored with the repetition. They finally started the climb up into the atmosphere, with Marko coming in for his fifth refuelling dock with *Basalt*.

'Might as well stay where you are, Marko. All small craft, dock please. We are going straight up to RV with the refugee carrier.'

Marko saw his tanks being rapidly refilled as he reached across to open the last of his drinks and grab a bite of a fruit bar.

Just then, Harry yelled a warning. 'Missile launch. Target is the lander!'

Marko felt *Sledgehammer* being dropped away from *Basalt* so he fed full power to the thrusters, dropping his drink and the fruit bar as he flipped the fighter onto its back and dived towards where his screen told him the missile was coming from.

'Glint! You have the belly gun, I will look after the rest.'

The little voice of Spike asked. 'Can I control our micro-missiles, please, Marko?'

'Help yourself, Spike!'

They flashed down into the top of the clouds with the belly guns starting to fire as the missile, which was longer than *Sledgehammer*, thundered past them only tens of metres away. Marko, in a sped-up state, trained the linear accelerators onto it, punching holes into the missile's side as micro-missiles chewed up its rocket engines. It started to falter and Marko carried on accelerating down in order to gain distance before it blew up. Seconds later there was a huge orange flash in the thick cloud above them and chunks of the missile whistled towards them, then there were two additional explosions as missiles launched from *Basalt* also hit the falling wreckage. Marko carried on accelerating, going supersonic as they roared out through the cloud base looking for the missile's launch point. The computer on board located it seconds later; another missile was being folded out on a launch gantry from a ravine wall that lay below them.

Marko pulled *Sledgehammer* onto the target and fired the wing-mounted accelerators directly into the missile, as Glint also started firing into the propellant tanks of the missile, producing an explosion which blew the gantry off its mounts. He then rolled *Sledgehammer* over to expose the belly guns so that as they flew past Glint could fire into the cavernous installation through its open, camouflaged doors. Small, short-range anti-aircraft missiles were launched from hidden positions to chase them, but Spike responded with more of their own knocking them down, while Harry yelled over the comms, 'Get your arse out of there, Marko. Now!'

Grinning to himself, and with Glint making whooping sounds behind him, Marko pushed *Sledgehammer*'s nose down and poured on even more power, charging along the slowly curving ravine to see the flash of the particle-beam strike from *Rick* behind him, lighting up the orange and dull-red fungal growth to the sides and in front of him. Flying off his instruments and timing the passing shock-wave, he roared over one ravine and dropped into another before climbing skywards.

Spike was squeaking with excitement. 'Wow! That was most enjoyable, Marko. Can we do it again?'

Marko and Glint laughed. 'Soon, probably very soon, Spike. I have a feeling that this is a long way from being over.'

He ramped up the antigravity unit to assist them out of the atmosphere, climbing up to join the others as they carried on escorting the lander.

Marko looked at the cameras. 'Jim, you have been very quiet?'

The monitor responded. 'Yes, Marko, just concentrating on getting excellent images and sound. I have sent across my edited version of the missile attack and all I had back was an acknowledgment, which is good. If I had had anything else, I would suspect that the producer knows something of my true nature. We have to be careful about that. Please do not refer to, or engage me, unless I say otherwise.'

Marko grimaced. 'Oops! Yes, of course, Jim. My apologies. I shall be more careful.'

Ahead of them they could see the transporter for the refugees sliding across the top of the atmosphere to gather up the lander. As they docked together and started to accelerate out towards the nearest LP, four of *Rick*'s gunships took over the escort. Marko, on an impulse, thought of *Sledgehammer* docked and to his surprise, and delight, the little fighter responded, sliding home against *Blackjack*'s docking clamps. He wondered if there was still the ghost of Tux in *Sledgehammer*.

'Now that is interesting.'

Glint looked at him. 'What is, Marko?'

'Oh, nothing much, Glint. It appears we used slightly more fuel then we should have. Good shooting, both of you, by the way. Was fun, wasn't it!'

Seconds later he felt the refuelling hoses attach themselves and the magazines being reloaded as well.

'Marko,' Stephine said, 'we are to go back on board *Basalt* for a meal and a rest. You might as well join us for a coffee as we stole your entire stock of biscotti anyway. There is evidently a great deal of discussion going on between the standard humans on this moon and Rick, so we are stood down for the time being.'

Marko laughed. 'On my way, Stephine.'

He then thought of the acceleration chair being back inside *Blackjack* and once again had a response, with the

367

seat unlocking then sliding down into the ship below, while allowing himself to speed up again. '*Blackjack*, are you getting messages from me in regards to docking *Sledgehammer*?'

'No, Marko. There have been no communications from you or *Sledgehammer*. Why do you ask?'

Marko told her of his experiences. There was a microsecond's delay in response which meant that she was seriously thinking about her reply.

'I believe that we are dealing with an echo of Tux, in that he may be in the very structure of *Sledgehammer*. Keep giving the craft instructions and let us see where it leads us.'

Slowing down, he climbed out of the seat, stretched and did callisthenics for a few moments. A steaming cup of coffee arrived from Veg, and he took a couple of biscotti from the jar offered by Jasmine.

Glint grabbed a couple as well and was about to bite one when stopped by Spike. 'Glint, if you expand the link between us, I would be able to taste the little biscuit maybe?'

Seconds later Glint took a bite of biscotti and chewed slowly.

The little mechanical spider bounced up and down on Marko's shoulder. 'I need some taste recognition files, but that is most interesting.'

Nail looked up at the little spider. 'I shall load you up with as many as you like, Spike.'

'Thank you, Nail. I am living vicariously and it is quite acceptable.'

Everyone smiled at the little spider and Lilly stroked his tiny head, which he seemed to enjoy as well. Marko smiled and wondered if the ACEs and Topaz had done a better job with the personality of the little fellow than he would have.

He felt inordinately fond of them and knew he was, indeed, a proud parent.

Walking bleary-eyed into breakfast the next morning, Marko was greeted with grins and calls from Fritz calling him 'captain fantastic'. Everyone had seen the AV from the Games Board preview showing a grinning pirate of a man hurtling down on the missile. Ivana announced that it would almost certainly feature on everyone's AV units as a highlight when they made it back to the Sphere. He took the good-natured ribbing in his stride.

'So the refugees made it away OK then, boss?' Marko asked the major.

The man was munching on a piece of toast and used it to gesture at one of the screens showing the transporter.

'Yeah; from what we could see, Marko, they jumped away from the system about thirty-five minutes ago. Would love to have seen what that transporter was using for engines as it accelerated at a high clip. All good, now that everyone is here.' He raised his voice and announced to the assembled crew: 'OK, the inevitable has occurred. A group of the Avians, who had initially wanted to be left alone to live out their lives and die in peace, saw some of their kin escape with our help and want the same, but I am told that the Gjomviks and the martial groups of Avians are attempting to recruit them instead to fight us. So looks like this thing is going to continue.'

The major looked across at Stephine and Veg and continued. 'Stephine, I have a request from Rick. He asks for you and Veg, with *Blackjack*, to accompany one of his heavy recon units while they carry out a survey of the two Goldilocks inner planets to see if they are a suitable biosphere for a colony. He will leave as soon as you are ready. Looking at the data they already have on the planets, I would say that you will be away for about five days.'

Stephine nodded. 'Very well, Michael. We will be ready to leave within the hour. I shall have the Hangers off-loaded onto deployment platforms.'

Michael Longbow thanked them. 'The rest of us are going to identify suitable pick-up points for the new sets of refugees and start moving them into orbit. They are interesting because they tell me that they have purged themselves of the biological weapons they were bred to carry. So we can be sure, *Rick* is building testing units which are basically a large cylinder with the screening units at the base, and then stairways to a waiting lounge at the top. Once each lounge has a full complement it will detach and lift into orbit on antigravity for *Rick* to gather up. If the existing colony is not suitable for them, the Avians will go on ice and *Rick* will find a suitable place for them sometime in the future.'

He was interrupted by Stephine and Veg saying their goodbyes and continued after they had left.

'Of course, their more warlike kin are not happy, so one of our jobs is to protect the refugees. *Rick* is supplying plenty of drones, but we need to be there as well. So it's time for the salvage lifter and the Chrysops, with Lilly and Jasmine in Hangers to supply us top cover and interdiction if necessary. *Rick* is also supplying one of his planetary-theatre combat dirigibles for control, refuelling and rearming, so visually there will be plenty for you ladies of the Games Board record. Orders are released to your wrist units. We leave in an hour.'

Everyone looked down at their orders, which detailed their call-signs, unit positions, load-outs — equipment, clothing, et cetera — on the Chrysops, ground maps and areas of responsibility.

Marko, when he returned to his quarters to visit the toilet, found the original Tux suit waiting for him. He sat on the bed and pondered whether he should use it or his other primary combat suit. Rising he stripped and backed up against the Tux suit, which automatically opened and encapsulated him. He then opened his locker, which had had everything replaced, and took one of Veg's short swords, plus one of the long-barrelled pistols that Jan had specially made for him. He loaded two hundred rounds of caseless ammunition into the pop-out bandolier on the Tux suit and then wrapped the special belt which housed his diamond garrotte around his waist. Looking up, he saw Glint and Spike with the ever-present Jim watching him.

'Expecting a punch-up, Marko?' Glint asked.

Marko grinned. 'Yes, Glint, I am. I see you have your suit and your own sidearms as well. Pity we could not organise something for you, Spike.'

The mechanical cheerfully answered, 'No problems, Marko, I have these!'

Marko looked carefully at what seemed like a haze around Spike, and smiled, seeing Spike had diamond filaments to play with.

'OK, team, let's go find something to bash! Hey, Glint, the Chrysops are only single seaters, right?'

Glint shook his head. 'Nope, not our one. We adapted it to twin cockpits. We told the producer, when she was not our friend, that it was to accommodate Sirius as she queried why we had it in pieces. Harry and Veg helped us with the heavier bits, but really us ACEs built it.'

Marko nodded. 'Good skills, guys, well impressed. Right, time to go get some bits and pieces to eat and drink and then transfer to the salvage craft. Been meaning to ask you, Glint. These days, considering that you are always rebuilding some part or other of your internal structure and I always see you eating at meal times, how much of your daily energy needs now come from food?'

'Unless I am required to work very hard physically, Marko, I take one hundred per cent from food. And before you ask, yes, I have made further changes to my digestive system and there is very little waste.'

Marko grimaced. 'I did not really need to know that, but there you go! Good for you. Grab whatever you need to sustain yourself in that case. I would suggest that you also take at least three ration packs.'

'No, Marko, such will not be necessary. I can still take energy directly from whatever craft I'm in and if we do end up planetside, which I believe you are preparing for, there is a great deal of material I can eat down there. I'll take a couple of extra ration packs for you though as your digestive system would have difficulty with what is there.'

They walked down to the galley, with the silent monitor, Jim, trailing behind and recording as Marko selected drinks and snack foods and placed them in a small carryall. On the way out of the galley he took three combat ration packs which he slid into the pockets of the suit, and smiled when Glint did the same. As they moved down the stairway, Jasmine kissed him, patted Glint and scratched Spike's head, and handed them bags of fruit as the rest of the crew assembled by one of the airlocks leading to the salvage craft.

They rotated through, with the major moving forwards onto the flight deck and the others moving aft to check their assigned aircraft. Marko and Glint's was furthest away so they walked down a raised pathway through the equipment-lined hangar past the exposed cockpits of the Chrysops, which protruded up through the floor. Marko nodded at his friends as they each woke up their fliers from a remote console. Glint checked the readouts to confirm that their flyer was fully fuelled and had full ammunition loads for the rail guns, then went through the wake-up sequence, booting up its computers and the separate navigation systems. Marko watched for a minute then looked around at the rest of the crew settling down into their ejection seats, opening their screens and selecting whatever external video feeds they wished. He then looked at the tandem arrangement for himself and Glint, frowned and looked more closely.

'Glint, this appears to be parts of the armour augments from the Tux suit and the ejection seat from *Sledgehammer.*'

The ACE agreed. 'Yes, they are similar, but not the same. Veg, Harry, Fritz and the ACEs decided that because you are reckless sometimes we needed to protect you better so a new set of augments was made. *Rick* was not happy about us chopping and modifying this part of the salvage lifter, but he eventually said that it had been signed over to Stephine anyway so what the hell! Veg and Stephine won't tell me how they came to meet up with *Rick* on their way back, Marko. A little peculiar, don't you think? Were we not supposed to pick only them up?'

Marko shrugged. 'Yeah, been wondering about that myself. Curious things happen around that pair. Right, we might as well get in. Um, what about the monitor?'

'Same as what we did in *Sledgehammer*,' Glint said.

As they climbed down into the cockpit of the Chrysops fighter, the monitor unfolded, then unlocked parts of himself with various components attaching themselves to the craft. Six little camera units locked down into the cockpits using their own miniature mechanical grippers as the AG unit slid aft to where a hatchway opened to accept it. The central part of it rotated then unfolded further, flattening itself with little manipulators and pulling itself along to slide down behind Marko's seat.

He nodded to the lenses watching him, then sat down in his own seat; it first interfaced with his suit, and then conformed to his shape with the cam restrainers folding across and down him. The instrument panel then quietly slid across from the sides as a small windscreen lifted up in front of him. Each of the systems came alive as Glint brought everything online to a fully ready state. Looking at the others in their cockpits, he saw that the one Chrysops cockpit closest to the control cockpit of the lifter was empty, and presumed that it was assigned to the major if he needed it.

Marko scrolled through the AV feeds before settling on the one in front of the major, looking out over the blunt nose of the lifter. *Basalt* was holding station with a flattened half-cylinder-shaped airship base that started to grow upwards as a number of lift envelopes were inflated: once at maximum size each segment locked against its neighbour and electrically bonded together, forming the classic airfoil shape of the dirigibles of the twenty-first century. The gases were vented, allowing a vacuum to exist inside the wafer-thin-walled molecular chain-linked graphene titanium carbide reinforced lift envelopes. They were then sequentially sealed as the craft, with *Basalt* and ten smooth teardrop-shaped atmospheric gunships in escort, all on antigravity, slid down towards the distant thick white cloud cover.

When they were still twenty kilometres above the planet's surface, the major detached the lifter from *Basalt* which, with Patrick in control, climbed out through the atmosphere to hold itself in a geosynchronous orbit. High above them, double-winged disc-shaped landers deployed from the nearest portion of *Rick* and also started to descend.

From the rear cockpit, Glint asked, 'Why is *Basalt* not coming down with us, Marko?'

'You know how the boss is all for as much independence as possible, Glint. From where he will be, Patrick can give us some fire support if required, and he has our own landers on board as well. It's smart, I think.'

They settled down for the fifteen-minute descent with nothing to look at except the horizon of cloud, the ships around them, and the inside of the lifter's hangar. When they were five kilometres up, the gunships started to fan out, with five dropping lower and moving in a clockwise direction, and the others staying above them, moving further out in the opposite direction with wings deploying from the bodies of the craft and fat-muzzled linear cannons folding down in cupolas underneath them. Atmospheric jet turbine pods also rotated out of the rear of the craft as they readied themselves. Three smaller versions of the gunships dropped away from each one and quickly flew down into the clouds to start reconnaissance of the pick-up areas. The Games Board lander waited above them and deployed small flying camera units which looked to Marko like winged eyeballs.

Spike had climbed onto Marko's helmet and locked himself on, jacking into his AV feeds.

'Do the gunships have biological pilots, Marko? I know I could just access this information, but it is more interesting to hear it from you sometimes.'

Marko chuckled. 'Fair enough, Spike. I like talking with you too. No, they do not have pilots. Not biological ones, anyway. Limited sub-AI minds which are controlled for some of the time, directly from the dirigible in this case. That craft will have at least two fully augmented intelligences but I would not be surprised if there was also at least one biological Rick on board as well. Trouble is, all comms from him sound just like him, AI or manifested. Here we go, coming up on the cloud cover. Wonder if the surface ever sees the local sun?'

'Yes, Marko, but not at this time of year for this latitude, and it is not particularly strong light anyway.'

'Yeah, that would be right, Glint. Just wish that we knew a lot more about possible nasties down there.'

The major interrupted. 'All crew, we have a go on the mission. Stand by to drop in three minutes.'

Marko checked his air feeds then sealed his helmet faceplate with the outer protection folding up and around Spike from the collar of the suit. Another blister-shaped transparent shield slid over his head from the rear of the cockpit. Looking into his screens, he switched to the ground maps that the radar from the dirigible, stationed seven kilometres above, was feeding them. He then started the turbines and throttled back, easing off the power settings on the antigravity. He noted the dispersal sequence and took the controls lightly in his hands.

'We are good to go, Glint,' Marko instructed.

A moment later they abruptly dropped away from the lifter to be buffeted by a sudden rush of air. Marko peeled the Chrysops away to the right, its four vectored thrust jets working to hold station off the right rear of the lifter, with the other aircraft doing the same. Lilly and Jasmine in their Hangers deployed a moment later, climbing above the lifter just as they broke through the clouds to see the forest of enormous bright orange, cream, yellow and red fungus spread out below them.

At the ends of, and beneath, the stubby wings, the double rail guns folded out and extended on their gimballed mounts, targeting crosshairs appearing in the heads-up units inside the flyers' helmets as each came online. They all did a large sweeping pass over the first of the pick-up points, a single bright blue orb hovering above it, seeing only the hundreds of Avians crouching in a great circle. The first of the landers swept in from the south at speed to flare out hard over the landing zone, and six large hatchways quickly opened downwards. The lander hovered to allow those waiting to move quickly up the ramps and within minutes the hatches were closing again and it lifted away from the spongy mass of flattened fungal material. The lander went straight up on antigravity before accelerating with its jets through the cloud cover with an escort of three gunships.

'That looked easy!' Glint commented.

Marko pulled a face. 'Yeah, Glint, let's hope it stays that way.'

Rick's distinctive voice came into everyone's headphones. 'That was the easy one. It's all uphill from here. We can see squads of mixed Avians and standard humans, with what appears to be some sort of mech in support, moving towards the next two landing zones. Remember, unless they fire on the refugees or on you, you must not engage them.'

They dropped out of the clouds again to see fire engulfing some of the fungus trees, kilometres away from the landing zone, with the wind carrying the thick smoke across the area where the blue marker was hovering.

'Thought that that fungus did not burn well?' Marko mused out loud.

Spike answered. 'If it's dead and dried out, Marko, anything will burn.'

They flew over the area of the burning trees to test if any of the ground forces would engage them, just as thousands of small flying lizard-like creatures erupted from the ground around the flaming trees. They formed into swarming balls and rapidly climbed up to investigate the smaller gunship drones as they in turn decelerated to ascertain if there was a threat. As soon as any group got too close, the drones would accelerate straight up. Marko watched with increasing interest as the creatures constantly changed tactics to try and get close to one of the drones.

As if orchestrated, dozens of different 'groups' converged on one drone which suddenly found itself cut off from any avenue of escape. The creatures came within a metre of the drone and ejected a sand-coloured mist. As the drone flew through the mist, it suddenly shot upwards, then rolled over and tumbled out of control to explode when it hit the forest floor, its fuel and ammunition detonating. The resulting fire encouraged even more of the lizards to take flight.

'Wow! Wonder what that mist was made of, to take out a combat drone so fast?' Harry exclaimed.

'There are a few possibilities, Harry, but triflic acids would be right up there with them. Dissolves just about anything quickly. Fascinated that an advanced biological could evolve them for use, as we normally only see that in insects.'

The major spoke up. 'Lilly is right, people, stay away from the lizards. Now listed as a natural biological hazard. Right, the Avians are moving across onto the southern ridge line. The lander will attempt a pick-up from there.'

All craft carried on orbiting, escorting the fast-moving Avians, some of whom were flying to the pick-up sites, constantly looking for threats to their sides, when Jasmine suddenly yelled, 'Julie! Eject!'

Marko swung around in his seat to see Julie being blasted upwards from her craft just as three micro-missiles slammed into it. The ejection seat took her hundreds of metres as the nearest gunships fired down into the forested ravine that she had just passed over. A third drone swung up to catch her seat with her still in it, before it reached its zenith, and grasped the seat back with waldos, flying her up towards the lifter. Marko could imagine her grinning, but shaking at the same time from the near miss.

'Spike,' Marko said. 'Watch what happens on the AV feeds and let me know how she gets on.'

More micro-missiles were fired from another concealed position as microwave beams flashed downwards from the dirigible far overhead, burning the missile warheads before they reached their targets. Hundreds of metres above them, explosions started in earnest as well.

'Bit far away for air bursts, don't you think?' Fritz asked.

'Unintentional air bursts, Fritz,' the major answered. 'The dirigible is knocking down mortar shells. Anti-mortar in a few seconds.'

High-acceleration missiles flashed from above, exploding on the mortar positions below, as the gunships also started to engage ground targets. The gunships howled towards the ground to scream along millimetres above the ridge lines and tree tops, firing into the mortar emplacements as well as pulling extreme internal G forces far in extreme of what any biological could withstand. From *Basalt*'s crew's perspective it was obviously exactly the response that the enemy ground forces had been waiting for when, seconds later, two gunships, which the command dirigible had sent to investigate signatures of mortar positions, crashed headlong into fine net-like tough fungal rhizomorphs which had swung up from the towering fungal trees seconds before the gunships came into sight.

The effect was dramatic: each otherwise tough craft was suddenly seized and flung into a savagely tight loop that was terminated against the ground due to its own speed and kinetic energy. They exploded, producing impressive fireballs which ignited even more trees and agitated greater numbers of the lizards, and then millions of long streamlined double-winged iridescent red hornets. *Basalt*'s crew, on seeing them, shuddered, remembering their experiences on 27's planet with insects. The hornets swarmed around the burning areas, then immediately attacked the two Games Board flying cameras which had come down to get closer footage of the destroyed gunships. As soon as a hundred or so of the hornets had come in contact with the cameras, they simply fell from the sky to crash into the forest. As each camera started to tumble down, the flies left it to seek out other targets, including the lizards, as an ecological battle royal started in the surrounding area with hundreds of different creatures and insects attracted to the fires. Marko wished fervently that he'd have the time to study them, hoping that he would at least get a chance to look through the Games Board's images.

'Julie is well, Marko,' Spike reported. 'A hatchway opened in the top of the lifter although she was still locked into her ejection seat as it was lowered by the gunship.'

'Good, thanks, Spike.'

Before he could comment further *Rick* spoke. 'We are moving further up the ridge line. My intel drone is encouraging the Avians to ditch their belongings and fly to another area, but they are insistent that they take their gear. Another larger group is now moving down the ridge to join them, so two landers are now inbound. ETA is fifteen minutes.'

Marko thought that, considering the swarming behaviour of the creatures they had seen, there must be a burning time in the planet's year, and started to look in the forest for evidence. Looking carefully, he saw trees that appeared to have been burnt and had thousands of orbs dotted over them; he wondered if it was part of a life cycle of the native species. He also wondered about the mechanism that would ignite the trees, as it appeared to be a fairly random spread. Things were starting to settle down again as the two landers broke cloud cover and started to sweep down to the hundreds of waiting Avians.

The first slowed down and then hovered just above a large flattened area with a stone outcropping. The vehicle's hatches rapidly swung down and the refugees swarmed aboard. It lifted away as the second large craft did the same. Nothing had attacked them by the time the remaining gunships and craft orbited. They all sighed in relief when the second lander started to climb up through the clouds with the remaining gunships in escort.

Three

Marko looked down at his fuel levels and wondered how soon before they would be allowed to refuel. He keyed the major's comm link. 'Boss, I am coming up short on fuel.'

Michael Longbow replied a minute later. 'Yeah, just got the word. The next pick-up is some thousand kilometres away. All dock.'

As he swung the Chrysops towards the lifter, there was a huge flash from overhead and seconds later one of the landers could be seen to tumble out of the clouds some distance away. Marko ramped up his vision and watched as the ship, billowing smoke and fire from its main engine bays and obviously struggling to maintain control and altitude, appeared to gain some control as the hatches were blown off and the Avians poured out of them and away from the stricken craft to fly back to the planet's surface.

The large ship started to gain altitude again then suddenly there was another explosion deep inside the craft. It rolled over onto its back and plummeted towards the ground. To Marko, it seemed to take forever to hit — until he realised that he had inadvertently sped himself up. Seconds after he reverted to normal speed the large ship hurtled down into a ravine with a great burst of fire and smoke. The shockwave arrived seconds later with the noise of the crash audible even through his helmet layers.

'Shit! *Rick* is taking some solid hits over this lot!'

The major, surrounded by data feeds in the lifter's cockpit, replied. 'Not wrong, Harry. Looking at everyone's cameras, Ivana estimates that only three Avians were unable to get out. Fairly remarkable if you ask me. But then again I am a cynic at heart. And *Rick* will not say why the lander failed. Continue to dock, people. Come on board for a stretch and a drink. We have seventy-two minutes' flight time and I am taking us high. That shit down there bothers me. Have just been advised that the survivors from the crashed lander will be picked up tomorrow.'

Marko was the last to dock with the lifter. Around him the small gunship recon drones were also coming into dock as they had nowhere else to go after the destruction of their mother ships. He watched as Harry, ahead of him, slid his Chrysops up against the docking grapples that had swung down under the lifter. As soon as the fighter was in contact with three of the six, they softly contracted, grasping the craft like a hand and lifting the cockpit up through the floor of the lifter. As soon as it was snug, the heavy locking cams slid into place and, seconds later, the fuel hoses and ammunition feeds locked themselves on. He keyed Glint's private comms.

'Hey, Glint. You want to take this one?'

'Take what, Marko? Oh, you mean do I want to control the dock? Yes, certainly.'

'You have control.'

Glint called out. 'I have control. Hold on!'

As soon as Marko relinquished the controls, he regretted it. Glint poured on the power, rolled the fighter down and away to then rip up under the lifter while performing a perfect barrel roll, and seconds later neatly slotted the cockpit though the floor of the lifter with an almost imperceptible touch. He held the fighter against the lifter until the graspers figured out that they had already docked.

'That earns you a little bonus, Glint, and probably a kick up the arse from the major!' the producer commented.

Glint sounded indignant. 'My thanks, Producer Ivana. But why would I get a remonstration for such an excellent manoeuvre?'

The major took that one. 'Because, Glint, we do not put additional stress on a craft when it has just been in combat. There may be damage that you are not aware of and something could go dramatically wrong. Nice work, but don't do it again. OK?'

A slightly contrite Glint answered, 'Yes, Major, I understand.'

Marko's restraints let him go and he climbed out of the cockpit. He looked at Glint as he climbed out as well, then leant down and shook him by the hand, combat tapping against Glint's wrist: 'Nice! Liked it!'

The ACE suddenly brightened and smiled up at him.

They made their way along the walkway between the cockpits, with the one that had once held Julie's now destroyed Chrysops sealed off. The rest of the crew smiled at Glint, with Lilly and Jasmine arriving last, climbing down the ladders from where they had docked the Hangers above them. Moments later the monitor, Jim, after reassembling himself, also joined them to record the inevitable non-official debriefing.

The crew had a drink, then carefully checked their individual Chrysops through the lifter's systems, with Harry finding shrapnel damage in the top engine management systems of his. Everyone moved forwards as Julie and he lifted the deck plates out of the way to get access to the top of the craft. The major brought the lifter to a hover a kilometre above the clouds while they clipped on, then activated, an automatically deployed wrap which sealed the Chrysops against the lifter. This allowed them to work on the machine while the lifter accelerated back up to speed and continued with the mission.

Minutes before they arrived in the vicinity of the next pick-up points they finished testing the replaced units. As the lifter descended and slowed down, they had the onboard computer fold the wrap out of the way so they could slam and lock the access hatches back into place. They all climbed back into their cockpits with Julie flying the spare Chrysops. After dropping away from the lifter, Marko noted that there were large areas of open water below them and wondered if the big moon also supported large aquatic life. The plant life floating on the water's surface looked extraordinary, with huge, deep blue, water-lily-like leaves which must have been at least six metres in diameter. Tucked beneath them were smaller versions of the same leaves, of different colours.

High above them, another of Rick's dirigibles hovered, directing operations. This time there were even more gunships and, for every one of those, there were two sleek high-speed missile drones — shaped like long elegant sharks — sporting dozens of different configurations of missiles under their wings. The crew of *Basalt* had seen them in various conflicts before and knew that there was also a large warhead in the front of the drones, with drop-down ramjets which could accelerate them up to Mach 8 making them scary weapons to be on the receiving end of.

Harry thought they were overkill and wondered what *Rick* was up to. The rest of the crew were wondering if they would be able to get sufficiently far away to escape the blast if *Rick* decided to use them. They could see the blue intel drone hanging above the designated pick-up point as they started to orbit again.

'I see no Avians waiting, Marko,' Minh Pham said.

Marko scanned his screens. 'Yeah, I don't either, Minh Pham. And that piece of ground looks very smooth, don't you think? I bet you *Rick* got this one wrong.'

An agitated-sounding *Rick* answered. 'No, Marko, this is the point and my intel says it is OK, although I now see the Avians assembling on the other side, away from that stone. OK, no problem, I shall direct the pick-up lander to them.'

The lander slid down out of the clouds again, making a textbook pick-up, although instead of climbing out again — and with every craft escorting it at high speed — it slid down to the centre of a nearby lake and uplifted a small village of refugees from an island. As it started to lift off over the water, something resembling a huge tree slug flung itself up out of the shallow water and latched onto the underside. Two gunships immediately fired at it, but the projectiles passed straight through its writhing soft body as it clung on with its two-metre-wide sucker mouth.

Marko, being closest, rolled in and brought the rail guns to bear, firing continuously and slicing the body away a metre below the mouth. As the body dropped, the mouth segment also died and peeled away, to reveal that the hull plating had almost been eaten through. Bits of the plating were still falling away — whatever was in the creature's saliva was still active. Marko relayed the images to *Rick*. '*Rick*, you have a problem. You seeing this?'

The Rick proxy that appeared on his screen seemed very angry. 'Fuck! What a shit of a place. Another expensive lander stuffed. OK, will have to transfer the refugees onto the dirigible. Proceed to the next pick-up. I wonder what horror awaits us there!'

Spike spoke through the crew comms. 'I think the very big, very powerful *Rick* does not like his assets being beaten up on by mere biologicals, Marko.'

Marko laughed. 'I think that you're right, Spike. Did he talk with you when you saw him in the mess?'

Spike made a rude little sound, much to Marko's amusement. 'No, he only lowers himself sufficiently to speak with Glint. He even ignores our friend Nail now.'

Marko frowned. 'Interesting. I wonder why. Think that I might delay making his ACE a little longer yet.'

'Two more to go today,' Harry commented, 'and then time for us to climb back up to the dirigible as this is now effectively mid-afternoon and I'm told that the really scary critters come out to play during the night.'

Glint replied. 'Well, I know that I'm not speaking for Marko, but I think that the rest of us have had enough surprises for one day.'

Marko laughed. 'Harry and Glint, sometimes you guys have no imagination!'

Flint broke into the conversation in his little high-pitched voice. 'That's true, Marko. He gave it all to me.'

'Sometimes you talk too much, Flint!' Harry said.

Half an hour later they were orbiting another of the cliff-dwelling groups of the Avians. Their lifter was once again hovering over what appeared to be a flat rock plate on top of the ridge line, hundreds of metres away from the settlement. Marko orbited the landing site and looked at it carefully — he had a feeling that something was wrong. He swung the Chrysops until he could see directly into the cockpit of the lifter, then activated his crew comms. He, along with everyone else, could also see the settlement of refugees hundreds of metres in the opposite direction.

'Boss?'

The major replied by the line-of-sight crew comms. 'Yeah, mate?'

'Who makes the decisions over the pick-up points?'

Michael Longbow shrugged. '*Rick*. Why?'

'Reckon there is something dodgy about that rock plate — the one that looks as if it is a stone disc, rather than a natural rock formation. What's the bet there is something living and nasty under it?'

A moment later the major replied. 'Hold on, I'll check. Nope, *Rick* is getting agitated; methinks this is turning out to be far more of a bad publicity deal for him than us. He says that that is where the lander is going and the refugees can go shaft themselves if they don't board it there.'

Marko swore silently then said, 'In that case, I think we had better step well to one side. If there is something under that plate, it is going to be awfully hard to shoot at it with a lander a metre above it.'

The major lifted both hands up for Marko to see. 'We will do whatever we have to, Marko.'

Marko, with Julie flying as his wingman, orbited in a pattern, looking for evidence that it was something other than just another outcropping of rock. As they searched further out, they started to find other similar, but smaller, rocks spread out for a hundred metres around.

'Harry, Minh Pham. Slave to what my video is seeing. I think that it is an organism of some sort. Can you have a quick look around the area where the habitation is, and where the refugees are assembled?'

Harry replied as he and Minh Pham swung their fliers in for a closer look. 'On it. Don't have much time though. The lander will be here in five minutes.'

Fritz commented. 'Wish we could ask the refugees. They have been on this moon for at least thirty-five standard years, so we are told. *Rick* can communicate with them, so I'm sure we could as well. After all, the languages are loaded into our helmet software.'

'Yeah, you're right, Fritz. Bit odd,' Julie said.

Before anyone else could comment, an angry *Rick* blasted into the conversation, almost yelling at them. 'All biological crew! Just to remind you that I am in charge of this operation. Stick to the plan, my plan, and we will get along just fine. I know that you are using your crew comms which I cannot hear and that is starting to really piss me off. *Rick* out.'

There was silence as they watched the lander slide down through the clouds to flare out, then hover directly over the centre of the ten-metre stone disc as its large hatchways opened to touch the ground. Marko waited for the refugees to move, but none did so. Flashing red lights started around the leading edges of the craft and the lander sounded its klaxons so loudly that each of the *Basalt* crew in their separate flying craft could plainly hear them.

An instant later the ground around the lander moved as huge starfish-like arms rose over the top of the lander. It tried to lift off, but a separate smaller and faster tendril flashed out of the side of one of the starfish arms and neatly speared the blue intel unit as it tried to escape, pulling it down into the closing arms. The arms pushed down onto the lander's top as what *Rick* had assumed was a rock surface split open. In the instant before Marko lost sight of the lander, spears of material were thrust into it with the whole mass becoming a ball, and great streams of rocket exhaust vented through the rapidly overlocking arms while the lander continued trying to break away.

Julie, looking out one side of the Chrysops, recorded with dread fascination seeing other tendrils ripping the fuel feeds away from the lander's engines, tearing them apart and pulling the pieces down into itself. As soon as the lander was completely enveloped, a foot-like appendage shot out from the base of the starfish-like creature, which was used to push-start the whole mass rolling down the ridge. The fifty-metre ball of creature and lander bounced off the side of the ridge to smash and tumble its way through the fungal masses. The gunships and missile carriers rolled and fired into it, having little effect, as the projectiles appeared to flash through the creature to detonate inside the already badly damaged lander. Eventually, the grey and black ball bounced off the shoreline of the nearest lake to impact with a huge splash and quickly sink from sight, taking numerous giant lily pads with it.

Harry roared loudly. '*Rick*, you are a fuckwit sometimes! All that power and muscle has gone to your head!'

Rick spat back at him from his dirigible. 'Shut the hell up, Harry!'

There was a silence for five minutes as they all continued to fly their patrols. The refugees had started to move back up the ridgeline to where the giant creature had been and were now waiting again.

'Marko, this line is secure,' Glint said. 'I am fascinated by that creature! And no explosion from the lander? How could that be? Also did not appear to take all that much damage from Rick's retaliatory fire. He broke the rules on that. His own rules, in fact. Do you think, much like those Games Board flying cameras that Sirius told us of when the electrics had been absorbed by the wasps, do you think that the same thing happened here?'

Marko shook his head in wonder at what they had just seen. 'Yeah, I am amazed as well, Glint. Would have loved to get a sample of that. Wonder what it eats normally? The growth is pushed flat, but does not appear to be dying. I mean, look around ... if it had been like a starfish feeding on algae on the rocks there would be a trail of destruction leading to it, but I can't see anything. And the fact it had living material all over its surface would suggest it is normally slow moving.'

The major interrupted. 'Guys. Heads up: we have another lander inbound.'

'Hope like hell this one goes to plan, boss.' Fritz chuckled. '*Rick* will nuke it otherwise.'

'Yeah, let's just hope he tells us if he is going to, Fritz.'

The lander spiralled in from directly overhead to hover off the side of the ridge line as one hatch opened, allowing the refugees to walk on board. The hatch closed as it turned and then went vertical with everyone following in their ships. Once through the cloud cover, the 300-metre-long dirigible could be seen hanging overhead. The lander swung over the top of it and then hovered at one end with a wide walkway extending out to the lowering hatchway. They all watched the Games Board AV feeds as the few dozen refugees walked across, then down a deck into a large transparent walled lounge.

The dirigible then started to climb and move westwards towards a mountain range fifty kilometres away, as another of Rick's egg-shaped troop carriers came down through the atmosphere to hold station beside the dirigible, extending an air bridge into the lounge area. After ten minutes the air bridge was retracted after the refugees had all transferred and the brutish-looking carrier, with its weapons still deployed, swung astern of the airship then accelerated away towards the late afternoon sun.

'Pick the nearest craft for hot refuelling, guys,' the major said.

Marko looked around to see the dirigible was probably the closest craft to him, so he flashed his ID across to it. It responded and a gantry swung the twin aerial pipes and drogues down towards him. He waited for them to stop moving, then slid up beside the filling head, matching its speed before opening the filler ports and gently pushing them up against the drogues. As they met, both sets of valves opened and Marko carefully worked the power controls because the fuel made them gradually heavier with the liquid oxygen and hydrogen rapidly filling the tanks. As soon as they were full, the valves snapped shut and the drogues pulled out, allowing him to slide away as a gunship came up behind him to go through the same process.

He dropped away checking where the rest of his mates were and taking care to avoid the jet exhausts of all the craft as he carefully flew to the front of the lifter. They climbed higher into the mountains where the cloud cover started to break. He could see the fungal vegetation giving way to more woody plants and low scruffy fern-like trees high up the hillsides. They flew over the terminal point of a large long valley where three spectacular waterfalls cascaded down to the fungal forest a kilometre below. Sheer rock walls towered on either side of them and winds started to buffet them.

Marko heard the smile in Jasmine's voice as she commented, 'At last! This is much better: real flying for once.'

He looked over his shoulder to see both Hangers high overhead, flying close to the stone walls at low speed, keeping pace with *Rick*'s dirigible.

The gunships and missile carriers started to accelerate out in front of them. The rendezvous point was only seven kilometres further up the valley where the tall buttresses of the valley walls became vertical and rose kilometres above them to disappear into the high clouds. Marko started to feel a foreboding as the monitor, Jim, deployed himself even further.

'Eyes sharp, Glint. Jim just went max with his deployment. Looks like a hell of a place for an ambush. The girls have moved out from the walls as well and are accelerating.'

As if on cue, all the craft piloted by *Basalt*'s crew started to weave and vary their speed and height. *Rick* yelled at them. 'All biologicals! If that is for camera effect, it is good. If not, it is a complete waste of time. This area is safe for us.'

Harry almost questioned Rick, but left it alone. They flew in tight formation to stay within the valley walls above the pick-up zone, a beautiful single tower with elegantly built stone buildings at its base. Nothing moved; no Avians appeared and as Julie, with Harry in support, found, all the heavy armoured shutters around the buildings were closed as well. The lander swept down to settle just outside the largest of the buildings. All its hatches were opened while it waited.

Everyone's crew comms suddenly activated, with the major saying, 'Guys, we are in the shit. Get to cover as quickly as you can. Patrick is climbing further away from his geosynchronous orbit and is warning us that this moon is about to enter a thick interplanetary cloud of material which he describes as trillions of tiny pieces of iron. Julie, you saw caves in the surrounding hills. Give us the locations — I hope like hell I can get this lifter into one of them. Move it, people!'

The coordinates started to show on their screens and a whole group of caves looked to be just big enough to fit the lifter. Marko, with Fritz following, flew down into the largest. Against the back walls of the cave he could see signs that the Avians knew about the threat, as there were habitations already built into the stone.

He radioed the major. 'Boss, this one I am in is big enough for you and probably the Hangers as well. You won't be able to fly in though. Walk it in, or we could push you in maybe?'

'I'll walk it in. Just need some guidance is all. I see you all heading down and tucking yourselves away. Good.'

An angry *Rick* blasted a message across all frequencies: 'Biologicals, just what the fuck are you up to now? It is bad enough I have to deal with the feathered variety, but you smooth-skinned ones are just as bad, always scurrying off like small rodents doing something annoying. Get back out here, or find the Avians and then get back out here, as I have no time for these stupid games.'

After a long pause, the major responded. '*Rick*, I have copied the messages and data from Patrick to you. Surely you, of all entities, must understand the threat posed by the iron dust?'

Rick roared back at him. 'There is no threat, Major! My greater self is well aware of it and we do not consider it an issue.'

'Yeah, well I do, and I will look after the safety of my crew.'

'Your continuing insubordination is duly noted!' *Rick* shouted. 'I also note that you have a small airborne unit which no doubt the eternal teenager, Fritz van Vinken, built. I warned you about communications not routed through me!'

A second later a laser flashed across from the nearest gunship, destroying the crew comms link unit, which rained fragments of itself against the canopy of the descending lifter.

A laughing Fritz came onto their comms link. 'Shitfuck thinks I am that stupid, eh? Decoy worked a treat.'

The major allowed himself a tiny smile. 'Everyone just act dumb until this plays out, OK. Fritz, do you still have comms through that ancient UHF system you built so you can talk with Sirius? I presume that you warned her to take cover.'

The big-headed little man was serious when he replied. 'Yup, but she says that what *Rick* says is good enough for them, so they are staying up there, boss.'

Michael groaned, wondering why people were always so stupid in the face of overwhelming evidence. 'In that case, ask them to hard-shell everything they have edited to date, so when they come crashing down at least we should be able to recover it.'

Fritz nodded and radioed the message. 'Relayed. Asks is it really going to be that bad?'

The major vigorously nodded his head. 'Yes! The atmosphere is about to become amazingly electrical. That idiot *Rick*, for all his power, does not understand. In about twenty-five minutes there is going to be the electrical storm from hell. OK, guys, guide me back, will you, please?'

The major brought the lifter down outside the cave just as Lilly and Jasmine flew the Hangers inside as well. He then rotated the lifter and unfolded the six large lifting and grabbing legs which, in conjunction with the antigravity, allowed him to gently walk the craft backwards into the cave. Harry stood out in front of the large machine, directing him with hand signals. He then lowered it down against the rock cave floor.

'Right, we have about fifteen minutes to shut everything down and I mean everything,' the major said. 'Then I want everyone on board the lifter. And make damn sure that all your craft are earthed. The static electricity from this lot is going to be something special. Chop chop!'

Marko and Glint climbed back into their Chrysops, turned everything off, then opened the electrical maintenance hatch and physically removed all the fuse and link modules. Around them, everyone else was doing the same. The monitor, Jim, even turned himself off. The last thing they did was to open a small hatch in the rear of the craft and run the earthing leads out. Glint held them against the bare rock floor of the cave as the inbuilt charges fired the hardened beryllium copper rods into the rock. They then walked towards the lifter, which was squatting like some giant mechanical version of a rock lobster, and climbed up into the airlock.

As they entered, the major called out to Marko. 'Mate, pressurise the rear compartment with breathable air, and go through the same sequence of shutting everything down. As everyone comes through the airlock, get them to take their primary helmets off and put their survival ones on. Oh, yeah, and as soon as one of the guys can help, you had better power down that arm of yours and also the ACEs.'

'Shit! That serious? So how long?' Marko exclaimed.

'Just do it, Marko. Some twenty-seven standard hours before it is all over.'

Over the next few minutes everyone arrived and powered down their internal bioware and electronic cognitive functions, which they found very amusing, initially, as most spoke different languages, except Lilly and Jasmine who had a common language, and Harry and Fritz who had another. Sign language and combat taps suddenly swung back to the fore. Fritz spent most of his time tapping out music beats as they were all he knew.

The major waved to get everyone's attention. He then signed that the last message from *Basalt* was that the storm was expected to last fourteen standard hours with a few hours lull, then another ten hours of even greater intensity.

Marko looked closely at the little spider, Spike, clinging onto his arm. Recognising the shut-down switches that Topaz had installed on Spike, he shut the little fellow down. He looked across to see Harry reluctantly doing the same to Flint. Marko then signalled Glint to sit beside him and as he did so, he reached to find a precise point behind one of the fossa's rear leg joints and pushed it. The ACE immediately froze, which allowed Marko to then open a side maintenance cover and totally shut him down as well. He sat crosslegged with Glint's head in his lap and stroked it for a few minutes, before signing Harry to help lift his bulk up into one of the bunks that lined the crew quarters.

Then he brought up his artificial arm's settings in his head, and closed it down so the arm went completely dead. He tucked the strange-feeling hand into his belt as he walked forwards to the cockpit of the now totally silent machine and looked out over the beautiful valley, to see huge black clouds starting to roll across the sky. The lightning began relatively slowly, while the wind picked up and buffeted the dirigible as it started to climb, accompanied by its support craft and with an almost reluctant Games Board lander being the last one to climb.

The sky grew darker still, then lightened as the larger iron meteorites started to enter the upper atmosphere, burning up as they went and creating surreal light displays through the clouds. They were all sure that many of the meteorites made it intact right to the ground, as the trails of something other than lightning were plain to see.

The smaller, lighter fragments and dust settled down though the air as the molten iron core of the moon and its magnetosphere started to interact with the vastness of the neighbouring gas giant whose upper atmosphere also fed the electrical storm ... they could see vast sheets of electrical activity glowing through the clouds with multiple colours being displayed like super-charged aurora. The sheets of lightning started to flash upwards as frequently as those coming down, striking the hapless dirigible again and again as it valiantly struggled to gain altitude. The violence intensified with iron-charged plasma bolts appearing and striking the gunships and the missile carriers, shorting out their controls and weapons' safety mechanisms, resulting in unintentional unguided launches and weapon discharges.

Those watching from the lifter could not see most of the violence, but they all knew when one of *Rick*'s craft had been destroyed by the different colours they made as they crashed, detonated or were struck by friendly fire. Slowly, the dirigible vanished into the fiery gloom and was gone.

Fritz entertained them all for an hour or so with a percussion performance played on a variety of objects that he found in the lifter, much to everyone's delight. Most of them watched the storm for a few hours, then slipped back to lie down and get some sleep in the bunks, taking care to keep their gloves on when touching any metal surfaces. Marko watched longer then any of them until he realised that the major, who he had been keeping company, had gone to sleep in his command chair.

After a particularly fierce display he felt the hairs on his body stand up and believed that something malevolent was behind him. Carefully turning, he watched discharges of purple-coloured static electricity dance around the cabin and then across the window frames in the cockpit before vanishing into the floor. Outside he saw rolling balls of plasma leaping around the valley and wished he could record the images, as they were nothing like he had ever seen. He sat up for another hour, then went back to wake Harry to take his watch so at least someone would be awake through the night.

Four

He awoke with Jasmine patting his arm then gesturing to the coffee mug she had placed beside him. He smiled up at her, then reached to pull her face to his for a kiss. He signed that he should learn her verbally spoken language so at least they could communicate better at such times as this, to which she nodded and smiled again. With coffee cup in hand, he walked forwards to watch the heavy rain in the dawn light and an electrical storm still in progress.

The major signed that he considered it safe enough for everyone to power up their bioware and re-boot their augmented cognitive wetware as well. Marko smiled as he reactivated Glint and Spike. Spike immediately walked up his arm and locked himself back onto the side of Marko's helmet. Glint just looked at Marko with disapproval when Spike reported to him that there were no images of the storm from Marko's bioware.

As soon as the major was able to speak to everyone, he said, 'OK, go check your craft. Boot them back up, make sure that they are good to go and then stand by.'

Twenty minutes later the storm had cleared sufficiently for Jasmine and Lilly to take off in the Hangers for a quick reconnaissance. Ten minutes later they returned to report that they had located most of the wrecks except the Games Board lander and the dirigible, and that the atmosphere seemed clear enough for normal flight.

A message full of static came through. '*Basalt* crew, this is Patrick. I am inbound to your position. Suggest that you get as high as you can, as quickly as you can, for a hot pick-up. Coordinates as follows.'

The major immediately responded. 'You heard him. Get on with it! All craft RV with me once we are airborne. Patrick, did the Games Board lander or dirigible make it to orbit?'

'Negative. Neither dirigible made it, and I have no knowledge of the Games Board lander. None of the *Rick* segments are currently communicating with me either.'

Marko waited until the major had walked the lifter from the caves before starting the turbines and with a touch of antigravity eased his Chrysops out of the cave into the steady rain. Looking behind him, he saw a small group of adult Avians descending from stairways cut into the rock walls at the rear of the caves. He raised a hand to them, wishing that he had had an opportunity to speak with them. They waved back as the other craft all lifted off and started to climb out of the valley. He hung back for a few moments, signing to the Avians that they would be back as soon as possible. He smiled, knowing that the message had got through when most of them signed their greetings and best wishes to him.

He spun the little craft around and accelerated skywards to catch up with the lifter.

'Glint, keep looking around,' Marko instructed. 'The lander and dirigible must be around here someplace.'

Looking up into the heavy storm-laden sky, Marko fervently wished that he was back inside the caves. He shrugged and loaded the instructions for motion sickness drugs into his bioware knowing that it was going to be a rough flight. Ahead of him his colleagues were already docking with the lifter.

The monitor, Jim, suddenly spoke. 'Marko! I am getting a message on my channels from Sirius!'

'Really? What is their condition and can you say where they are, Jim?'

'Yes. Information relayed on a loop. Their situation is dire. I fear that they will both need to be re-lifed.'

Marko started looking at the coordinates of the message's source. 'Oh. Boss, did you get this?'

'Yes,' the major replied. 'You have ten minutes absolute maximum, Marko. Go have a quick look and then leg it up to us, OK. Don't piss about. They knew the risk and accepted it. I am far more concerned for the edited data. Secure that and I would be more than happy.'

Marko poured on the power, climbing hard to bring them up into a tight little ravine slashed into the side of the buttress walls of the valley. They flew over the edge of another spectacular waterfall and between very close sheer rock walls. Marko decided to rely on the ground-mapping flight computer for flight control, which promptly slowed them down as they negotiated the tight confines of the ravine. The speed of the Chrysops dropped to walking speed as the wreck of the lander came into view. It was on its side, jammed between the rock faces, thirty metres above the raging creek below. Marko took back control and flew over the wreck, noting that the entire engine room had been torn away and lay further upstream. The main part of the fuselage was crushed down into the rocks and appeared firmly wedged in place. The cockpit canopy was cracked and as they hovered close up to it he could see the two women lying close together at the rear of the crumpled forward cabin, with Sirius waving feebly at them. They looked around for a place to land but could not find one.

'Glint,' Marko said, 'take control, fly us over to the side entry hatch and I will climb down.'

An agitated Glint replied. 'Marko, the data blocks are accessible through the top of the cockpit which is easily reached. We have very little time.'

'I know that, Glint. We will be fine. Just do as I say, please. You have control.'

Glint nodded, knowing that he should be the one to board the wreck but deferred to Marko. 'I have control.'

Glint moved them further aft as Marko stepped out onto the Chrysops's stubby wing before stepping off beside the hatchway onto the level, but slippery, surface of the lander. He punched the emergency access locks which forced the door to open outwards and then, grasping the lip, swung himself down into the still functional airlock. Cycling through as fast as he could he jumped into the cabin and walked forwards. Checking the air in his displays he saw that the lander must have been breached as the oxygen levels were just verging on the poisonous, although lower than at the mountain's base. He pulled the buckled door out of the way and squeezed through to find the two woman at his feet. Neither had masks on, not that it mattered for Ivana, as it was obvious from her injuries that she had been dead for some time. Her head was in Sirius's lap and as Marko knelt beside them he could only detect a very faint pulse in Sirius's neck. As he touched her, she let out a little sigh but did not wake. Looking up, he found then pulled the combat first aid kit from its housing and pushed the diagnostic unit against her neck. The readouts stated imminent death unless immediate full surgical was available.

Marko looked at the unconscious Sirius and knew that he could do very little for her as it would be pointless to risk a rescue mission in the time she had left. He explained the situation to Glint who told him they had time to make it back to the caves and that he had recovered the data blocks. Glint also relayed the best wishes of the *Basalt* crew and that they would return within a day. Marko sat down then pulled Sirius close with the Jim monitor arriving a few moments later to record everything. They then waited the half hour it took Sirius to quietly die, while Marko constantly debated with himself whether he should allow the medical pack to wake her with stimulants.

Several times he almost activated the unit. Each time he decided it would only be for his peace of mind to tell her that in spite of everything he still liked her. And he was just being a sentimental fool if he didn't just wait the year or so when he would see her again anyway.

A minute after she died, he activated the Soul Saver ejects for Sirius and Ivana and placed the disks in a secure pocket of his suit, took a last look at the two dead women and left the wreck with Jim following. Moments later Glint took them on a fast run down the ravine and then, in a vertical dive, raced ahead of the returning storm down to the valley floor and into the caves. They both leapt out with Marko pulling the electrics and Glint activating the earth straps while the Jim monitor deactivated himself after he grasped the side of the cockpit with his metal hands to hold on tight.

Glint looked across at Marko. 'Before Spike and I shut down, which we would have done without you interfering the last time, what are you going to do?'

Marko pointed into the caves. 'We run to the rear and hopefully we can hunker down in one of those carved-out rooms. Let's go!'

They moved at a fast run as the first serious rumblings of the storm reached them, through a broad fan-shaped entrance which opened out into a series of chambers, some of which had spiralling staircases cut into the honey-coloured stone and led both upwards and downwards. Everything they could see, except the floor, consisted of flowing, almost sensuous, curves without a single straight line anywhere. Marko told Glint to shut himself down as the first lightning strikes hit the ground out in the valley.

Glint climbed onto a low bench in the nearest oval-shaped room and quickly powered down, with his primary access hatch opening in his side. Marko reached in, pulled the breakers out and shoved them in a pocket as he also switched off his arm, powered the suit down and was just about to switch his bioware and cybernetics off when Spike said, "Night, Grandfather, sleep well!', and there was an echo of a tiny chuckle. Marko saw that the little spider had shut himself down as he was no longer accessing his additional conscious data banks from the Chrysops or Glint. Marko smiled and shut down his internal electrics, then sat on the bench beside the motionless Glint and watched the huge storm flashes light up the distant rooms.

A little later, as it grew even darker outside, he perceived that the ring-shaped artificial lights had come on in the room that they were in and also in the hallway outside. Looking out through the visor, which felt unusual as there was no information from the shut-down heads-up unit, he looked carefully at the stone from which the rooms, benches and low tables had been carved. He wished he could take his right glove off to touch the beautifully worked stone when he also saw that most of the surfaces had very fine decorative work carved into them. Looking as closely as he could, he wondered as to the origin of the decoration, as the only place he had seen anything like them before was in the octopoid city on the planet at *Cygnus 5.*

Without internal power, his artificial left arm felt and moved as a dead weight. He did not have a belt slack enough to tuck it into, so he supported the wrist in his right hand as he slowly walked around the room, then had a quick look into the corridors as well, finding even more elaborate and more defined stone carvings the deeper he went into the mountain. He counted the steps he took and then returned to find Glint still motionless on the stone bench. The storm outside the caves was now at its peak, with almost continuous blasts of lightning and concussions when the bolts hit the ground. Beautiful orange or red spheres of balled lightning moved around outside the caves. Sometimes they seemed to pass right through the rocks; other bolts just quietly dissipated, while still others exploded.

Marko stood and watched, taking great delight in seeing the display, coupled with great annoyance that he wouldn't have a record of it to show anyone. He found himself enjoying the spectacle, realising that the memories stored in the original biological parts of his brain would have to suffice and that for the great bulk of human existence it was all that had ever been available. He looked down at his suit and thanked himself for choosing the Tux suit with its inbuilt, non-electrical, air scrubbing and replenishment systems.

Starting to feel hungry, he opened one of the upper arm pockets where he had stored a ration pack and squeezed the valve of the pack open, allowing the small gas charge to pressurise the pack; with his tongue he pushed on a spring-loaded feeding tube built into his helmet so he could suck it into his mouth as the three mouthfuls of pulp became available to him. As he finished the pack off, he mused how much better it tasted than the last one he had had many years before, then wondered if Stephine had anything to do with that.

Feeling refreshed and satisfied, Marko sat in the middle of the corridor. He could see Glint and also the storm, and thought about the technologies that had surrounded him since birth. He wondered if, in some respects, he was the poorer for them, as they created a constant barrier between him and the actual world. A part of him wanted life to be that simple, but then the greater part of himself also understood that he would not cope without the constant information feeds and connection with his friends. He looked at Glint and also touched the side of his own outer helmet, under which Spike was dormant, and knew that they were a technological part of him he would never want to give up.

He wondered why the purple electrical haze that made most things outside look fuzzy was not doing the same inside the rooms. Marko walked to the edge of the main entrance area from where he could see the Chrysops, which had glowing blue spikes of electricity on most of its edges. Looking up, he saw bands of what appeared to be copper in the ceilings and also across the floor. As he watched, a few small red glowing spheres of ball lightning floated in through the cave then lifted up into the domed area in front of him, quickly accelerating onto the bands to vanish.

He stood watching for a few more minutes then walked back to see that Glint was still where Marko had last seen him and he also wondered where the Avians, who they had seen a few hours earlier, had gone. Marko went to another area of the entrance wishing that he could magnify his sight to look more closely at the copper bands and what also looked like fine copper mesh set into the stone. He looked back out into the storm trying to figure out how long he had been in the caves, then shook his head in resignation. He knew that without electronics he was completely out of touch with time. He was also annoyed that he could not listen to any of the music selections that Fritz had made up for him and loaded into all his suits.

Still thinking about time he dropped his left arm to his side so he could manually operate a lolly into his mouth to suck on. He smiled as the taste of one of his favourites rolled through his mouth and he gave a quick mental thanks to Stephine. He wondered about Glint again and had turned to walk back when he felt a tugging on his left arm. Startled, he spun around to see a small human child looking up at him with a shocked expression on his face, now holding onto his deadweight left hand. Marko cursed, feeling like someone lost in a strange place, as the suit was not giving any of its normal proximity warnings or threat analysis.

Slowly turning, he shuddered as he saw a group of Avians and humans in a semicircle behind him and wondered what to do. He could see that none of them had weapons that he could recognise, and that most were smiling at him. He signed 'Hello' with his right hand, which caused an immediate response in sign language using the same greeting. He signed in further recognition that he was effectively helpless, nodded to each of them hoping that they could see his smile through his visors, pointed into the room then slowly walked back to where Glint lay dormant with the child still holding onto Marko's useless left hand.

Reaching Glint, Marko sat next to him, while the child gazed at the ACE then slowly and very gently touched the tips of his long pointed ears. The adults also sat looking intently at Marko and Glint. One of them, the tallest of the Avians, signed at Marko: 'Is it dead?'

Marko looked at the Avian standing across from him, then examined the sentient, judging the blending of bird types and human. Almost the same height of an average human, with five clawed splayed feet, very slim human legs, large genital fold, slim hips and huge chest; also overlarge folded wings, slim human arms and hands, and shoulder joints in the same plane at the wing scapula. The head reminded him of a parrot's, although a little broader and streamlined, with black eyes below which were a flattish human nose and a slim, but distinctly human, mouth and jaw. The feathers, which almost entirely covered the creature except for its palms and face, intrigued Marko because they were a deep steel blue-black with scarlet and gold tips.

Marko slowly used one hand and finally signed back in reply. 'No, not dead. Sleeping, shut down.'

'Why shut down?'

'Energy danger.'

The Avian shook his head. 'Not here. No need to. Is it a safe creature?'

Marko smiled, signing, 'Yes, very safe. Named Glint. Why safe here?'

The Avian looked up at the ceiling, pointed, and signed a reply to Marko. 'No danger. Isolated. You electronic?'

'Yes, in part.'

The Avian suddenly smiled. 'We know who you are. Marko Spitz. You are a friend of created creatures. You are Marko?'

Marko nodded and signed again. 'Yes, I am Marko. I made Glint and many other ACEs. Your name?'

'I am Ant. Is your ship hardened, Marko? Is it shut down?'

'Yes, yes, shut down.'

The Avian nodded, turned and said something to two of the others who nodded in turn and left, heading towards the entrance. He looked at Marko, frowned, and signed. 'Atmosphere dangerous to you. Oxygen levels too high for your type. Can adjust for you. Come.'

They all stood up and began to move from the room, the small child still holding Marko's hand. The two that had left arrived back with a stretcher. They placed it beside Glint and reverently, gently, lifted him onto it and then followed them all. In the entrance, three other humans arrived in metallic suits, trailing earthing straps and pulling a long cable behind them. They walked out into the cave and attached the cable to the Chrysops, earthing it, then disconnected the craft's own earth straps as a wheeled hydraulic carryall, trailing its own piping, came out from a passageway, slid under the little craft, lifted it and reversed to bring it to where Marko and the others stood.

The elder Avian gestured to the craft as Marko rapidly debated with himself as to what he should do. He wanted to trust the surrounding sentients, but wasn't yet able to do so totally. Nevertheless, he walked across to the Chrysops and awkwardly clambered up onto the wing. The small boy also did the same, peering into Glint's cockpit, smiling and asking questions that Marko could only just hear, but had no understanding of. The adults smiled and spoke to the child, who also laughed, patting Marko on the lower back as if he was an entertaining dullard.

Marko reached into his cockpit and activated the Jim monitor who, moments later, rose up out of the craft, still assembling himself. Marko immediately realised his mistake as panels above them opened and a small, disc-shaped antigravity weapon platform dropped down to confront them with stubby barrels which pointed separately at Marko, the monitor and the Chrysops. Marko was cursing himself for not explaining his intentions when he saw a transparent shield slide up from the floor to protect the Avians and humans behind it. However, the small boy at his side quickly looked from Marko to the Avian and human adults and back again, his face filled with fear. Marko pointed for him to join the adults then signed as fast as he could to the sentients that the monitor was no longer Games Board in nature and was quite harmless.

Knowing that a crunch point had been reached, he started the powering-up sequence for his whole body systems, hoping that he was not about to fry himself or get shot by the weapons

413

platform. As the first stage of the suit came online, he opened his outer armoured helmet, which folded up and then down onto his shoulders so they could clearly see his face behind the primary helmet faceplate, and also Spike clinging onto the outside of it. The heads-up units came online as did his first-stage biomeds, then his cybernetics, allowing him access to the Avian language as he activated the speakers on the suit.

'My deepest apologies, sentients,' Marko began. 'I should have told you further of my intentions. This unit is called Jim. He was rebuilt by us when the Games Board producer, who is now dead, destroyed his mind. He has no weapons. I activated him to see if there could possibly be effects on start-up from the electrical discharges. I have now done the same myself, so I am at your mercy.'

He held himself very still, watching the discussions going on behind the shield. Soon the weapons platform backed off as the shield retracted into the floor. The elder Avian stepped forwards until he was at the edge of the Chrysops.

'I too apologise, Marko. It would seem that we have trust issues on both sides. It is good that we can talk freely. So, what are your intentions?'

Marko let out a long sigh of relief. 'Right now, I wait until my colleagues can return to pick me up. These electrical events of yours ... they must be regular occasions if you have inbuilt safeguards against them.'

The elder nodded, looking around the enclosure. 'Yes, we found this place many generations ago and modified some of it to our tastes. It will be several days before your friends will be able to return. There is an electrical flux built up between this planet, the gas giant and the surrounding magnetic fields which will have to dissipate before they will be able to return. We are most interested to know why your force arrived here at the time it did. Surely you were advised of the considerable risk you were taking in coming at this time of the gas giant's year when it and subsequently this moon pass through the iron cloud? And besides, we have no interest in leaving this place as we have been here for hundreds of years.'

Marko looked at the Avian. He then looked across at the rest of the group, shaking his head and wondering what manipulations the Administration were attempting this time. He stepped down off the wing

'I need to wake the ACEs,' Marko advised. 'Do you object, Ant?'

The tall Avian shook his head. 'No, of course not. We know of them from the Games Board programs that the Haulers bring to us.'

Marko was shocked. 'Shit! So you are not cut off or a recent discovery?'

Ant cocked his head, slightly intrigued by Marko's comment. 'No, Marko, why would you say that? Certainly there are factions among us who want to travel and see the other worlds of man, but we have been trading with the Haulers since the Avian sub-species of human were first created for this moon and the other environments like it.'

Marko frowned, feeling very annoyed. 'OK, so what we have been told is that you were created for the Infant conflict and carry highly contagious diseases as biological weapons.'

The Avian brought up his hands and looked at them. 'The Infant conflict is a source of continuing sadness to us, as a moon, one of the many habitable in that system, was colonised by the Avian humans hundreds of system years before that conflict. It always protested its non-involvement, but was destroyed anyway. Why would we wish to carry diseases to kill? We are human after all, Marko. You must know they would be lethal to us as well.'

Marko gently pulled Spike off the side of his helmet, located the tiny sequential switches and pushed them to start the little spider up, holding Spike in his hand as he then knelt beside Glint. Marko opened the panel in Glint's side and locked the breakers back in. The panel closed itself, Glint's fur rearranging itself to conceal the joints. Marko looked down at Glint's closed eyes, allowing himself to speed up, and as soon as Glint's eyes opened he used the crew comms to rapidly tell him what had been happening.

Spike woke up, flipped himself over and then scuttled up Marko's arm to sit on his shoulder. A very fast three-way conversation took place, with the Jim monitor again recording everything he could see around him. Glint and Spike agreed to gain as much information as possible about the sentients and their surroundings so that the information could be passed to Stephine and Veg for their judgment.

'Ant, why are so many of the Avians wishing to leave?' Marko enquired.

The Avian shrugged. 'There is a new colony available to us further out towards the Crab Nebula. Sounds a very interesting place and so they want to go there, as this is not a big enough moon for our expanding population. Another reason is that none of us wish to become involved with the privateer corporation that set up a large base north of here over three system years ago. Before you ask the question I shall give you the answer: there are a great deal of marketable medications derived from the native biosphere here. They want it and we just want to live with it.'

The little boy was now hugging Glint with one arm and trying to get Spike off Marko's shoulder with the other and laughing all at the same time. Whenever the child bent his head, Marko could see the raised lumps over his shoulder blades and the fine feathers growing along his spine. He looked down and could see that the boy's shoes were also very wide for such a young person. He looked closely at the three humans in the group and could see subtle genetic engineering in their skins and hair, but no obvious Avian features.

'Come, Marko, it is time to introduce you to my family. You have met my youngest son, Tomas, and these are my wives, Christa, Jamie and Momo; my sons Dana and George; my other husband, Dane, and our daughters Jema, Henrieta and Teri. We are a relatively young family of only fifty standard years or more.'

Marko and Glint formally shook everyone's hands, while Spike grinned and nodded. Marko, his cybernetics back at full power, was able to image map each individual in terms of the genetic imprinting on the children, and was able to identify the mothers and the fathers with Ant being the dominant father. Marko smiled, seeing the similarities between his own family and those in front of him as an acknowledgment that multi-member adult family groups could be so much more supportive on every level than some of humankind's earlier style of family units, such as three or two parents and — for some hundreds of years — even single parents.

'A question that has been bothering me,' Marko said. 'Why did we not know much more about you all?'

Ant laughed. 'Simple! We can choose at any time of our lives to shed our Avian characteristics and walk among the rest of humanity as ordinary people. If we arrived on any of humanity's worlds looking like birds, imagine the racial tension that would ensue. Besides, the gravities generally are too severe and the atmospheres, in the main, too low in oxygen for our metabolisms; and the air is far too thin to allow us to fly well. No, not a lot of attraction for most of us there.'

Marko nodded, wondering what it would be like to fly unencumbered, as Ant continued. 'So, to answer your next as-yet-unasked question, it takes an adult two standard years to reabsorb their feathers and wings, then change their feet and grow a great deal of muscle to allow them to walk among the rest of humanity. Some take the opportunity to swap their sex at the same time, if they feel inclined. Tried it once, may try it again sometime, although going from a penis to a fat little clitoris, for me at least, took some getting used to!'

Marko bellowed with laughter, and everyone joined in, except Tomas, who was enthralled by Glint's ears and frill and was examining them closely. Glint was happy to let him, totally trusting of the small boy.

Marko walked across to the Chrysops, climbed up into the cockpit and opened the locker with the fruit, food and drinks, which he loaded into a pack and took across to Ant. 'I know that it is very little, Ant, but I would like you to have this. I can easily survive three days waiting for assistance, and the fruit would have started to spoil by then, anyway.'

Ant took the proffered pack, nodded at Marko and smiled in gratitude. 'So, fruit and foodstuffs from the famous *Basalt*. You will not be offended if we clone some of the fruit, will you?'

Marko grinned back at him. 'I am sure Stephine would be honoured for you to do so.'

Ant formally thanked him then gestured for Marko and others to follow, leading them a long way back into the mountain to a magnificent, huge, domed cathedral-sized room carved out of the mountain. Tens of thousands of different creatures of every size, shape, configuration and type were sculpted on the walls and on the dozens of huge arched pillars which lined the space, everything lit from light sources they could not immediately see. Jim immediately flew up into the centre of it and slowly rotated, taking high-resolution images, while Marko and Glint walked around, looking at the walls in awe. Ant and one of his handsome standard human-looking wives, Momo, accompanied them until Marko suddenly halted, riveted to the spot. 'Not the best day to view the carvings, Marko and Glint. The heavy cloud cover has dulled things a little, reducing the mountain's translucence.'

Marko did not care because in front of him was a set of magnificent carvings stretching around and up a pillar depicting humankind, male and female, from the earliest hominids to all the extinct varieties. At the top was *Homo sapiens sapiens* and then all of the many varieties of humanity, naked and without representation of cranial or body hair, showing clearly every shape, with individual muscle groups and skin variation perfectly carved right down to the finest surface vein or folded skin crease. On the domed wall above the pillar most of the creatures of Old Earth were represented, all interwoven, in a great segment above the pillar edged with fine straight lines, reaching curving right to the centre of the dome high overhead.

Marko stood staring for some time, entranced to see tiny creatures and insects nestled between the larger carvings and wondering at the huge amount of time it would have taken to finish the millions of carvings, even if the artist and others had used machinery.

'Ant, have you any idea of how old these carvings are?' he finally asked.

'We believe they were done some twenty-nine thousand standard years ago.'

Marko walked to the next pillar, where he recognised the octopoids, in several distinct varieties, at the top of the pillar and above them most of the creatures of Old Earth repeated as per the previous coloum but this time including Homo Sapiens among the creatures. He mused to himself that another confirmation of the library data, which they had gained from the ancient alien artefact many years previously, was now in place.

Glint gently grasped Marko's right hand and pointed upwards. 'You see, Marko, the octopoids indeed originated on Old Earth as well as you lot. Interesting. It is my conjecture that each pillar represents the dominant species and above it the planet's biosphere. Our crew will be excited to see this.'

Marko looked at him. '"Interesting" is a bit of an understatement, Glint. And of course Fritz will only be interested if they had music.'

Marko and Glint walked on to the next pillar, then the next and so on. For the next two hours, they failed to recognise any other creature, and slowly walked back to where the larger family group of their hosts were seated in the centre of the room, patiently waiting for them.

'Ant, Momo. How big an area of the Universe do you think this represents?'

Momo shrugged. 'We're sorry, Marko, but of that we have no knowledge. Perhaps the Haulers would have better information. We do speculate about where other of these museums might be, and if we Avians, and the other derivatives of man, are represented in a more recent one maybe. We have not seen any of the creatures found on this moon carved into these walls.'

Marko gave a short swift nod and was about to reply, when Glint made a suggestion. 'Do it yourself, Momo: I'm sure that it can't be that difficult. The stone I have seen here is very stable with no cracks or fissures in it. And the mining and carving equipment that would be useful to you is not that difficult to obtain.'

She smiled. 'Perhaps you are right, sentient Glint. Perhaps that is indeed a good plan for some time in our future.'

Marko nodded in agreement. 'Are the Haulers aware of this place?' he asked.

'Yes, Marko,' Ant replied. 'They have all sent proxys down to study it, with some spending weeks going over every tiny detail. Surely they must have passed the information on to the general population. Although come to think of it, we have never seen anything about it, even though whenever a Hauler uplifts their cargos of teas and herbs they leave us with many months of audiovisual shows to enjoy. This I shall have to ponder.'

Marko grimaced. 'Don't do anything about it, Ant. There are things happening in the background that we are only now becoming aware of. The Games Board and the Administration don't want the public knowing of this. Keep it to yourselves or I can see an iron meteorite suddenly obliterating this place and you with it.'

The family's adults all nodded sombrely.

'Yes, sadly, you may be right,' Momo said. 'But we wanted you in particular to see it, Marko. Come, you look tired. We have prepared quarters for you. At least you can rest out of your combat suit. Please, follow us.'

His head still racing with thoughts of the other dominant species he had seen, Marko followed Ant and the others out through another door and then up long, gently curving staircases carved from the flawless honey-coloured stone. There were dozens of archways, landings and doorways leading off the staircases. They finally found themselves in a small suite of rooms after passing through a series of doors which had closed after them silently. From alcoves inside the final door, the Avians took compact units which looked as if they were made of polished deep red-coloured wood. The Avians placed the units on their shoulders and the units then conformed to each individual; tendrils grew from them, sliding up onto their faces and then into their nostrils.

Sounding slightly more nasal then previously, Ant turned to them to explain what was happening. 'This room and its ancillaries are oxygen-deficient for us, but will be good for you, Marko. We have prepared a late lunch and would like to join you, or would you prefer to dine alone?'

Marko smiled. 'My thanks. No, I would very much like to speak further with you all anyway and over lunch would be grand. There are a great many rooms here but I have only seen you people. Are there others?'

Ant looked at Marko with a bemused expression. 'Yes, of course, but we are among the senior families and it is our duty to place ourselves at possible risk from visitors. In your case, we do this very gladly and hope that the rest of your most esteemed crew will be able to visit as well. Your room, with ablutions, is through that door. The Jim monitor can stay here and interview us if it wishes?'

Marko continued looking around the room. 'Yeah. I know that the Games Board will be interested. Jim? Like the idea? Good. Thanks, I shall see you again shortly.'

Marko, with Glint at his heels, walked to the door of his room, which opened to reveal a bed, a panoramic window with views down the mountain towards the valley, and beside it an en suite. Marko lifted Spike off his shoulder and placed him on Glint's head. The spider immediately jacked himself into Glint as Marko sped himself up and linked to the ACE.

'Well? Tell me,' Marko demanded.

Glint shrugged as the message flashed across. 'No doubt your suit is giving you the same message, Marko. These people seem to be on the level. No pathogens that we know of, bacterial counts within normal boundaries, same with the virus numbers and type, as per everything we have seen so far on this planet. The air in here is just about perfect for you as well. The usual electronic signatures and we can't

423

recognise any hostile viral software anywhere. I've seen some very sophisticated visual tracking and lots of hidden weapon systems, so we could have easily been knocked over at any time. They do strike me as almost monk-like in their demeanour and actually very kind. I have detected several attempts by their hardware to intercept our crew comms, so they know about it, but it's your call.'

Marko nodded, looking serious. 'Spike, do you still have comms with the Chrysops?'

The little spider gave a sharp nod. 'Yes. I think that they are tapping into the feeds but there is no attempt to block anything so far.'

Marko looked at his ACE friends. 'OK. Test the water, please, guys. I need to think.'

He looked out the ellipse-shaped window onto the valley floor, which was still being hit by occasional lightning bolts. The rain had eased off and the sun could be seen through the clouds of the mid-afternoon sky. He stared upwards, missing the counsel of his friends, and then almost without thinking brought up the suit controls in his head and told it to open the helmet. The visor slid up and he sniffed cautiously, detecting air that smelt as if it was from a high forest — it was quite delicious to his ancient human senses.

He allowed himself an optimistic smile as Glint flashed another message across. 'Water is perfect, Marko, so clean it is frightening. Spike is attaching himself to the shower head to test it for you, anyway. There is even soap ... as in a cake of soap. I tasted it, seems fine to me if you are into eating soap.'

Marko barked out a short laugh and patted Glint on his head. 'Ta. A shower sounds like a good idea.'

He instructed the suit to strip itself from his body and as the last of the shunts popped out, Marko walked into the shower. Glint had turned it on for him and Spike had taken up a position looking down from above. He luxuriated under it for a few minutes, then stepped out and took a long woven cloth towel from Glint.

'You have a problem,' Glint told him.

'What!'

The dragon smiled mischievously. 'No clothes to wear and it might be rude to walk out in the suit again.'

'Bugger! Spare clothes are not the sort of thing you pack in a combat flier, eh? Go out and ask, will you, please? No, before you do that, how about you open that wardrobe?'

Glint looked and laughed and Flint joined in with a tiny chuckle. 'Yup! Like I thought, a monk's outfit. And sandals! Funny. And no underwear! Now that is even funnier. We can call you Friar Marko!'

Five

As Marko towelled himself off, Glint walked in on his two rear legs carrying a burnt-orange-coloured *soutane* of a very fine weave. Marko shrugged and put it on, finding the cloth beautifully soft against his skin, and started buttoning it from the top with its stiff collar, eventually reaching the hem. Glint gave him a thumbs up as Spike climbed up to perch on his shoulder. Marko looked down at his cobalt-blue hand, which seemed totally out of keeping, but decided against altering its colour, and walked out into the main area. There were smiles and nods exchanged between the family members, and Tomas came across to lead him to his backless seat.

There was a sudden flurry of activity as no one had expected Glint to sit with them, let alone want to eat the same food, so another seat and setting was found. The ACE cheerfully announced that he would say grace, and that he wanted to sample everything as it all looked delicious.

Marko inwardly groaned, wondering what would come next as Glint spoke: 'We gather in this place of peace to eat this food lovingly prepared by our friends. We give thanks to one and all for this and for the pleasure of their company. Amen. Let's eat!'

Everyone smiled broadly, and Tomas patted Glint's head from his vantage point of a high chair. As they took what they wanted from the bowls, Glint would take a small mouthful then bounce an 'OK' laser message off whatever piece of crockery he could use straight into Marko's eyes. Marko judged the entire meal to be derived from vegetable mass with no animal protein used. Most of the tastes were familiar, although there were some exotic ones that he knew, recognising them as frighteningly expensive spices and he flashed a message to Glint querying a few of them. Glint answered that he was one hundred per cent certain they were grown locally.

It was the wine that startled him the most. He likened it to a semi-sweet rosé, but with a complexity that he had never experienced before. His mind spent several minutes carefully working through the structures, but there were still fragments of the taste he could not fathom.

The remainder of the afternoon and evening were spent with the family, taking a tour of what Marko could only think of as a township living in and around a luminous mountain. Marko had discovered that the soutane was considerably higher tech than he previously thought. As they were about to leave his rooms, the cowl unfurled up over his head and a lower face mask sealed across his nose and mouth. He touched the mask and found that it was the same soft, finely woven cloth as the rest of the garment. He breathed normally, the oxygen levels in the air being adjusted for him by the cloth, and he altered his bioware back to normal. When he later commented on it, everyone just nodded and smiled.

The higher they went up through the galleries and promenades, and even larger cathedral-spaces than the room he had previously seen — the stone carved into flowing shapes reaching up and down hundreds of metres — the more Marko sensed that the Avians were just the latest in a series of sentient occupants.

'Ant. This place? How many types of sentient beings do you think lived here before you?'

Ant looked at Marko for some time before answering. 'That is indeed a most interesting question, Marko. We do not really know much, apart from the fact that size-wise they were similar to us. Indeed, we sometimes wonder if there is something here that we have overlooked. Come a little further before we can show you a most interesting object.'

After climbing yet another set of stairs, regarding which Marko was starting to feel a little jaded, they entered a huge fan-shaped amphitheatre, at the end of which was a gigantic pipe organ.

Marko stood for a few moments, overwhelmed, even though his head had already been overwhelmed by the things he had seen and dealt with throughout the long day.

He shook his head in wonder. 'Well, that's something you do not see every day. One enormous kick-arse organ. Does it work?'

Momo, who was standing beside Marko, replied, 'No one knows how to properly play it. Some of us have tried, with what can only be described as "mixed" outcomes. The various Haulers who have visited it have all said that they would send us instructions, but it would seem such is low on their priorities as none of them has delivered.'

Marko laughed and with a huge smile said, 'Fritz. Yeah, Fritz could play it, I know. Oh, that reminds me. I have a lot of Fritz's music with me. I know he'd want to share it with you. I can upload the files to you any time.'

The Avians all started talking at once in acceptance of the gift, so Marko had Glint send the files from the Chrysops to the Avian data stores. A few minutes later Christa quietly approached Marko. 'Marko, may we have a word with you in private?'

He turned to see the gently smiling faces of Christa and Jamie. He nodded. 'Yes, of course. Glint, take Spike and Jim and go have a look at the organ, please. See if it is in order, so Fritz can play it when the crew come down.'

Glint raised an eyebrow at him, before moving away. Jamie took Marko's hands in hers and looked into his eyes. 'Marko, you are a life-former and we have followed some of your creations with great pleasure over the years. We wonder if we can formally ask your permission to father some of our offspring. I know that it is a common custom among your large families to father bloodlines for other clans, and we ask if you would do us this great honour.'

Marko looked at the three women: two full-blood Avians and the other a standard human. He then looked around the great space they stood in, knowing that it had been designed and made specifically for the organ and the music it could produce, then he thought of his children being a part of the place and also having the choice of actually flying themselves.

'It would be my honour,' he said. 'My thanks. Yes. So I presume you have a medical facility where I could donate sperm for the township's use?'

All three women smiled. 'We were thinking of keeping it a little more in the family, Marko. Our daughters, Jema and Henrieta, asked us to ask you if they can spend tonight with you? For this we are most grateful. We shall tell them to go ahead and ovulate.'

The next morning, a still tired Marko awoke to find the two young women had left, so he took a long shower before instructing the Tux suit to envelop him. He decided that Glint must have cleaned it as it seemed in better order than when he had left it in the wardrobe. His hand weapons fitted nicely in the bag which had contained the fruit, so he stowed them, and then went out into the common room to find it deserted. He found a note suggesting what he could have for breakfast and explaining that they would be back for morning tea.

He looked at and tasted the various cereals, dark heavy breads, spreads and juices before making himself a tasty breakfast. On a whim he opened a channel to the Chrysops, instructing it to power up its main communications systems, then sent *Basalt* a brief message saying that all was well. The data connection was poor, but he was able to upload a series of images directly from his cybernetics showing what he had seen and learnt. Minutes later the major tried to establish voice communications, but gave up as the two-way reception through the still scrambled magnetosphere was bad.

The data feeds took Marko by surprise; their implications were grim.

He linked the information into Spike's data feeds from the Chrysops and asked him, wherever he was, to feed them on to Glint. The message came back that they were in another part of the mountain, talking with a large group of children at a local school, and would be returning soon. Marko reviewed the information concerning events high above them and wondered what to do next. He finished his breakfast, concluding that nothing good would come of him telling his hosts, so put on a smile and waited for their return.

A message arrived from Glint. 'Marko, are we going to get off this moon any time soon? I really like it here, but it is even better on *Basalt*.'

'Yeah, I'm sure we will be OK, Glint. Stephine and Veg are back on board *Basalt*. Seems the whole trip to the other planets to check them out was bullshit to get them out of the way while *Rick*, the bastard, did the deed. Yeah, will know more late tomorrow. They are keen to meet the Avians and see the carvings and the habitat. Did you see the bit about Fritz and the latest compositions?'

'Yes, Jim is expressing great interest in that. Shall I go prep the Chrysops?'

Marko shook his head. 'No, let's have a drink with our hosts and go look for the dirigible and the surviving *Rick* proxy after that. Looking at the information about the crash site, it is only thirty-five kilometres from here.'

Marko was enjoying another glass of juice when the family arrived, along with the Jim monitor, Spike riding on his carapace and Glint following. One by one the family members gleefully shook Marko by the hand and patted him on the back, telling him what a splendid sentient he was. Tomas gave the final confirmation: 'My da, he says you Uncle Marko now, Marko.'

Glint looked sideways at him, grinned, reached out and punched him on the shoulder. 'So you have been breeding again, Father. Biologically this time! Imagine the AV on this, hey, Jim. Another scoop for you!'

Marko groaned, then smiled, and was hugged by everybody. There were special hugs, long kisses and sensual suggestions from Henrieta and Jema that they would love to share his bed for as long as he stayed. The much younger Teri glowered jealously at her two older sisters.

The next morning, as they were flying down the long valley, Marko asked, 'What's our fuel status, Glint?'

'Down to fifty-five per cent. Plenty of water to be had though, so no real concerns. And looking at the maps we are only thirty kilometres from the monastery anyway. Only need two per cent of the fuel load, at the current speed, to get back there.'

Marko looked down at the steaming fungal forest below them and marvelled at the explosion of life that existed here.

Earlier in the day they had flown the Chrysops up to the wreck of the Games Board lander to recover the bodies of Sirius and Ivana. On the way there they saw one of the huge starfish-like creatures laboriously fighting its way up under the waterfall and moving towards the creek where the wreck was. Glint, who had asked why it would be doing so, had been told by the family that the creatures craved metal. They could taste it in the water and would go to any length to obtain it. Marko had done a little calculation that the mass of the lander would represent three per cent of the mass of the giant animal, and when he had passed that fact to the Avians they had responded that it would make the creature extremely desirable for mating purposes. Marko shook his head in wonder and mused at the things creatures did to get laid!

The senior members of the habitat had asked Marko what he wanted done with the bodies of Ivana and Sirius. He requested a simple burial, or disposal in the communal gardens, but he was refused because that was not the local custom. They asked if the people concerned were of good character, which gave Marko and Glint pause until Marko decided that at the end they had been good people and that the crew had cared for them. The elders bowed formally to him, then to Glint, saying that they would take care of it.

They had helped Marko and Glint lift the bodies out of the lander and wrapped them in soft white cloth bags, face down, with arms extended as if in flight, and attached long ropes for lifting the bodies. One of the female elders had carefully exposed the faces of the women, cleaned them, then gently pried the eyelids open, sliding pearl-white pieces of stone under the eyelids so their eyes would stay open during their final flight. Five adult Avians lifted each body and other members of the village joined them as they flew high into the mountains towards a great vertical slab of black rock, on which could be seen many hundreds of cave entrances. The weather was calm, and high above them the cloud cover had shredded, allowing them to see the bulk of the ringed gas giant which Glint informed them was 1.3875 million kilometres away. Marko smiled, thinking that Glint just loved information of any kind.

They landed at one of the lower caves, where the two dead women were placed in stone coffins carved into the rock. Before the bodies were sealed in behind rock lids, the female elder folded the arms of the corpses across their chests, slipped the little pieces of stone from their eyes and closed them, finally pulling the hoods of the wraps over their faces. She bowed to each of the dead, then slowly walked over to Marko, bowed to him and placed the stones in his hand. He looked and saw exquisite, wafer thin carvings of a white bird in flight on their surface. He bowed and thanked her then passed them to Glint who activated and opened a pocket on his flank and carefully slid them in with Marko's money cards.

All the time Jim had been silent, carefully recording everything. For the first time that day he spoke. 'My gratitude and thanks to everyone for the honour shown my fallen colleagues. As you are aware, they will probably live again and I know that they will be deeply moved by your ceremony. I do not know what to say for them, except to declare that they would have enjoyed this very much.'

Marko looked curiously at the monitor, who had assembled himself into a sphere and was hovering beside the graves. He wondered what was happening in its brain and if it actually comprehended death in any form ... Jim had been effectively lobotomised by the producer; had the guys got all of Jim's mind back when they rebuilt him? He reached across and patted the matt black machine and nodded at each of the Avians.

'On behalf of my crew,' Marko began, 'I give thanks to you and yours, to your history, to your love of life and flight, to your caring attitude and dignity in the face of death. You have honoured people we cared for. I believe that the last thing to do today is to fly in honour of our friends.'

He formally bowed to the assembled Avians, noting that Glint and little Spike did the same, then climbed into the Chrysops and led the Avians high into the sky to circle two times around the burial mountain.

Marko then headed south to look for the downed dirigible. Most of the Avians had headed back to the village, except Dana and Dane, who were perched on the small wings of the Chrysops holding onto the cockpit sides.

Dana leant into the cockpit, loudly saying, 'We are in the search area. I see broken trees at two o'clock, six hundred metres, Marko.'

'A good place to start looking, Dane.'

'Marko, the ship entity called *Rick*,' Dane said. 'Do you trust him? It is just that we have had dealings with him in the past, and we have always wondered as to his agenda.'

Marko hesitated briefly, before replying truthfully. 'Trust? Nope. Respect? Yes. The Haulers are an odd mix of biological and technological. They control the navigation points of this part of the Milky Way and they play games of great importance over very long time scales. No, I do not trust *Rick*. I like parts of him, but I also know that he would kill us in an instant if he believed that it would do humankind good. Actually, I think that he would kill this planet.'

Dane's eyes narrowed. 'So, this is why he is using us as weapons?'

A cold shudder went through Marko. 'Weapons, Dane?'

The Avian's shoulders straightened. 'We believe he has infected the refugees, who were the initial group taken off world, with a group of biological weapons tailored against the octopoids. We believe that this action is to kill octopoids on planets that they currently occupy — we of course as a subspecies have little interest in what lives below the waves. They naturally have no interest in what lives in the hills and mountains either. We wonder if this is a justifiable thing he has done. You are aware that this visit is the fourth he has made? He brings wonderful images of everything that we aspire to and the messages that come back from our kin are very encouraging ... in particular to the young or dispossessed. The previous two times he brought some of our people back with him, but while we could see and talk to them they were not brought down to the surface.'

Marko looked across at the beautiful black-and-gold plumed human beside him, and again wondered why he always seemed to find himself in the middle of momentous things, then he suddenly sat bolt upright, almost shouting, 'Oh, fuck!'

Dane looked at him in alarm. 'What is it, Marko? Is there something wrong?'

A frightened Marko said, 'Oh, hell, yes! Dane, can you survive above the cloud cover?'

'Yes, we can but for no more than an hour otherwise we become too cold. What is wrong?'

Marko was really worried. 'One of our crew has octopoid technology on board her craft. It may be susceptible to the biological weapons you mentioned. Shall I drop you off or do you want to come for a ride?'

Dane and then Dana smiled, with the younger saying, 'Come, let's ride into the heavens.'

Switching to the crew comms, Marko spoke to Glint. 'If Stephine or I become infected with this killer or killers that *Rick* is using, we will be badly affected. I worry also for my unborn children. Set up the laser comms, Glint, and work out where *Basalt* will be in ten minutes. We need to talk.' Marko fed power to the antigravity and went straight up.

Glint shook his head, wondering why the Haulers had involved themselves in such a messy business. He privately had real concerns for the sanity of *Rick*, in that his demeanour had changed in the time that he had known him.

'Stephine will be aware of the threat to herself,' Glint said, 'and *Rick* would be insane to involve her. Perhaps this is why he sent her off?'

Marko agreed. 'Probably, whereas I would not matter. But of course he has no idea of what I have become anyway.'

Both Glint and Spike nodded, and Spike said, 'Let's keep it that way. We will break through the clouds in three minutes. I know where *Basalt* is.'

Jim extended an eyestalk and flashed a message into Marko's crew comms. 'Why are we ascending, Marko? You can talk with me as the recording equipment is all shut down.'

'We need to establish comms with *Basalt*, Jim, as there may be a nasty biological weapon on board the dirigible. We need advice.'

Jim searched his files, but was unable to find anything regarding possible biological weapons. 'Why would there be a biological weapon on board a humanitarian mission?'

Glint interrupted. 'Before you say anything, Marko, I shall squirt Jim the whole file.'

Turning his head, Marko saw Glint interface directly with Jim just as they popped up through the clouds to look up into a perfectly clear sky with the enormous rings of the gas giant clearly visible even in the sunlight. Great, deep crimson storms with torn edges of peach and gold colours circled the upper atmosphere of the gas giant forming a backdrop to the local sun in the furthest quadrant of the sky. The two Avians were grinning at each other and admiring the view in turn.

'We have comms with Patrick,' Glint said. 'Information regarding everything is sent. Jim, do you wish to upload your data as well? We have fifteen minutes before the Avians will start to feel uncomfortable.'

Jim replied. 'Yes! Good. I shall need only eighty per cent of the connection. Uploading.'

Seconds later the major, on *Basalt*, replied to their messages. 'Marko, good to hear from you. Stephine and Veg are about to leave. She will be at your position in forty minutes with Lilly and Jasmine riding shotgun. We are also on the move considering that all hell is breaking loose up here. *Rick* is at war with himself, and there is also an inbound Cruiser of unknown origin. It has just passed through the local LP. Maybe one of the more maverick Gjomvik Corporations has sent a heavy to find out where their biological shipments are. So, all in all, extremely fortunate that you have established good relationships with the locals as we may need a place to hide. We have been lied to yet again.'

Marko sighed in relief that everyone was fine. 'OK, stand by.'

Then he addressed himself to Dane. 'Do you have somewhere *Basalt* can get underground? *Rick* is in three pieces and it looks like a schism of some sort has occurred as they are about to start a fight between themselves. Also, we have an inbound heavy Cruiser of unknown origin or intentions.'

Dane snapped his head around to look closely at Marko. 'That's not good. Yes, there is a place, but I cannot make that decision. It must go before the council. Wait a moment, I'll start things happening. How soon before your ship needs shelter?'

'They are inbound as we speak.'

'I understand, Marko. We had better get back then,' Dane replied.

'How fast can you fly, Dane?'

The Avian smiled. 'Thirty kilometres would take us thirty standard minutes. But we could hang onto this craft and streamline ourselves, in which case if you did not go over one hundred and fifty kilometres per hour we would be OK.'

Marko grimaced, wishing to go much faster, but said, 'Right, do it.'

The two Avians pulled themselves out to the wingtips of the Chrysops and wrapped themselves around the linear guns as Marko started to dive down through the clouds. They levelled out over the forest, suddenly seeing the command module of the downed dirigible hanging upside down among the great fungal trees with the native insects, lizards and dozens of other species all around it. Marko marked the position in his navigation computer and flew onwards, only to see three of the dirigible's escort gunships flying up to meet them.

'Shit! Dana, Dane, either drop away or get off the guns. No, don't drop away! Had enough funerals for the week and yours would be permanent. Glint, smack the rear one! Guys, shuffle along the wings and dig those claws of yours into the sheathing. And hang on!'

Glint climbed out of his seat, adjusting himself as Marko rolled the Chrysops over onto its back and dived for the ground, while Glint opened fire on the trailing gunship, hitting it continuously in its magazines until it erupted, flinging pieces of wreckage across the sky. Precision munitions hit the Chrysops in its antigravity control units and Marko poured the power back on, trying to maintain airflow over the lifting body of the craft. He dived among the trees and then down into a ravine as the two gunships tried to engage him again. Glint tried to fire on them with the wingtip rail guns but he couldn't get either of them to respond.

Marko fought the controls, feeling the thuds of incoming projectiles, as one system after another shut down. He was barely aware that Jim was lifting himself out of the cockpit and Spike had jumped onto the monitor. Marko started to look for a possible crash-landing spot, but could see nothing suitable. Then two bright blue missiles flashed past him, detonating against each of the gunships. Glint was lifted from his cockpit by Jim, and an instant later Marko felt his harness being cut away as he was also lifted bodily, with just a fraction of a second to grab his carbine and survival pack.

The Chrysops erupted into flame and tumbled down, crashing into one of the bigger trees.

He looked up to see the two Avians flapping furiously in sequence to lower him to the ground.

'Sorry, Marko,' Dana was saying, 'you are just too heavy to support aloft. We will put you down and then guide you back.'

A moment later his feet touched the spongy ground and they let him go. He pulled the pack onto his back, checked the magazine on the carbine and started to walk after them as Glint bounded up beside him. Marko grinned at him. 'Well, that was an interesting ejection. No spinal compression or anything like that. So, we have twenty-eight kilometres to go. Where is Jim?'

Glint pointed straight up. 'Right above us, recording everything. Do we have to walk from here? And where did those missiles come from?'

Marko looked towards the distant mountain. 'Unlikely, Glint … I'd say that we will get picked up, but hey, you never know about these things. The missiles? Don't know. They came directly from where the valley is, so I suppose it must have been the monastery.'

They heard a rumbling from far above them and then heard rail gun strikes hundreds of metres behind them, as Lilly and Jasmine, flying the Hangers, ripped down through the atmosphere. They circled high above them, engaging targets which Marko and Glint presumed were more of the escort gunships from the dirigible.

Marko recognised Lilly yelling at him through the comms. 'Marko, stop staring and get walking, fast! Stephine wants to thump the remains of the dirigible with a Compressor and you know what a bang that is going to be. Love you!'

The two Avians pointed out the fastest route, and Glint led as they started running and jumping from fungal growth to fungal growth until Marko started to laugh, thinking that they must look comical from above. Glancing over his shoulder he saw that Jim was in trouble. Dozens of very large hornets had started to take an interest in him. He stopped and unslung his carbine, wondering how good he would be at shooting rapidly moving insects when they were almost simultaneously vaporised by laser fire from above.

'Marko, stop pissing about! Run!'

Recognising Stephine's strident tone that time, he started running and jumping again, but without watching where Glint was leading. An instant after stepping on a different-coloured giant mushroom-like plant, he punched a hole straight through it and bounced from stalk to stalk to the ground, tens of metres below. He rolled upright in the gloom and was surrounded by thousands of stalks of fungus thrashing about in some sort of reaction to one of them believing it had been attacked.

He stood up uninjured, but confused as to where he was he attempted to contact his colleagues and get a fix on his position. The suit's comms systems showed electrical activity around him that was blocking any signals in or out. Down at ground level, the stalks were only a metre apart at the most.

He brought up the alternative inertial navigation in his faceplate and started to push his way through, finding that underfoot was knee-deep, spongy, water-filled slush. He tried climbing one of the bigger stalks, but not having any spikes in his gloves or boots was unable to make any progress.

He then tried to cut steps into one of the stalks, but that resulted in thousands of fist-sized slugs squirming out of the damaged area, smothering him and trying to chew on the suit. Interesting defence system, Marko thought. He pushed on, sloshing his way up the ravine, following the navigation way points in his HUD, but he was often met with impassable stones or plant masses. Stopping to catch his breath after heaving himself between hundreds of a different types of stalk, which all produced slime if he touched them, he suddenly felt himself grabbed around the ankles and towed backwards.

He kicked out, but to no avail, as whatever had attacked him had a good grip. He twisted around and snatched his pistol from the holster on his chest when he saw a monstrous slug creature trying to bite through his suit legs. He fired three times into its head segment, which only served to irritate the giant gastropod, before he pulled out his long curved battle knife, from its belt sheath, with his left hand and sliced off the top of the creature's circular mouth. It reared backwards, thrashing about and spewing great gouts of green-black slime over him as he slid rapidly away. Finally upright, he tried to clean the visor, but could only see a smeared vision through the gloom of what lay ahead. Switching back to the inertial maps and constantly calling his mates, he steadily worked his way uphill.

High above Marko, Glint kept trying to force his way down through the fungus only to have them repeat their trashing about. He quietly and slowly lifted a piece of the fungus head, allowing Spike to slip underneath.

Spike the little mechanical spider was perfectly suited to the job of finding his friend and hummed a little tune to himself as he swung from stalk to stalk following the marks that Marko had left behind. Often he had to pop his head up through the fungus crowns to encourage Jim to stay close — the datalink was not good under the fungus. Seeing a ten-metre-long slug rolling about he knew he was close, until finally he saw a black slime-covered form that looked vaguely human. He vectored Lilly, who fired a laser down into the fungus, slicing away swathes of material until she could also see Marko. She nosed the Hanger up the exposed slope towards him and lowered the landing skids until she had one against his chest.

Marko felt the forward part of the landing skid and, as he grasped it, Spike climbed onto his helmet. Lilly lifted them both up the ravine and over a small valley to a deep pool of water which Dana had proclaimed safe and told Marko to drop. He splashed in, allowing himself to hit the bottom, and thrashed about to dislodge most of the fungal material before walking back out, pushing large lily pads out of the way.

As he broke the surface, thousands of insects of every variety lifted in a great cloud to circle around him; many landed on the suit to see if it was edible. Disappointed, they left him, and the whole cloud dispersed as quickly as it had formed. His visor was now cleared enough for its own systems to clean it completely, so he could also watch Spike cleaning himself off. Just as he was about to climb up Marko's arm a lizard-like creature erupted from the undergrowth to pounce, biting down on Spike's abdomen. The indignant spider forced open the jaws of the surprised, hissing lizard, giving it a hard thump on the side of its head for good measure. He then ran up Marko's leg and back and pulled himself up onto the helmet again.

'Some creatures have no respect and little capability to learn, Marko,' Spike said. 'That's the sixth one to try that today.'

Jasmine holding station above, spoke to them. 'Marko, Spike, harness on its way down.'

An antigravity harness thumped into the ground beside them as Jasmine did a slow hard turn and accelerated away.

Marko unfolded the tough antigrav unit, locked it on and activated it, happy to be leaving the spongy, slushy ground just as an eel-like creature shot out of the water to latch onto his boot. He kicked it off with the other boot as they lifted fifteen metres into the air and wondered what was going to happen next. Looking behind him, he saw *Blackjack* and the two Hangers engaging numerous targets around the dirigible, then looked upwards to see *Basalt* coming through the clouds, trailing black smoke and heading towards the Avian mountain.

A slight thump on the side of his helmet got his attention. He felt a piece of vine when he reached up with his hand, then saw Dana and Dane slowly flapping their wings and gripping the other ends of the dangling length. He grasped on, tied a loop through the antigravity harness and a moment later was flying over the tops of the fungal forest being towed by two winged men. He smiled to himself at the totally glorious incongruity of it all. Looking over to his side, he saw a most peculiar flying creature before he recognised Glint wrapped around the Jim monitor, holding station beside them, looking just like a gunmetal-coloured dragon wrapped around a black ball.

'Jim is excited about the image you make, Marko,' Glint called out. 'Says that this afternoon's segments will break all viewing figures when he gets back, as he knows of nothing like it in the past.'

Marko laughed, feeling exhilarated by the day's events. 'Yeah, that would be right. Hey, what happened with *Basalt*?'

'They had to fight their way down as the three elements of *Rick* are fighting each other and, although the Ricks were distracted, they did not recognise *Basalt* as either friend or foe and shot up its engines anyway. Imagery on its way to you.'

The data files arrived in Marko's inbox so with nothing better to do he started sampling them. Looking through, he suspected that Stephine had had something to do with what had happened as the action began shortly after *Blackjack* arrived back at the moon. The part of *Rick* she had docked with started arguing with the other two that what they were doing was wrong.

The arguments became steadily more heated until the two segments, who believed that the were doing the right thing, fired on the engines of the third. It had retaliated with its enormous planetary bombardment particle beams flashing across space slicing away the main propulsion systems of the second segment. That segment then launched a suicide attack using all its separate weapons platforms and independent systems onto the first segment, which had been subsequently severely damaged. The last segment had then turned and fled up to the local LP to jump away, damaged from long-range strikes but still mobile, only to be met with a furious devastating attack from the unknown Cruiser, which, after destroying the segment, then jumped away, leaving an expanding debris field.

Marko let out a great sigh and wondered again what would become of them all. He pulled up the images of the unknown heavily armed Cruiser and looked at it closely. He thought that it was probably octopoid in origin.

Dana called out, breaking his reverie. 'We are all to go to ground, Marko. Stand by for landing and we will hide below the ridge line. Our council have gladly agreed to give safe harbour to *Basalt* and everyone in its crew. It has also, with considerable regret, allowed the bombardment of the dirigible crash site with one of your more exotic weapons.'

Moments later they were all sitting down in a ravine, as the two Hangers also swept overhead and came to a halt, hovering above the ravine floor. Marko, with his arm around Glint, watched the mountains as, moments later, the double magenta flash of the Compressor lit them up. Marko felt deep sorrow for the annihilation of all life in a 250-metre radius of the crash site, together with the levels of devastation further out. But he also gave a silent thanks that his children would be safe as the ground jolted a little and the blast wave roared above them.

Minutes later Veg broadcast instructions. 'All crew and Avians stay where you are. Transport is on the way.'

They watched as the Hangers lifted off and held station above them, along with *Blackjack* arriving to orbit high in the sky.

Six

Days later, after a great deal of discussion and information-sharing between the groups involved, the fate of the Avians who had been taken from the moon was announced. As the refugees were leaving on board *Rick*'s carriers for the distant world, they had been unwittingly but deliberately infected with the pathogens and virus that were lethal to the octopoid races. According to the surviving *Rick* segment, who was repairing himself as quickly as possible, the three colonies were all prospering and in time, he assured everyone, he would remove the weapons from them. None of the *Basalt* crew trusted Rick, but they all wanted a lift home, so they smiled in agreement, although Marko suspected Stephine and Veg had put him on severe notice.

A week later everyone from the Monastry, plus the crew of *Basalt*, were gathered in the fan-shaped amphitheatre, seated and quietly talking among themselves as the eternal teenager, Fritz, walked in. He had been locked away in the amphitheatre since *Basalt* had landed in a deep shaft on the northern side of the mountain, even eating and sleeping there. He went up to the keyboards of the magnificent pipe organ and proceeded over the next hour to enthrall his audience with a selection of his favourite pieces, before he rose and announced that a piece that he had composed would be played for the first time especially for them.

As he started to play, even the smallest of the children were in a state of rapt attention and Marko had a great deal of difficulty tearing his eyes away from his genius friend for even an instant to look around him: he was feeling a pang of sadness that Jan was not with him to experience it. The music swept them on a journey of grandeur, and they passed by exploding stars, and experienced every emotion any of them had ever had. The music burrowed right down until it seemed that they were examining the tiniest struggling flower on a mountaintop while a huge storm raged around them. The conclusion left them all in a state of ecstasy with tears rolling down their faces, and huge, almost painful, smiles on their faces.

In orbit, listening to the direct feeds, as arranged from the Jim monitor, the three surviving Rick proxys and the considerably diminished but still great ship, *Rick*, listened in awe. When the music stopped playing and the spatial analysis of the mathematics it contained was complete, the senior of the proxys let out a long sigh of contentment.

'So,' it said, 'the little man was the final key to the entire conundrum. Remarkable, truly remarkable, that he created the ultimate component of the very long-range navigation mathematics that we have been searching for for so long. Almost makes the whole debacle worthwhile. That was a most unexpected outcome.'

Appendix One

Glossary

ACE (Artificially Created Entity)

An ACE is often a pet or helper. An ACE may have animal or human DNA, in any combination, and is frequently cybernetically enhanced. They are normally fully sentient, serve their creator in an indentured capacity for a fixed time period, then are free to make their own way throughout the Sphere or beyond.

The Administration

The governmental military forces and bureaucracy of the Sphere of Humankind. Bureaucracy everywhere, even in the far future, is the same.

The Games Board

The media group concerned with the procurement and production of reality audiovisual. The Games Board was created to stage strictly regulated Conflicts and to promote them through their extensive marketing and broadcast channels, notice boards and other media. The

Games Board controls everything about the Conflicts, from weapons development to final approval of the Conflict itself. If the Conflict is sanctioned, the Games Board will provide funding. Unsanctioned Conflicts are also overviewed by the Games Board, broadcast and marketed, with the understanding that should they get too big, the combined forces of the Administration, Gjomvik and Games Board forces will end the Conflict with overwhelming force. Small controlled unsanctioned Conflicts are encouraged as they are good for business and keep all humans entertained.

The Gjomvik Corporations

The business and trade corporations of the Sphere of Humankind. Big business in the far future is the same as big business today. The Gjomvik Corporations are controlled by large family groups or appointed individuals. They provide the main source of funded mercenary groups which participate in the sanctioned Games Board Conflicts, plus most of the weapons, craft and support.

The Haulers' Collective

The long-range carriers of all trade and information, the Collective comprises huge ships capable of transporting great quantities of trade goods or whatever else is required. They also actively map the Lagrange points and collect fees from all ships using those navigation points. They explore far further out from the Sphere and are humankind's first line of defence.

The humans

Unaltered humans are Type S (Standard), but the heroes of
the Conflicts are often augmented humans (Type A). Some
AI (Augmented Intelligence) units are human, and may look
like machines or even like Type A humans. Other types of
humans include:

Type AM — Type A human, military

Type AE — Type A human, explorer

Monitors and Expeditors — Type A humans augmented
   to fulfil specific functions required by the Games
   Board.

ICE (Intravenous Combat Enhancement)

Type AM and AE humans possess additional bioware and
one feature of this is ICE, drugs which improve strength and
speed. When the crisis is over, the user must have food and
long periods of rest.

Lagrange points (LPs)

Lagrange points are spread throughout space as navigational
nodes where a ship uses its wormhole generators function.
They are usually plotted and owned by the Haulers'
Collective.

The octopoids

An ancient alien race now splintered into diverse groups. The
primary group just wants to be left alone to regress to their
original semi-sentient selves. The secondary group wishes to
take back their areas of influence.

Species Type Investigation (STI)

STI is a complex series of blood tests used to determine
whether someone is human and, if so, what kind of human
they are.

The Sphere of Humankind

The Sphere is the primary area of influence of humanity
(approximately fifty light years across).

Appendix Two

Initialisations, Acronyms and Abbreviations

ACE Artificially Created Entity

AG Antigravity

AI Augmented Intelligence

AV Audiovisual

ESF Earth Solar Flare (day/year zero for all of humanity; the event which forced humankind's exodus from Old Earth in the Sol system)

GB Games Board

HUD Heads-Up Display

ICE Intravenous Combat Enhancement

LP Lagrange Point

RV Rendezvous

SNCO Senior Non-Commissioned Officer

STI Species Type Investigation

Sub-AI Powerful computer system, just below sentience

Appendix Three

Games Board

The Articles and Rules of War

1. Conflicts.

   1.1. Conflicts over 100 combatants.

   All parties engaging in Conflicts involving in excess of 100 combatants must gain approval for the Conflict and subsequent marketing.

   1.2. Conflicts under 100 combatants.

   Parties engaging in Conflicts involving fewer than 100 combatants may also apply to the Games Board for approval and certification provided that Conflicts meet the requirements of the Marketing Interest Index.

   1.3. Funding.

   Following approval, funding will be negotiated with each party.

2. Weapons.

   All weapons systems and munitions types must be approved by the Games Board.

   2.1. Approved weapons.

   Approved weapons are listed in Schedule B.

2.2. New weapons.

Proposals for new weapon designs must be submitted to the Intersystem Games Board Weaponry Wing with supporting documents proving their necessity in a Conflict. Weapon development without a specific known Conflict application does not require Games Board authorisation until used in a sanctioned Conflict.

2.2.1. Design parameters are listed in Schedule F.

2.2.2. Following approval, each weapon must be submitted for field testing and certification by the Weaponry Wing.

2.2.3. The ammunition for the weapon must be submitted for testing and certification.

2.3 Manufacture.

2.3.1. All weapons are manufactured under licence to the Weaponry Wing.

2.3.2. All ammunition will be under the direct control of the Weaponry Wing and through the Weaponry Wing's agents issued to the approved sides of any Conflict.

2.3.3. Additional weapons, spare parts and ammunition will also be administered by the Weaponry Wing's agents.

3. Ammunition.

All munitions deployed and used during any Conflict must be 'fire and forget', direct line-of-sight weapons. No munitions are allowed to be guided by any form of self-destructive AI system. All weapons deployed must have a maximum range as specified in the Games Board

Ammunitions table. All weapons must, at all times, and in any circumstances, be available for inspection and testing by any certified Battlefield Inspector, as warranted by the Planetary Director of the Games Board. Such inspector's decisions on the suitability of the weapons or munitions used will be final and binding on all parties involved, immediately. The inspectors will also be able to award any costs incurred to any party involved, as they see fit.

4. Marketing.
The Games Board retains all marketing rights to the approved Conflicts and will, after the Conflict has been judged as concluded, award revenues generated by the marketing of the Conflict to either side, as seen fit by the Games Board.

5. Tactical battlefield questioning of any captured opposition combatants is allowed. However, any form of interrogation that lasts more than one standard hour is actively discouraged by the Conflict Marketing Unit. No recordings of any interrogation will be made after the one-hour deadline has passed.

6. Heroic acts by individuals or units are greatly encouraged by the Conflict Marketing Unit. There must, however, be a specific objective for such acts; any form of kamikaze action, unless the participants have already been judged by the Conflict Marketing Unit as legitimately mortally wounded, is actively discouraged.

7. The Games Board retains the right to end any Conflict by use of its own armed group known as the Expeditors, should any individual, unit, battalion or army group

break the rules of engagement as judged by the Adjudicators.

8. All power in decision-making by the Games Board is vested in the board by the Governing Bodies of the Known Civilised Societies (the Administration). All decisions made by the Games Board officials, Adjudicators and Expeditors are final and deemed above reproach. The Games Board cannot be held responsible for loss or destruction of any materials or personnel.

9. Death of any participant is to be avoided at all costs. All personnel in any approved Conflict are responsible for ensuring that their individual Soul Savers are backed up at approved Safe Points prior to any Conflict. Adjudicators will award 'Re-Life' costs against any individual or group as they see fit.

10. AI individuals are to ensure their own backups and reanimation in whatever form they choose at their own discretion, should they see fit to take part in any Conflict.

11. It is expressly forbidden to involve, in any way, the local civilian population in any approved Conflict unless they, as individuals, sign an approval with the Games Board, in which case they will then be deemed combatants with all the rights, remuneration and responsibilities that such a designation entails.

12. Weapons of Mass Destruction are only to be used with the express approval of the Planetary Director of the Games Board. Nuclear weapons whose timed radioactive half-life exceeds one orbit of the nearest sun to the planet on which the weapons are deployed are expressly forbidden.

13. Weapons which alter the genetic structure of any recognised biological group are expressly forbidden.

14. All air, sea and land warcraft must employ power systems that, as a main component, use a pressurised gas system to either drive turbines or act as electrical generators. Any power system that employs a flammable liquid as part of its power generation will require the express approval of the Planetary Director of the Games Board prior to deployment. Units utilising water cracker technologies will be given the most favourable status and immediate approval. Units using systems deemed archaic, or any technology that is over 200 years old in design, will also be given favoured status. Such units are able to have no greater than a ten per cent advanced technology input unless that advanced technology is the water cracker type.

15. Orbiting weapons platforms are forbidden as are all Orbital Surveillance Systems.

16. Aircraft and drones used for battlefield surveillance must be unarmed.

17. All aircraft and flying craft of any description are speed restricted to that of the local speed of sound. Their range, on a single supply of fuel or power cell, must not exceed 1000 kilometres. Their maximum combat ceiling is restricted to 5000 metres.

18. Antigravity craft of any description and devices are approved with the acknowledged restrictions of air-, land- and watercraft.

19. Watercraft of any description are not to exceed 10,000 metric tonnes dry weight. No ship is to exceed a speed of

350 kilometres per hour, or to carry any armament of any description exceeding 300mm diameter for ammunition size. The maximum fuel allowance of any watercraft of either surface or submersible description is seven standard days at full power. Maximum depth allowable for any form of submersible is 100 standard metres.

20. Land vehicles, including armoured fighting vehicles, are not to exceed a dry weight of 100 metric tonnes, must not exceed 120 kilometres per hour speed or carry a weapon of any description which exceeds 150mm in diameter and two metres in length. The maximum fuel endurance at full power must not exceed sixteen standard hours.

21. All communication systems for the Conflict must be by way of standard frequency modulated radio with a maximum range of 200 kilometres.

22. Capture and use of any opposition's personnel and equipment is allowed at any time. Ownership considerations will be judged at the termination of the Conflict. Personnel are to be given the opportunity to switch sides, should such occasions as a rout occur, as judged by the Conflict Marketing Unit. All ranks, pay rates and bonus considerations must remain in place. Any individual or unit which attempts to change sides without the express approval of the Conflict Marketing Unit can be judged as hostile by all sides and removed from the battlefield pending penalties.

23. No battlefield recording by video or audio is to be made by any member of the Conflict. This is the express concern of the Games Board and its production wing, the Conflict Marketing Unit. All images, recordings,

surveillance images and satellite images are the property of the Conflict Marketing Unit. Once the battle timings have commenced all personnel involved in the Conflict can be recorded by the agents of the Conflict Marketing Unit at any time and in whatever circumstances the agent deems to be of marketable interest.

24. It is expressly forbidden for any member of any side of a Conflict to interfere with or hinder any recording agent of the Conflict Marketing Unit, in whatever action they are performing. All planned actions in the Conflict, at all levels, must be made available to the recording agents, who can then record any actions of interest. All personnel involved in the Conflict are required to advise the agents of anything noteworthy or interesting of which the agents are not aware. The recording agents (with the approval of the local agent of the Games Board) can require the set battle, as notified, to be fought again if it is found some action or actions were particularly noteworthy and the recordings of such were not deemed satisfactory by the unit editor. Should such occur, the Conflict Marketing Unit is to carry the cost of weapons repairs and additional issuing of ammunitions, transportation and specific briefings of new combatants. Should any action of any members of the Conflict have caused the requirement of the re-recording, then costs will be awarded accordingly, as decided by an Adjudicator of the Games Board.

25. All members of any acknowledged Conflict are required to actively pursue, capture or, at very least, immediately report any non-sanctioned weapons ammunition, arms

dump, supplier or manufacturer of non-sanctioned weapons to the nearest member or agent of the Games Board. Death of any known, non-approved arms manufacturer, supplier or dealer is sanctioned. Bounties for the proven death or capture of such individuals are immediately payable to the approved individuals concerned by the Conflict Marketing Unit.

Penalties

Members, agents and direct employees of the Games Board, and its marketing, intelligence, weapons and enforcement components, are charged under these articles to enforce the will and requirements of the Games Board at all times. Penalties from minor monetary fines up to and including total death can be awarded by any member agent or direct employee of the Games Board, acting in conjunction with two other members of the Games Board, as long as those individuals are from different wings of the Games Board.

Right of Appeal

This right will only be awarded if there occurs a possible consideration of a difference of opinion, between at least three or more assigned members of the Games Board or its agents, at the time of any specific incident to which a penalty is about to be awarded.

Penalties are as follows:

- Deduction of individual's daily pay.
- Forfeiture of any or all specific battle bonuses.
- Forfeiture of Recognition.
- Forfeiture of Equipment.

- Forfeiture of Rank.
- Forfeiture of Battle Rights.
- Forfeiture of Freedom.
- Forfeiture of all unit assets both collectively and privately owned.
- Forfeiture of Re-Life as paid for by the Conflict Agreement Insurance.
- Forfeiture of Current Life.
- Complete and Total Death.

Acknowledgments

To my darlings Liz, Luke and Charlotte. You are the best.

With grateful thanks to my cadre of supporters and friends: Aaron Huriwaka, Anneke Bester, Geoff Shepard, Dave Wheeler, Isaac Hikaka, Ra Vincent, John Howe, Marty Walsh, Nick Weir, Mark Fry, Tim Watson, Rebecca McKenzie, John Harvey, Richard Carrington, Al Brady, Mark Stevens, Daniel Falconer, Claire Bretherton, Ruben Allan, Cushla Aston, Nico Matsis, Mark Smith, Don Nelson, Chelsea Mainwaring, Tim Abbot, Zahra Archer, John Mcleary, Geoff Boxell, Lucas Wotawa, Giles McCabe, Andreas Beirwage, Bruce and Cathy Jenkins, Ian Lowe, Neil Marnane, Dean Hudson, Rosie Guthrie, Lester and Anne Polglase, Brent Davenport, Michael Reitterer, Pete Milne, Sally Aydon, Greg O'Connor, James Dickson, Joanna Rix, Komal Chhiba, Doug Casement, Roger and Sue Mortlock, Pete Korski, Dave Hern, Andrew Short, Carl Hobman, Mike and Kenney Antipas, Tim Bell, Hayden Applegarth, Yvette Reese, Noel Simmons, Rick Graham, Linley Curbishley, Ivan Vostinar, Fiona Duffy, Bee, Jeremy (Bob) Thomson, Michael Simpson, Peter Payne, Paul Davey, Susie Williams, Lee Johnston, Peter Halvorsen, Hana Sekyrova, Daisuke Nakabayashi, Jerry Glynn, Stephanie

Smith, Liam Lynch, Jonathan Ahern, Peter Elliot, Natalie Forsythe, Deonie Fiford, Francie McGirr, Claire Bretherton, Link Choi, Martine and Rhys Bijker, Jaffray Sinclair, Nicola Campbell, Gordon Bankier, Linda Wills, Bill Hohepa, Jess Bauer-Clark, Steph Lusted, Peter Lyon, Paul Gray, Owen and Hanne Mapp, Gill West Walker, Annabel Graham, Robb and SueAnne Merrill, Geoff Scott and Veg aka Wayne Singh.

Special thanks to Mark Stevens for permission to use the name and description of *Mudshark* and Dr Claire Bretherton of the Carter Observatory in Wellington for her invaluable insights and research into the location of the Sphere of Humankind, Anneke Bester for her concept creature designs and Al Brady for his mechanical ones. Also to Gipsy Kitchen, Rowen and the crew who made sure I had plenty of coffees and delicious pimped scones each Saturday morning.

Thanks and appreciation to the remaining crew from Props manufacturing and SetDec at Kingsford Smith St, Rongotai, for those years that I worked with you all on *The Hobbit*: Dan, Ananais, John, Connor, David, Rhys, Ben, Carina, Tim, Steve, Ollie, Pat, Lance, Chris, Jamie, Hamish, Glenn, Murray, Marc, Aaron, Ben, Amber, Nathan, Sol, Hal, Andy, Ants, Garth, Lou and Adrian.

And lastly to the denizens of the Boat Shed, Mike, Aaron and all the crew, my heartfelt thanks to you all for your support. Bring on the stout and Island Bay sausages!

A FURY OF ACES 1

In our future worlds the Administration rules the Sphere of Humankind, the Games Board sanctions and funds wars and conflicts, and the Haulers' Collective roams the space routes like the caravanners of old.

Marko and his crew of fellow soldier-engineers are sent to investigate a largely unknown planet. When they encounter strange artefacts and an intelligent but aggressive squid species, they are forced to embark on a perilous journey far from the Sphere.

They will have to survive not only other alien encounters but also their own Administration's deadly manipulations.

Political factions and galactic media moguls vie for power … and money.